UNDER THE COVER
OF DARKNESS

Also by

Duane De Mello

The Wave of the Future

The McCarthy Era: 1950-1954

Was American Society Threatened?

Under the Cover

of Darkness

Duane De Mello

iUniverse, Inc.
Bloomington

Under the Cover of Darkness

This is a work of fiction. All of the characters, names, incidents, organizations, and dialogue in this novel are either the products of the author's imagination or are used fictitiously. The use of names of actual persons, places, and characters are incidental to the plot, and are not intended to change the entirely fictional characters of the work.

The Central Intelligence Agency's Publication Review Board has reviewed the manuscript for this book to assist the author in eliminating classified information and poses no security objections to its publication. This review however, should not be construed as an official release of information, confirmation of its accuracy, or an endorsement of the author's views.

iUniverse books may be ordered through booksellers or by contacting:

iUniverse
1663 Liberty Drive
Bloomington, IN 47403
www.iuniverse.com
1-800-Authors (1-800-288-4677)

ISBN: 978-1-4620-4585-3 (sc)
ISBN: 978-1-4620-4586-0 (hc)
ISBN: 978-1-4620-4587-7 (ebk)

Library of Congress Control Number: 2011914850

Printed in the United States of America

iUniverse rev. date: 08/22/2011

For Joan,
who paid an unfair price for all of this.

We are so accustomed to disguise ourselves to others
that in the end we become disguised to ourselves.

Francois de La Rochefoucauld

CHAPTER 1

As soon as he opened the hotel room door, Mitch realized something was wrong.

Whenever entering a darkened room, it was his custom to shut the door behind him first, and then move his hand to the light switch to turn it on. Before his hand touched the switch, he glimpsed a shadow moving towards him. Mitch enjoyed ambushing his prey, but he hated to be on the receiving end.

Mitch had come to know that violence is indeed the proverbial crap shoot. When in it, the best you can expect is to make sure you have stacked the odds in your favor, knowing that if you find yourself in a fair fight, your tactics are not good at all. Now, he thought, what do you do when you find yourself in the dark, and the demons have come for you? He knew the answer was to be prepared to move fast and violently in reaction.

With the shadow closing in, Mitch quickly dropped to the floor and lashed out with the side of his right foot. He could hear the sharp crunch of a broken leg bone, just below the knee, accompanied by the howling cry from the now disabled assailant lying on the floor next to him. Mitch jumped up, turned on the light, and looked down at what appeared to be a male dressed in all black with a balaclava mask over his head and face, with only his eyes showing.

The assailant, writhing in pain as he tried to hold his broken leg in both hands, glanced up at Mitch. Before any words could be spoken, Mitch's second kick landed squarely in the rib cage of the downed man, causing another howl of pain and anguish.

Not knowing if the guy was armed, Mitch needed to keep his assailant on the ground. He kneeled and placed his left hand on the target's ribcage. He ripped off the balaclava to reveal a now sobbing mass of a young man with blond, short-cropped hair, blue eyes bulging and tears streaming from an unshaven face with about three days of growth.

"Who are you?" Mitch asked.

"Fuck you," was the reply from the man contorted in pain on the floor.

With that, Mitch placed one of his knees over the injured rib cage and pressed down hard.

"Stop, please stop, please," the man cried out.

"Alright, let's try again. Who are you and what are you doing here?

"I was trying to steal whatever I could find in the room."

Mitch grabbed him by the shoulder with one hand, a leg with the other and rolled him unceremoniously over on his stomach, accompanied by more crying out from the man. After quickly frisking his rear pants pockets, checking down his legs and ankles for whatever the man might be carrying, Mitch rolled him back over on his back and checked the front pockets of his pants, his black jacket pockets and inside shirt pockets. Nothing whatsoever was to be found, not even a scrap of paper.

"You won't find anything. I'm clean," was the only reply between moans.

Mitch grabbed both of the man's hands, checking for any rings. He found nothing. Next, he checked his neck and wrists for jewelry or a watch. Again, nothing.

"What's your name?" Mitch asked

"Nobody you'd want to know," was his reply.

With that, Mitch removed the man's black leather belt. Tying the belt at the ankle of the broken leg, resulting in more howling, Mitch dragged him over to the desk along one wall of the room. Noting that it was firmly anchored to the wall of the room, he securely fastened the other end of the belt to a leg of the desk. It was a sloppy job, but it would hold temporarily while Mitch used the room phone to dial outside, followed by 911 for the police.

After telling the 911 responder what had happened, who he was and where he was staying, Mitch suggested an ambulance come as well, since he believed the man suffered at least a broken leg in the melee that followed the apparent robbery attempt. Mitch hung up the phone. He noticed that the man was no longer moaning so loudly from the pain in his leg and ribs, so he moved over to the window to watch for the police. He hoped they'd arrive quickly. He wanted to be rid of this man.

"See what you've got yourself into. You failed in your mission, whatever it was supposed to be, and now you're going to be arrested."

"Fuck you again," was the response. "I'm not saying anything."

The Marriott Residence Inn, located on Peachtree-Dunwoody Road in the fashionable Buckhead district of Atlanta, Georgia, was in an area of upscale shops, hotels, restaurants and popular bars. Just going on midnight, Mitch had earlier finished his meeting with his supervisor, Jack Benson, at his hotel located six blocks away, and was looking forward to a good night sleep before flying back home to Italy the next day. The situation now though worried Mitch. Was the assailant waiting for him, or was it indeed a robbery attempt gone awry? To make matters worse, the man had no wallet, no ID, nothing. That screamed professional hit, belying the man's claim that this was a simple robbery.

Just under five minutes after placing the 911 call, Mitch spotted the blinking red, white and blue lights of two police patrol cars pulling up outside the hotel. During the short wait for them to arrive, he checked over the room. Nothing appeared to be missing. The few clothes he brought on the trip were still in the closet, just as he left them. Nothing was disturbed or out of place in the bathroom. Not having brought his laptop on this trip to meet with Jack, he instead was relying on his encrypted Blackberry for communications with Jack and the Agency, and he was carrying that in his pocket.

With the knock on the door, Mitch opened it to find two Atlanta police officers standing there. He identified himself as staying in the room, invited them in and showed them the man dressed in all black lying on the floor next to the desk. The officers looked the man over and asked him to identify himself.

"I'm not saying anything. Just get me out of here and to a hospital for treatment. I'm in a lot of pain," was his only response.

Mitch explained to the officers the circumstances he found himself in upon opening the door to the room a short time earlier. He described the tussle that took place, his attempts to question the man and not finding any kind of identification on him. Both officers had wry grins on their faces as they looked at the man on the floor with the belt still holding him to the leg of the desk.

"Just how did you take this guy down?" one asked Mitch.

"Well, first of all, in the dark I couldn't be sure about the size of the person, nor if he or she were carrying a weapon of some kind."

"Good thinking. Go on."

"I dropped to the floor and applied a swift kick outwards to where I thought the person's leg, probably around the area of the knee, would be."

"Good move. Where did you learn to do such a thing?"

"I work out and exercise a lot, and I also watch too many action movies."

"Nice job," was the officer's reply.

The next knock on the door was two ambulance attendants wheeling a gurney. With the police officers still unable to get the man to identify himself or tell them what he was doing in the room, the two attendants took over at that point. They unfastened the belt from the man's leg and carefully lifted him onto the gurney. As they moved him toward the open door of the room, Mitch was tempted to whisper a few choice words into the man's ear to let him know how he felt about his botched attempt to succeed in his mission. However, with the police officers standing right there, he decided otherwise.

One of the police officers accompanied the attendants out of the room and downstairs to their ambulance. Mitch, after identifying himself and showing the remaining police officer a California driver's license, explained that he was a job recruiter visiting Atlanta for purposes of conducting a series of interviews. He also said he was due to depart from the city in the morning, and asked the officer if this apparent robbery attempt, or whatever it was, require him to remain behind. The officer said he saw no reason preventing Mitch from leaving as planned. With that, the officer left the room carrying the assailant's belt and balaclava mask.

With the door now shut, Mitch was finally alone and done with this ugly incident. He called Jack, apologized for waking him up, and explained what had happened.

Unable to figure out if it was more than just a robbery attempt, they agreed they were bothered by the lack of identification on the man, his apparent good physical appearance, except for his now broken leg and probable fractured ribs, and his unwillingness to identify himself, even to the police.

"Mitch, you're a tiger," Jack said. "All I can say is try to go to sleep and then get out of town in the morning," He then added, "I still like the way you work. Do continue to stay in shape, old buddy."

*   *   *

Downstairs, outside and across the street from the entrance to the Residence Inn, two men, also dressed in black, were sitting in a late model dark blue Chevrolet Suburban SUV. They watched intently as the police cruisers arrived, then by the ambulance, followed by the man being brought out to the ambulance and taken away. Using a pair of binoculars, one of them clearly saw his face, under the lights of the arcade of the hotel, before he was placed in the back of the ambulance.

"That stupid son-of-a-bitch," the man with the binoculars said to the other. "He was supposed to beat the shit out of Vasari, not the other way around."

The other nodded in agreement, saying, "Wait until we call this one in to the brass. It won't go over very well at all."

"I agree. However, you're senior to me so you make the call. Tell them to get one of the legal types over to the nearest emergency hospital and get our guy out of there, assuming he's not at death's door or on a respirator."

CHAPTER 2

The 10-hour, non-stop flight from Atlanta to Rome provided Mitch the time he needed to digest the last two days of his life. The incident with the assailant in his hotel room, as violent and disturbing as it was, he could tuck in the back recesses of his mind for the time being. It was the earlier meeting that same evening with Jack, and his revelations about the new operational direction of their work together, that really intrigued him.

"Mitch, I've always been impressed with your ability to be flexible and responsive to change," Jack had said to him. "I've seen you on the street alter your profile and demeanor while walking forward, never looking back. What a set of skills to have available whenever needed. I've also admired your willingness to focus on new opportunities when confronted, employing a different array of weapons when called upon."

"Jack, stop right there. Why do I feel coolness on my face from the light wind, or, better yet, should I say I hear a song in the wind from the bull shit you're throwing at me right now?" Mitch replied.

"Mitch, what poetic grace you're able to muster. You are forever my poet of choice. Listen, I have a lot of good news to give you today. At least I'm hoping you'll see it that way."

"No, I've got no interest in volunteering to go on the next mission to Mars."

"The powers that be at the Agency, up on the 7th floor at Langley, have been given a new set of marching orders from the White House. It's a presidential finding that places us back in the business of conducting executive action or as we prefer to call it, lethal operations. The section of old Executive Order 12333 that bans assassinations is now voided. It is not for us to ask why. I know for sure that it will never be publicly acknowledged that we are going back to the use of these kinds of ops to eliminate hostile elements opposed to our government."

"Well, I know I'm up for it, but what about you, Jack? Furthermore, what's with all the superfluous words about my responsiveness to change?"

"Well, for one, we both will be moving from the Counterterrorist Center and reassigned to the Special Activities Division. For more sensitive black-type ops such as this, SAD is better equipped to provide the kind of logistics and overall support that we will need. By the way, Mitch, we are not talking about the same finding years ago during President George W. Bush's tenure, when lethal ops were allowed against select terrorist targets. I believe that was around 2004. This time it's different."

"Regardless, Jack, it will be no problem for me. Something does come to mind though. What about the kinds of ops that are currently conducted by SAD?"

"Well, the primary focus of their teams is to engage in clandestine insertion and extraction ops, kidnappings, renditions, false-flag ops and providing covert assistance to foreign governments. Nothing will change for them, and they will be separate from us.

Our team will be a stand-alone unit within their organization. We will only make use of SAD's logistics capabilities, and possibly require the use of some of their personnel to be on a stand-by basis, should we run into problems requiring assistance with extraction, for example. They are truly superlative in ops support, and I am very glad to have them at our six."

"What does SAD have though, in the way of direct on the ground support, particularly for conducting the pre-hit survey, setting up for the hit, the logistics involved, as well as my extraction once a hit is concluded?" Mitch asked.

"Good question. This is the part I am sure you are going to like. Our own surveillance and ops support team from CTC will be coming over to SAD with us, all seven of them that you and I have worked with since we first formed up together several years ago. We cannot get better support than having our own dedicated people remain with us. As you know, they remain clean and uncontaminated from our previous ops against the radical Islamic terrorist groups, plus they all continue to live, when not on assignment, completely away from the Hqs area, and literally spread out all over the U.S."

"Of course, Jack. That's the good news. What else have you got?"

"Being on our own, we will undertake whatever is required to plan, launch, make the hit, and then return to wherever is necessary. At that point, Mitch, you will go into your sleeper mode until called upon for another op.

"That's fine with me, provided it means that I return to Rome and continue to function in my non-official cover role as a businessperson under deep cover."

"You're correct, Mitch. No change on that score."

"What about the special covert ops teams from the Department of Defense? How will this finding from the White House affect them?

"Not much," Jack replied. "The DOD teams will continue to run their own aggressive covert military type ops as approved by the National Security Council and the Office of the Vice President, particularly as it applies, for example, to destabilizing Iran. If you recall from some years back, before former Secretary of Defense Donald Rumsfeld was finally forced out, these teams were referred to as operatives from the Strategic Support Branch. Subsequently, they have become known as Special Mission Units. Derisively, I still prefer to call them the Secret Army of Northern Virginia. Since they engage in military ops, they are not subject to the same requirements for congressional authorization as it applies to us. In this new finding for us however, we also will be circumventing having to advise Congress.

"Well, if DOD is not subject to this kind of congressional scrutiny, why not let them be the primary force in running lethal ops? They certainly have the talent and capability."

"Yes, they do indeed have both. Nevertheless, when you learn more about the specific targets and circumstances involved for us, you will quickly realize that these military units would be hard pressed to try and succeed due to the size of the footprint they usually leave on their ops. They just can't move around and operate in the necessary stealth-mode like we can."

"I take this to mean then, that a DOD or SAD element, our team will be composed of only our surveillance and support members, and me as the only single active shooter who makes the tap on the target, escapes and evades, and is extracted from the area."

"You've got it, Mitch. Our team will conduct the pre-shoot target area survey and take care of all the required logistical support. The team will also arrange for the shooting nest location for you, and handle your ultimate extraction. That means we have only a small footprint, go in and conduct the op, and leave expeditiously."

"What can you tell me about the high profile targets?"

"At this stage, Mitch, just accept that they will be very senior, high level targets, and let it go at that. I will provide more information later. Are you still onboard?"

"Of course, Jack, you know I couldn't stay away from this one. I'm able to put aside the royal screwing from our Deputy Director Steve Capps, when he gave away to the Brits the identity of our access agent during the Jihadist truck bomb attack on the Sellafield nuclear waste processing facility. While it was a screwing I will not forget, I have put it behind me. With you giving me a chance to get back into the mode where I operate the best, I realize it's time to move on."

"Mitch, I'm glad to hear it. As you know, my preference is for targeted killing ops, especially when the President realizes it is one of the few left after all attempts at diplomacy have failed."

Jack knew exactly what it meant to be going back to the ways of old. When properly planned and correctly pulled off, a successful hit on a high-level target is perceived as coming out of nowhere. The resultant confusion allows the shooter to make his measured escape to safety. With Mitch being the best one-shot kill man in the Agency, his proven record of accomplishments favored new successes when directed by the President.

*   *   *

Mitch Vasari, a 38-year-old operations officer of the Central Intelligence Agency, was known as a deep cover NOC in Agency parlance, working totally away from Agency facilities while posing as a businessperson. In seven years of service, he had never been inside the Agency's Langley headquarters, or even in the metropolitan Washington, DC area. Because of the sensitivity of his operations, particularly when working against radical Islamic terrorist groups, only a few senior level officials inside the Agency knew his true name identity. His personnel file was known as a black tape file, and like the terrorist group ops he previously engaged in, was restricted reading for just those Agency officers with a need to know what he was doing.

Jack Benson, who was Mitch's inside-Agency point of contact, supervised all of Mitch's operational activities. Both were consummate operations officers dedicated to serving the Agency and the orders they were given. Where Mitch was fluent in Arabic and Italian, being born of an Egyptian mother and an Italian father, Jack was fluent in Russian and had spent 22 years working against the Soviet and Russian targets the world over. They had just completed five years of working together in counter-terrorist operations on the eve of this pending transfer to the SAD and a return to the kinds of ops that the Russians liked to refer to as wet work. Both were highly gratified to know that accompanying them would be Jack's best surveillance and operational support team in the business—their eyes and ears that served to keep them safe and out of harm's way.

Jack had inside access to all Agency stations and facilities throughout the world, while Mitch, while had been the singleton operative purposely kept at arm's length on the outside in order to ensure his security and operational capabilities. In other words, the benefit of working this way is that it kept him alive to do his kind of work. None of that would change with the return to lethal ops.

Before the previous stand down on executive action ops instituted by the President immediately after taking office for his first term, Mitch was able to exhibit his proficiency on two occasions. The first was in downtown Cairo, Egypt, where he took out a visiting senior intelligence officer from Iran's Revolutionary Guard Corps—the anti-west group of militants who, when not engaged in supporting terrorist acts around the world, were also in charge of Iran's nuclear program. Mitch employed the classic Mozambique technique, or double tap—two rapid shots to the middle of the chest. The ensuing scramble of people around the Iranian, however, did not give him the opportunity for the third shot—raising his aim slightly upwards in a straight line and placing the last round in the head. The second successful hit, in 2007, was a single, long-distance half-mile shot, along the Corniche Beirut, the seaside promenade in Beirut, Lebanon. Shooting from high up in an apartment building along the waterfront, Mitch took out the predecessor to the notorious mastermind of the Hezbollah terrorist group, Imad Mughniyeh. One year later, Mughniyeh himself was killed by an Israeli KIDON hit team in Beirut.

His reputation thus firmly established with the few senior Agency officials aware of his existence, with the stand down on lethal ops, Mitch was assigned to working with Jack on counter-terrorist ops. There, he engaged in the recruitment and handling of agents functioning as penetrations of radical Islamic terrorist groups, or Jihadists as they were also known. Now, presented with the opportunity to return to his much preferred hunter-killer mode—basically an ambush hunter living out on the edge—he would not only be able to push himself to the limit, but also practice what he valued the most—methodology, concealment and setup. Mitch knew that further success awaited him.

CHAPTER 3

The perfect cover office has to meet certain requirements. In the past, a business office location within line-of-sight of the local U.S. Embassy was the primary requirement for a NOC deep cover officer such as Mitch. A relatively close in location meant being able to use an infrared laser beam device between the cover office and the embassy that would provide a secure means of voice communications between the NOC and Agency station personnel inside. But this was no longer necessary. Instead, Mitch had available for everyday use the latest in both a secure laptop computer and a BlackBerry for use anywhere in the world. This was especially useful in that he could communicate directly with headquarters in Langley and local Agency station in the U.S. embassy, wherever he was.

In Rome he did not want an office anywhere near the embassy anyway—downtown along the Via Vitoria Veneto—where many security cameras covered movement on all the surrounding streets. In addition, Italian police were throughout the area and numerous intelligence operatives from hostile countries plied their trade there as well.

Mitch was able to locate his cover office on Via Ventiquattro Maggio, a mile and a half away from the embassy, in an upscale area of fashionable commercial offices and shops. With no other American firms operating in his modern, seven-story building, where he was in one of four offices on the fifth floor, he felt comfortable and free to move about as he saw fit. He employed one full-time Italian office manager who handled all his calls and correspondence, as well as setting up meetings with executives from companies interested in hiring Mitch's firm to find suitable job candidates for filling vacant positions.

The cover company, McKinsey and Trotter, was home-based in San Francisco, California. As a successful executive search and personnel recruiting firm, M&T engaged in the placement of technically qualified candidates into electronics, computer hardware and software companies from around the world. After working undercover for the firm out of the San Francisco office for five years, the Agency suggested moving Mitch to Rome, at Agency expense, where he would set up an M&T European branch office. There, he would be able to continue his work against terrorists and targets of high priority interest. The firm readily agreed and Mitch was ready for his new assignment.

When out of the office on cover company work, Mitch traveled throughout the European Union, and parts of the Middle East, visiting firms interested in contracting for M&T services, as well as conducting personal interviews with potential job candidates. While he found the job satisfying and full of new challenges he much preferred to engage in operations for his real employer, the Agency. With eight months behind him since setting up the office in Rome, he looked forward to Agency management deeming him firmly established there and ready once again for operational tasking. Mitch felt comfortable that his movements and activities all made him appear to be a legitimate businessperson engaged in real commercial business.

Italy was known as a hotbed for numerous terrorist groups, mostly those that came out of the Middle East. And Mitch could easily fit in with the Italian populace given his own Italian ethnic background and fluency in the language. Now that he knew he and Jack were back in the lethal ops business, he was anxious for an assignment so he could once again demonstrate his ability to conduct a hit.

When he received and quickly scanned the secure, encrypted message on his laptop late one evening at his near the office, Mitch realized that Hqs had finally judged him successful in maintaining himself in Rome in both running a business as well as now being able to conduct himself in a clandestine mode. He could tell from the cable message that it came from SAD at headquarters, and instructed him to be prepared to travel to a suitable meeting with Jack within a week's time. Without actually stating it, Mitch knew the message meant he was ready for an upcoming operational assignment. He now expected a secure cell phone call from Jack, once he was outside the U.S., giving the location and time for them to link up.

*   *   *

October in Barcelona is not a bad time to meet in a bar half full of locals and an occasional tourist or two. The Ambar Café, located in the city's Gothic Quarter, afforded plenty of privacy with its expansive outdoor seating overlooking the sea. The mild sunny afternoon weather and tasty tapas further added to the relaxing ambiance.

"Jack, this place represents one more good choice on your list of pre-arranged locations for our meetings. I like it," said Mitch.

"Only the best for my number one," Jack replied.

"Oh, oh, now I know you have good news."

"You bet I do. And a lot of it. Let me start by saying I am highly pleased with your effort to get yourself up and running in Rome. I know the city and the many difficulties involved for an expatriate trying to establish a business there. Your success in placing candidates for your cover firm is an added bonus. I'm sure the home office is quite satisfied as well."

"It hasn't been all that hard. Just time and a little bit of perseverance. It's paid off and I'm now ready to get down to some real work."

"You should know at the onset, Mitch, that our newly configured team in SAD represents not only the first in the Agency to return to be sanctioned for lethal ops, but also the first designed to be completely on the outside of Langley, with no known ties or connections of any kind, assuming we have set it up correctly. This will enable us to engage in truly black ops and be totally deniable and disavowed by our government."

"Well, Jack, except for the fucking experience involving the Brits in Scotland, I believe my work with you in counter-terrorist ops has been productive and rewarding. Therefore, I accept your endorsement of SAD and look forward to any involvement they bring to our future assignments."

"Good. The remaining members of our team, as you know, are independent contractors ostensibly working for existing companies located in various parts of the U.S. Fortunately, none of these companies have any kind of association with the private firms that make up the Washington beltway bandits—hired to fulfill government requirements. Therefore, we are as clean as possible. In addition, our own ambassadors in the countries where we'll be traveling or working in will not be advised of our presence or the kinds of ops that we will undertake. That means they can publicly state that, except for high-value terrorist leadership targets, our government is clearly on the record as being against targeted assassinations."

"I understand, Jack. That means we are going to go after other high-value and obvious leadership targets of the foreign government kind. Correct?"

"You're right on target, Mitch. As you can recall, it was some time ago that the President approved stepping up the remote controlled Predator and Reaper aerial drone missile attacks against al-Qaeda, Taliban and Pakistani Taliban targets in Afghanistan and Pakistan. These attacks represented classic targeted killings. What the President has done now, after entering his second term of office, is to extend that policy to include individuals, in this case leaders of governments, who are found to be pursuing actions opposed to U.S. interests."

"Jack, I am fully prepared to live with the assignments given me, especially when they are sanctioned by the President. However, we have a weak link in providing for our covert capability to remain totally outside of the Agency, and be denied and disavowed by our government. That link Jack is you."

"I believe I know where you are going with this, Mitch. Continue."

"For you to go on holding high level meetings with senior Agency officials inside Agency facilities, and be given by word of mouth only, our targeting assignments, you yourself represent a threat to our team's operational security. You are also in your true name identity in your dealings at headquarters, and make use of an assortment of alias identities when working abroad. Regardless the names used, you are known by many individuals and intelligence organizations as a career Agency operative. With all of that awareness out there, aren't you stretching it a bit in terms of our team's ability to securely operate when you are involved with us on a mission?"

"Mitch, I agree with you that this is the weak link. But by limiting my contact with other team members to select out of the way locations inside the U.S., and severely limiting my meetings with you as the shooter and primary team member, I believe we will still be able to function securely in terms of persons involved and support required."

"Alright, Jack. Let's put that aside a moment. It sounds like we will be a hit team operating along the lines of the Israeli Mossad's 'Kidon' teams, or even the British 'Increment' and 'UNK' hit teams."

"Correct, Mitch. I am actually organizing it as a single team version of a Mossad Kidon team. We will only be a fraction in size though, in terms of persons involved and support required."

"This is all good news for me, especially knowing we will be operating at an extremely high level of compartmentation and operational security. With that being the case, Jack, and your own recognition of being the weak link, I want this meeting today to be our last face-to-face as long as I continue to work for you and engage in lethal ops. I don't like making this request, but my personal security and an optimal chance for success as the shooter really requires it."

"Mitch, I also don't care for dropping direct contact with you, but know that it has to be done. I'm glad you spoke up about it first, and I didn't have to initiate this part of our conversation. I took the liberty to prepare for you this list of new secure cell phone numbers of our team members for whenever you need to arrange to link up with them for any kind of direct contact and ops support. This will include passing to you the weapons and other necessary equipment when inside the countries where the ops will take place. Our only contact will be for emergency or non-scheduled reasons, and you already have my latest secure cell phone numbers. We will not make any changes in the use of your laptop and BlackBerry for communicating with headquarters and overseas stations. Keep in mind though, headquarters has chosen to restrict the stations that will be knowledgeable of you and the other team members in their countries of responsibility."

Saying their goodbyes to each other seemed awkward. Both had a lot of trust and faith in each other after working many years together. Mitch viewed Jack as not just his immediate supervisor, but also his longtime friend and confident. He knew though, that he made the right decision. After walking the half a mile to the Las Ramblas area of Barcelona, Mitch joined the Saturday crowds of locals and what remained of the tourists from two cruise ships berthed nearby. He then returned to Rome, but remained bothered by the way the meeting with Jack ended. The only thing that buoyed him up was prospects for the ops assignments to come. He knew he would not have long to wait.

CHAPTER 4

The recently appointed Director of the Central Intelligence Agency, Dr. Benjamin Wicksford, and Secretary of Defense, Leon Panetta, rather than come together for their newly established monthly meetings at their respective headquarters offices, this time met in a secluded Agency facility located in Warrenton, Virginia. It was a Saturday morning in late April, the first shirtsleeve weather of the year. They sat outside in a gazebo behind the brick colonial home that also served as an Agency safe house, on a large expanse of neatly cut, vibrant green lawn. After coffee was served, they turned to discussing what brought them there, the conduct of sanctioned lethal ops, and whose teams were going to do what and to whom.

"Were you as surprised as I was last week when the President told us of his decision to go after the three sitting heads of state he considered up to their ears in sponsoring acts of terrorism against the U.S.?"

"Leon, I was flabbergasted," Wicksford replied. "I knew something was up when he asked us to step outside the Oval Office to the secluded privacy of the basketball court near the West Wing. With only the three of us, no advisers or anyone else present, I knew it was going to be important."

"I have never seen him conduct business like this before, Ben. You can be sure we are not going to see anything in writing, as in a Presidential Finding, for example."

"That immediately came to mind when we got onto the court outside," Ben said.

"We are just going to have to fudge on that and say we have one when we spell out the President's wishes to our teams," Panetta replied.

"Being relatively new on the job, I may have to learn to live with this kind of action by the President, especially given his recent decisions on personally involving himself in how to conduct the war on terrorism. I just hope that the results fulfilling the President's orders will have a major impact on the senior leaders of those countries that are behind the terrorist attacks against us."

"I could not agree with you more, Ben. However, I want you to know that I personally do not like receiving orders from the President this way, and never have, including what your predecessor, Robert Gates, experienced when he was Deputy Director serving under DCI William Casey years ago."

"I remember about that back then, when I was Casey's personal aide, and Gates use to come into his office from the side door where his office was located. He always wanted Gates to feel free to sit in on his meetings any time he wished since Casey did not want to keep anything from him. As I recall though, Gates would step in, listen to Casey describe the private operation run out of his back pocket, and then quietly return through the door to his own office."

"Good memory, Ben. Gates knew that if Casey was to continue running his own black ops, and avoid involving the Deputy Director of Operations, Clair George, it was just going to be a matter of time before the crap was going to hit the fan. It was just plain and simple: all intelligence collection operations are to be approved and run out of the Directorate of Operations, not out of the DCI's office. Casey however, persisted in going around George and doing it his way."

"You were right, it did hit the fan. It was unfortunate though, it had to be a brain tumor and stroke that silenced him. I was with him in the office that fateful morning just minutes before he collapsed. I had returned to my office and, within minutes, could hear the ambulances coming onto the compound through the gate of the main entrance."

"Ben, you obviously see a parallel here between what the President has ordered us to do and the apparent unhindered approach Casey took towards running operations?"

"Well, both were trained as lawyers and should have more respect for the law, rather than finding ways to circumvent it. Actually, Casey was also a Jesuit-trained Knight of Malta. That alone should have resulted in respect for international law and the sovereignty of nations. I do know though, that he did not care at all for The Geneva Convention. He commented to me one time that the Convention was nothing but a set of rules governing atrocities committed in the name of political ideology."

"That is an unusual stance for a man trained in the law," Panetta replied.

"I know. I agree with you, Leon. Like Casey though, could it be that the President has come to believe that to wage a war with rules only results in prolonging human suffering?"

"If that is the case, Ben, all the tools and tricks we have available to us are going to be used in this war against terrorism. That brings me back to why I am against what the President wants us to do. The trick, in this case, is the President sanctioning the use of lethal ops. The tools, unfortunately, I see as the two of us. With nothing written down, no record of his orders to us will exist. We will have nothing leading back up the chain of command to the President, and could be left hanging out there to dry in the breeze."

"What choice do we have if we want to keep our jobs, Leon? I happen to like mine, especially since we both only recently got appointed. Tell me, what would you prefer to do?"

"Well, Ben, I believe we should just quit postulating about it and get on with the show? We have orders from the President. How about we just proceed to carve up the pie of targets on the President's hit list?

"That's fine with me. Let's start with the one he named first, Venezuelan President Hugo Chavez. Keep in mind that the President said he is leaving it solely up to us on the order and timing of the three hits."

"Ben, I would like to propose that one of DOD's Special Mission Unit teams be responsible for the Chavez op."

"I like that, Leon, and I will certainly go along with your choice. However, something just came to mind. I recall the President mentioning to us about using joint ops, where applicable, in going after the targets on his list. I wish he had a better understanding of what actually is involved in running these kinds of ops and the turf battles our two agencies always seem to want to play with each other. Although the CIA originally came out of the U.S. Army's Office of Strategic Services, to this day it still continues to operate primarily along military lines. However, that is where the similarity ends. We perform at our best when operating with a different set of rules, structure, and level of speed and application of force compared to your war fighters in DOD."

"You know, Ben, I think the President is giving us something of a fig leaf when he used the term, joint ops. How about we try and apply it in a way that still allows for us each to go our separate ways on the conduct of the hits, but keep an emergency standby, or small reserve backup unit prepared to get directly involved in assisting each other, should it become necessary?"

"I can agree to that, Leon, although I don't care for enlarging the footprint of an op with too many people on the ground. I would prefer to limit the Agency's involvement in one of your ops to as little a number of my people as possible. For example, we could be on standby and prepared to assist in the extraction of a shooter in an extreme emergency, say during the exfiltration phase. We are stepping out on relatively new ground here and I can see it is going to require some detailed coordination. At the same time, given the strict secrecy called for in these hits, the less number of people with knowledge of what we are doing, the better."

"That will work for me, Ben. I recall that before I was sitting in your chair as DCI, back in the early 90's, the Bosnian War brought our two agencies together in a degree of cooperation on the ground that actually worked out quite well. Your Agency provided all kinds of logistical support in Tuzla to the Army and the Air Force, for example, on numerous occasions. In Sarajevo, one of your Agency teams also rescued an Army colonel and his driver during a kidnapping attempt by a bunch of radical Islamists."

"I remember that as well, Leon. Let's work together at furthering that kind of cooperation. As far as you taking the lead on the Chavez hit, we will also continue to share with you the real-time intelligence coming out of Chavez's security apparatus as a result of one of our best recruited agents working in place on his personal protection staff. The staff is highly trained and competent but suffers from Chavez all too often changing his own movements, making unscheduled appearances, and having his protectors rush to keep up with him on short notice. Our agent reports that the staff is frequently frustrated trying to cover him effectively when he makes these changes. He thinks he is better at protecting himself by not revealing what his ultimate plans are."

"I've seen some of the reporting from that agent—its top notch. Since Chavez frequently has outdoors speaking engagements, we should be able to work up a flexible pre-hit survey and ops support setup to make the hit at one of those events, especially given your agent's timely reporting."

"Without question, our agent there will be the key to keeping us apprised of his schedule. Have you noticed that when he reports on upcoming events for Chavez, he also comments at the end on how Chavez previously changed the timing of engagements already completed?" Chavez seems to think that by moving up or down by an hour or two a planned event, he improves his survivability status. That it indicates a high level of paranoia about his own personal security."

"I noticed that, Ben. However, I believe we will still be able to accommodate him and put an end to that paranoia."

"You know, Leon, before the President called us to the meeting on the basketball court, that intel report issued by NSA on the intercepted conversation between Chavez and his minister of the interior was probably the key piece of information that convinced the President of the need to remove Chavez from office."

"I couldn't agree more," Leon replied. "In the report, when the minister acknowledged that Chavez's idea of wanting a poison used to kill our ambassador in Caracas was a good one, which was all the excuse that the President needed to order us to undertake the hit. By using a poison that makes it appear the ambassador has suffered a massive heart attack, Chavez decides to give the go ahead to put the plan into action. That serves to elevate Chavez and his minions in Venezuela to outright terrorist status."

"Our ambassador there is known for speaking out about the poor state of the Venezuelan economy, including the dire straits the country is in as a result of Chavez's policies that favor the wealthy elite at the expense of the vast majority of the much poorer populace. So for now, obviously, Chavez has concluded that the ambassador's remarks represent a degree of meddling in his country's affairs that he will no longer tolerate."

"The good news though, is that with the President telling us that our own Department of State is not to become privy of his lethal ops instructions to us, State is nevertheless playing into our hands by planning to recall their ambassador whenever the President believes the time is right."

"Actually, Leon, we may be able to let the President know when that time comes if we are fortunate to either be given a heads up from our agent in Caracas, or, NSA picks up another intercept."

"I agree. Ben, how about we switch gears now, and turn to the second target on the President's hit list?"

"That's fine with me. For this one, Leon, I prefer that my Agency handle the assignment. I know that your SMU teams continue to work on the periphery of the country involved, Iran and, on occasion, conduct forays inside it as well. However, I am looking at a plan on hitting the target individual when he leaves the country and goes abroad on one of his relatively regular state visits."

"Ben, although DOD and our SMU teams have a whole host of military options and contingency plans on the shelf for going after leadership figures there, I am not going to be greedy and ask for this one as well. You can be my guest. Iranian President Mahmoud Ahmadinejad is all yours," Leon replied.

"It is payback time, and we at the Agency look forward to this assignment. I liked what the President said to us in justifying the hit on Ahmadinejad. Namely, you know, the line was crossed by Iran when, barely over a year into the President's first term, NSA intercept reporting confirmed that Ahmadinejad was directly involved in ordering his Revolutionary Guard Corps to undertake the op that resulted in the deaths of seven Agency officers, including our base chief, in eastern Afghanistan."

"Ben, we both know that although no state of war exists between the U.S. and Iran, we have actually been in one for some time. The RGC has supported too many terrorists' attacks all over the world. It's about time they and Ahmadinejad be considered fair game for us. When the terrorist issue is combined with the growth and weaponization of Iran's nuclear program, including RGC control of it, I can understand the President wanting to drastically up the ante."

"And fair game it shall be, Leon. I know the President said he wrestled in his mind with the question of legitimacy in going after heads of state," Ben added. "But, in the end he concluded that it would not be illegitimate to kill such a leader as a means of hastening the destruction of his regime."

"I am glad he recognizes though, that the elimination of Ahmadinejad will still mean the theocracy of the mullahs will remain but, according to your own Agency's latest estimates, Ben, the Iranian people are now prepared to finally move against both the RGC and the mullahs on their own terms."

"Yes, they are," he replied. "And fortunately, no one is under any illusion that the elimination of Ahmadinejad will mean a new administration that is friendly to us and the west. It merely means his demise will hopefully give rise to a more moderate theocracy that will not play such an important part in policy decision making. And that the government of Iran will seek to develop their economy more at harmony and in tune with western fiscal and nuclear development policies."

"Best of all, and fortunately, except for a very limited amount of covert support to a select few moderate individuals, including at least one who is a ranking and popular mullah in his own right, we have largely stayed out of trying to influence events in Iran," Leon said.

"You know," Ben replied, "although the President did not spell out any specific action for either of us to take against elements of the RGC, they are not going to go down easily, especially once Ahmadinejad is eliminated. We should not expect that the RGC, as well as their regular military units, will go away quietly. Both our agencies are going to have to be fully prepared for dealing with the RGC and the military on a much more intensified scale, once the hit on Amhadinejad takes place."

"I totally agree, Ben. I have a feeling we will be meeting like this again, many times over in the future, and it will be about much more than just increased ops against the RGC and the military."

"Leon, what about the third and last target on the President's list?" Ben asked. "I wonder if you feel the same way as I do about it."

"How's that?"

"I would like to defer assigning, for the time being," Ben replied, "the hit on North Korea's Kim Jong-Il. It will be by far, as I view it, the most complex and difficult hit to pull off in the history of both of our agencies."

"I couldn't agree with you more," Leon replied. "How about we hold off for a few weeks, or a month, in order to see just what we have available in the way of our own capabilities, including agent assets on the ground and in place, that can assist us in this kind of assignment?"

"For starters," Ben said, "as we both know, the personal security around him is intense, to say the least. In addition, he rarely leaves North Korea and, when he does, he only travels by armored train, actually two or more of them spaced out and running in line along the same tracks. To make it even more difficult to plan a hit, he is only known to take the train as far as his next door neighbor, China."

"Even if we have someone that can get close to him inside North Korea," Leon added, "he even has tasters, for example, sample all of the food and drink that he consumes."

"We had better stop there, Ben said. I feel a terrible headache coming on at any further thoughts about this third target. You know, I believe we actually accomplished a lot here today in this beautiful Virginia countryside setting," he added.

"Yes, I agree," Leon replied, "and we both still have a lot of work ahead of us. Take care of yourself, Ben."

"Will do. It's been good meeting with you again, and I know we will be back together soon."

CHAPTER 5

With a light bronze complexion, and short, combed-back golden blonde hair, she is a stunningly beautiful Puerto Rican woman. Standing five feet eight inches tall and weighing 130 pounds, she was born and raised in Ponce, the second largest city after San Juan. Gabriela Rivera Torres excelled throughout middle and high school in the sciences, particularly biology, the English language and sports, most notably soccer. Graduating from high school at the top of her class, her parents sent her to live with an aunt and uncle in New York City, where she attended Columbia University. Fluent in Spanish and English, she enrolled in the university's Middle East Institute and majored in Modern Standard Arabic language studies. After graduating with a Bachelor of Arts degree, and returning home to Ponce to spend a summer with her parents and friends, she decided her future would be in living and working overseas, thereby making use of her formidable language skills, including her newly acquired Arabic.

Nearing the end of the summer, she met up with a high school classmate who had also returned to Ponce on leave from the U.S. Army. Gabriela learned that her friend, assigned to Fort Bragg in North Carolina, worked as a communicator in a Joint Special Operations Command unit. Curious, but not overly enthusiastic about prospects for serving in the military, the friend convinced her to visit the U.S. Army recruiting center, in San Juan, to see what kinds of positions of interest might be available to her. Possessing what she considered a strong independent streak, Gabriela surprised herself when the Army recruiter, also a female multi-linguist, suggested she take the qualification test and she agreed. The result was an offer to join the Army and attend Officer Candidate School at Fort Benning, in Georgia.

With the encouragement of her family and friends, she accepted the Army offer, completed the twelve-week long OCS course, and was commissioned as a Second Lieutenant. Her first assignment was for further training at the John F. Kennedy Special Warfare Center and School, at Fort Bragg. With a psychological evaluation indicating she was an exceptionally strong performer when working as a singleton, which supported her own contention of herself as highly independent, she finished her training at Fort Bragg in the top tenth percentile of her class. When subsequently offered a coveted slot to become an intelligence officer, she accepted and went on to complete a one-year long Field Tradecraft Course that certified her as an operations officer, also known as case officer.

For the next five years, Gabriela proved herself a skillful, talented and professional case officer during numerous assignments throughout Latin America and the Middle East. Trained as a deep cover operative, she frequently worked under business cover as a NOC. Not having any occasion or reason to meet up with Mitch, her Agency counterpart, she nevertheless was DOD's version of him, working operationally the same way when separated from her military colleagues during assignments overseas.

During the summer of 2012, after returning from a three-month assignment working against the FARC guerrillas in Columbia, she was promoted to Captain and temporarily posted to the Joint Special Operations Command headquarters staff at Fort Bragg. Less than a month into this assignment, she was introduced to a visiting Defense Intelligence Agency officer from Washington, Colonel Wallop Little, the commanding officer of the DIA's Strategic Support Branch. To her surprise, she found herself trying to engage in a conversation with an overbearing, pompous, and obvious physically out-of-shape commander in charge of running elite teams of intelligence operatives designated to serve alongside SMU teams in the field when engaged in sensitive black operations. After Col. Little told Gabriela that he had looked over her military record and was considering her for an assignment at DIA headquarters, she feigned her surprise and appreciation for his offer. Explaining that she had only been in her current position at JSOC for one month, she asked for time to think over the prospects of such a quick change in assignment and the impact it would have on her career. Showing difficulty at hiding his displeasure that she would not literally jump at the chance to move over to the DIA, they agreed that she would get back in touch with him within the next couple of weeks.

Gabriela wasted no time in ferreting out the kind of assignment she would be undertaking should she accept the Colonel's offer. Navy Commander Rory Grimes, a former SEAL team commander now serving as the senior staff member of the Naval Special Warfare Development Group assigned to JSOC, had become a friend and mentor to Gabriela beginning when they first met six years earlier at Fort Bragg.

"To tell you the truth, I'm not surprised at all about Little's offer to you," Rory told her. "He makes these little, excuse the pun, forays down here every couple of months, trying to line up new personnel for his branch at DIA headquarters. Many of us here go so far as to question the need for his branch to even exist."

"Rory, not only does this guy totally look and act out of his element, he came across as highly unprofessional. He obviously expected me to be overjoyed at the invitation to join his branch, but he went totally sour when I did not respond the way he wanted."

"Let me give you a short backgrounder on why we here at JSOC do not take too kindly to when he ostensibly comes here to discuss his branch's involvement in support of our SMU teams operational assignments, and then proceeds to conduct himself in a totally different way."

"Go on," she replied.

"I'll try and keep it brief. Before Rumsfeld finally retired, he succeeded in creating Little's Strategic Support Branch within the DIA as a means of eliminating almost total reliance on the CIA for the collection of human intelligence on the ground. By using the branch's ability to deploy overseas teams of case officers, interrogators, technical specialists and linguists, in tandem with JSOC's teams, Rumsfeld was able to control his own version of running clandestine operations around the world. By the way, Gabriela, a number of these kinds of joint ops with Little's branch subsequently became a major embarrassment to DOD, and also totally at odds with what previously had been the province of the CIA's Directorate of Operations, now known, as you know, as the Agency's National Clandestine Service."

"I spent too many years working down in the Southern Hemisphere to appreciate, much less understand, the turf wars going on up here between the agencies," said Gabriela.

"You will be on a steep learning curve now, in coming to realize what is at stake here."

"What is the perception within JSOC, including your SEAL comrades, Delta Force and the Special Ops guys, on having been designated by Rumsfeld to work with Little's SSB?"

"I am happy to report that fortunately, under the current Sec Def, Leon Panetta, we are now in more capable hands, and no longer tied to SSB as we once were. JSOC is now able to decide when we need to deploy with the assets of the SSB, whether it be their case officers, tech types, linguists, or whatever, for our ops. Ever since the startup of Little's branch back in 2005, JSOC has never been comfortable in working with these people. Without elaborating any further, I hope you can see what I'm saying."

"I understand completely, Rory. Does that mean that with my background as a case officer and a linguist, I was selectively chosen to report for duty here last month, instead of a direct assignment to the DIA?"

"That is especially so in your case, Gabriela. Not only do you already have a Special Ops background and a well-illustrated string of successes already in your record, you also give JSOC a case officer's HUMINT collection capability as well. And then there's your background in languages."

"I certainly would prefer the JSOC style of ops over anything to do with the SSB. However, I do need some clarification on what I can expect in the future if I decide to request that my temporary assignment here become a permanent one."

"Of course, Gabriela, what's on your mind?"

"I assume you are aware of my preference for working as a singleton as much as possible. Obviously, I take my orders like everyone else, and operate within the chain of command as instructed. However, my best strengths lie in what I bring to an op when I am alone on the ground and in control of as much of my own operating environment as possible."

"Gabriela, one of the best things about working with the teams of the SMU is that your background is particularly suitable to operating as you prefer. In many cases, this will include you out in front and taking the lead in sizing up the opportunities to provide the necessary direction to make sure our ops succeed. This would include conducting pre-operation surveys, directly participating in the ops as assigned, and involvement in the exfiltration phases as well."

"Rory, you are still an upfront kind of guy. Thank you for the information and the advice."

"While I am not privy, at least at the moment anyway, to any upcoming ops currently under consideration, Gabriela, you definitely will fit in with us here at JSOC based upon your specific capabilities. For us, you represent a value-added asset that will be able to make needed contributions to what we do best—black ops, including lethal ops, in the most covert of circumstances."

"Rory, this is what I most wanted to hear."

"Now you know why you were temporarily assigned here last month in the first place. You represent a known quantity, but we wanted to look at you directly in order to see if there is a fit. If you like, Gabriela, I can make the necessary arrangements for your permanent billeting to JSOC."

"Please do so, Rory."

CHAPTER 6

"I'm really only comfortable when I'm alone," Mitch thought to himself following the return to his apartment in Rome after a late afternoon meeting in the Hotel Hassler, at the top of the Spanish Steps above Piazza di Spagna. His overt work as a personal recruiter, running his own office in the country of his birth and living a bachelor's lifestyle, certainly appealed to him. He also was looking forward to his flight the next day back to the US, since it meant he was one-step closer to his upcoming assignment as the Agency's lead shooter to target a sitting head of state.

After making himself a light dinner of veal scallopini, a tossed salad of lettuce, tomatoes and basil with vinaigrette, a slice of crusty Italian bread and a bottle of Pinot Grigio, he further mused at prospects to come in his work. In remembering a couple of his favorite lines from *Alice in Wonderland,* he would apply two of them from the grinning Cheshire cat to himself: "I'm rather clever at appearing . . . and I'm even better at disappearing."

"These two lines," he decided, "I will take to heart since they will be the hallmark to my return as an ambush hunter."

Years earlier, when first joining the Agency and ultimately being chosen for training as a shooter, he put himself through a laborious mental exercise on whether he was suitable for such work. He started by considering the religious aspects of killing. His deceased father, a Catholic, was born and raised in Italy. However, this did not have much impact, since he passed away when Mitch was 12 years old. His mother, though, an Egyptian and practicing Muslim, did instill in him a significant number of the tenets of Islam. However, his learning of the teachings of the religion did not include any formal teachings at Muslim schools or the practicing of the faith in mosques.

After concluding that people of all religious faiths throughout history have regularly used their beliefs as justification for killing, he decided he would have no problem living with his own conscience, since he believed rituals only work for those who need them. The trappings that went with the practice of a religion would have no impact, since he knew that, deep down, inside himself, he could use his exceptional skills with rifles and handguns, whether it be for firing at paper targets on a shooting range, stalking animals in the forests, or even the hunting down of humans as assigned to him. It did not matter.

Before finishing this exercise on determining his suitability for squeezing the trigger, he considered his mental state of mind. Having studied the psychological write-up on a number of assassins of the past, including those successful in killing heads of state, he found that the schizoid personality, in many instances of a paranoid type, a common factor present in many of them. Mitch noted it was a general conviction among psychiatrists that in today's world, schizophrenia is one of the most prevalent of all the human conditions attributed to such individuals. This led him to conclude that, in a macabre sense, almost anyone is therefore, capable of being an assassin. He then reversed that logic as a question: Who is out there that is sane enough to be incapable of killing? This rationale became his justification that he was both sane and capable of the actions he would take in his operational work. As far as he was concerned, he reasoned, it did not matter if he was a sharpshooter serving in the military or a police department, or, his current role as an intelligence officer with the Agency.

*   *   *

The following day's 16-hour flight, from Rome to Denver, was uneventful. Mitch had told his office manager that he would be in the U.S. for at least four days, in the Denver area, to meet with prospective clients who were interested in hiring electrical engineers to work in their production facilities. In actuality, the encrypted cable Mitch received on his laptop told him to plan on two days at a long-distance rifle range in northern New Mexico, and two days in a planning session back in Denver. He could expect to be picked up at Denver's International Airport by the lead member of the Agency's support team that Mitch worked with a number of times in the past, Gene Claggett.

Although the headquarters cable mentioned nothing about the target individual, the location or circumstances for the upcoming operation, Mitch was queried about his sniper rifle preferences to use at the range. Mitch replied with his three favorites: The British-made L115A; The Finish-made Sako TRG-42; and, the Canadian-made PGWDI Timberwolf Tactical. Depending upon the details for the operation, Mitch knew that one of these rifles would be suitable for him to use. He also knew that it would be good to be back working with Gene again. Whether it was leading a surveillance team, or providing protection for Mitch in evading enemy forces in a hostile environment, Gene was the best.

Standing five foot nine inches tall, weighing in at 175 pounds and having a tanned complexion from spending much of his time outdoors on the streets, Gene had earlier spent a 20-year career working indoors as an accountant. However, he had a well-developed avocation in photography, such that he easily could pass as a professional photojournalist. So that is what became his commercial business cover when, six years earlier, he became an outside contractor for the Agency.

After Mitch cleared Immigration and Customs in Denver, and retrieved his one checked bag, he made his through the secure area and immediately spotted Gene standing outside the barrier doors.

"Hey, old buddy. How are you? Gene asked.

"I'm fine thank you," Mitch replied. "What about you?"

"I'm great. No changes for me. We're going to head over to the domestic side of the terminal where I have an aircraft waiting to take us for a short flight south, to Taos, New Mexico. A vehicle will meet us there and, along with the three favorite instruments you requested, get us situated in a nearby hotel for the evening."

"Sounds fine," he replied. "Is anyone else from the team going to be with us?"

"Not this time. Given the sensitivity of our mission, particularity insofar not wanting to take any chances of compromising your personal security, it is just going to be you and me. Even Jack is out of this one, given your request for no further meetings with him after the last one in Barcelona."

"Gene, I'm glad you know about that. I also hope you agree with my concerns, not just for me, but for all the team members involved."

"I couldn't agree with you more. You and I, along with the rest of the team, have never been exposed to the headquarters setting, much less anything else around the Washington area. You made the right call. Jack has just had too much time spent at headquarters to be able to participate in this kind of sensitive op."

"Where will we be going tomorrow?" Mitch asked.

"The Agency has specified that since you cannot be brought anywhere near one of their firing ranges, or other facilities, I have made arrangements for a nice private setting for you to show your stuff."

"That's good. I can go for that."

The two of them flew on board the Beechcraft Model 200 Super King Air for the short one-hour flight to Taos, where an Agency support officer met them. After a ten- minute drive to a nearby motel, Gene signed them in and the support officer disappeared for the rest of the evening. Following a late-evening dinner of local Taos Mexican food specialties, they sat out on a veranda overlooking the foothills of the Sange de Cristo Mountains and a cloudless sky full of dazzlingly bright stars overhead. It was here that Gene briefed Mitch on the operation to take out a sitting head of state whose country is the world's leading state sponsor of terrorism and currently developing plans to unleash their newly developed nuclear weapons against the west.

"Mitch, I'm going to walk you through the op chronologically. You jump in whenever you have a question or point that requires clarification. Sound good?"

"Yes."

"First off, since this operation is posed to represent one of the most restricted or special access programs in Agency history, the people made witting of it is extremely limited. It goes something like this: The DCI, his deputy, and the director of the National Clandestine Service."

"That's restricted enough for me."

"After that, Jack, of course is privy, but he will remain at headquarters for any day-to-day responses or guidance required. Our own team supporting you, of course, also will be fully witting."

"Good. What roles will each of them have, and what will their covers be?"

"Starting with me, due to the latest intel reports we have received, I'll deploy within five days. This will enable me to start the pre-hit survey of the overall area around the hit, and also begin arranging for your shooting-nest location and setup. After that, I will lay the groundwork for the extraction phase after the hit is completed. For cover, I will be in my clean, established alias as a professional photographer on free-lance assignment."

"Let me stop you right there. Tell me who the target individual is going to be for the hit, the location of it, plus the timing. That way I can better appreciate and relate to you and the rest of the team members who will be in the area."

"The target is Iranian President, Mahmoud Ahmadinejad, and he will be in Paris in approximately six week's time."

"Wow. That's fine with me since it is certainly overdue. This bastard has been playing games against us for way too long."

"One of our few highly placed agents in Iran's Revolutionary Guard Corps has reported on Ahmadinejad's upcoming trip to Paris. Further, NSA intercepted reports have confirmed it, including the dates and purpose for the trip. He will initially fly to Vienna where he will give a speech at the IAEA headquarters on Iran's peaceful intentions in furthering their nuclear energy program. Then he will fly to Paris for two more scheduled functions. One will be to receive an award from a left-wing journalists association, where he will speak on the openness of Iranian society and the protection of the democratic process there."

"I have trouble believing that one. What's the other function?"

"This is the one we are interested in for our purposes. He is expected to give a short speech and have a photo ops session while surrounded by a large number of Iranian students currently studying at French universities. It will take place directly in front of the Eiffel Tower in a spot that offers a picturesque view of the lower portion of the tower as background."

"That is great news, Gene. It could open up some good possibilities for us. I know that area—grassy, open parkland area that heads southwest towards the Ecole Militaire, the Military Academy and lined with many apartment buildings along both sides.

"Good memory, Mitch. I plan on extensively checking it out as part of the survey. The open parkland area is the Parc du Champ de Mars. I thought the same as you—the buildings on both sides of the park. I expect to have a number of building choices for our team members to check out under cover of inquiring about short term apartment rentals in the area."

"I bet I know who you plan to use to check out their availability, particularly those up high enough in the buildings for direct line of sight towards the foot of the tower. It has to be our favorite married couple from the Middle East."

"You got it right. Our Lebanese couple, Hassan and Rena, will make the initial inquiries, and I expect they will be able to spot a couple of good ones, depending upon the projected distances to where we anticipate Ahmadinejad to be standing for the photographs below the tower."

"You know, Gene, irrespective being in their late 70s, that are able to get the job done easily without drawing any kind of attention or suspicion. The are very bright, with lots of awareness of what is taking place around them, full of energy and also fleet of foot when moving out on the streets."

"Actually, I'll be meeting with them three days from now to brief them up and get them on their way to Paris as soon as possible. Their Lebanese passports are in order and Paris is like their second home. They will be invaluable for us."

"Also, with their native French language capability, they will move around with ease. What are your initial thoughts about the apartments themselves?"

"Depending upon the shooting distance involved, Mitch, I have an idea to run by you. If time will allow for it, I am considering constructing a false wall concealment area inside the chosen apartment. It will enable you to stay behind for a few days, after the hit, in order to avoid the immediate commotion difficulty in clearing out of the area."

"Go on."

"Most of the apartment buildings that line the Champ de Mars leading away from the tower are rectangular in configuration, six to seven stories in height, and with front sides that provide excellent views facing the tower. The rear of the buildings, do not have a view of the tower at all. This is where my idea comes into play. If we find two suitable apartments, I would like you do the hit from the side of the building facing the tower, then move down a flight or two of stairs to another apartment in the rear of the selected building. This second apartment is where the false wall will be installed."

"I'm with you on this. I would expect that even with me making a suppressed shot, the confusion and commotion that ensue will result in a massive police search of the many buildings along the Parc, especially once the trajectory is established for the path the round travels before impact. It should result in the police focusing on the upper floors of those buildings whose apartments are above the trees lining the Parc and have an unobstructed line of sight to the foot of the tower. In a worst-case scenario, the authorities are able to pinpoint a building or two correctly and do a thorough search of all the apartments in the buildings under suspicion. I would expect the search would not be as thorough on the opposite side of the building. Any individuals found in the apartments, however, can expect to be questioned. This is where the quality of the false wall comes into play."

"The wall will be the key to pulling this off successfully. If done right, it would not have to be any more than 18 inches in width, with a dresser, table, or armoire in the front of it to conceal the small entrance way that allows you access. Only a very sharp eye would spot what, in effect, is a slightly narrower room."

"A bed with a large solid wood headboard, for example, could also serve to conceal the small doorway."

"Whatever we use, we could even place sliding coasters on the bottom of the legs, allowing for movement if it becomes necessary, and they would not be that noticeable. With you entering the second apartment from the shooting nest upstairs, the doorway to the concealed area would be ready and open for you. Once inside, a member of our team would slide the armoire, bed, or whatever, in place."

"I can live with that for awhile."

"You would probably need to be in that second apartment, including inside the concealed area when necessary, for several days until it is judged time to get you out of there and into the escape and evasion phase.

"If we luck out in finding a suitable building with two or more vacancies, I believe we can make this work. Who else besides Hassan and Rana will be involved in renting the apartments?"

"Our Luxembourg-born, former New York City schoolteacher, Laura, is available for this one. She will pose as a schoolteacher on a sabbatical, planning on a one-month stay in Paris. Monica, our French art and history doctoral student, is also going to participate as well. The two of them, along with Hassan, Rena and I, will make up the part of the team responsible for the pre-hit survey. Excluding me, the four of them will also handle the search for the apartments, with Laura and Monica doing the actual renting, if we are lucky enough to find two in the same building. The remaining member of the team will be our carpenter and handyman, Beau. How does that sound to you, Mitch?"

"That's fine with me. I assume that means Beau will be responsible for assembling the concealment wall when not performing in his surveillance and counter-surveillance roles. Actually, knowing that all of them have excellent street surveillance skills, they will be invaluable to us."

"Speaking about being of value, you have a big day on the range tomorrow. I know it won't take much to confirm your penchant for accuracy, but in terms of having you at your best, let's call it a night."

"With a good night's sleep behind me, I'll be ready."

CHAPTER 7

The topic of death never particularly interested Gabriela as a subject for any kind of serious study. As a U.S. soldier and Special Forces intelligence operative, killing when necessary is something to face in the line of duty. In the few previous combat ops she engaged in while on assignment in Latin America, she found no pleasure or desire to celebrate following the taking of an enemy's life. While she was prepared to lay down her own life for her country, she made damn sure it was the enemy, instead, that gave up theirs.

Traveling north from Fort Bragg to Washington, and entering the Pentagon's third-floor, super-secure National Military Intelligence Center, was quite an experience for her. Following the briefing there and her induction into one of JSOC's most accomplished SMU teams, she was escorted into the large fifth-floor, sumptuous mahogany wood-paneled office of SecDef Panetta. After they sat down and the basic pleasantries were over, she found herself alone with the SecDef, except for one of his aides who moved to a chair in the far rear of the room.

"I realize this is considered a special kind of meeting for the both of us. However, we are experiencing unusual times in many parts of the world now, and I wanted to be the one to welcome you into what I have found to be the best SMU team we have in JSOC," Panetta said.

"I cannot thank you enough, Mr. Secretary, for this opportunity. I will not let you or our country down."

"Your record speaks for itself, Captain. Because of the recommendation from the JSOC Commander that you join up with this particular SMU, and because I have given specific orders for a sensitive operation to be undertaken by this team, I specifically asked for you to be present today so I could be the one to brief you on it."

"Sir, my fellow team members are really going to be envious when they learn I am meeting with you here today."

"Your CO is envious too, since a meeting like this is almost always inappropriate. Rest assured, he is fully briefed on us meeting today, as well as aware of the nature of what I am about to tell you."

"Thank you, sir."

"The first assignment is going to take you back to Latin America. I can see from your record that you have extensive experience in Columbia, Peru and Chile, including getting high marks for your singleton efforts, as well as a fine record of combat ops against militant guerrillas and terrorist groups there."

"I did what I was assigned to do and was fortunate enough to succeed. It still required a lot of support and assistance from my team members."

"It is because of your penchant for working alone and being the point person, that I am sending you and your team to Venezuela this time. I see you have not worked there so far."

"That is correct, sir."

"This operation will result in the targeted killing of Venezuelan President Hugo Chavez. Do you have any kind of problem with this kind of assignment, Captain?"

"No sir. Not in the least. However, it will be a first for me in going after such a high-level target. All of my previous assignments, as you just noted, were against guerrilla cadres, terrorists and drug runners. None of them were that high up on the food chain."

"Your CO, Major Green, was in this room with me the day before yesterday for the same briefing. As we speak, your SMU team has now been made aware of my orders and is already working on the planning phase for the mission. Because of the ops sensitivity and necessary compartmentation that are involved, all subsequent orders and instructions of any kind will also by word of mouth, with no cable traffic or written orders to be issued. As I understand it from your CO, you will be serving as his Executive Officer."

"Yes sir and it is an honor for me to serve in that capacity."

"He will brief you further upon your return to JSOC at Fort Bragg. Let me add here and now that I believe your role is perfectly suited for you, Captain, since you will be the first of your team to leave for Caracas and conduct the initial pre-hit survey on your own. We also have the benefit of running a couple of recruited Venezuelan agent assets on the ground there who are part of Chavez's security apparatus and report out to us regularly. You and your team will have the benefit of their reporting on the schedule of events he will be participating in, including dates, times and locations. Furthermore, NSA intercepts will also be available and forwarded to your team as well.

"I look forward to this mission, sir, and will do my best."

"Your CO and team members will work out your cover details and see to it you will have everything required. Do you have any questions, Captain?"

"No sir. Thank you again for this assignment."

"I realize this is a lot for you to absorb, especially with you just joining SMU, let alone meeting here today with me. However, with what I have been told about you, and what your record shows, you will indeed do us all proud."

*   *   *

Throughout the President's first term in office, he regularly received detailed briefings on Venezuela, Iran and North Korea. It included the President's Daily Brief from the Director of National Intelligence, consultations with his National Security Adviser and the National Security Staff, and meetings with the country's senior-most military and intelligence leaders. With the same kinds of meetings now taking place in his second term, and no noticeable improvement in our relations with any of the three countries involved, he decided it was time for a change. After much personal deliberation on his part, he determined the need for an entirely different course of action to take against all three rogue states. With Chavez, Ahmadinejad and Kim all continuing down their paths of sponsoring international terrorism groups, plus directing and supporting specific terrorist acts, all three in joint concert threatened to bury the U.S., Israel and other close allies. The deciding factor, moreover, was when all three set out in pursuit of developing and acquiring nuclear weapons. Therefore, and once and for all, he reasoned, the U.S. would move to stop them in their tracks through regime change, thereby eliminating their capacity to be a threat to any country in the future

The President noted, from briefings on Iran and North Korea, that the CIA and DOD had, for a number of years, been regularly tracking the physical locations, movements and activities of Ahmadinejad and Kim Jong-Il, always looking for a time and set of circumstances whereby they could be successfully eliminated, should such orders be given. In the case of Chavez however, while a contingency plan was on both the CIA and DOD's shelves in the event of a regime change in Venezuela, consideration for eliminating him was not included. Now, with Chavez committed to Venezuela providing direct support to international terrorist groups and embarking on a nuclear weapon acquisition program, the President added him to the list.

If nothing else, as the President rationalized, such planning on the part of certain government agencies made the process of going into action less complicated than having to start from scratch. The difficulty lay in the President concluding that such action had become necessary. When he first was elected to the office back in 2008, the President hoped his administration's policies, for both domestic and foreign affairs, would embrace the concept of "fair play." As idealistic and admirable as a goal can be, it was no longer practicable in today's world. Instead, U.S. action towards its enemies would have to be more sophisticated, more aggressive, more clever and, as a result, more effective than the death and destruction being wrought with the American government and U.S. citizens at home and abroad.

No sooner than first taking office, the President surprised himself with the ease it was to increase drastically the use of drone aircraft to eliminate Afghani and Pakistani Taliban, along with assorted militant Jihadists in the border areas of both countries. The Bush administration's military policies against these same terrorist groups, which the President criticized while campaigning for election, were barely successful when compared to the significant upsurge in drone attacks and cross border raids on the ground ordered by the President after assuming office. As he mused to himself on more than one occasion, "So much for fair play. I'm in it, I like the results, and it will continue, as fundamentally repugnant it may be for many of my critics."

* * *

The National Rifle Association's Whittington Center, located on the south-western outskirts of Raton, New Mexico, is a target-shooting gun enthusiast's paradise.

Comprised of 17 assorted types of ranges, for all types of weapons, the expansive facility also includes 33,300 acres of natural beauty for hiking, camping, and wildlife viewing. However, it was not the beauty of the area, or the assortment of ranges, that convinced Gene of its suitability for Mitch's use. Instead, it was the 1,000-yard high power rifle range and his old Marine Corps buddy, who happened to be the facility's chief range master and was willing to close off the range for Mitch's personal use.

Arriving on range with a cloudless blue-sky overhead, at 10 o'clock in the morning, the range master kept his word to Gene and not a soul was in sight. The Agency support officer, who served as their driver, unloaded the rifles and supporting gear from the SUV, and helped Gene and Mitch to set up on the range's firing line. He then drove off, with instructions to return to pick them up at one in the afternoon. By prior arrangement with the range master, Gene had 18 cardboard silhouette targets on stands delivered ahead of time for Mitch's use. Normally, at the facility's high power rifle range, only four kinds of NRA silhouettes are allowed: a Gallinaa (chicken), a Javelina (pig), a Guajalote (turkey), and a Borrego (ram), for distances of 200 to 500 meters. Instead, in their place were full-view, black-on-white images of a person holding a handgun. These silhouettes were placed, three to a line, at 300, 500, 600, 800, 900 and 1,000-yard firing lines. The use of these images, plus their placement, was unusual, another reason for having the range closed to all other shooters.

Ideally, Gene would have preferred that Mitch be able to use the secure and restricted 1,000-yard range at the Quantico Marine Corps Base in Virginia. That range would also have been reserved for Mitch's exclusive use, and mechanized steel targets that automatically reset upon being hit would have been used instead of cardboard. However, with the security restrictions and desire for Mitch not to be anywhere near a federal facility, the Whittington Center's location in a relatively remote part of New Mexico was an excellent alternative.

Once the three rifles and ammunition were placed on the bench rest at the firing line, and Gene had set up a Vortex Razor HD spotting scope, Mitch was ready to begin firing. He did not expect to be rusty, even though he was only able to practice two to three times a year since he moved from San Francisco to Rome. He was an accomplished shooter with an uncanny knack for accuracy, and he expected nothing less for this day's shooting effort. The game plan called for the use of only two types of ammunition: .338 Lapua Magnum armor-piercing and incendiary rounds. Mitch was to fire a minimum of three shots of each type of rounds, from the three rifles, at all the three targets on the six firing lines. At that point, depending upon the overall degree of accuracy achieved, Gene and Mitch would decide if more firing was needed.

Starting out with the British L115A sniper rifle at 300 yards, he placed six rounds of both types of ammo inside the center of the chest of the silhouette, within a grouping of only two inches in diameter. Using a titanium suppresser and a Zeiss Hensoldt ZF 4-16x56mm variable scope, he could not ask for much better accuracy to begin with for the day. He worked his way through the 500, 600, 800 and 900-yard target lines, six rounds into each target. Gene, alongside him, used the spotting scope to call out the degree of accuracy, size and location of the groupings. Mitch continued to achieve two to three inch diameter groupings on all the targets, with all rounds placed in the center of the chest of the silhouette. For the 1,000-yard silhouette target, two of the rounds, in the center of the chest, were so close together that Gene had difficulty discerning the slightly larger diameter of the hole for the two rounds. The third round was six inches off the center of the chest. As a result, Mitch fired four more rounds at 1,000 yards, all landing in the center of the chest within a three-inch diameter grouping.

Next, he turned to the Finnish Sako TRG-42 rifle, with a stainless steel barrel threaded for its titanium suppresser. It was topped with a Nikon Monarch X 2.5-10x44mm scope. Mitch fired 36 rounds into a new set of silhouettes, all at the same distances used with the L115A rifle. Since all the groupings at the various distances were within 2-3 inches in diameter, including the 800, 900 and 1000 yards targets, he was satisfied.

Lastly, Mitch turned to the Canadian C-14 Timberwolf rifle, also equipped with a titanium suppresser, and mounted with a Leica ER 2.5-10x42mm scope. The results were identical—18 rounds all grouped within 2-3 inches in the center chest of each silhouette on all of the six distances.

"All right, fella, are you as pleased as I am?" Gene asked.

"Yeah, I feel real good. All three rifles are still my favorites. If I had to choose one to serve as my all-around choice, it would be a tough decision. In the end though, and leave it to the Brits, it will be the L115A.

"What about for Paris?"

"Since right now we have no idea of a location for the shoot, let alone the distance, I will still go British."

"I can arrange to have all three rifles on hand and, once we have a suitable apartment location chosen, you can select which one to have in place for your use."

"That will be perfect, Gene."

"All three rifles will be boxed up in separate concealment devices, tripods included, so as not to look like rifle cases. You know the drill. It will be the same as in the past. Another thing I have been thinking of is to have one of our team members leave the ground floor exit of the apartment building a few minutes after the shoot, and run a surveillance detection route away from the area to see if he or she attracts any attention. I know it is taking a chance; however, they will have a well backstopped cover story and not have any gunpowder residue on them should they be stopped, questioned, and examined."

"Gene, the idea is good; however, I would like it if they had a cover story that placed he or she in the company of someone, preferably French, in their actual apartment at the time, in order to withstand police scrutiny should it become necessary. I don't like having any of them out on the street immediately after the shoot, unless it is strictly for static surveillance purposes."

"I'll work on it when I follow-up with the other team members once they are on-site in Paris."

"I know I will be in good hands with you taking the lead there."

"Do you want to fire any more rounds? We still have 20 minutes left on our reservation time. How about doing some box shooting groups on the corners of the targets in order to test your adjustments on the three scopes?"

"Having used all three of them in the past, and except for that one round that went a little astray on the 1,000 yard target, my adjustments are just fine. Let's call it quits for the day."

"Our driver is due back anytime, Mitch. I'll have him take you to the motel separately. I'll stay here with the gear and also have some time to visit with my old Corps buddy, the range master."

"How about if we use our secure phones over the next couple of days to work out any final details before I head to France?"

"That'll be fine, Mitch. Since we will not have any occasion to directly link up once you are there, our phone conversations will have to suffice."

"That's worked in the past, and it will work again. Best wishes, Gene."

CHAPTER 8

Manolo Diaz, the Cuban smuggler, was called out of semi-retirement by the leader of the SMU team, Major Dexter Green, to play a role in the operation to remove Chavez from office in Venezuela. Fifteen years earlier, when Manolo was specializing in the use of small, fast boats for moving people, weapons, supplies and assorted contraband materials into and out of Cuba, he was recruited by Green as a source of information on the island nation. With much of his smuggling operations either starting out from Venezuela, or ending up there, he was on close and friendly terms, especially where money was involved, with a number of ranking Venezuelan military officers, customs and intelligence personnel who were all susceptible to his requests for favors.

Now, however, living on a 60-foot fishing boat berthed in the Mexican port of Vera Cruz, the only operations Manolo ran were hiring out for local fishing charters in the Gulf of Mexico. Green hoped that when he called, Manolo would consider it a good omen, since it would offer up the opportunity for a little excitement in his life. Green, knowing that Manolo was known to the Mexican authorities for his past smuggling activities, decided to meet with him to the south of Vera Cruz, six miles away in the more modern area of Boca del Rio.

When Manolo arrived at the Hotel Mocambo, an old Spanish-style edifice built in the 1940s and located on the high ground of Mocambo Beach, he called Green on his cell phone and was invited upstairs to a small suite where the two would be afforded the needed privacy. It was three in the afternoon on a hot, sultry day. Green opened the door and greeted him with a hearty bear hug since they had not seen one another for several years, and then served up ice cold Coronas. They began their discussion.

"Manolo, you just do not age. You look great, how have you been, old friend?"

"I'm growing long in tooth and not busy enough these days," was his reply.

"I hope," Green said, "to be able to remedy that situation."

"I knew you didn't come here just to offer me a beer. My boat is paid for in full, and the few fishing charters that come along now and then provide for its upkeep, pay the berthing fees and keep me in food and drink. That's about it. Not much excitement anymore."

"How would you feel about spending some time over in Caracas? Are you still on good terms with your many official friends there?"

"Always, my friend. When it becomes necessary, greasing their palms still does the trick. What do you have in mind for me?"

"I'm planning on having a few of my people go there and take out a couple of government officials. Actually, it will be a couple of senior officials. Your role will be strictly as a decoy; actually, a distraction right after the hit is made. You will not have any actual direct involvement in it at all."

"A few more details, please."

"Sure. With the hit coming from a specific location, your role will be to make a commotion, a distracting noise from a nearby hotel parking lot, to draw the attention of the police and security authorities toward you instead."

"Go on."

"For example, Manolo, thirty seconds to one minute after the hit, with you sitting at the ready inside your rental car, I will call you on your cell phone. This will be the signal for you to squeal your tires noisily as you drive away fast in an opposite direction from where the hit was made. This will serve to draw their attention, and you may be stopped. With the smell of some of that lousy Venezuelan rum on your breath, you will be questioned and subsequently released to return to your own hotel."

"So, I play the role of having been drinking, but not enough to be arrested for drunk driving and a little recklessness, as I start the drive back to my hotel. Correct?"

"That's it, Manolo. Exactly."

"You are right about their rum there. No comparison to Cuban rum."

"The key here, old friend, is the distraction you make may initially draw attention to yourself. This will provide the time for my shooters to start to move out of their area for the escape and evasion."

"How long will I be on the ground there?"

"With a good cover story to justify your being there, I would say a minimum of one week, and no longer than two weeks."

"If I fly down from here to Caracas and back, sure, that will work for me. Are boats of any kind to be involved?"

"No, not directly this time. However, how about a cover story of you going there to look to attract fishing boat charters up here in the Gulf of Mexico? With you as an actual charter boat skipper, would that be a plausible reason for you to be in Venezuela?"

"Yeah, it would be. I can do a canvassing survey of travel agents in Caracas and the marina operators in nearby La Guaira. The purpose would be to determine, for example, if it makes sense to bring my boat down from Vera Cruz in order to charter it out to the many wealthy Venezuelans that enjoy sport fishing in the local waters. The offshore fishing is comparable in both places, and a good charter boat is always in demand."

"You have not changed, Manolo. You still know how to make things work. I will be linking up with you by cell phone throughout your stay in Caracas. However, we will, for obvious reasons, not have any kind of direct contact. At some point during your canvassing survey, I will give you a heads up to be in a certain hotel parking lot and wait for my next call to begin the noisy departure heading off in a particular direction. If it turns out no one tries to follow and intercept you, so be it. Just return to your hotel and await further word from me."

"What about my old contacts there in the government?"

"They should not have knowledge of your presence there at all. However, if you are stopped and questioned later, and they do become aware of you, the cover story of doing the survey should be plausible. Subsequently, if any of the police and security types do not buy your story, and believe that you are connected or involved some way in the hit, your naming of your old contacts in order for them to vouch for you may work out. Since you will not be directly involved in what we will be doing there, no one will be able to connect you in any way with our operation."

"I can live with that. What about you and your team? Will you be able to help me out should it become necessary?"

"I don't see that happening in this op, Manolo. Just being a decoy and making the distraction will be the extent of your role. Your cover story of the survey, followed by having a drink or two in the hotel, should be enough to hold up."

"Who do you plan on taking out? Is it anyone I might know?"

"You may hear about it while you are still there in-country, but I doubt you are familiar with any of them."

"Alright then, old friend, now the important part—what's in it for me?"

"I'm glad you asked, Manolo. This part you will like. For your round-trip air travel, hotel, rented car and food, $10,000 dollars. For your time and effort, which I'll call your honorarium, you get $15,000 dollars more. I will give you half now, followed by the remainder when you return here to Vera Cruz. How does that sound?"

"For me just to serve as a decoy distraction, you must be making a hit on the man himself, el Presidente Chavez."

"No, not at this time. It will be a little down the chain of command, instead."

"Count me in. And keep in mind though, I am prepared to do more for you, if need be."

"Manolo, that is what I like about working with you. You are always willing to go that little extra distance. You have not changed at all."

"It's all part of the service I provide, my friend."

As they finished their third round of Coronas, Green gave Manolo a manila envelope stuffed with $12,500 dollars, in crisp $100 dollar notes. They made arrangements to be back in contact, via cell phone, when the trip to Caracas should begin. They said their goodbyes and Manolo departed from the hotel by taxi for the port area where his boat was berthed.

Before leaving the hotel himself, to have dinner alone in a nearby restaurant, Green further mulled over in his mind the projected use of Manolo in the op. He was pleased with the way the meeting turned out, and he knew from his previous work with Manolo that he would perform as instructed. No more or no less than agreed upon, he felt comfortable that the distraction from the noisy car could well serve to draw the attention of the authorities away from where the shooter would be exiting the hide position in a nearby hotel location.

Should it turn out that Manolo was detained for investigation and interrogation, his cover story would have to suffice in explaining the purpose of his trip and presence in Venezuela. With no evidence found linking him to the hit, he should be released. If all went according to plan, he might not even find it necessary to contact any of his government friends to prove his bona fides and vouch for him. Green accepted that, should Manolo be detained, for whatever reason, it could certainly put a damper on their relationship when he returned to Vera Cruz to pay him the remaining monies. However, knowing how well they worked together in the past during some tense encounters with Cuban security and military types, he knew Manolo was one very strong person when it came to handling himself under difficult circumstances.

When Green was originally given his oral orders by the JSOC command to plan and execute the hit on Chavez, he accepted it with relish, since it came with him having complete control for formulating the plan of the op. Now, however, as he thought further about the use of Manolo, and the extraction of the shooter and the rest of the team out of Venezuela, he realized that he and the team still had heavy-duty planning ahead in order to bring the op into better focus. DOD, like the CIA, maintained on-the-shelf contingency plans for literally each country of the world. Name the country and something was spelled out in a detailed ops plan on how to handle every conceivable type of situation, whether it was to be a full-scale war scenario or a limited direct action lethal op. This scenario, however, for an SMU team of limited size to engage in a directed action killing of a sitting head of state, was unusual.

CHAPTER 9

"This op is going to be of the classic shoot and scoot variety," intoned Green to his fully assembled team back at Fort Bragg. "Unlike the kinds of direct action ops we've engaged in over the last couple of years, this time each of us will travel separately, as singletons, and return the same way. Unless we run into enemy action that impedes any of us during the op, and it requires one or more of us to intercede to assist a team member, we will remain as singletons throughout.

"Each one of us will make our way to Caracas from different locations in the U.S. and Central America. Your alias documents, tourist passports included, will be forwarded to a U.S. city, like Los Angeles, Dallas, Chicago, or New York, for example, where your ostensible cover company is located. You will pick them up there and commence your travel on round-trip tickets. Some tickets will have an open return, and some will have specific dates for the return leg, which can be changed in Caracas, should it become necessary. Once the hit has been made, and providing you are not prevented from departing for whatever reason, you will either go onward to another South American destination for a few days before returning stateside, or return directly to the point of origin on your ticket. There, you will exchange your documents for true name ones, and fly back here to Bragg. What are your comments?"

"Sir," Gabriela said, "As you know, we have worked out my cover story and purpose for traveling to Caracas. As for the other team members, I am currently working with them in finalizing their backstopped cover and all the necessary documents for them to function securely."

"That's fine, Captain. I like the way you have stepped up to already become an integral part of this SMU. Since you have only recently joined us, let me make a few general comments, some of which you are probably already aware. Except for you, Captain, we are all snipers qualified. You, as an experienced SF officer as well as an intelligence case officer, are particularly well suited for this op. That is why I selected you to be the XO. For the benefit of your other team members, the Captain is also an expert marksman in both rifles and handguns. As a value added plus for this op, she has directly participated in several similar direct action lethal ops in Latin America in the past.

"I have assigned her to be the first to hit the boots on the ground in Caracas, having about a four to five day head start on the rest of us. That will enable her to conduct the pre-hit survey. Once we know the locations and circumstances for upcoming events that Chavez will be participating in, she will be able to direct us to the best hide locations for the shoot. I am confident that these locations will be hotel rooms with upper floors having a direct line of sight to the target. Captain, pick up on this thread and continue the discussion."

"Thank you, sir. First off, I encourage all of you to maintain your current hairstyles and trimmed beards. This op calls for us to look anything but military, both in our actions and physical appearance. Being that we are all Spanish speakers and, except for two of you, are Latinos as well, we will blend in quite naturally. After you arrive in Caracas and have a chance to observe what the local men are wearing, I encourage you to go out and purchase some indigenous local clothes, particularly shirts, for example, to blend in with the populace.

"For me, I will be posing as a travel consultant, visiting Venezuela for purposes of scouting out new tour possibilities for tourists who are seeking more offbeat types of destinations. For example, tours that focuses on the foods of Venezuela, with particular emphasis on the latest avant garde cuisines being offered there. Other examples that I would explore with local tour agencies are arranging for white water rafting, paragliding, long distance mountain bike touring, etc. The point is, I will be able to move around in both the city and surrounding area using this kind of business cover. It will enable me to engage in the actual operational goal of conducting a detailed search reconnaissance and systematically observe the targets areas and potential hide locations from which to make the hit."

"Captain, let me interject here," said the Major. "This morning I received a detailed cable from the military attaché in our embassy in Caracas. He cited some of the favorite venues Chavez likes to use when making his frequent speeches outdoors to the people there. It will serve as a starting point for your initial forays around the city until we learn from our two recruited agents in his presidential security detail the specifics of the upcoming venues he will be using."

"Thank you, sir. The information from those two agents will be crucial to our plan. Several years ago I passed through Caracas on a couple of occasions and was impressed with the numerous park areas downtown and their proximity to high-rise hotels and apartment buildings. I believe Chavez frequently makes use of these parks for outdoor speeches."

"Captain, let me interrupt you again, since this is a good time to talk about our means of communicating during this op. Instead of our usual tactical, hand-held secure transceivers, which would be our death sentence if discovered on us, we will all be using normal looking cell phones with encrypted capabilities. We will use them throughout the duration of this op. Captain, should you leave for Caracas before the agents report in, we will get their information to you, via the cell phones, as soon as received."

"Thank you, sir. Once I receive their reporting and am able to check out likely locations, I will be prepared to offer up a number of hide locations, depending upon Chavez's projected schedule of events. I will be carrying with me, inside a small traveling case concealment device, an additional set of alias documents, including a passport and driver's license. Should I find a hotel, for example, that overlooks the area from which Chavez is expected to speak, I will rent a room that provides for the best shoot location. Sgt. Major Garcia will then be able to move into this hide location and prepare his set-up.

"After previously talking with several of you and finding out you have not worked an op that is reliant on this form of cellular phone commo, let me reassure you that this kind of system works exceptionally well. I have been involved in a number of ops in the past using it, and it will not be a problem for any of you."

"Captain, before we end this meeting, what are the remaining details that are still outstanding insofar documentation and cover for the rest of the team?" the Major asked.

"Sir, this week two of the men will be traveling to the locations of their new cover companies that our support people have arranged for backstopping. While there they will also obtain alias driver's licenses from the DMVs in those states where they will purport to live and work. By the first of next week, the team will move into ready-to-go status."

"That's good news, Captain. Are you satisfied these guys can pull off their cover legends should they be stopped and questioned?

"Yes sir, I am satisfied. Although I have yet to see them in action in the field, I did put them through some mock drills of entering a foreign country, going through immigration and custom controls, and being interviewed on their cover stories. I am confident they will do quite well."

"That's good news. Lastly, let me mention something about our shooter and the weapons we will have available to us once inside Venezuela. When I selected the Sergeant Major as the shooter for this op, believe it or not, he is not that much better than the other qualified snipers on this team. That is because all five of you are outstanding expert sniper shooters. However, his preference for a particular rifle type sold me on making him my choice for this hit. After the shoot, he will be able to leave it behind, thereby making it appear as though he barely got out of the hide location before being discovered. With the local security, police, and intel types subsequently finding it in the hide location, it may serve to throw them a curve ball as to who is responsible for the hit. A curve ball they are not expecting."

"How's that, Major?"

"Captain, what do you know about the Dragunov sniper rifle?"

"Sir, it is Soviet-made, fires a 7.62 caliber round, is semi-automatic and not thought to be in use by U.S. forces. I believe that in the past, it was primarily limited to the Soviet Union, the former Warsaw Pact nations, China and Iran."

"Captain, that's excellent. Not being known to be in use by the U.S. military is what makes it my choice. It just so happens that our Sgt. Major is truly an outstanding shot with that weapon in his hands. He uses it with a custom designed and fitted titanium suppresser and when fired from 300 to 1000 meters out, nobody can touch him for accuracy."

"Sir, I certainly like your idea for its use. Since this SMU team is operating quite differently for this op, compared to a more normal deployment, configuration and armament, a Dragunov makes for an unusual choice. I look forward to moving out to Caracas next week and conducting the survey that will result in just the right location for the Sgt. Major to show his stuff.

"I can see though," the Captain continued, "that since he will be leaving the weapon behind in a hotel room that I will be renting in alias,

I will need to be long gone and on my way out of the country when the hit is made."

"You're correct on that one, Captain. Moreover, based on your record in past ops, I have no doubt that you will not encounter any difficulties in making your way back home here."

"I will be up to the task, sir. As for the rest of the team, what weapons will we be carrying in the event their use becomes necessary?"

"I have arranged for a diplomatic pouch shipment to our embassy there containing seven SIG-Sauer P-226 handguns, along with 9 millimeter ammo and two magazines for each of us. Once we all are on site, and using our encrypted commo, I will arrange for members of the military attachés staff to deliver them to us. They will conduct brush passes with each of us in out-of-the-way locations on the outskirts of the city."

Gabriela, along with the rest of the team that had sat silent throughout the discussion between her and Major Green, were pleased to know that they would each be in Venezuela carrying their own weapon. In the SIG-Sauer semi-automatic, they would have an excellent one: Superbly accurate, ruggedly built by master Swiss craftsmen and smooth to operate. They nevertheless hoped they would be able to complete the op successfully and leave the country without having to use them.

CHAPTER 10

The last thing that the President wanted, when contemplating the upcoming hit on Iranian President Ahmadinejad in Paris, was to put in jeopardy the rarely acknowledged close relationship with the French government. If there was anything particularly good that was inherited from the previous Bush administration, dating back to the September 11, 2001, terrorist attacks, it was the new relationship between the two governments in dealing with international terrorism. Forget the criticism and negative hyperbole against the French from former SecDef Donald Rumsfeld over them not doing enough to fight terrorism. Furthermore, dismiss that even members of the U.S. Congress showed their displeasure by renaming French Fries as Freedom Fries in their cafeterias on the Hill. That was all nothing more than a cleverly designed smokescreen that aptly served to conceal what the President, after he took office, came to appreciate and benefit from in the form of the top secret Western Counterterrorist Intelligence Center, known by its codename, Alliance Base.

Headquartered in the center of Paris, in the military barracks at Les Invalides, and primarily funded by the CIA's Counterterrorist Center, Alliance Base is comprised of case officers from the intelligence services of France, Great Britain, Germany, Canada, Australia and the U.S. It is headed by a French General from the 12,000-strong external intelligence service, the General Directorate for External Security (DGSE). The purpose of Alliance Base is twofold: to regularly exchange intelligence information on international terrorism, and to plan and conduct operations against terrorists the world over.

Since its startup in early 2003, Alliance Base operations have made extensive use of extraordinary renditions to apprehend and move known and suspected terrorists from one state to another for interrogation and subsequent incarceration.

In the immediate aftermath of September 11th, then French President, Jacques Chirac, issued instructions to all the French secret services that henceforth they were to fully cooperate and share all available applicable information with their American counterparts. His edict included mentioning that U.S. counterparts were to be treated as if they were part of the French services. No sooner had Alliance Base become operational, than another highly secret agreement between the French and the U.S. took place. The French government agreed to place 200 of their Special Forces troops, under U.S. JSOC command, to fight alongside U.S. forces in Afghanistan. Subsequently, as the President has duly noted, that number has grown to over 500 French troops that are separate from the 1,800 regular French army troops in the NATO contingent there.

A further sign of the collaboration between the U.S. and France that remains increasingly active to this day is the Agency's use of an air base, in the former French colony in Djibouti, to fly Predator drone missions against high value terrorist targets in Yemen and elsewhere in the Middle East. As for French detainees at the U.S. base in Guantanamo Bay, in Cuba, France is the only European ally who takes them back to French soil where they continue to be imprisoned. No matter how the relationship is viewed, it remains one of the modern stories of what cooperation between two states can achieve in the war against terrorism.

It was for this reason that the President was willing to take the gamble with the hit against Ahmadinejad in Paris. Even if the French government could determine that an American hand was behind the killing, Iran's support for terrorist attacks around the world, including some costing the lives of French citizens, the President reasoned, would enable the government of France to turn a blind eye to his removal there. Nevertheless, the hit operation itself should make every effort possible to avoid any sign of a U.S. hand and instead make it appear some other enemy of the Iranian state was behind the killing. The clincher that convinced the President that the risk was worthwhile was when he was told what French President Nicolas Sarkozy said before Parliament, while serving as the Minister of the Interior in 2003, on the apprehension of September 11th mastermind, Khalid Sheikh Mohammed: "This arrest took place thanks to the perfect collaboration between the services of the great democracies."

*   *   *

The cryptic call to Jack, from DCI Wicksford's office, as unusual as it was, did not surprise him. Jack knew the request to stop by the DCI's nearby home in McLean, the following Saturday morning, was for no other reason than to provide an update on when the hit on Ahmadinejad would take place, while at the same time providing for the security of their discussion by not having any written record of their meeting on Agency property. With the DCI obviously seeing the incoming intelligence reports on the schedule of events during the visit to Paris, Jack would be pressed for a status report. He knew the DCI would want to be current on the plans for the hit should he receive a query from the President.

Jack was prepared to tell the DCI that Mitch was sent the information on the dates and locations for the two events where Ahmadinejad would be speaking, one of which would be held outdoors at the foot of the Eiffel Tower, the other at a conference for Islamic scholars inside the new Islamic Center in the suburbs of Paris. Mitch was preparing to depart from Rome for Paris within the next two days, and planned, for cover purposes, on conducting several interviews with clients there who were interested in filling some high tech engineering positions. His business visa for entering France was good for ninety days and, once the hit was made, he hoped to leave Paris one week later. He scheduled one last business meeting in the southeast of France, in Lyon, before he planned on leaving the country from the Mediterranean port city of Marseille.

Meanwhile, Jack dispatched Hassan and Rena, the Lebanese couple, to Paris so that they could begin scouting out suitable apartment locations near the Eiffel Tower. He, likewise, scheduled Beau to leave for Paris at the same time and begin to locate sources of materials for the temporary concealment wall to be assembled once the second of the two apartments was rented. Lisa, posing as a divorcee with money, and Monica, as a doctoral student studying French history and the arts, were also preparing to leave and take part in the pre-hit survey and the search for the two apartments to rent for use in the op. Each would be rented anywhere from two to six weeks, depending upon what looked plausible as part of their cover story for being in Paris.

The game plan also called for the members of the team to purchase some of the tools, materials and decorations for the second apartment, so as not to draw attention to a single person buying everything needed, and then carrying it all to the apartment. Beau would also be purchasing a large bolt of black felt cloth for the apartment to be used for the hit. The cloth would be stretched over the inside of the shooting window, about a foot inside the room, with a slit cut in it through which Mitch would be able to shoot from inside the room. Along with the titanium suppresser on the rifle, little noise, if any, would be heard outside the window of the apartment.

*   *   *

Back in Rome following his meeting with Gene and practicing with the rifles at the shooting range in New Mexico, Mitch finalized his plans for the trip to France. He met with his office manager and had him make air, train and hotel reservations for Paris, Lyon and Marseille. Mitch also had him re-confirm the schedule of appointments in Paris and Lyon Three days later, on the eve of his departure for Paris and what he knew would be the most notorious hit of his career to date, he treated himself to a sumptuous dinner at one of his favorite Italian restaurants near Villa Borghese, on Via Margutta. Dining like this was his usual practice before undertaking missions of this type. The quiet and solitude he found in eating and drinking alone allowed him to set the stage for thoroughly thinking out what was soon to come.

By the time he was halfway through the main course, Mitch found he had come to terms, once again, with becoming the key player in the taking of a human life. He fully believed that the act soon to take place at the foot of the Eiffel Tower in Paris was justified based on Ahmadinejad's role in ordering acts of terror to be undertaken against innocent civilian lives. As his executioner, Mitch felt no moral conflict whatsoever in his elimination. Regardless how the job of the assassin was viewed, the preparatory stages and the intricate planning and timing of the unfolding chain of events, all served to provide Mitch with an experience he found to be perversely enjoyable. In carrying out the orders of his commander in chief, Mitch believed that he represented the finest of the foot soldiers doing their duty, including, if need be, to lay down his own life. However, as he had come to practice his craft of enabling death, it would be Ahmadinejad that was going to lay down his life instead.

At the end of his meal, Mitch skipped dessert and instead ordered a glass of twenty-year old Port. He thought of the first moves to take place following his arrival in Paris, turning to the initial efforts to reconnoiter the area around the Eiffel Tower. Although he knew that Gene, along with Hassan, Rena, Laura and Monica, would be conducting a thorough survey of the entire area, including all of the side streets and apartment buildings overlooking the Parc du Champ de Mars, Mitch would still have to satisfy his own predilection for wanting to have at least a partial hand in it as well. He knew though that he would have to stay completely clear of the tower area the day before and day of the hit. Those days the other team members would be there conducting their own counter-surveillance of what the French and Iranian security forces were establishing in the way of observation posts, counter sniping positions, police and security vans, video cameras, traffic re-routing barriers, etc.

With the exception of his birth city—Florence—the sights, the lights and activities taking place in Paris were at the top of Mitch's list of favorite places to visit and enjoy. After arriving there and checking into his hotel, he planned to limit his visit to the Eiffel Tower to accomplishing only two things: one, a walk around the base of the tower, much like he had done in the past; and two, a double-decker excursion bus ride that would take him along the Parc du Champ de Mars, around the tower and alongside the numerous apartment buildings that, from their upper floors, provided excellent line of sight views of the tower itself.

Returning to his apartment in Rome following dinner, Mitch was hopeful of getting a solid night's sleep. While dozing off though, he gave himself a cautionary warning of something to carefully follow and be aware of regarding his changing perception about the taking of a life: Namely, his track record as a highly successful assassin was producing in him a strong sense of being able to kill with joy. He had now come to the stage where he was able to take pleasure in the use of his exceptional skills, and to celebrate each time he achieved success.

CHAPTER 11

"What is the purpose of your visit to Venezuela?" asked the portly, pockmarked immigration officer at Maiquetia International Airport, outside Caracas.

"I am a travel consultant visiting here to see about arranging new vacation locations for eco-tourism adventurers," replied Mariangel Delgado, in actuality, Gabriela in her commercial alias.

"I see you have a new Argentine passport. Where do you live and work?" the officer asked.

"I live in Buenos Aires and work there for several of the local tour companies."

"I see you just arrived on the flight from Lima."

"Yes, it was a connecting flight from Buenos Aires.

"How long do you expect to be here in Venezuela?"

"Approximately two weeks," she replied.

"Do you have a confirmed hotel reservation? If so, what is the name of the hotel where will you be staying?"

"Yes, I do. I will be staying at the Tamanaco Intercon, in Caracas."

"Have you ever visited Venezuela before?"

"No, this is my first time."

"What is the name of your company?"

"Eco-Tours Consulting Associates."

"How long have you worked for them?"

"Next month it will be three years."

"What did you do before that?"

"I sold cosmetics while finishing up my college degree."

"Will you be traveling outside of Caracas during your visit here?"

"Yes, I plan on visiting Maracay, Valencia and Catia la Mar."

"Enjoy your stay in my country."

Following the retrieval of her checked luggage, and an uneventful bus ride from the airport into downtown Caracas, Gabriela checked into her hotel, unpacked and immediately began planning for the pre-hit survey.

Knowing the importance of the survey to both the personal security of the team as well as the success of the hit, she proceeded to map out in her mind what she would accomplish over the next several days. Before leaving Fort Bragg, on the long circuitous trip via Buenos Aires, she worked with the team members in selecting their hotels, their duties while working separately on the ground in Caracas, and their escape routes for leaving the country following the hit. Now that she had learned what the arrival procedures and immigration questions were, she'd pass that information back by secure phone to the team.

As a member of the Special Forces, she prided herself, like all SF personnel, on her individuality and fierce streak of independence. Strong faith in one's own capabilities had become a hallmark of SMU ops. Combined with the use of highly aggressive behavior when dealing with threats to their lives, this self-reliance resulted in the qualities demanded of all SF personnel engaged in guerrilla warfare. Whether operating in the urban environment, like that now called for in Caracas, or applying those same skills and resources against whatever they would face during their individual escapes out of the country, they would be able to cope successfully. The best part to come would be after the return to Bragg and the brief realization that their faith in their own omnipotence and invulnerability was deserved.

Starting out fresh the first morning after her arrival, Gabriela, armed with a list of the numerous outdoor speaking locations President Chavez favored for his boisterous and boastful litanies that served to feed his well-known ego, worked her way around the city checking out each of the six locations on the list. This foray around the city also served to provide her with a layout of the physical characteristics of the overall area. She remembered, from previous visits, several of the city's lush parks that she found now to be near some of the locations Chavez preferred.

In the afternoon, Gabriela checked out a number of the hotels around some of the favored locations, particularly those offering suitable lines of sight on the upper floors. By the time she returned to her own hotel—one that was fortunately not close to any of the possible hit locations—she had come to some conclusions about the most suitable ones for the hide spot from which to make the hit. She knew that upon receiving the information reports from the two agents that detailed the dates, times and locations of upcoming venues for the president, she would be able to follow up with additional reconnaissance. For example, the presence of grandstands and the layout for any rostrums that he would use. In addition, and of high importance, would be the direction that Chavez might be facing in terms of interference from the angle of the sun. Depending upon the time of the event, would the sun be in front or toward the rear of where he could be standing? Knowing that he did not like to get down into the crowds, due to previous assassination attempts, he might only walk where crowds were cordoned off. If so, could nearby trees or the presence of grandstands pose a problem?

The following day was spent out on the streets again, this time studying traffic patterns in a highly congested city with too many cars, buses, trucks and motorcycles, all accompanied by the haze of gas, diesel and oil fumes. By late afternoon, she could identify several suitable escape routes out of the city. These included routes to near and distant towns and cities that could provide brief haven until the team members were able to move toward the borders.

Still on her list, but on hold until a specific location for the president was known, were technical surveillance and observation posts, and potential counter-sniper positions. At this point, she had already accumulated a great deal of information that, by necessity, could not be committed to pen and paper, much less on a laptop computer. Instead, she would be communicating the details to the appropriate team members via secure cell phone, enabling each one to complete their required tasking.

Gabriela would also be responsible for selecting the hotel from which Sgt. Major Garcia would make the hit. Using another alias and passport, she would rent a room in the hotel on a high enough floor to serve as his hide location. Using charm and her good looks, she would make sure she was given a room facing the necessary direction. While the president was speaking and the hit was imminent, she would remain there with the Sgt. Major and assist him in leaving and making sure nothing incriminating was left behind.

She had no plans to return to the first hotel, where she was registered in the Mariangel Delgado alias. Instead, she would pre-position a small bag of clothes and personal items to be used in the escape phase of the op. She would select a hotel on the outskirts of the city, in the direction she would be heading, and arrange to leave the bag in the checkroom for subsequent retrieval.

Sgt. Major Garcia had a different escape plan, as formulated at Bragg ahead of time. Although all of the team's escape plans were obviously subject to change, depending upon conditions in Caracas after the hit, their basic plans would remain in effect, unless it became necessary on the ground to make changes. After leaving the Dragunov rifle behind in the hide location hotel room, accompanying by a Russian language magazine on military arms and ammo, and Russian-made shaving gear in the bathroom, the sergeant major would make his way downstairs to the hotel lobby. He would not appear to be in a rush, since the round fired from the rifle was suppressed and would be basically soundless outside the hotel room window. Two other team members would be in the lobby area to provide backup assistance to the sergeant should he be stopped or detained in any way. At the rear of the hotel, in a parking lot near the hotel tennis courts, an additional team member would be in a rented car to pick the sergeant up and start him off on his escape route toward one of the outlying towns. From there, he would catch a bus and work his way toward the border with Colombia. He would only carry a backpack with change of clothes and personal items for a couple of days. The additional clothes he brought to Venezuela will have been disposed of before the hit on Chavez. Another team member, also in a rented car, would be cruising in the immediate area of the hotel, and would be in cell phone contact with the two members inside the hotel lobby. This team member would be their backup and pick them up after the sergeant was driven away from the hotel.

The remaining member of the team, team leader Major Dexter Green, would be a rover, driving between the hide location hotel, and the spot where Chavez would be speaking. He also would be responsible for keeping track of Manolo Diaz after he was called and instructed to begin the noisy exit from one of the nearby hotel parking lots. Should it work, with security police forces going after him on suspicion of possibly being involved in the assassination, Green would be able to observe Diaz's car antics and inform team members afterwards as they proceeded into their own escape phases.

Posing as a vacationing golfer, complete with his own set of clubs in his rental car, Green would, after observing Diaz, proceed to a local golf course for a leisurely round of 18 holes. He also planned to be the only team member to leave Caracas, two days later, from the main international airport at Maiquetia, provided all went according to plan.

*   *   *

Gabriela, back in her hotel for the evening, waited for the information on the location for Chavez's speech. Then she would be able to complete the remaining loose ends in the pre-hit survey, followed by the arrival and set up of the rest of the team. She felt good about all she was able to accomplish to date and believed that a successful op was in the making. Even if this particular SMU team was not functioning as a typical SF engagement in enemy territory, due to the singleton tasks assigned to them, she knew they were all still bonded by their fellowship of fighting and surviving. It would especially prove itself to be true as they made their separate ways out of the country and met up together afterwards, back at Bragg.

Chapter 12

It was a cold, wet evening when Mitch arrived in Paris after the short flight from Rome. As the taxi pulled up to the front entrance of Hotel La Villa Saint-Germain, the doorman immediately ran out with a large black umbrella in hand, to shield Mitch from the rain.

"Bonsoir Monsieur Vasari," came the greeting from the front desk clerk as Mitch stepped inside to the warmth of the hotel's small lobby.

"Salut to you too," Mitch replied. "It's good to be back in Paris."

"I am holding your previous room, the one that looks down the boulevard toward the Seine. Will that be satisfactory, Monsieur Vasari."

"Of course it will. I would not have it any other way."

"I see your reservation with us is for two weeks. Is that not longer than you usually stay?"

"I will be conducting a number of interviews and I want to give myself plenty of time. If I don't need the full two weeks, I'll give you as much advance notice as possible."

"Very good, Monsieur Vasari. Welcome back to Paris."

Located on the Left Bank in Paris, in the district of Saint-Germain, the hotel is situated in the artistic and literary heart of Mitch's favorite city after Florence. The following morning, after a light breakfast of croissants and coffee, Mitch started the first of two days of scheduled appointments. Under a clear blue sky, and a light crisp breeze, he moved about the city by taxi to make calls on three French electronics firms interested in the executive recruiting services of Mitch's company, M&T Inc. The firms were located in different sections of the city, on the outskirts of the 15th, 18th and 20th arrondissements. On this first day of work, he avoided the 7th arrondissement, where major landmarks and government institutions dominate the district, including the Eiffel Tower where Ahmadinejad would soon be coming on his fateful visit.

Knowing from an intelligence report sourced to the recruited Revolutionary Guard Corps agent of the date and time for Ahmadinejad's photo session with the Iranian students at the foot of the tower, Mitch scheduled all of his meetings well ahead of the session, thereby leaving plenty of time for what would appear to be some leisurely tourist pursuits. The first of these would be to ride on the top of a double-decker tour bus whose route included a drive along the Parc du Champ De Mars to the Eiffel Tower. There, he would be able to get off and walk around the tower area on his own. Looking like a typical tourist with a camera hanging around his neck, he could take his time to get a feel for the overall area.

The second pursuit, one practiced by so many Parisians and tourists alike, would be jogging. Wearing his running clothes, Mitch planned to run and jog throughout the Champ De Mars area in order to reconnoiter the apartment buildings that line the entire distance from the tower eastward to the military academy at Ecole Militaire. His main objective was not to spot suitable shoot locations. That would be the job of fellow team members, Hassan, Rena, Laura and Monica. Which checking out apartments for rent in the area, the four of them would check out the inside of apartments and determine the specific views of the tower from windows. Instead, Mitch's goal would be to get a feel for some of the distances and shooting conditions between the foot of the tower and the buildings along the Champ De Mars.

On the morning of his third day in the city, with all five of his scheduled appointments over with, Mitch walked two blocks from his hotel on rue Jacob, over to Boulevard Saint-Germain where he boarded one of the L'Open Hop-On-Hop-Off tour buses. With four interconnected routes covering most all of central Paris, he went from his Montparnasse-Saint-Germain route over to the front of Les Invalides, the large complex of buildings that house a hospital and retirement home for war veterans, as well as museums and monuments relating to the military history of France. He alighted there, and hopped aboard the Paris Grand Tour route bus to continue the ride westward to the Eiffel Tower. Getting off on the back side of the tower, he strolled around the entire base area that anchors the massive edifice, marveling at the amount of steel that went into its construction.

He knew that by now all the other team members were on the ground in Paris and going about their individual assignments for the pre-hit survey. Looking eastward at the assorted apartment buildings lining the north and south sides of the Champ De Mars, he visualized Hassan, Rena, Laura and Monica checking out available apartments for rent inside them. He knew Beau, the team's professional carpenter, woodworker and amateur sketch artist, would be checking out stores where he might purchase the materials for the false concealment wall. From a brief phone conversation the night before, he knew Gene would be out and about checking on potential backup escape routes out of the city for the team in the event the operation went bad.

Mitch knew that Gene was also responsible for making a brush pass directed by the Chief of Station from inside the embassy. The purpose was to deliver Mitch's sniper rifle which had arrived at the embassy in the diplomatic pouch. The COS was not fully briefed up on the operation, just instructed by headquarters to expect a classified package in the pouch that was not to be opened by anyone in the station staff, including the COS himself. Instead, once the outer wrappings were removed, the package was to be given to the station officer responsible for counterterrorism operations who would, in turn, make arrangements for the secure transfer of the package, in an out-of-the-way part of the city, to Gene. Subsequently, he would see to it that Mitch would find the rifle all set up in the chosen apartment on the day of the hit.

Before getting back onboard the tour bus at the tower, Mitch strolled out onto the Champ De Mars, walked out several hundred yards, and noted the angle of the sun in relation to the various nearby apartments. It was late morning and he knew that on the appointed day Ahmadinejad would be with the students for the photo session early in the afternoon, starting around two p.m. Therefore, Mitch planned to return to the area about that time the following day to further check on the angle of the sun.

Reboarding one of the tour buses and riding further into the center of the city, he got off once more, this time at the Louvre Museum. Whenever on a trip to Paris, he always stopped by. This time the Louvre was having a month-long exhibition of Near Eastern Antiquities and being of interest, he decided to spend the rest of the afternoon viewing it.

Three hours later, after returning to the hotel, he showered and freshened himself up for the evening. Next, he walked several blocks to his favorite Parisian dive bar, Le Piano Vache, located on rue de la Montaigne-St Genevieve.

"Monsieur Vasari, how good to see you. It has been several months," said Paul, the regular bartender known to Mitch for at least the past five years.

"Paul, you look the same as ever, and better than me on any day of the year," he replied.

"What may I serve you?"

"Absolut rocks, please."

"My pleasure." Paul glanced at the entrance behind Mitch. "An old friend just came through the door and is heading over here to see you."

"Mitch, how are you?" said Dirk, an American writer who lived nearby in the Latin Quartier.

"Dirk, why did I know you would be here tonight? Good to see you, man."

"How long will you be here this time?'

"I still have a few more days work, and then will move on to Lyon before returning home to Rome. How about you? Making any money these days?"

"Not as much as I would like. I'm still working as a stringer for the *Christian Science Monitor*, plus continuing to sell feature stories for several U.S. magazines.

Making just enough to get by and enjoy this place as much as ever."

"Dirk, I'm getting a call, and I am going to step out to take it. If I don't come back, how about I meet you back here tomorrow or the next night?"

"Sounds good. I'll call you tomorrow."

*   *   *

"Gene. Good to hear your voice. How are things going? Is everyone here and gainfully employed?" Mitch asked.

"Everything's fine. Hassan, Rena, Laura and Monica are all checking out apartments and Beau, although not yet having a shopping list of items to purchase, is scoping out stores for the best sources of supply."

"That's good news. I see the date is set for the man's visit, and we've got eight days to go. Will that be enough time?"

"Yes, I checked with an old friend here, plus heard back from Hassan and Rena that, upon signing a short-term lease for a minimum of two weeks to one month, they can move in within two days of signing. A police check is required and that only takes 24 hours."

"Is Beau comfortable he can assemble everything in that short a timeframe?"

"Once a foundation is laid for a house, that guy can have it all framed up in a matter of a few days."

"Gene, I like what can be seen along the Champ De Mars. Literally anything on the top two floors of about eight buildings there would appear to be suitable."

"Yeah, that's my view of the situation as well. The rental price for the apartments higher up will be high, but that won't be a problem. It's what we are here for that counts."

"How about contingency planning?" Mitch asked.

"We will continue to try and rent two locations, and also still have you remain behind in one and eventually depart on your own as planned. Meanwhile, I have Beau working on a couple of innovative ways to get you out of the building when ready and moved out of the city and on your way out of the country. I'll let you know should we have to do a rehearsal. Stay in touch."

CHAPTER 13

When he was running his best times, 20 years ago, Mitch could run a mile in four-and-a-half minutes. Today, however, he planned more of a combination run and jog, covering the two-and-a-half miles' distance from his hotel to the Eiffel Tower in a leisurely 20 to 25 minutes. With his days of regularly participating in marathons and triathlon events behind him, this particular route, primarily along the Seine and most all the 7th arrondissement, or Palais-Bourbon as it was also known, should not be covered in a hurry. It is too beautiful to pass by quickly and can best be enjoyed while taking in the gorgeous scenery that is all along the Seine River. Exiting the hotel, he ran around the corner onto rue Bonaparte and headed down the short two blocks to turn left on Quai Malaquais. From there it was basically a straight route along the river to the tower.

Upon reaching the tower from the back side, along Quai Branly, he turned left on Avenue De Suffren, and found himself standing underneath the tower, facing eastward down the Champ De Mars. From there he had a beautiful view all the way to Ecole Militaire and the tower of Tour Montparnasse in the distance behind it. What immediately caught his attention were the rows of apartment buildings, with upper floors above the majestic tree line on both sides of the Champ De Mars, the same buildings he drove past on the tour bus the day before. Based upon his count of buildings from the bus ride, he estimated there were 20 apartment buildings between the tower and the Ecole Militaire, covering a distance of about 1,000 yards, give or take 50 yards either way.

Until he heard from Gene or any of the four team members who were out seeking to rent the two apartments, all that Mitch could do for now was to wait it out. He knew the apartment selected would be well chosen and quite acceptable for his purposes. With so many buildings out there, he felt confident that the perfect one was just waiting to be rented. He also felt good about the distances involved. Unless the weather was to intervene and make shooting conditions more difficult, or cause a change in Ahmadinejad's photo session at the tower, anything under 1,000 yards should pose no problem for him.

*   *   *

Beau Andrews, master carpenter, amateur artist and highly professional counter-terrorist operative specializing in surveillance and counter-surveillance, was thoroughly enjoying himself the past four days. Canvassing the do it yourself hardware stores and antique/restoration shops all over Paris could hold his attention for days on end. Best of all, he was being introduced to a whole new world of French gadgets, tools and ideas for projects that he would be able to enjoy for years to come. Fancying himself a pretty good amateur cook as well, Beau went to a store recommended to him by his girlfriend back in the U.S.—E. Dehillerin—located on rue Coquillere, and arguably the finest kitchen utensils store in all of France. He was only in the store for an hour when he realized he was spending a significant amount of his own money on items that he just could not resist buying. He knew that once the operation to take out Ahmadinejad was finished, and he had additional free time on his hands, he would be back at Dehillerin's for more shopping.

Back to reality though, he knew his job for now was to source materials for a temporary concealment wall that would be constructed in record time, leaving inside the 18 to 24 inches wide space where Mitch would take initial refuge following the hit. Finding at least a half a dozen construction materials and hardware stores around the city that sold everything needed for the job, Beau awaited a call from one of the team members directing him to a specific apartment address. There he would be able to see and select the most suitable room, take measurements and decide on the materials to be used to construct the wall. Once the job was completed, his primary function would be to serve as a counter-surveillant outside the apartment building on the day of the hit. Should the police in any way turn their attention to the building, he would use his phone to warn Mitch to hide inside the concealed area and await further word.

Born in Billings, Montana, and raised in Portland, Oregon, Beau was taught by his college-educated parents to be an independent thinker and decision-maker. The result was a disdain for authority and a penchant for doing things his way. He studied fine arts at Reed College, and initially considered becoming a painter, primarily working in oils. However, a fascination with the myriad types of wood found throughout the Pacific Northwest led him instead to become a professional carpenter. Detail-oriented, and with an obsession for preciseness and order to all things around him, he found that he was not a people person. He concluded he could best survive in today's world by staying on the margins and working, as much as possible, on his own.

A boyhood friend of Beau's from Portland, who also studied at Reed, turned away from the system of liberal independent thinking so valued at the college, and joined the and became an intelligence analyst. He encouraged Beau to apply to the Agency, but upon finding he did not have a graduate degree or skill sets to qualify as an operations officer, Beau was ready to settle down as a carpenter on the west coast. However, when the friend mentioned Beau to a manager in the Counterrorist Center, who was looking to recruit a new surveillance team member, Beau found himself with an offer to travel a lot and spend many hours on his own on the streets of all sorts of hospitable as well as inhospitable locations around the world. With seven years of more excitement than he ever dreamed of behind him, including roaming Parisian shops of fun and interest to him, he now figured that his friend from Oregon did him quite a satisfying favor.

*   *   *

Luxembourg-born, now living in New York City, Laura Nys worked nine years teaching world history in the New York City school system. Within a year of going through an unfortunate divorce, she moved in with a schoolmate from high school, Monica Marshall, a doctoral student studying French art and history at Columbia University. They enjoyed travel in Europe together, whenever they could scrape up the funds to finance a new trip. Upon seeing an advertisement in the *New York Times* for travel writers, they applied, only to learn that the ad sponsor was the Agency in search for people with keen observation skills, a college education, and a spirit for adventure. On a what-the-heck whim, they both applied and were considered for employment.

Following extensive background investigations, polygraph examinations and psychological evaluations, they were offered jobs as independent contractors in the Agency's National Clandestine Service, and assigned to the Counterterrorist Center.

There, they were given six months of training in intelligence tradecraft, surveillance, counter-surveillance, small-arms weapon training, high-speed defensive driving skills and the overall conduct of counter terrorist operations. For the next three years, the two of them built up their proficiency by serving on teams of highly skilled intelligence operatives. Sometimes they worked on the same team, at other times they were separated. They had a shared amazement how much they continued to enjoy what they were doing, and their degree of curiosity and appreciation for the countries where they were assigned to work.

Working for Jack, their supervisor throughout their entire time in CTC, proved to be a bonus for them as well. He appreciated and admired their growing skill in intelligence tradecraft. Their imaginations and ingenuity employed in street demeanor and the use of disguises when conducting surveillance impressed him to no end. By the time that he, along with Gene and Mitch, were asked by the DCI to move to the SAD for the return to lethal ops, it was a given that Jack would take his best surveillance team, Laura and Monica included, with him.

When assigned to participate in the operation against Ahmadinejad in Paris, the two of them were ecstatic to be in a European city they enjoyed so much. Laura, posing as a high school teacher on sabbatical looking for a Parisian apartment to rent for two to three weeks, set about her task of locating one of the two apartments to be used by Mitch during and after the hit. With part of her cover story being true, in this case being a professional educator, it enabled her to easily sell the story line. Monica, also with a strong element of truth in her cover as a post-doctoral student of French art and history, sought an apartment for a two to three week period as well.

The remaining team members in Paris looking for an apartment to rent, Hassan and Rena Hijazi, brought a plausible background and cover story to the task at hand as well. Both were born and raised in Beirut, spoke French fluently and projected an air of being a happily retired couple of wealth who enjoyed traveling across the world. Bringing their advanced age and apparent moneyed status to bear when making inquires on properties available for rent, they were expected to have an easier time in finding their choice of lodging for a third honeymoon in the City of Lights.

With the day approaching for Ahmadinejad's appearance at the foot of the tower just a little over one week away, all team members directly involved were moving quickly to locate the apartments, submit detailed application forms, provide a substantial rental deposit, clear 24-hour police checks and, subsequently, move in. Fortunately, springtime in the city is when many apartments begin coming on the market for rent. In the meantime, Gene maintained secure phone contact with the team, and was regularly updated on the progress they were making. The operation was proceeding according to schedule, and he liked playing team members off against each other in order to see who would be able to produce the two desired apartments of choice.

CHAPTER 14

Casa Natal and Museo Bolivar, two homes from Venezuela's colonial era, are the birthplace and museum of Simon Bolivar, "El Liberator," who succeeded in wresting independence from Spain for not only Venezuela, but also other South American countries as well. The two restored buildings are located side by side in downtown central Caracas at the intersection of Avenidas Universidad and Norte 1.

Chavez, who is obsessed with what he believes is his direct relationship to El Liberator, had the remains at Casa Natal exhumed several years earlier in order to prove a genetic connection. At cabinet meetings, he also has an empty chair near his side for Bolivar's "spirit." He will not make public the DNA testing on the remains since his warped mind knows full well he is not a blood relative by any stretch of the imagination.

When Gabriela received the secure call from Major Green that this would be the site for Chavez to make a major address to the populace the following week, she immediately set about completing the remaining items on the pre-hit survey, including choosing and renting the hotel room to be used as the hide location for the team sniper, Sgt. Major Garcia. The major also told Gabriela that the Casa Natal location is one of Chavez's favorites for making his pronouncements, due to the wide expanse of open grounds in front of the home where a speaker platform is customarily set up directly in front of the main entrance. She planned on taking a leisurely stroll through the grounds the next morning, in order to check out lines of sight to the upper floors of nearby hotels that overlook the expanse of park grounds directly in front of Bolivar's birthplace.

April in Venezuela, nearing the end of the dry season, caps an eight-month period that is the most pleasant time to visit there. The following morning for Gabriela was no exception. The taxi ride from her hotel, the Gran Melia Caracas, to the entrance to the grounds at Avenidas

Universidad and Norte 1, lasted only ten minutes. Upon walking the short distance from the intersection to the front of Casa Natal, she found no indication or evidence of plans for Chavez to make his speech there the following week. No signs were posted nor was any kind of grandstand or podium in the process of being set up. She knew this to be the case ahead of time, based upon reporting from the two agents working in his security detail. With a number of attempts having been made on his life in the past, he subsequently became unpredictable as to time and place for speaking engagements, travel itineraries, etc. In fact, the agents reported that the typical advance notice to newspapers, television and radio stations to be only 24 to 48 hours at most before any of his appearances. Therefore, Gabriela planned to use the last-minute setting up of a speaker's platform and podium as the indicator that Sgt. Major Garcia needed to get in place and ready for the shoot.

Walking up to the front entrance to Casa Natal, she stopped to read the sign that was posted several feet off to the left of the entrance. It listed some of the dates and details in the life of Simon Bolivar. Turning directly around and starting to walk back across the open ground towards the intersection, she scanned the treetops and immediately could spot at least five high rise buildings that looked like hotels nearby. She noted that each had six to ten floors easily above the tree line. Best of all, one of them had a direct line of sight visibility starting on the fourth floor and going up to the tenth top floor. The windows on these floors provided a clear view looking straight down the Avenidas Universidad. She was also able to estimate that the distance from them to the podium area ranged from 600 to no more than 700 yards to the podium area from which Chavez should be speaking, all considered relatively short distance shots for the Sgt. Major. Noting the colors, styles and building decors of the five, she proceeded to spend the rest of the morning and early afternoon visiting each of them to consider their suitability for locations from which the Sgt. Major would complete his mission.

Late in the afternoon, Gabriela stopped by another nearby hotel, the Four Seasons, and made calls to each of the five hotels—the Hilton Caracas, Hotel El Arroyo, Altamira Suites, Caracas Palace Hotel, and the Pestana Caracas Hotel and Suites. Using a cover story of seeking the best prices for a tour group needing ten rooms, including rooms on the upper floors that commanded good views of the city, she determined that all five would be able to accommodate her, since it was just at the end of the tourist season and many rooms were becoming available. Before going to sleep that evening, she called Major Green to reconfirm that the hotels the team members would stay in were different from the five up for consideration in her survey. The major confirmed this, noting that team members would start arriving over the next several days and would be familiarizing themselves with the overall area, plus finalizing their escape and evasion routes.

The next task for Gabriela would be to rent a room in the hotel of her choice for the Sgt. Major's hide nest. She planned to use a different alias and to stay in the room as well, alternating with her room in the Gran Melia Caracas. This would make each of the two hotel rooms looked lived in for housekeeping purposes. The remaining measures still to be checked on were of the threat kind—possible presidential threat countermeasures that Chavez's protective security and intelligence personnel could mount in order to compromise the team's success and ability to escape the country. Unfortunately, Gabriela would not be able to locate these measures and determine their significance until the day before and day of Chavez's speech. Included would be the specific personnel there to guard Chavez and observe the crowds of people around him; the standoff personnel nearby, including counter-snipers that would be observing surrounding buildings as well as occupying some of them; the vehicles, primarily armored; a medical ambulance for moving Chavez out of the area to a hospital; aerial and electronic measures, including protective helicopters for surveillance monitoring; and, counterintelligence measures, the ongoing means and methods employed to gather and evaluate threat information against Chavez.

Gabriela knew that on the day of the hit, downtown Caracas would resemble a militarized zone, and the people and vehicles around Casa Natal would be at a standstill. She also knew that no one could predict how the crowds of people there, much less the security, intelligence and military personnel that would be present, were going to react once the hit on Chavez took place.

* * *

Sgt. Major Ernesto Garcia is a celebrated SF sniper with six tours of duty, two tours each, in Bosnia, Iraq and Afghanistan. Born and raised in El Paso, Texas, of Mexican-American parents, he attended two years of community college there before enlisting in the Army. Easily qualifying for Ranger School and SF training, he subsequently went on to Fort Benning, where he excelled in sniper school. Graduates there are expected to achieve scores of at least 90 percent in first-round hits when firing at a distance of 600 meters. In the sergeant's case, he achieved 97 percent, thereby setting a school record still standing to this day.

After completing his second tour in Afghanistan, he returned to SF headquarters at Fort Bragg, where he joined one of the SMU teams. Participating in half a dozen direct action targeted killings in the Middle East and South America, he was selected by Major Green for the current op to remove Chavez from office. Except for Gabriela, other members of the team, all snipers, could easily have been chosen by Green for this particular assignment. However, Garcia's considerable experience using the Russian-made SVD Dragunov sniper rifle made him the obvious choice.

A quiet, serious and no-nonsense sergeant major, Garcia nevertheless easily mixed well with the team, which admired and respected the versatility of his shooting skills. He also was the oldest team member and this, along with his tours in the hostile areas of Eastern Europe and the Middle East, meant he was accorded the respect he deserved.

Garbriela had Garcia make his hotel reservation in an older hotel located on the outskirts of Caracas. Upon receiving the call from her at least a day in advance of the planned hit, he would check out, take a bus into downtown Caracas and move to the hide location in the hotel of her selection. Plans were in place after the hit for another member of the team to take him by car to the outskirts of Caracas, where he would catch a bus for one of the distant cities in his escape route.

Leaving Fort Bragg in true name, Garcia flew to Los Angeles, where he picked up his alias documents and flew onward to Venezuela via Mexico City. After arriving at Maiquetia Airport, he took a taxi to the nearby Costa Real Suites, a small hotel located in the suburbs of La Guaira, near the beach. After the first day there he found that he was comfortably fitting in well with the local populace. On his second day, he joined a small tour group and visited the nearby National Park El Avila that separates the city of Caracas from the sea. He also found time to lounge about the hotel's outdoor pool and to take his meals in the cantinas in the vicinity. By the end of the third day, with little else to do of interest, he was ready to receive Gabriela's call and move to the hide location.

*   *   *

While Garcia was enjoying his first full day in the country, Major Green arrived and took up residence at the Hotel Centro Lido Regency, in the business area of downtown Caracas. Accompanied with a set of golf clubs as part of his vacation cover story, immediately after arrival he booked a round for the next day, at the Izcaraqua Country Club which was located only three miles from the hotel. He also checked out the hotel's Nouveau Grill, on the top floor, noting the excellent views of the entire city. From there he could view the park area housing the Casa Natal; however, it did not have an unobstructed view of the actual building from where Chavez would be speaking.

The remaining team members, Sergeants Vargas, Diaz and Thompson, all in alias, arrived at Maiquetia Airport the following day, coming in at different times from Mexico City, Port-of-Spain in Trinidad and Cheddi Jagan in Guyana. After arriving at their separate hotels in Caracas, Sergeants Vargas and Diaz rented cars to use as part of the team's separated escapes out of the city after the hit. With all three of them being fluent in Spanish, they quickly settled in and could move about the city with ease. Sgt. Vargas included in his luggage a bag used for tennis gear, since he was designated to meet with an embassy military attaché who would provide him with Garcia's sniper rifle which, having a collapsible stock, would easily fit into the bag. In the few days left before Chavez's scheduled appearance at Casa Natal, the team continued familiarizing themselves with travel routes outside the city and traffic patterns inside, noting the significant vehicular congestion throughout most of the city during daylight hours.

Chapter 15

Running any kind of intelligence operations out of France—Paris, in particular—is decidedly risky business, to say the least. Many of the world's intelligence services consider France a hostile environment in which to operate, treating the environment there much the same as in Moscow, Beijing and Havana. French thinking is colored by the persistent idea that a number of countries, especially the U.S., is engaged in economic warfare with France. Regardless the success of the U.S.-French counter terrorist efforts dating back over a decade to the 9/11 bombings, the French continued to believe that U.S. intelligence agencies support competitors of French firms.

To give French businesses an edge, French laws do not restrict economic developments in the way that many laws in the U.S. affect U.S. firms. In addition, French society does not have a history of fair play and will use every advantage available to gain an upper hand. The French, at times including the government, are conduits of technology and information to anyone who is willing to pay for it.

France's various intelligence services also play a role in helping French firms to succeed against the U.S. They are aggressive, sophisticated, heavy-handed, and pose a significant threat to U.S. interests. They are also full service organizations, able to mount various types of operations, technical collection ops in particular, and are considered on the same level as their U.S. counterparts. Without hesitation, the French government will direct its intelligence services against the U.S. when it believes that national interest, especially economic ones, are threatened.

The Directorate of Territorial Security, the DST, an internal service that is part of the Ministry of Interior, represents the biggest threat inside the country. With over 3,000 employees, their primary interests are the foreign intelligence services that operate within their borders. The DST also gathers information on the legitimate business activities of foreign firms, with particularly U.S. firms. While the Directorate-General for External Security, the DGSE, maintains a cordial, yet compartmented relationship with the CIA on counterterrorist operations, it also is involved in collection ops against the U.S., including science and technology and sensitive economic issues and information. An additional intelligence player inside the country is the Information Directorate of the National Police, the RG. With close to 5,000 employees, they pose a significant threat in their exploitation of telephones, telephone taps, cellular telephony, faxes and all forms of mail package services. The RG efforts at surreptitious entry are, by tradition, their best source of business information against the U.S.

It was because of the RG's excellent technical collection capabilities against cellular telephony, that Gene, Mitch and the rest of the team exercised constant caution when using their secure cell phones. They knew their calls would definitely come to the attention of the RG, but would confound and irritate them to no end because they were encrypted. They would only be able to intercept and record the jangle of sounds and tones from the encrypted traffic as long as the calls lasted. With the team keeping their calls brief, and practicing a high level of operational tradecraft by moving discreetly to new locations during and after all calls were made, their personal security should remain intact. While their calls would not be decrypted, the RG would, nevertheless, be able to, within a few minutes, pinpoint the locations from which the two parties were talking.

The capabilities of the French to successfully work against the U.S. and other countries even extend to their military intelligence officers. In response to requests from analysts, French officers regularly pose as NOCs, under business cover and in civilian clothes, to elicit and collect information from, for example, the U.S. businessmen they meet at technology exhibitions, air shows, conferences, etc. They are able to assess, develop and attempt to recruit the people they meet as new sources of sensitive and proprietary information. Their strongest areas of interest are high technology developments, with emphasis on electronics, communications, aerospace and submarine technologies. Operating against the U.S. and other countries to acquire information on these technologies is considered normal tasking by French intelligence.

So Mitch, every time he visited France under cover for executive recruiting purposes, could expect to come under the watchful eye of at least one of the French services as he made his way about the country to hold meetings with senior French corporate officials interested in his firm's abilities to locate experienced personnel with high-tech skills for their companies. It is for this reason that he did indeed conduct legitimate personnel search activities on behalf of his firm. Except for being able to spot and initially assess a particular French corporate or senior engineering official who exhibited potential vulnerabilities of interest to the Agency he avoided giving the appearance of anything but a real executive search professional.

He also exercised a high level of surveillance consciousness, constantly being alert in his observations as he went about his business. On occasion, he would notice he was being followed to and from business meetings, but never made any alerting moves that would indicate his awareness to his followers. Twice, during previous visits to Paris, once at a technology trade show and another while having a drink in a hotel bar, he was approached by friendly and congenial Frenchmen seeking to engage him in conversation. One of them claimed to be a successful corporate business official acting as a technology broker and looking toward establishing a relationship involving the exchange of information of interest to his firm. On another occasion, a Frenchman claiming to be a trained electrical engineer, like Mitch himself, expressed interest in the kinds of scientific and technical information he was prepared to talk about in depth. The giveaway, to Mitch, was that on both occasions, the Frenchmen ended their conversations by wanting to have another meeting while Mitch was still in France, or wanting to arrange to meet again, upon his return. He knew the drill too well to not be able to detect obvious attempts to establish and sustain contact for further assessment and development purposes.

*   *   *

Going through a local real estate agency, Hassan and Rena met with a rental agent and accompanied her to the seven-story apartment building located on the corners of Avenue Charles Floquet and Avenue Joseph Bouvard, where the building intersected with Allee Thomy Thierry. The agent greeted the madam building supervisor at the ground floor entrance, next to her office, and was given the key to the apartment located on the uppermost floor of the building. They rode the elevator to the top and entered spacious, well-furnished seventh floor apartment.

The living room had two sets of double French doors that opened up upon the Champ De Mars. Rena, in her usual jovial and friendly manner, moved smoothly around the four rooms of the apartment, including the bathroom and kitchen, with Hassan in tow behind her. Returning to the living room, she went over to one set of the French doors and swung them open. She said to the agent that she just had to see the view with the windows open. Exclaiming how beautiful the view was, Rena asked Hassan to come and stand next to her and enjoy it. He did so and was able to easily see, over the tree tops and directly in front of them, the splendor of the entire Eiffel Tower, including all the area underneath it.

Showing definite interest in wanting to rent the apartment for a two-week period so that she and Hassan could enjoy another of their Parisian honeymoons, she asked the rental agent for the best price possible for the period. The agent, reminding the couple that the apartment, being situated on the top floor commanding a superb view from one end of the Champ De Mars to the other, said the non-negotiable price for the two weeks would be 3,900 Euros. Rena, looking at Hassan and obviously posing as the one responsible for the purse strings, said that it would not be acceptable to them. The agent then asked if another apartment in the same building, on the opposite side, would be of interest to them. Rena replied that they were hoping for something with a view, but it would have to be at a lower cost. Offering her apologies for not having anything else that could be of interest, the agent suggested the couple try some of the other agencies to see what they might have available. With that, Rena and Hassan both thanked the agent for her time and effort and departed from the building.

Walking across the Champ De Mars under a noontime clear blue sky, to the other side, along Avenue Emile Deschanel, Hassan called Laura and said that, unless she or Monica had found what they thought would be a suitable apartment on their own, he and Rena had found the perfect site from which Mitch would be able to complete his work. He gave her the telephone number of the rental agent's office and suggested she call and inquire about vacancies available in the Avenue Charles Floquet area. Laura replied that she had looked at a number of apartments, but none were suitable. She added that she would check with Monica before calling the rental agent Hassan had suggested. It was agreed that if Laura could rent the seventh floor apartment Hassan and Rena had viewed, she would go ahead and rent it, followed by Monica, the next day, inquiring about the second apartment in the same building.

Late that afternoon the pieces began to fall into place as Laura viewed and proceeded to rent the top floor apartment. Claiming her recent divorce settlement provided her with the funds with which to enjoy her return to freedom after a nasty relationship with an ogre of a husband, the same rental agent laughed and said she went through a similar episode in her life a few years earlier. They filled out the paperwork after Laura agreed to the 3,900 Euros price for two weeks. She provided her alias passport and drivers license for the required two forms of identification necessary for the subsequent police check. She also provided half of the 3,900 Euros, in cash, as an advance deposit, with the remaining amount to be paid upon moving into the apartment, hopefully within 24 hours after the police check was completed.

The following day, in mid-morning, Monica called the same real estate firm and inquired about apartments in the area near the tower, either in the 7th or 8th arrondissements. When told about two available in each of them, she asked about the two in the 7th, and arrangements were made to view each of them early that afternoon. Given the address of the first apartment, located on rue Edgar Faure, she met with a different agent and was shown a run-down, sparsely furnished apartment of three rooms. She expressed no interest and the agent walked her over to the other apartment located in the same building where Laura had rented the previous day. The apartment, on the opposite side of the building on the second floor, and facing out along Avenue Charles Floquet, was well furnished and definitely suitable. The single bedroom, relatively spacious, housed a double bed with a large headboard, along with a sturdy 19th Century French armoire. She noted that the area behind the headboard might well be suitable for the false concealment wall to be constructed by Beau over a day or two period, once she could move in. The agent also produced the necessary paperwork and, after Lisa agreed upon a two week price of 2,000 Euros, she filled out the application and provided identification and half of the rental amount as an advance deposit. Once she could move in, hopefully the following day, the stage would be set for Beaux to come in and choose the location for the concealment wall. He could then make up his list of materials needed for its construction, and divide it up among himself, Monica, Laura and, possibly Gene. Hassan and Rena would not be able to participate in the purchasing of materials, since they had been in the building earlier themselves and seen by the madam supervisor at the ground floor entrance way. It would be too risky for them to be seen associated in any way with the apartment Monica had rented.

*   *   *

As planned out with Gene ahead of time, and prior to making any moves to go to the apartment rented by Laura for the hit on Ahmadinejad, three of the team members would counter surveil Mitch during two well-planned and detailed surveillance detection runs in select portions of the city, well away from the Eiffel Tower. Mitch would make specific stops in shops and stores along the routes and purchase a particular item or two or make an inquiry about a service the shop might provide. Spending at least two to three hours on each of these runs, the way he visited the shops and went about his business while inside, and exited and continued along the routes, was all designed to reveal to his three team members any hostile surveillance that was watching Mitch and tracking his movements and actions. The team members, knowing the details of the entire routes, including where stops would be made, would take concealed, static positions from which to observe who might be focusing on Mitch.

Early in the afternoon of the third day before Ahmadinejad's visit to the tower, Mitch received a brief call from Gene. He gave Mitch the apartment number and address of the building rented by Laura for the hit, as well as the apartment number, in the same building, where Beau would shortly be installing the false concealment wall. Gene also gave the time of the day, late in the afternoon on the day before the hit, that he wanted Mitch to show up at Monica's apartment to view its location and the wall, followed by going upstairs to Laura's apartment overlooking the Champ De Mars and the tower. Gene said that the apartment for the hit was perfect and that Mitch would be satisfied. Gene's parting words were: "It looks like a nice comfortable distance of not more than 550 yards."

CHAPTER 16

When Major Green received the secure call from Colonel Singleton, the senior military attaché assigned to the U.S. Embassy in Caracas, he was walking to his car in the parking lot at the Izcaraqua Country Club. Having just finished a round of golf, he was looking forward to returning to his hotel room nearby for a shower and relaxing evening before making phone contact with Gabriela and other members of his team to get an update on their status.

"Major Green, this is Colonel Singleton. I believe you were told to expect my call."

"Yes sir, Colonel. I believe we met a couple of years ago during a conference at Fort Benning. Thank you for calling."

"Yes, I do remember you. Good to hear your voice. I have a package and want to give the pickup instructions for getting it to you. Another officer on my staff will be making the delivery, and I assume you will be having someone else take possession of it."

"That is affirmative, sir. Just tell me when, where and any particular circumstances."

"Tuesday evening, 1930 hours, next to the main entrance to Paraque Los Caobos, is a restaurant called La Atarraya. Behind the restaurant is a large parking lot. A good number of cars should be in the lot due to the popularity of the restaurant at that time of the evening. The lot will fill up by 2200 hours, but for our purposes it will be fine for 1930. At the far end, opposite the restaurant, have your person drive up and look for a lime green Ford minivan with a broken window on the passenger side. Try and park on that side, next to the sliding rear door. If that is not possible, park behind the van. The exchange will take place there. Your person should say they represent the gold and silver exchange. My person will reply that they wish to make a deposit. If the parole does not take place like this, my person will leave the lot with the package. Am I completely clear, Major?"

"Yes sir, very clear."

"It if does not go down as planned, we will repeat it the following night, at 1900 hours, same place."

"I fully understand, sir."

"Major, take care of yourself, enjoy Caracas, and I hope we are able to meet again one day in the future."

"Thank you, sir. I hope so as well."

∗   ∗   ∗

Three days before the hit on Chavez, Sgt. Garcia received the phone call from the major. He was relieved to know that Sgt. Vargas would pick up the sniper rifle the following night for delivery to the hide location in Gabriela's hotel room. He was anxious to move on with the operation, check out of his hotel and go, the morning of the hit, to the hide location. He could now begin his preparatory routine to get himself into a well practiced frame of mind, becoming relaxed and at peace with himself over the act he would soon be committing on behalf of service to his country.

Even though he was raised as a pious Roman Catholic, albeit now a non-practicing one, he had no conflict in his mind over the taking of a life such as Chavez'. He had already participated in joint military ops with the Colombian military across the border from Venezuela, and personally witnessed what the insurgents were doing to the people there with weapons supplied by the Chavez's government. He preferred to view the upcoming op as just one more success to come and leave it at that.

No sooner had Sgt. Garcia spoken with Major Green, than Gabriela received word from Sgt. Vargas that he would be delivering the package to her hotel room in two days' time, the evening before the hit. She also let out a sigh of relief to know the op was moving into its final stages. She planned on holding off, for one more day, paying a final visit to the area around Casa Natal in order to confirm that the anticipated speaker's platform and podium were in place in front of the historic building. Instead, she would spend a good part of the following day on additional reconnaissance around the Casa Natal area, checking on any noticeable security preparations and enhancements that might begin to appear. Of particular concern would be signs of any countermeasures, like counter sniping positions in the process of being set up, and any increased security in and around the high rise hotels nearby that offered direct line of sight to the area in front of Casa Natal. She would also be on the lookout for any new presence of military and government vehicles being pre-positioned along the streets surrounding the Casa Natal.

*   *   *

Ordinarily, whenever he wanted to be able to reach as many Venezuelans as possible in the country at once, Chavez preferred to give his public speeches to the people over national television, in particular the government propaganda stations. However, with public opposition to his strongman rule significantly on the rise, the populace was increasingly turning away from watching the government stations. To make matters worse, the privately owned and most popular station, Globovision, which is also the single all-news channel throughout the country, came under opposition control. Chavez could not tolerate that, and proceeded to go after a number of the opposition investors, throwing them in jail on trumped-up charges. Just when he thought that policy changes were coming into effect at the station that would be more acceptable to him, new investors bought into it and continued to side with the opposition. His patience had been tested to its limit, and he could no longer tolerate the rhetoric that the opposition was regularly using against him. Now was the time, he decided, to announce a series of major government pronouncements across the board that would affect the citizenry of Venezuela for years to come.

He decided that for his upcoming speech to introduce the new direction the country would be taking to return it to stability and bring the economy and populace further under his control, he would make this historic announcement from the birthplace of his idol, Simon Bolivar. Casa Natal, on the grounds he visited so many times while growing up, would be the most suitable location. There he would announce policies that appeared to provide for more freedom of expression, while at the same time enabling the government to crack down on what he termed were the undemocratic attacks from the oppositionists' intent on bringing down his administration.

As what was becoming his usual practice in planning for public announcements and appearances around the country, only a few trusted people around him were aware of his upcoming schedule. These were his long-time personal adviser, the scheduling secretary, the Minister for Internal Affairs, the Counterintelligence Director at the Bolivarian National Intelligence Service (SEBIN), and his trusted chief of the Presidential Security Guard.

The only weak link in this limited number with access to sensitive personal security information turned out to be the chief of presidential security. It was not a case of disloyalty on the chiefs' part, rather just the opposite. The chief had such a degree of loyalty to Chavez, and concern for his security at all times, he often gave out advance scheduling information to several of his subordinates, two of whom happen to be the recruited agents of the JSOC commander in charge of military intelligence at Fort Bragg.

Several years earlier, in two separate runnings of the nine-month long U.S. Marine Corps Command and Staff College course at Quantico, Virginia, the two Venezuelan officers, both senior majors at the time, honored the Venezuela military by being chosen to attend this prestigious course. As two of the limited number from foreign nations invited to participate each year and unbeknown to either of them, they were spotted, assessed and brought along to subsequent recruitment by a SF amphibious warfare officer who was an instructor on the staff at the college. He primarily developed them off base, during each of their nine-month periods at Quantico, especially during trips to various defense contractor firms and facilities around the country, as well as frequent social outings, in order to build up a strong personal bond with them.

Who would have known that upon finishing the courses, the two newly recruited agents would return to Venezuela and be given coveted command and staff assignments in their branches of the military? For over a year, following their return, they used covert communication systems to maintain the relationship with their recruiter, who by then had become the chief of military intelligence at JSOC. The irony in this development of having two agent penetrations, independent and unknown to each other in his presidential security guard, is that Chavez himself was responsible. With two highly trained professional military officers returning to Venezuela and projected for senior command positions in the future, they would, instead, be relegated to personal protection duties. Chavez's preference was to have them directly serve him in his security detail, since they were judged to be the best officers the Venezuela government had available. Therefore, he personally tapped these two officers to become part of the guard providing for his security.

*   *   *

The U.S. Embassy in Caracas sits in an imposing five-story red granite modern-contemporary edifice located on a 27-acre mountainside in the Colinas de Valle Arriba area overlooking the Las Mercedes valley. All the government agencies represented there are housed within the Embassy's chancery building, including the Defense Attaché Office, headed by Colonel John Singleton. Directly across the hall from the DAO is the suite of offices occupied by the CIA, and headed up by Station Chief, Donald Barnes.

Both the DAO and the Agency station are located on the fourth floor of the embassy, totally enclosed in a Secure Classified Information Facility, or SCIF, as it is known.

When Singleton received the pouch containing the sniper rifle for Sgt. Garcia, neither he nor Barnes were aware of what was shortly going to take place on Venezuelan soil. That was the degree of restricted compartmentation of need-to-know information concerning the operation that was unfolding. Barnes was not even aware the pouch had arrived. The limited amount of information available provided no hint at what was coming. It was only a restricted handling cable for Singleton, instructing him to contact Major Green and make arrangements to pass the package under the most secure of location and circumstance. Likewise, the recently arrived new U.S. Ambassador to Venezuela, Louis Sutherland, did not have a clue of what was going to happen either.

Barnes, in his capacity as COS, was the only person in the station to even be aware of the two recruited agents in the presidential security guard. He did not know their identities but did, on occasion, see some of their reporting. These two agents were the two top assets for the U.S. in all of Venezuela. The degree of security used with them even prevented their being met and handled inside the country. It was all done via secure comms with JSOC at Bragg, plus those few occasional times when they could take leave and go out of the country on brief vacations. The sensitivity of their positions inside Chavez's guard detail had to be protected at all costs.

In most countries where DAO and the Agency stations handled sensitive recruited agents in place, security is such that they could still be met, debriefed and handled in- country. In the case of Venezuela, the threat posed by SEBIN, the national intelligence service, precludes any form of inside contact. SEBIN intelligence officers are considered very good, based upon their training provided by the Cubans, the Russians, the Libyans and, more recently, by the Iranians. They also have a fairly high level of electronic signals collection capabilities throughout the country, as well as highly trained surveillance and counter-surveillance teams that frequently are seen on the streets working against DAO and station officers going about their own intelligence collection efforts.

Such was the situation on the streets of Caracas when the female junior DAO officer from the pouch and mail room found herself tasked with the assignment to pass the sniper rifle package to Sgt. Vargas in the rear of the restaurant parking lot at Paraque Los Caobos. Trained to treat the running of intelligence operations in Venezuela as if in a denied area, like those that could be found in Cuba, Russia, Libya and Iran, she skillfully conducted a three-hour long SDR into several areas of Caracas, before determining she was free of surveillance and able to proceed to the drop site with the sergeant. Skillfully making the pass, and with the sergeant already having run a similar, lengthy SDR himself, both of them separately exited the restaurant parking lot and continued onward to further establish that they were free of surveillance. The sergeant now only had to keep the package in his possession for one night, re-pack it the next day into his tennis gear bag and deliver it to Gabriela's hotel room hide location.

CHAPTER 17

No sooner had Beau walked into Monica's apartment and viewed the rooms, than he settled upon the bedroom for the concealment wall. The room, consisting of a double-size bed with a sturdy headboard, an antique armoire, a chair and a single nightstand, would easily be large enough to accommodate a 20 to 24 inch space behind the headboard and covering the entire wall. He decided to fashion a small doorway, directly behind the headboard, through which Mitch would be able to hide himself, as necessary, during the aftermath of the hit on Ahmadinejad. Noting that the bed did not move about all that well on the parquet flooring, one of the items on his list of materials to purchase were four sturdy coasters so that the bed could easily be moved in front of the doorway.

Taking the exact dimensions of the wall behind the bed, and noting the wallpaper on the opposite wall and painted surfaces of the two remaining walls in the bedroom, he planned to construct the temporary wall out of thin veneer wood panels. With the bed frame and headboard constructed of what appeared to be dark walnut or mahogany wood, he would try and match, as close as possible, similar coloring for the panels. Dividing up his list of materials, he would be responsible for the larger items, such as the paneling and the wooden slats used to brace and anchor the panels outwards from the real wall. Noting that the existing wall behind the headboard was bare of any pictures, Beau would task Laura to purchase two nondescript pictures to hang to each side of the headboard. For the opposite wall he would have Monica purchase a single larger picture, with a lot of color in it, so as to serve as something of a distraction should the police or anyone else come inside the room while conducting a search of the apartment.

With 48 hours available in which to construct the wall, Beau knew time would be of the essence. The only problem he was able to visualize would be getting the larger of the materials, the 3 by 7 foot panels and the 3 inch by 7 foot slat boards, past madam building supervisor downstairs at the entrance to the building. To determine how much of an issue it would be, he worked out a plan to utilize Monica and Laura. Each of them, during the coming evening, would make several exits and returns through the main entrance in order to see if madam supervisor paid them any attention If they timed it right, Beau believed he could be able to carry his larger items past her doorway unseen and proceed upstairs to the apartment to install the wall.

After giving Monica her assignment to buy a picture for the opposite side wall of the bedroom, he called Laura to ask her to purchase the two smaller pictures. Beau could now do nothing further but wait to hear from both of them early the following morning for their report on their late night forays past the supervisor's doorway. In the interim, he went to the "BigMat" building supplies store in the 15th arrondissement, and purchased a hammer, a small wood saw, some nails, screws and an electric power drill. Before returning to his hotel in the evening, he stopped by the nearby Castorama superstore, and purchased two pieces of black felt cloth, each 7 feet long by 4 feet wide. They would be hung by Mitch about two to three feet behind the open windows of the living room of Laura's apartment. His firing position would be from a small dining table and chair placed behind the cloths.

*   *   *

Two days later, as the time grew nearer for Mitch to check out of his hotel and make his way to Laura's apartment early in the evening of the day before Ahmadinejad would be appearing at the tower, Mitch organized all the clothes he had brought from Rome. Inside the single suitcase, he had an empty, flattened out lightweight backpack. He separated out the clothes he had been wearing during the trip to date and put them into the suitcase. The remaining articles of clothing and personal items, all that he would need after the hit, he placed in the backpack.

The next morning, after notifying the hotel desk clerk he would be checking out later in the afternoon, he left the hotel carrying the backpack. By prior arrangement with Gene, they met up on a back street near the Sorbonne, in the Latin Quarter. Gene took the backpack from him and, later in the day, arranged to pass it on to Monica, who would keep it for

Mitch in her apartment where he would subsequently be hiding following the hit. Around midday, after checking out of the hotel, Mitch took a taxi for the short ride to the Paris-Gare-de-Lyon train station, just as if he were going on the next leg of his business trip, this time traveling onward to Lyon. Inside the cavernous station, with over a thousand people typically arriving, departing or just milling about, he proceeded down one of the escalators towards the men's restroom. Spotting Gene at the end of the second escalator, he removed his identifying name tag on the suitcase and gave it to him. Now free of all accompanying baggage, Mitch could spend the afternoon in any of his remaining favorite areas of Paris in the springtime. Gene returned upstairs to the station's main luggage storage room and, after attaching his own name tag to the suitcase, checked it in with an estimated time of pickup in five days.

By late in the afternoon, Beau put the finishing touches on the concealment wall and, with decorative pictures hung on the wall, stepped back to admire his work. Monica, always making sure she was in the apartment throughout the times Beau was doing his work, agreed that he had done a wonderful job in a very short period of time. She noted, in particular, how the wood paneled temporary wall was indistinguishable from the real thing. She opened a chilled bottle of white wine, and they toasted the occasion.

About the same time Monica and Beau were enjoying their wine, Gene was on an extensive SDR through the 13th and 14th arrondissements that lasted just over two hours. Walking on foot, along with taking two taxis and a bus ride, he concluded that nothing of a suspicious nature was keeping track of him, and he subsequently was in the black, or surveillance free. He could now proceed into an operational mode and make his way to the brush pass site where he would meet with a NOC officer stationed in Paris and take possession of the package bearing the sniper rifle to be used by Mitch the following day.

The NOC officer, earlier in the day also went through an elaborate SDR in order to receive the package from an inside station officer who was not known to French liaison. It was up to the NOC to select the location for passing the package to Gene. Once selected, the NOC was able, through his own encrypted cell phone, to call Gene and give the location and time to him.

Of the three water canals that course their way through a good portion of Paris, Canal de l'Ourcq, Canal St-Denis and Canal St-Martin, the officer chose Canal de l'Ourcq. Of the three, this canal extends further to the outer reaches of Paris, into what is termed the wilderness, over 73 miles of woodlands northeast of the city. Inside the city is the start of the canal, at Bassin de la Villette, where it intersects with Canal St-Denis.

With walking paths on both sides, and a stately canopy of trees overhead, several park benches line one side, two hundreds yards past the canal's intersection with Canal St-Denis. Gene arrived at the benches precisely at 5:15 p.m. Only one person, a male, was sitting at one of them. He noticed that the man had a folded copy of Le Figaro on one side of him and a light brown leather case, looked to be three feet long, sitting on the ground on the other side.

"What a gorgeous day for a walk," said Gene.

"Yes, it is," was the reply. "I come out here at least three times a week," the man added.

"I used to come here a lot myself, but no longer do so," said Gene.

With their recognition signal and paroles between them successfully completed, they established their bona fides and could now proceed to make the pass.

"I have no idea what I'm giving you. And I was told by the inside officer that no one in the station is aware of the contents either."

"That's good," replied Gene. "That's just the way it should be."

Picking up the bag and starting to walk away, Gene added: "I appreciate you coming out here like this. Thank you very much and best wishes to you."

"And the same to you."

As Gene started to walk away with the leather case, the NOC stood up and immediately started back toward the start of the canal, at Bassin de la Villette. He subsequently would conduct another SDR, this time for at least one hour, to satisfy himself that he was surveillance free and in the black. Not called upon very often to engage in a brush pass like this in the open air, he knew the contents in the case had to be important, or else he would not have been tasked to do this.

Gene made his way further along the canal to the northeast. The case weighed just over 18 pounds. Besides the rifle inside, it included the suppresser, a tripod and a single magazine with five rounds in it. He would be glad to get this part of the op over with. Carrying a loaded sniper rifle, on the streets of Paris, of all places, was risky to say the least. Even if it did indeed look like a trombone case, Paris had too many watchful eyes at all hours of the day and night.

Following two taxis and one bus ride as he made his way from the canal area, Gene was glad to meet up with Laura standing outside her apartment building, around the corner where the building intersects with Allee Thomy Thierry. Wrapping one of her arms around his free arm, she escorted him into the building past the ever—present supervisor and up to her apartment. They too shared a nice glass of chilled white wine following the completion of one of the remaining steps in this complex operation to bring down a sitting head of state.

*   *   *

That evening, as Iranian President Mahmoud Ahmadinejad was giving his speech to the assembled body of Islamic scholars at the new Islamic Center in Paris, back in Tehran, the Islamic Republic News Agency released a government statement that revealed just how close the relationship between Iran and Venezuela had become. Immediately picked up for replay by the primary French agency, Agence France-Presse, it was subsequently followed by Associated Press and Reuters for rapid distribution around the world. Who would have known that the two assassinations about to take place would be done so in an atmosphere illustrating the close bonds and links between both countries' presidents, Ahmadinejad and Chavez?

In an unusual joint press release from two of Iran's ministries—the Ministry of Mines and Metals, and the Ministry of Energy—it was announced that the governments of Iran and Venezuela had signed an agreement for the production and transfer of Venezuelan processed uranium to Iran. Describing the locations of the uranium deposits in the western parts of Venezuela, as well as details of the extraction efforts that have already been underway there for over three years, the release cited the assistance provided to Venezuela by Iranian engineers and technical personnel throughout that period, and that both countries would continue their efforts to develop nuclear energy for peaceful uses and, as always, within the norms of the IAEA.

The press release also provided information on how the initial forms of Iranian assistance started with geophysical survey flights, followed by geochemical analysis of the deposits found. It ended by mentioning that radioactive thorium deposits were also being developed and would continue with further help in developing Venezuela's nuclear infrastructure of radioactive sources, facilities and the production of components and materials for the country's peaceful program.

What was not stated in the release and, of course, being the obvious issue of concern in such an announcement, is what clandestine reporting from both Iranian and Venezuelan agent sources had recently revealed: In exchange for direct access to Venezuela's estimated 75,000 tons of uranium ore reserves, Iran was providing not only their expertise and personnel on the spot where the extracting and production was taking place, they were also providing secret nuclear weapons advice and training to the government.

To add fuel to this already alarming development, clandestine reporting also indicated that Iran was providing the technical know-how and training of Venezuelan personnel in long—range missile technology. Russian involvement in weapon technology developments in Venezuela had become publicly known a number of years earlier. However, except for some minor arms transfers and technology agreements, nothing upped the ante as much as Iran coming into the picture with missile technology.

It was not as if the President needed, at least in his own mind, any further evidence to justify his decision to turn to targeted killings. However, it did serve to reinforce that the correct decision was made to eliminate from the world two leaders of countries who not only had come together in support of promoting and conducting terrorists acts, but also had come together to further their development of weapons of mass destruction.

CHAPTER 18

The British-made L115A3 Long Range Rifle is arguably one of the top sniper rifles in the world. It is a large-caliber weapon considered to be a state-of-the-art system with its telescopic day and night all weather sights. For the hit on Ahmadinejad though, Mitch chose his favorite sighting preference, the Zeiss Hensoldt ZF 16x56mm scope, accompanied by a titanium suppresser that should release no more than a "pift" sound upon the $.338$ Lapua Magnum round exiting the modified barrel to the target.

By the time Mitch started his two-hour long SDR prior to going operational and heading over to the apartment building near the tower, he was growing tired of having time on his hands as he further explored a city he had enjoyed so much during many previous visits. He attributed his growing restlessness to the nature of the task ahead of him. Never having engaged in such a sensitive op in Paris in the past and being fully aware of the formidable capabilities of the French security and police services, he now only wanted to move forward and get it over with so that he could proceed to execute his plan for exiting France and eventually making his way home to his own apartment in Rome.

The area of Montmartre, in the 18th arrondissement, while no longer the bohemian district it once was, still exudes a village-like appeal. The area also draws the largest number of tourists in Paris overall, compared to other parts of the city. As a result, he decided to spend the last few hours there, revisiting a number of shops and old haunts. With the tourist season rapidly going into full swing due to the onslaught of spring, it would be easy to mix in with the hordes of visitors. However, that alone would also make it difficult to spot any kind of directed surveillance effort against him. With his knowledge of the area though, particularly those shops and drinking establishments that had rear or side doors from which to exit, he should be able to move into positions from which he could spot anyone trailing behind, or possibly even out in front, ahead of him.

As part of the SDR, and following his lunch, he made a rear door exit at the Sancerre Pub and Brewery on rue Des Abbesses, and proceeded to walk through a geographical grid layout of streets just to the west and behind the primary tourist site in Montmartre, the Sacre-Coeur Basilica. A little over one hour later, he found himself at one of his favorite dive bars frequented during previous trips, the Au Rendez-Vous des Amis, on rue Gabrielle. No longer recognized by any of the patrons, but finding it seemingly easy to fit in with a few of the regulars he talked to, he enjoyed two leisurely beers, left and made his way on foot further north. Upon making his way to the nearby metro stop of Lamarck Gaulaincourt, he boarded and rode south, across the Seine, exiting at the Sevres Babylone metro stop. From there he walked the relatively short distance to Laura's apartment on Avenue Charles Flouquet.

Nearing the apartment building, he spotted a group of four people climbing out of a taxi and preparing to enter through the front door. Picking up his steps, he fell in behind them and was able to go past the supervisor without identifying himself or whose apartment in the building he was heading for. The timing was perfect and, once past the supervisor's doorway, as she turned back inside her room, the four people boarded into what quickly became a very crowded small elevator, while Mitch made his way around to the back of it and proceeded to go up the stairs instead.

He stopped first at Monica's apartment, where he would have said he was going should he have been stopped and questioned by the supervisor. After showing him in and providing a quick walk through of her apartment, including the concealment wall area behind the bed, he quietly left and once again used the stairwell to make his way further upstairs.

Laura let Mitch into her apartment and with few words spoken between them as well, showed him through the rooms. The emphasis, of course, was on the living room and the two sets of French doors opening up upon the Champ De Mars and the Eiffel Tower at the end of it. She opened one set of the doors so that he could get a good look at the overall tower area, and he spent a couple of minutes taking in the stunning view. The lights of the tower would be coming on in about a half hour, making the view even more spectacular.

"When Gene was here yesterday, he used a Leupold Digital Rangefinder to determine your shooting distance."

"Yes, he told me he would be doing it. Earlier, he said that his naked eye estimate was around 550 yards. What did it turn out to be with the rangefinder?"

"Good old Gene, he knows his stuff. Would you believe 552 yards? That's from right here at the window doors to directly in front of the foot of the center of the tower. That is the area typically reserved for photo sessions with groups of people."

"With the openness of the area, and the relatively short distance involved, I don't anticipate to have any problem with it at all. I checked the weather this morning at my hotel and found the prediction tomorrow is for basically dead calm, with no winds expected."

"There is nothing like good news, Mitch. By the way, I have a pair of surgical gloves for you. You know the drill; they need to be worn throughout your stay, as well as downstairs when you are in Monica's apartment. Leave this pair here when you exit tomorrow, and she will have a new pair for you there."

"Good."

"I also have a fresh change of clothes for you, along with your shaving gear. Monica has the rest of your clothes and stuff downstairs in your backpack. She and I will be tidying up after you and will see to it that whatever you leave behind is disposed of in different parts of the city, your clothes included. You know the routine."

"What about the rifle?"

"As soon as possible, after you head downstairs, I will bag it up and carry it down via the stairwell, which appears not to be used much on the upper floors. I will give it to Monica, and she will store it inside the concealed area that you will be in, when necessary. There it will stay until after you leave and, at an appropriate time after that, she will make arrangements for Gene to stop by late one evening, and take it for returning to the station."

"What are the timetables for you and Monica to depart?"

"We will both remain here for a couple more weeks but will not be seen together at all. Keeping our separate cover stories intact, we will eventually make our ways outside the country to return stateside.

"There's nothing like being in a wonderful city and enjoying it to the fullest," Mitch said wryly.

"By the way," Laura said, "we both have ample food and drink to take care of you for close to a week. Furthermore, Beau, Gene, Monica and I will all be out and about in the surrounding area, keeping track of any pending searches of apartments. We will immediately call to alert you, should it become necessary, in order for you to go behind the wall in the bedroom."

"I'll have no problem with going behind it when necessary."

"In the event you are seen in the apartment with Monica, the two of you can pass it off as the single guy from Rome, meets an American in Paris and all that can come to."

"After the hit, I will be getting out of my clothes and changing into a fresh set before proceeding downstairs," Mitch said. "The problem after that is, if I am subsequently discovered down there and subjected to any kind of forensic residue tests on my hands and face, it could all hit the fan."

"Yes, I agree. However, I wouldn't think it likely for someone to be tested that is found in an apartment on the other side of the building. On this side though, it's a different story, particularly up here in the upper floors with line of sight. The key thing is that you quickly get out of here and down to the other side of the building."

"Believe me, I will be moving fast. By the way, when you bag up the rifle, please remember to include the two black felt sheets as well. They will certainly be contaminated with residue."

"It will be done."

The two of them spent the rest of the evening talking about their previous work, the likes and dislikes of their job, and what it was that kept them so interested when engaged in operations that took them all over the world. They had been on the same team for close to five years, but it was always in terms of being separated and not out on the streets together. They rarely found the time, much less the circumstances, including while inside the U.S., to spend any amount of time in each other's company.

Nearing the end of the evening and thinking it was about time to turn in and get some sleep, Laura asked Mitch: "How are you feeling about this op? What are your thoughts?"

"First of all, it is not just another op. Talk about a high level hit, wow. However, once past all that entails, that's all there is—it is indeed just another op. What we go through, how we do it, how we leave the area, etc.—not much is different at all from the others we've handled in the past. As for me, I am going into it in great shape. My mind is at ease, and I firmly believe we are ridding the world of one more duplicitous bastard who has no place being here."

"What about who will replace him, back in Iran?"

"I believe it is safe to say that it will be someone as evil and intent on taking lives as much as this guy. But, the key here is in the message. When people like this are removed, the regime that is involved, in this case the ayatollahs in Qom, will quickly stand up a replacement. However, I do believe they will think twice about the need to take Iran in new policy directions, or else face a repetition of what is about to happen."

"I agree. Their long record of support for international terrorist movements, engaging in a multitude of horrific terrorist acts on their own, plus the real intentions of their nuclear program, has sounded the death knell of the current regime. I also know one more thing as well."

"What's that, Laura?"

"Unless Ahmadinejad is enjoying the same view of the tower right now that we are, all lit up and blinking beautiful, he will never be see it the future. Instead, he'll be on his way to see all those vestal virgins in what he believes will be a paradise."

CHAPTER 19

Having selected the Caracas Palace Hotel as affording the best line of sight for the shot down the Avenidas Universidad to the Casa Natal, Gabriela was able to rent one of the plaza level rooms on the 17th floor of the 21-floor Tower section of the hotel. In judging the distance from the leading edge of the tower to what she figured would be the speaker podium for use by Chavez, she did a geometrical calculation for the height of the room in the tower and then walked off the distance from the edge of the hotel building to the Casa Natal. She determined that Sgt. Garcia would have a shooting distance of 725 yards, easily within his capabilities.

While still maintaining her room two miles away in the Gran Melia Caracas Hotel, as Mariangel Delgado, she used a different alias at the Palace. After dividing up the clothes she brought with her into two parts, she checked in at the Palace with a backpack on wheels containing only about 20 percent of her overall clothing. By previous arrangement with Sgt. Garcia, when he departed from the hotel room after the shoot he would leave behind a set of clothing, along with an extra used razor and toiletry accessories, as well as a couple of Russian language comic books. Basically, he would leave the hotel with only the clothes on his back. The rest of his luggage and clothes would be in the rental car that Sgt. Vargas would be using to pick him up in the rear parking area behind the hotel.

In the days following her arrival at the Gran Melia, Gabriela consistently followed through with her cover story as a travel consultant surveying the Venezuelan tourist sector for the viability of new eco-tours and types of adventures. She called upon numerous travel agents, introduced herself and provided business cards and information about her commercial cover firm in the U.S. She also made it a point to talk up her activities with the staff in the hotel. This served to substantiate her cover in the event inquiries were made about her, for whatever reason, by the authorities after the hit. She even mentioned to one of the front desk clerks she had befriended that upon checking out, she would be heading to the cities and parks south of Caracas, She specifically mentioned that she would be visiting the Aguaro-Guariquito, Santos Luzardo and El Tama National Parks, along with the cities of Calabozo, San Fernando and San Cristobal. In reality, however, following the hit she would be heading eastward toward the border with Guyana.

By the time late afternoon rolled around on the day before the hit, all the pieces were just about in place. Gabriela was in her second day at the Palace Hotel, with only a final walk through in the area around the Casa Natal, to check on the latest security arrangements going into place by the authorities there. Major Green, likewise, did his own reconnaissance through the same area surrounding where Chavez would be speaking. He also checked the Palace Hotel to get a better feel of the area behind the hotel where Sgt. Vargas would be picking up the Sgt. Major in order to start out on their exit routes.

Green made sure that sergeants Diaz and Thompson had separately conducted their own recons through the area around the Palace Hotel, since they not only would provide advance notice if any police or security forces should move on the hotel following the hit but if necessary, they would provide counter fire in the event Gabriela or the Sgt. Major ran into difficulties. This would require not only Diaz and Thompson be right in the middle of it should a firefight break-out, but that they start their action from concealed positions around the hotel in order to best protect themselves. After discussing their game plans with them, Green was satisfied that they would be in the best setup that cover in the area afforded. If all went according to plan though, and no hostile action ensued, all members of the team would quietly melt away from the area and start their escape routes as originally envisioned.

Early in the evening, as Green was beginning to think about where to have dinner, he received a call from Fort Bragg. One of the agents on the Presidential Security Guard had reported in with a timetable for the next day's speaking engagement at Casa Natal, plus other events on the President's schedule for the day. The agent told his case officer handler at Bragg that Chavez was scheduled to be on the podium and ready to start speaking at 1010 hours the following morning. This information allowed Green to make not only what he hoped would be the final calls to the members of the team, but also to meet with Manolo Diaz, in order to get him into position at a decoy location near the Casa Natal. The game plan still called for him to drive away from a hotel, making noise with his tires and brakes, while exiting the hotel's parking area. Based upon the advice of Gabriela, the Hotel El Arroyo was selected as the best site for Manolo to use. Like the Palace Hotel where Sgt. Garcia would be shooting from, the El Arroyo also offered a direct line of sight. However, it also was the most distant in the area from the Palace, where Sgt. Garcia would be starting his escape route.

Later in the evening Green met with Manolo in a rundown tavern in the El Rosal area, on the outskirts of Caracas.

"Manolo, my friend, good to see you," said Green. "How are you getting along on your paid vacation in this crowded capital?"

"Comrade Major, it is also good to be back with you. I like the paid aspects of this vacation, but I am now ready to get to work."

"We are on schedule here and about ready to move into the final stages of our planned event."

"What do you have in mind for me?"

"Do you know the Hotel El Arroyo?"

"Yes, it is downtown in the central area of the business district."

"That is correct. I would like you to go there tomorrow morning and park your rental car outside, in the front parking area, as close to the main entrance as possible. If you show up around 0900 to 0915 hours, you should be able to find a space near the entrance."

"No problemo, my friend. What comes after that?"

"Go inside the main lobby area, visit the shops there and also have an excuse to go to the front desk and inquire about something. For example, vacancies this month, a list of their room rates, etc."

"Good. I can say that I have a number of friends coming to visit in a week's time, and we are going to go out on a fishing charter."

"That would be perfect. The point here is to establish yourself as being in the lobby during the period 1000 to 1015 hours."

"If need be, I could also sit down and take a coffee from where it is served in the lobby area."

"That will be perfect. However, by 1015, or no later than 1020 hours, you should be out of the front door of the hotel, in your car and ready to start your noisy exit from the parking area."

"That will be easy to do. I have decided that should I be stopped, I will say that I am not used to the way the car handles, and am experiencing some problems with the accelerator."

"That's excellent. It will be a good response."

"My friend, I take it that I can expect to be stopped. Is that affirmative?"

"The possibility exists that either as you are driving out of the area in front of the hotel, or shortly thereafter, on the streets nearby, you may well be pulled over and questioned."

"Any idea what the questioning will be about?"

"You may be asked, after identifying yourself, what you were doing in the hotel. The police or security authorities who stop you may even take you back to the hotel to prove your story about having a coffee in the lobby while you were waiting for someone to show. They may want to establish a time line for your presence in the lobby area."

"You have just given me an idea. I will call a fellow I met the other day, while I was doing some canvassing of charter boat agencies. He was friendly and we hit it off quite well during our meeting. I will invite him for coffee at the hotel, say at 1000 hours. However, I will give him the name of a different hotel in the area. He will go there instead, and not show up where I will be at the El Arroyo. Should the police ask what I was at the hotel for, I will say to meet a friend for coffee. I will then give them his name and phone number. If they contact him, he will say he went to meet with me, but I was a no-show at the other hotel. It will be explained away as a disconnect between us, but it will have myself placed at the El Arroyo at the time in question tomorrow morning. How's that, my friend?"

"I couldn't handle it better myself, Manolo. That will be perfect."

"What else can I do to help out?"

"Whether you are stopped after your noisy car decoy episode or not, you are doing plenty for us. You should just continue on for another day or two with your charter boat inquires, and make plans to check out of your hotel and return to Vera Cruz."

"You know, old friend, it has been good to work with you again, however, we have not really done anything together as I thought would be."

"I know what you mean. I also would have preferred more direct involvement of the two of us together, but, in this op, such was not to be the case. Your role though, is important, and I want you to think through the details of what we have just talked about and you are assigned to accomplish. Timing is the most important aspect for you to follow."

"You can be sure to count on me."

"One last thing before we part, Manolo. If there are any changes to this schedule for tomorrow, I will call you and give as much advance notice as possible."

"I have the times you have provided and, unless you say otherwise, I will carry out your instructions to the letter."

"After you have returned home, I will be in contact with you to make arrangements to visit and make the final payment."

"I thank you for that, old friend."

"Alright, how about we synchronize our watches and call it a night?"

*   *   *

By the time Sgt. Major Garcia ran an extensive SDR through the outskirts of Caracas, and made his way to Gabriela's room in the Palace Hotel, it was close to ten o'clock. Nightlife in the central downtown area was in full swing as diners and partygoers made their way in and out of the best spots the city had to offer. With the Dragunov sniper rifle already placed in the closet of the bedroom, where it would be safe until Garcia set it up in the morning, he and Gabriela made small talk for an hour or so before deciding it was time to get some sleep in advance of the next morning's main event.

Although this hit for him would be one of the few so far that was to take place inside the city limits of a capital, Garcia did not give it much forethought. At least in the room of the hotel he would have comforts available to him not usually afforded when carrying out his duties in the field. The only aspect of the op that caused him to rethink the plan before he dozed off was the exit procedure he would be using following the hit.

He knew it called for him to move quickly downstairs to the rear of the lobby and outside, where Sgt. Vargas would be waiting to drive him off. After thinking it though a couple of times, and exactly how he would do it, he put his mind at ease and went into a sound sleep, as was usually the case for him before a hit.

Chapter 20

President Hugo Chavez, the leader of the Bolivarian Revolution and self-styled inheritor of the reign of Latin America's greatest independence hero, Simon Bolivar, puffed up his chest and stepped up to the speakers' platform in front of the swelling crowd of Venezuelans in front of Casa Natal. He could feel tightness in his rib cage due to the substantial Level IIIA body armor protecting his upper body, but nevertheless, shrugged it off as a necessary expediency when facing a populace growing increasingly dissatisfied with his rule of the country.

The weather outlook for the day could not have been more beautiful. With a slight morning breeze of no more than three miles per hour, and a cloudless blue sky overhead, the band played the national anthem, "Gloria at Bravo Pueblo," as Chavez stood at attention. While the band was playing, Sgt. Major Garcia had his set up complete—the Dragunov was resting on what he decided to be the best soft surface platform from which to shoot, elevated just to the right height allowing for the downward angle from which he would be firing. The hotel room desk was moved to the edge of the open sliding glass door leading out onto the balcony. The edge of the balcony, composed of black wrought iron steel bars, enabled Garcia to be able to shoot between them at a downward angle of approximately one-hundred and ten degrees, to the speakers' podium.

Chavez decided to start his speech by announcing the time had come for a new direction and it would include the need for additional nationalization of key sectors of the economy. The time was ten minutes after ten and Chavez felt good about the way he was beginning on what he planned would be a speech lasting no more than one hour.

Garcia, on the other hand, was in a totally different world. He spent the preceding ten minutes concentrating on the task at hand. Relaxing and slowly lowering his breathing was paramount in his mind. Knowing that the placement of the rifle round into the target is all that matters, he exuded calmness as his level of relaxation increased. With the Dragunov in hand, he lined up the cross hairs with the middle of Chavez's chest, just above the bottom of the sternum. Neither aware of nor able to see any signs of body armor, he calculated his trajectory. Gabriela purposely stood at the opposite end of the hotel room, near the door, and, at Garcia's expressed preference, did nothing further than to guard the door.

He took in a deep breath and then began to let it out slowly. Nearing the end of his breath, and as he continued to squeeze the trigger, he felt the sharp quick snap as the hammer fell, producing that sought-after surprise feeling that all snipers experience as the round leaves the barrel. Holding the rifle tightly, the backwards slam of it into his shoulder produced no pain at all; rather it was like an old friend giving him a mild punch with a fist on his shoulder. With the titanium suppresser absorbing most of the sound, only a relatively small puff of smoke rose upwards towards the ceiling of the room as the armor piercing round started its 725-yard path toward the podium.

Garcia immediately refocused his eye through the scope, only to see that Chavez was completely gone from the podium. Instead, as he scanned the area, all he could see were three well-built men with their backs to the crowd from behind the podium as they looked downwards towards the ground. Garcia quickly stood upright, away from the table and his backpack rest platform, and moved forward toward the window as Gabriela, now standing next to him, slid the glass door shut and closed completely the drapes.

The crowd of people immediately in front of Casa Natal initially began to surge to the podium, believing Chavez had taken ill or fallen off of it. However, as several people in the front of the crowd could see some blood seeping out from underneath him on the ground, combined with security personnel looking up and pointing at the high rise buildings, these people cried out, "El presidente es muerto." What started as a movement of people forward quickly stopped and went into reverse. Moreover, as panic started to set in, the crowd all began to scatter away from Casa Natal. In the absence of any sound of gunfire, they nevertheless realized their president was dead. They began running for their lives. More security people closed in around the podium area, followed by uniformed police and military personnel. They quickly cordoned off the entire area, now void of the crowd, forming an oblong shaped circle as they faced outwards as if trying to spot where the shot had come from. With the numerous high rise hotels and apartment buildings in the area, so many with windows offering line of sight, it was a hopeless task to try and spot anything of consequence.

No matter that Chavez was wearing significant body armor, the armor piercing 7.62mm round impacted slightly higher than where Garcia was aiming, entering the body just above the top edge of the chest armor. The round slammed above the top of the sternum, shattering the manubrium and ripping through the jugular notch into one of the jugular veins. With dark, deoxygenated blood pumping profusely from a still beating heart, Chavez's body had crashed backwards off the podium to the ground two feet below. He was dead and close to being bled-out before he could be lifted onto an ambulance stretcher that had been positioned 75 yards away and taken for the short three—block ride to the nearby Cruz Roja Venezolana Hospital. Curiously enough, as the large crowd was rushing to all points on the compass, an eerie silence took over and only feet hitting the ground could be heard as they fled. No one was crying out or showing any visible signs of concern for their fallen president. Only a few of the older people in attendance, who had been standing near the podium area, appeared to be caught up in expressing emotions of despair at what they had witnessed taking place.

*   *   *

Not very far away, and right on schedule, Manolo received his call from Major Green and timed his decoy performance perfectly. Located six blocks away in the hotel parking lot, and not hearing any of the commotions from the Casa Natal, at 20 minutes past ten o'clock he started his car, popped the clutch and squealed on the tires as he pulled away towards the exit of the El Arroyo Hotel. He attracted the attention of a few people in the hotel entrance area, but that was about the extent of it. In the distance, he caught the first sounds of a couple of sirens, but no vehicles appeared to be approaching the hotel parking area from where he had just departed. Continuing to drive in the opposite direction, away from the hotel and Casa Natal, he drove out of the central district towards the suburbs for at least a good ten miles. About an hour later, after arriving back at his own hotel, he learned from the hotel staff and the lobby television blaring out the news, that Chavez had been assassinated.

Back in the area near Casa Natal, Major Green, from a distance of two blocks away, could observe what the security, police and military forces were doing to take up defensive positions as well as to start moving progressively outwards from where Chavez had fallen. He could tell they employed the classical layers or rings of security for their posture around Chavez. The members of the Presidential Security Guard were the closest immediately around him. They were the first to quickly scan the crowd as well as look to the distant areas away from the podium, since they would obviously be the best trained to react to any kind of a shooting, including that from a sniper positioned in one of the many high-rise buildings in the area. The Ministry of the Interior personnel, in civilian clothes, were in the next ring extending outward, followed by police and finally military personnel in battle gear.

Green could see several of the ministry personnel pointing fingers up at some of the taller buildings. However, nothing appeared to come of it. If the police and security forces were going to make any moves towards any of these buildings, it did not appear to be happening anytime soon. Except for some of the personnel from the Ministry of Interior, who could be seen talking animatedly on their transceivers, little else in the way of communications was observed in use. Curiously enough, Green also did not see any indications of counter snipers positioned on the roofs of any of the nearby buildings in the area.

Not wanting to try and move in any closer, Green fell in with what remained of the milling groups of people making their way out of the area. Seeing a bar and restaurant nearby, he walked there and called Sgt. Thompson, who, along with Sgt. Diaz, who, along with Sgt. Diaz, were parked at the Palace Hotel from which Sgt. Major Garcia should be leaving from after coming downstairs from Gabriela's hotel room.

"Sergeant, Major Green here. Report in. What is your situation?"

"Sir, I'm in the parking area in front of the hotel, near the lobby entrance. All appears normal. No unusual activity."

"I'm at least four blocks away, between you and Casa Natal. No movement is taking place here indicating that any forces are moving towards you."

"That's good, sir. I'll remain here until I receive a call from Sgt. Diaz indicating that Sgt. Vargas has picked up the Sgt. Major, and they are clearing out of the area. They should be behind the hotel near the tennis courts' parking area."

"Go as planned, Thompson. Have a safe trip home too."

Green no sooner ended his call with Thompson when his own phone rang. It was Sgt. Diaz.

"Sir, this is Diaz. The Sgt. Major just got into Vargas' car, and they are now exiting the hotel parking lot. The situation here is normal. No unusual activity."

"That's good news, sergeant. Once they are out of sight, you and Sgt. Thompson can proceed with the exit plan."

"Sir, I can stay around a while longer to see if Captain Torres leaves the hotel as well."

"That's a negative, sergeant. She knows the drill very well. You will proceed as directed and clear the area. I don't want you and Thompson on site there any longer than necessary."

"Yes sir. Have a safe trip home, sir."

"Thank you, sergeant, and the same to you too. I'll see you back at Bragg."

With that, Green went inside the restaurant's bar area, ordered a beer and watched the news of Chavez's death. As he expected, not only was it a noisy bunch gathered at the crowded bar, their reaction was barely short of outright jubilation. No one was jumping up and down expressing happiness, but they weren't depressed either. The looks on their faces provided the real sign he could read—it was as if a yoke had been lifted off their shoulders, and their country's poor, stagnant economy, along with a low standard of living, might just have turned a corner.

He thought about making his way over to the Palace Hotel in order to check on Gabriela himself. However, as with the orders he gave Sgt. Thompson, enough of them had been on the site around the hotel that he did not want to risk his own security by going into the same area. Knowing what the elements of her escape were and, after going over it with her in detail, knew she did not expect any assistance or intervention on his part, or even from other team members, for that matter. She was a thoroughly experienced and capable SF officer who was better trained than most in meeting the demands of difficult targeted killing operations.

At best, he thought, once he finished his beer and began making his way over to his own hotel, he would give her a call to check on her status. By then she should be well clear of the hotel following the Sgt. Major leaving and starting his escape route. She would have cleaned up after he left, including picking up for later disposal the surgical gloves he wore the entire time he was in the room. She would also leave behind the Dragunov sniper rifle on the table near the closed glass door. In the bathroom, she would leave behind his toiletry articles as well as the Russian language comic books.

As he neared his hotel, Green stopped in a small park about a block away. Taking a seat on a bench overlooking an overgrown stagnant pond of dark green water, he was about ready to call Gabriela. However, a gnawing feeling in his gut began to cause him concern. He wondered, in particular, if the whole scenario of leaving the Dragunov behind had been the right move. Would it really serve to throw the authorities off the team's trail? If it had been packed up in the same bag used to take it in, and taken downstairs with the Sgt. Major, for later disposal, would it have made any difference?

If the authorities had any reason to rush to the Palace Hotel after the shooting, leaving the rifle behind in order to make a quick escape would make sense. It all boiled down, he decided, on what was observed at the hotel. Of all the team members in the op, it was Gabriela and the Sgt. Major, who would stand out as the ones that could possibly be the easiest to identify. Regardless her using two different alias names in the hotels, plus the wearing of disguises and use of an elaborate cover story, it would be the technical collection aspects that the Venezuelan authorities could use to succeed in tracking the two of them down.

Namely, this would involve the hotel's use of inside and outside perimeter video cameras. Installed to provide for the personal safety of hotel patrons and the protection of hotel property and staff, these cameras, upon viewing by the authorities, could reveal key incriminating evidence linking the two of them to the room where the Dragunov rifle would be found. Gabriela could also be seen coming and going in the lobby area during the three days prior to the shooting, as well as getting on and off the elevator on the floor where her room was located. As for the Sgt. Major, while he would not be seen as much as her, his image ought to have been captured entering the hotel the night before the shooting, exiting the elevator on the floor of her room, and possibly departing from the hotel the next morning shortly after the shooting. In all, Green reasoned, it would all boil down to what the authorities could learn from the video images.

"Captain, Green here. What is your status?"

"I'm clear of the hotel and walking about six to seven blocks away heading south. In about five minutes, I expect to be catching a bus that will take me further south."

"That's good news. The rest of the guys are all clear and on their way as well. What about the disguises you and the Sgt. Major were using?"

"Sir, I am carrying a backpack that now includes the wig I wore at the hotel. I will dispose of it tonight when I find a convenient location. I will also be disposing of the clothes I am currently wearing. By tomorrow, when I am further away, I should be looking a lot different."

"What about the Sgt. Major?"

"The same baseball cap he wore into the hotel last night, pulled down snugly, he wore out this morning. Same for the pants and shirt as well. Once in the car with Sgt. Vargas, he would be changing to another cap, as well as into different jeans and a fresh shirt. He will also be dry shaving off his moustache. All of that should help him a lot when the hotel's video cameras are checked."

"Well, we all know it won't be over until we are back home, but for right now, so far so good. With all of you on your way, I am starting to feel better."

"What about you, Major?"

"As planned, I will be checking out of my hotel in the morning and flying to Mexico City in the early afternoon. Should I be stopped and questioned at any point here, I have solid alibis to account for all of my activities. Take care of yourself and be safe."

"Sir, see you back home."

"And Captain?"

"Yes sir?"

"Job well done!"

CHAPTER 21

He had no sooner rolled over on his back, when he could feel the slightly cool droplets of almond scented water falling on his face. As the droplets lightly brushed his cheeks and nose, he looked upward and strained his eyes in the early morning haze of the still partially darkened room. He could make out the small, tightly formed image of a young, angelic, smiling face peering kindly straight down at him.

Trying to shift his body by placing both hands to his side, as if to try and lift himself up, he realized she was gently straddled over him. As much as he tried, using both hands, he could not raise his body upwards to feel her lithe form. Looking intently into her face, he could make out short, golden hair that was wet, wavy and combed straight back. As a few of the droplets of scented water continued to fall from her hair, he began to feel that ever present ache in his groins with the realization that he had an enormous erection.

With no efforts on the part of either of them to speak, he continued to feel like he was paralyzed from moving his body in any direction. All he could feel underneath him was a soft cloud-like mattress of gentle support for his back. He didn't have a clue where he was or what he was doing with this woman who he could only perceive as beautiful and still looking straight down into his eyes. It was as if no words were necessary between them. He arched his back and strained once again to raise his groin and erection upwards. His one consuming thought was to enter inside this beautiful creature and fully experience the pleasures of her body.

However, he still was not able to raise himself off of the mattress, and she continued to remain motionless just above him. It was as if an unseen force was preventing their bodies from touching. Likewise his hands remained flat on the mattress as if glued there. He tried once more to slide inside her. With the invisible wall still between them, she began to lean forward and downward towards him, moving her face to one side of his head, as if to start to whisper something into his ear. It was at this point he thought he sensed the feel of her pubic hair on the top of his now throbbing erection. Knowing that success was momentarily going to be his, he heard a door lock open and a voice spoke out softly:

"Hey, Mitch. The coffee is ready and you have a big day ahead of you," said Laura.

"Damn it. Why are you waking me now?"

"What's the matter fella? Did I catch you in the middle of a good dream?"

"Yes, and what a dream it was. What time is it?"

"0900 hours and a beautiful morning as well."

"Any word yet from Gene?"

"He called a few minutes ago. He didn't say where he got his information, but it appears he was able to determine that Ahmadinejad is not due to be at the tower for the photo shoot with the students until early this afternoon."

"Is the weather forecast still calling for zero to two miles per hour winds?"

"Yes, the same as we heard last night before turning in."

"I can certainly live with that."

"Yesterday, when I last talked with Beau, he said that Gene asked him to be in a position nearby the photo shoot area. He will be seated and, with a small easel and pens in hand, he will be whiling away his time doing some sketches as his cover."

"Now that is a great idea. It will give us timely reporting not only on the results of my shot, but also how the security forces around Ahmadinejad are positioned and what their reactions are, including indicating whether it represents any kind of threat to us."

"From the expanse of the Champs De Mars, Beau should even see down toward this building and be able to give us a heads' up depending on what happens."

After a light breakfast of coffee and croissants, Laura and Mitch spent the rest of the morning in the apartment. Using her new pair of sports binoculars, she regularly looked out the apartment windows at the foot of the tower. Mitch moved the kitchen dinette table over in front of the double set of French doors in the living room. The L115A3 rifle was set up in place with its tripod open on top of the table. The two black felt pieces of cloth were still folded on a nearby sofa and would not be hung on top of the windows until Ahmadinejad and his party was seen arriving at the tower.

By the time the early afternoon rolled around, Mitch had showered, shaved, put on a fresh set of casual clothes and, once again, put back on his surgical gloves. Laura busied herself in the small kitchen and showing off some of her cooking skills, prepared bowls of hot leek and potato soup, a lettuce and tomato salad plus thick slices of crusty French bread.

Both were beginning to feel the tension of the long wait but were doing a good job trying to hide it from each other. With the television set on, they occasionally glanced at the broadcasts from the "France 24" international news channel. By three in the afternoon, Hassan and Rena had called Gene to report that they had just strolled underneath the tower. They noted that several large carts of metal folding chairs had been wheeled out to the front of the tower facing down the Champs De Mars. They also noted that three black SUV's, with blackened windows, were seen slowly crisscrossing the numerous streets in the area surrounding the tower.

When Beau called to report that he could see a number of what appeared to be young college age Iranians milling about and talking together near where workers had just started to set up the folding chairs into several rows, Mitch knew it was time to open the double windows and hang the black cloths from the top of them. He draped both down onto the edge of the table in front of the rifle on its tripod. This gave him a slit-like opening to shoot through that, by molding them around the barrel of the rifle, measured a foot and a half in height by five inches in width. From a sitting position behind the narrow dining table, he sighted in through the scope just as two workers carried a small portable podium to the front of where the assembled chairs were being placed. The end of the suppressed barrel of the rifle was three inches inside of the slit opening. He had a clear view of where Ahmadinejad would be standing behind the podium and facing down the Champs De Mars. He would be directly in front of what were the currently empty chairs.

Beau, seated on his stool and balancing his sketching easel on his lap, was also facing towards the front of the tower. However, he was over on the other side of the Champ De Mars and, like Mitch in the apartment window, at a slightly diagonal angle to the tower. From this position, he had a clear view of where the students would be seated, in front of the podium, approximately 125 yards away. He noted what appeared to be a professional photographer taking some distance, light settings and angles with his camera, from different sides of where the chairs had been placed.

Hassan and Rena had moved away from the tower and went over to sit in an outdoor café within a half block of the front entrance to Laura's apartment building along Avenue Charles Floquet. This would be their observation post from which to report in the event any police or security personnel came into their area and appeared to be making moves to enter the apartment building, whether before or after the hit was made. Since the building entrance was on the opposite side from where Mitch was, up above in Laura's apartment, this was the side where Monica's apartment was located on the second floor. From her living room window, she could see directly below onto the sidewalk, thirty feet from the building entrance. As usual, Hassan and Rena were engaged in animated conversation, along with enjoying glasses of one of their favorite Pinot Noirs. However, from their café vantage point, their keen eyes would not miss any of the comings and goings around the apartment building area.

Arriving from Avenue De Suffren, and turning onto Avenue Gustave Eiffel, six Renault Espace series SUV vehicles, all black in color and with blackened windows, pulled up to the southeast leg of the tower, approximately 90 feet away from the podium. Seeing the vehicles arrive, Beau could hear the cheers and clapping from the 38 or 40

Iranian students standing around the chairs in front of the podium, signaling they knew that Ahmadinejad had arrived. Every single one of them was either the son or daughter of a senior Revolutionary Guards Corps official and all loyal to the former low-level radical student RGC militia member, and now the President of the Islamic Republic of Iran, Mahmoud Ahmadinejad.

From where Beau was sitting, he could also count eight Iranian security personnel, in dark suits and forming a circular perimeter around the students and podium. As Ahmadinejad exited the third of the lined up vehicles, and started to walk toward the podium, he was accompanied by four more security personnel, two on each side. Respectfully, and as if having been instructed beforehand, the clapping and cheering ceased, and the students sat down in the chairs facing Ahmadinejad as he stood in front of the podium. Beau could also see about a dozen additional security types, in plainclothes, on the outer reaches of the Iranian perimeter, milling about at least 80 to 120 feet away. He thought these could be French security. Because of the trees beyond, along the edges lining the Champ De Mars, he was unable to spot the presence of any counter snipers on the rooftops of nearby buildings.

Gene was also on duty nearby in the area, sitting in an outdoor café on the corner of Allee des Refuzniks, where it crossed with Avenue Gustave Eiffel. This gave him a good vantage point looking toward where the Iranian vehicles were parked. It would also be the direction by which any of the French authorities would come past should they correctly perceive the shot coming from the side of Champ De Mars where Mitch was located in the nearby apartment building.

Sighting through the L115A3's scope, Mitch focused on the top of the podium that he estimated to be only four and a half feet high. This height would be perfect to accommodate the diminutive five foot six inch president of Iran. He was born in Aradan, Iran, to Jewish parents named Sabourjian. They converted to Islam when Mahmoud was four years old and changed their name to Ahmadinejad as their way of condemning their old faith.

Trained as an engineer, he received a doctorate in traffic management. Growing up with feelings of inferiority, due to his Jewish background, Ahmadinejad's life has been filled with vitriolic anti-Israeli statements, consistently questioning the right of the state of Israel to exist. This track record of hate-filled attacks on Jews is his way of compensating for his own insufficiencies by embracing the fundamentalist Shia sect of Islam. By succeeding in projecting an image of a leader whose every decision reflects his total devotion to the highest authority, he uses his religion to advance his one true agenda—the wiping of the state of Israel off the face of the earth.

Breathing deeply and slowly, with a look of utter calm on his face, a certain level of serenity overtook Mitch as he proceeded to sight in on Ahmadinejad himself as he stepped in front of the podium. With both arms in the air enjoying the adulation of the Iranian students gathered in front of him, he planned on giving a short speech to thank them for their seriousness in attending to their studies that took them away from their families and their homeland. With that and a few minutes of pictures with the students around him, he would be out of there for the day.

For a brief moment, while allowing for Ahmadinejad to settle down the small crowd and begin speaking, Mitch jokingly envisioned himself as a purveyor of fine teas in the Iranian city of Meshad. Upset that the box of tea in his hands, the one with an image of Ahmadinejad emblazoned on it, had by far passed its sell-off date, it was time for it to be disposed of permanently.

His senses increased dramatically as he continued his rhythmic breathing. External considerations became secondary and he targeted on Ahmadinejad for a head shot. Slowly squeezing the trigger, he knew the snap to come would be felt straight back into his shoulder. The culmination and subsequent release that came with the suppressed "pifft" sound, told Mitch instantly that he had struck successfully. It was only then that he regained all of his normal senses and focused back into the scope at the podium where Ahmadinejad had been standing.

The podium was flung to the side of Ahmadinejad's body as he now lay six feet back from where he had been standing. He was gripping both sides of it with his hands when the Finnish-made .338 Lapua Magnum Scenar hollow-point bullet impacted squarely on the tip of his nose following its almost perfectly straight trajectory of 552 yards. The entrance point on the nose was barely three eighths of inch in diameter. The exit point behind the head at the base of the cranial cavity was a gaping hole that defied description or measurement.

Mitch and Laura could see none of this pandemonium developing underneath the tower. He slowly closed the double French doors, as she slid the two pieces of black felt cloth downwards off the top of them. He stepped back away from the windows and pulled off the surgical gloves. Picking up his backpack containing extra clothes and toiletry articles, he said goodbye to Laura and went out the apartment door in order to proceed downstairs to Monica's apartment on the second floor. Laura packed up the rifle, gloves and felt cloths, stuffing everything into the musical instrument case. Next, she moved the table and chair back into the dining area and quickly checked through the rest of the apartment, making sure no evidence of Mitch was left behind. Lastly, and as a precaution just before going out the door herself, she turned up the air conditioner in the event any lingering smells of cordite residue were left behind. Carrying the instrument case down the stairwell, she also made her way down to Monica's apartment.

Provided no warning calls came from any of the other team members observing nearby, Laura would give the case to Monica and immediately exit the building and head on foot further into central Paris towards the Notre-Dame Cathedral. She planned on spending the rest of the afternoon and early evening in the Latin Quarter, browsing book and antique shops, before making her way back to the apartment. She felt good about how smoothly their plan played out after Mitch completed his mission, and they worked their way separately downstairs.

It was Beau, from his vantage point of only 125 yards from where the podium had stood, who watched the chaotic scene unfold at the foot of the tower. As the students panicked and started to run away from where Ahmadinejad had just started speaking, they ran into the eight Iranian security personnel that were collapsing their perimeter inwards toward where he lay on the ground. Once past them, the fleeing students next ran toward the dozen French-appearing police or security officers which remained in place in their own perimeter over 75 yards away and did not yet start their own advance. Not making any effort to head them off, they were allowed to pass through their cordon.

Beau noticed an Iranian male step out of one of the vehicles and move toward where Ahmadinejad lay. Quickly moving over next to him, he bent down on one knee and gently rolled the body over, turning the face down into the grass. Observing the condition of the back of the head, he rolled the body over onto its back. He motioned to three other Iranians who was part of the inner perimeter that was closest to him, and they advanced to pick up the body. Holding Ahmadinejad by the legs and arms, they picked him up and immediately rushed him to one of their vehicles. Within seconds after the body was inside, all the remaining members of the security details climbed into the rest of the Renault SUVs and sped away across Avenue Gustave Eiffel directly in front of the tower.

With his stool and easel in hand, Beau cautiously started to walk forward toward where the French plainclothes officers were closing in to establish their own perimeter around the podium and scattered chairs laying nearby. He quickly stopped when one of them raised his hand, as if to say advance no further. The blaring of sirens could be heard and within minutes, additional French authorities, including several dozens uniformed police, were converging on the scene of carnage.

As he strained to see through the legs of the police that were now forming the single perimeter around where Ahmadinejad had fallen, he was able, for a brief moment, to make out the tell-tale signs of the results of Mitch's perfectly placed bullet. In the middle of a pool of vibrant red blood, measuring about ten inches in diameter, he could make out what appeared to be a clump of scalp, tissue and dark hair on the edge of the grass next to the light gray pavement. That told Beau everything that he needed to know—The Iranians had carried away a dead man.

Throughout this scene of what started out as a photo session with the students, and was turned into the death of a head of state, a news truck from the French Euronews television channel, with a video cameraman standing on its top, was broadcasting live from a position on the Champ De Mars two hundred yards from where Beau had been sitting on his stool. Directly facing the tower and the podium from where Ahmadinejad was starting to speak, the cameraman was able to catch the entire event from when Ahmadinejad arrived by car, walked over to the podium, was shot, and subsequently lifted up and carried away and placed inside one of the vehicles.

In an eerie turn of events, as this scene was being broadcasted live, inside the news van on a monitor, a live satellite feed was coming in from Latin America. In a initial breaking news story from Caracas, it reported the assassination of another president, Hugo Chavez, that had preceded by 30 minutes Paris time the inglorious end of Mahmoud Ahmadinejad.

CHAPTER 22

The news broke around the world with as much surprise and concern as that when John F. Kennedy was assassinated in Dallas almost fifty years earlier, in 1963. With the presidents of two oil-rich countries now lying dead from the hands of unknown assassins, threat alarm levels were escalated in numerous countries and military forces were put on alert. The countries that still maintained "hot line" contact between their leaders activated them in order to reassure and assess their previous commitments of working together towards peace in the world.

When DCI Wicksford and SecDef Panetta received the news and subsequently viewed the reporting on TV, they could not help smiling. They also knew that with the success of these two well-planned targeted killings, it was time for another in-person meeting.

Three days later, Major Green and his team, except for one member, were in the final stages of making their separate ways to Fort Bragg. Similarly, Mitch, Gene and their team were in various stages of pulling out of Paris and returning, either to Italy as in Mitch's case, or, back to the U.S. The green lawn at the safe site in Warrenton was more vibrant now than a couple of months earlier, as Wicksford and Panetta met and considered the results of the recent events and the choices and options for the last remaining assignment given by the President.

"Were you as surprised as I was," asked Panetta, "that the timing for the hits would turn out to be within a half hour of one another?"

"Considering that neither team was aware of each other's assignment, it was incredible."

"What's the latest word on your team, Ben?"

"The two officers who rented the apartments in Paris, Laura and Monica, remain there as part of their cover story and in fulfilling their rental agreements. They will stay at least one more week. As best we can determine, the French authorities visited no apartment at all in the entire building. We have no hint that the building even came under suspicion as the source for the shot."

"What about the rest of the team?"

"The other members, Gene, Hassan, Rena and Beau, all departed and have returned stateside to their respective homes around the country. Mitch departed from Paris without incidence, and currently is in Lyon where he is making one more business cover call before returning to Rome. We subsequently learned in a call from Gene that with no moves made by the authorities toward the apartment Mitch was hiding in, he hardly spent any time at all behind the concealed wall of the one on the backside of the building."

"What's the word from Paris Station?"

"I received cables and secure calls from both the COS and our Alliance Base Chief, detailing what they learned from their French counterparts. This is where it gets real interesting. With the Iranian security detail immediately removing Ahmadinejad's body, the actual crime scene left little to investigate. Instead of taking the body to a local hospital, their own doctor, who knew when he turned the body over that the man was dead, did not bother to get any kind of examination at a hospital. Instead, they went straight out to Charles de Gaulle and quickly departed for Tehran."

"Our senior milatt at the embassy cabled me, saying that he learned the French police were advised by their president's office to maintain only a minimum of security coverage for the photo shoot at the tower due to the current poor state of relations with Iran. In fact, the milatt said that the Iranian embassy asked just for police escort of the motorcade and a single outer perimeter around where they would provide their own coverage."

"Our man on the scene, Beau, posing as a sketch artist, said that no sooner had the French forensics team arrived, and viewed the gore on the ground and the scattered chairs, when a cleanup crew arrived with a water truck and hosed the whole area down. Within an hour after the hit, you would not have known anything happened there."

"The milatt said he asked if counter-snipers had been employed, and the reply he got back was that none were asked for and therefore, none were supplied. That says something about the warm fuzzy feelings the French have for the Iranians."

"One of the last things Beau noted in his report was that two members of the forensics team could be seen looking outwards down the Champ

De Mars and at the surrounding apartment buildings on both sides. However, without a body to view, and therefore, unable to determine the angle of entry for the bullet in the head, it would be a fruitless task to try to determine where the shot came from."

"Being a suppressed shot certainly didn't help either, Ben."

"The COS also mentioned that the French Minister of Foreign Affairs called in the Iranian ambassador and curtly told him that removing the body from the crime scene and taking it out of the country violated French laws, and prevented the authorities from being of any assistance at all."

"You know, Ben, given the way these directed hit assignments were given to us by the president, and the latitude we both gave our teams to handle them completely on their own, how would you evaluate the way they turned out, notwithstanding their obvious success?"

"I am extremely pleased with the Agency's team and how they went about their planning, execution and nearly complete withdrawal from France. The need-to-know restrictions and compartmentation we could maintain, no doubt, contributed to our successful completion of the mission. Now, Leon, tell me about your team and the situation as it unfolded in Caracas. We certainly followed it closely from our vantage point, but I want to hear it in your own words."

"First off, Ben, I'm also highly pleased with the results. Instead of having several layers of senior witting military officers all privy to what was coming down, we instead had our single SMU team calling the shots and doing it all, basically on their own. Major Green, our team commander, was the first to make it back to Bragg. He departed from Caracas the day after the shooting and got back home the following day. While he would have liked him to be the last out, such was not the case.

"The shooter, Sgt. Major Garcia, as you have been able to see from your own as well as our reporting, turned in an enviable performance. For him, it was the expected one-shot, one-kill kind of action. We could not have asked for more. He also proved to be very adept at making his limited disguises work to his benefit. This morning I received after action reporting from the two agents on President Chavez's security detail. They reported that they were shown the video recordings from the hotel where the Dragunov rifle was found. Sgt. Major Garcia was clearly visible entering the hotel the night before the shoot, getting off the elevator on the floor of the room used for the shoot, as well as leaving the next morning after the hit. He is considered by the Venezuelans to have been the assassin.

He wore identical clothes each time, including a baseball cap pulled down well on his head. However, by keeping his head facing downward, nothing of his facial features at all was captured on the video recordings. Coming out of the elevator on the lobby floor, he dropped out of sight of the video cameras when he exited out a rear door of the hotel and rounded a corner near the tennis courts. Once Sgt. Vargas picked him up in the parking lot, he changed pants, shirt and cap, plus shaved off his moustache. After two days of traveling out to Maracaobo and into Colombia by bus, he flew from Bogota to Mexico City and arrived back at Bragg yesterday.

"The three sergeants, Vargas, Diaz and Thompson, likewise, experienced no difficulties leaving the country. Two of them came out via Guayana, and the third caught a boat for Trinidad and flew from the Port of Spain to Miami. They performed exceptionally well and, from the agent reporting, they did not come to the attention of anyone during their entire time in the country."

"That is wonderful news. You mentioned though, that one team member has yet to return."

"Yes, one member, Captain Torres, has not been heard from since she last reported to Major Green. She told him that she was several blocks away from the hotel, after the shooting, and would soon be catching a bus to head southwards."

"What do you know about her planned escape route and return home?"

"She indicated she would travel by bus southwards and make her way either into Brazil or Guyana, depending upon what appeared to be the safest for her. Once she made her choice, she was to have called in order to let us know."

"Travel can be hazardous due to road conditions and crime there. She also is a female traveling alone. What is your level of concern at this point, Leon?"

"If we do not hear from her within another 24 hours, we will have to go into a search mode and consider her missing. Let me add though, she is the most capable on the team at using a commercial cover. She also is physically very good at taking care of herself. Nevertheless, that part of the world is rife with nefarious people and potentially life-threatening situations."

"Did the two agents from the presidential security guard have anything to say about her?"

"Yes, they did. They saw videos of her checking into the Caracas Palace Hotel where she registered as Ivonne Lopez, and traveling on a Costa Rican passport. She can be seen in the lobby a number of times during her stay, plus getting on and off the elevators on the floor where her room was located. She and Sgt. Major Garcia are the two most sought-after people in all of Venezuela right now. While the videos did capture a limited glimpse of some of her facial features, the wig that she wore, along with a couple of large, floppy-type hats, served to conceal her pretty well.

"What were the last videos taken of her?"

"They showed her getting off the lobby elevator five minutes after Sgt. Major Garcia, and heading towards the main entrance. However, she turned down a corridor nearby the front entrance, where a number of shops are located, and exited the hotel through a side door leading out in the direction of the far side of the rear parking lot. That is the last seen of her."

"If you recall, we never revealed to either your milatts or my station chief at the embassy in Caracas any of the names that team members would be using, much less about what they would be doing there. Therefore, unless we see pictures of her plastered on TV and in the newspapers, we will have to exercise caution in citing any names. We don't want to compromise her true identity either. What about her alias name when she entered Venezuela?"

"She entered as Mariangel Delgado, a citizen of Argentina. She used that name when registering at her primary hotel, the Gran Melia. At best, I believe the way to go is to have your station and my attaché office there query their sources throughout the country on a missing Latino woman, name unknown, who may be implicated in the event that killed Chavez. It should appear as though the U.S. Government is attempting to assist the Venezuelan authorities with their own investigation. What do you think of that?"

"For now, Leon, we don't have many options. I do believe though, that we should wait for another 24 hours and then query our embassy in Georgetown, Guyana, as well as the consulate in Brazil, up in Manaus, which is fairly close to the border with Venezuela, and see what they might be able to do to help out. Manaus is along the primary road route running south out of Venezuela."

"That's a good idea, since she told Major Green that she wanted that option, when heading south, to cross either into Guyana or Brazil."

"Thank you, Ben. This officer is too valuable to lose. She is young but already well experienced in SF ops, and has a bright future ahead of her. I personally met with her in my office and give her the assignment to JSOG's SMU. So I have a personal stake in this and want her back soon."

"We'll work hard on it and make sure she is located. Let me comment now on what the president told me yesterday morning, before we both went into the cabinet meeting. I was providing him with the daily brief and when we finished, and were about to make our way out of his office for the cabinet meeting room, he motioned for me to step outside to the edge of the rose garden."

"I recall seeing that take place. I had just entered the cabinet room and could see you and the President through the windows. It's interesting the way he likes to have these little private moments completely out of earshot of anyone and anything that might be listening."

"Well, he said he had seen all the reporting on the events in Caracas and Paris, and just wanted us both to know that we were to continue moving forward with our planning the op against Kim Jong-Il as soon as possible. He asked, Leon, that I tell you what he said and apologize for not talking directly with you."

"I completely understand. He also does not want the three of us to be seen alone together anymore in what some may consider or construe as some kind of special meeting."

"I can understand his concern. How about we start working on this remaining task that's ahead of us?"

"We at DOD have no reporting assets at all inside North Korea. I also know from what I see of your reporting, you only have a limited number of agents reporting out from there, and none that are directly close to Kim."

"We thought we had a possibility of recruiting a female on his personal staff that was involved in food preparation, but the North Korean vetting process she went through before getting anywhere near his food revealed she had a boyfriend who defected and was able to escape to Japan."

"I would think that resulted in her losing any chances she had of being able to serve, much less be a taster and food screener to him."

"You're right on that score. We were meeting with the boyfriend in Tokyo, and he told us about her in Pyongyang. He even said he was confident if she had gotten the job, she would cooperate with us, including if it meant she had to be sacrificed in the process."

"What about the logistics side of trying to run that kind of operation?"

"With the cooperation of some of our best foreign liaison service partners who maintain diplomatic relations with North Korea, we would have been able to not only contact the woman but also get to her the necessary means for poisoning the bastard as well."

"Well, even if that were possible, the level of security screening around him, especially in his personal quarters and among his immediate staff, including those involved in the serving of food and drink, no doubt entails several people who sample anything that gets near his mouth."

"Let me bounce off of you another possibility. In the past, we made use of two NOC officers who were actually husband and wife. Their cover jobs, as well as personal avocations, provided them with the access and justification of being in specific areas of interest to us. It resulted in them obtaining extremely valuable intelligence information for us."

"You mean like both being nuclear engineers attending an international conference together and bringing along their golf clubs to play a game or two at a particular course near, or next to, a sensitive facility of interest?"

"That's it exactly. They could obtain what we wanted not only at the conference, but out on the golf course as well. In fact, it was the soil and water samples they collected on the golf course that actually had the most value."

"I believe I know where you are going next."

"What I have in mind is to use our shooter, Mitch. He is our NOC who made the hit on Ahmadinejad in Paris. If we can match him up with a suitable female NOC, and they have plausible cover and pretext for being together at a particular location, we may have the making of an op that could succeed in this case."

"That gives me an idea, Ben. Our two agencies have jointly conducted a number of sensitive ops together in the past. SMU operatives have teamed up with your SAD operatives, and successful ops have resulted. In this case however, I would propose a scaled-down team, probably out of necessity, due to Kim Jong-Il's very limited travel outside of North Korea, and the intensive security forces that are always around him."

"Leon, I believe you are on to something here. It makes me think of a report on his last trip out of North Korea to China."

"Sure, we probably both read about it in the same report. However, not only will the hit be one of the most all-time difficult shots to make, it will also provide a very limited window of time during which the shot must be taken."

"To top it off, it will also require some very sophisticated support from both our agencies, including special extraction assistance for getting our people out of there once the hit is made."

"How about we select the primary team members, give them all the information available to us and let them pick the rest of the team and brainstorm it from there?"

"Leon, are you thinking about a possible partner who would be suitable to team up with Mitch on this one?"

"I sure do, Ben, provided that she can be found safe and sound in South America and, after some R&R time, come back to duty prepared for a new assignment."

CHAPTER 23

"What happened to me? I've been on the worst bus trip of my life," said Gabriela, in Spanish, to the doctor at the Roraima City Centre Hospital in Boa Vista, Brazil.

Replying in a combination of Spanish and Portuguese, the doctor said, "Thank God you are back with us. You have been unconscious and delirious for the past two days. You were found behind the bus station on the other side of town."

"I remember getting off the bus in Boa Vista, and asking an old man where to go to catch the connecting bus for Manaus. He pointed towards the end of the building and said to go around the corner and straight ahead to where the buses park. I turned the corner and was walking toward the buses. Suddenly, I felt a blow to the back of my head and neck. That's all I can remember."

"You apparently have been robbed since we did not find any identification on you," replied the doctor.

"What about my backpack and Blackberry cell phone? Do you have them?"

"No, we don't. Besides the clothes and shoes you were wearing, the only other things of value on you were three U.S. 100 dollar notes found inside one of your socks. That's all."

"When can I leave here? I must be on my way."

"You have a mild concussion and a bad contusion at the base of your head. I want you to stay for at least another 24 hours."

"I need to make a phone call."

"That will have to wait. First, I am having the nurse come in and get the details of who you are, where you are from and all that you can remember about coming here to Boa Vista."

No sooner had the doctor left the room than Gabriela thought about her predicament: namely, under what alias would she identify herself? She thought it best to revert to her alias of Mariangel Delgado. That was the one used to enter Venezuela two weeks earlier on her Argentine passport. Unfortunately, the passport was in the backpack that was taken in the robbery.

When she left the Caracas Palace Hotel, after Sgt. Major Garcia made the hit on Chavez, she disposed of the passport in her second alias, Ivonne Lopez, a citizen of Costa Rica, while making her way across town to the bus station. Subsequently, without any access to TV or newspapers during the bus trip, she had no way of knowing if her picture or name were publicized as being wanted for involvement in the assassination.

As her thoughts became clearer and the minutes passed while waiting for the nurse, she knew that she would have to use her Mariangel Delgado alias since, besides entering Venezuela with it, it was again used just a couple of days earlier to leave the country and enter Brazil. She remembered arriving in the town of Santa Elena, on the Venezuela side of the border, and then taking the shared taxi a mile to the border. Then she went through the immigration and customs station portals for both countries. After that, it was a five-hour, bone-shattering ride to Boa Vista on another bus, this time an old local one from the Eucatur Bus Lines.

*   *   *

The next morning, feeling much better, Gabriela was able to make a call to the secure number previously used with team members when she still had her Blackberry.

"This is not a secure line call. Who is this? Who's calling?" Major Green asked.

"Sir, it's me. I no longer have my cell phone, since I ran into a little problem."

"You're overdue and we have been worried. Are you alright?"

"I'm on the mend now but am going to need some assistance."

"Where are you?"

"Boa Vista, in Brazil."

"That's good news. At least you got that far. What's your condition?"

"After arriving here I was in the process of making another bus connection that would take me further south, to Manaus. As I walked around the corner of a building, I got whacked from behind. I woke up two days later in the local hospital. Other than a sore head and mild concussion, I'm fine."

"Do you have any money or credit cards?"

"Credit cards are gone, but I have 300 dollars in cash. What about you and everyone else?"

"We're all back, in good shape and relieved to hear from you. Are you in good enough shape to leave the hospital now?

"Yes, I believe so. I think the doctor will agree to let me go now."

"Will you be able to move about on your own?

"Yes, sir."

"OK. That's good. Get yourself over to their airport there. It's called Boa Vista-Atlas International. Call me back once you arrive there. I'm having an aircraft leave soonest from Panama. It is only a couple of hours away."

"Thank you, sir. I'll be calling you back soon. I'm anxious to get back."

*   *   *

"Where is he? Shouldn't we have heard from him by now?"

"Jack, listen up old buddy," Gene replied. "Think about our use of the secure phones while in France. We must have been driving the French nuts. They could tell encryption was involved but were unable to do anything about it. However, they sure as hell could use their GPS capability to pin down our locations."

"I realize that, but of all people, we need to know that Mitch is alright."

"I last talked to Laura late in the morning, just before boarding a bus for Charles de Gaulle. She said he walked out of her apartment carrying his backpack and planned to work his way over to the Gare de Lyon station where you left his suitcase at the reserve baggage counter. From there he would catch a train for Lyon, finish his cover business, and then fly back to Rome."

"What was the situation around the apartment building when he left there?"

"It was quite normal. Laura told me that Monica, from upstairs in her apartment was watching the Champ De Mars side of the building, while

Hassan, Rena and Beau were outside and regularly observing the scene from Laura's side."

"What do you make of the French response to the hit?"

"I would say uncharacteristic. It appears that says something about the current state of play in France's dealings with Iran. Cool to say the least."

"That's our read from this side of the pond. Cable traffic coming in indicates that with no body to examine, along with the quick exit of the whole Iranian contingent back to Tehran, the French were very upset and just not prepared to do much more than a cursory investigation of the scene at the tower and the surrounding vicinity."

"Beau said he had a ringside seat to the unfolding of the whole event."

"Yes, he did indeed. Best of all, his accurate reporting on it was corroborated later by the French services' reporting as well. Apparently, they had a couple of people quite near the bottom of the tower and facing toward the back of the podium. The French said that Ahmadinejad began to speak and a second later he was flat on the ground on his back. No sound from the shot and best of all, no indication of the direction from where it came."

"If the Iranians hadn't moved so quickly, and the French had the time to examine the body on the ground, even for just a few minutes, a good medical examiner would have been able to determine the trajectory. If he had, it would have pointed down the Champ De Mars in the direction of Mitch's location in the apartment."

"So much for the way the Iranians responded."

"Just so you know, Jack, at no time did any of us feel a threat of any kind from anyone. The whole op played out beautifully."

"Gene, save that for the post op debriefing. When you hear from Monica and Laura that they have left the country on their way back, make sure they call me after arriving stateside.

"I don't know where the debriefing will take place yet. I'll probably set something up in the middle of the country since you guys will be spread out all over the place."

"That'll be fine," Jack replied. "I'm back in Boston now, and will remain here until you call. What about Mitch? I expect that he will call me once he arrives back in Italy."

"If you recall from the last one of these ops, he will have to undergo his own special debriefing with one of our medical examiners and, since

I don't want to bring him back here to the states for it, I will have to set something up in Europe. He shouldn't mind that at all."

"Let me tell you this, Gene, he remains one cool, collected man who has his act totally together.

"What do you expect? We wanted the best and that is what we have in him."

"What's up next? Is anything coming our way soon?"

"Now that you mentioned it, rest up my friend. It won't be long now."

CHAPTER 24

Le Richemond Hotel, along the Quai du Mont-Blanc on Lake Geneva, had changed little since Mitch's last stay two years earlier. The small junior suite reserved in his name on the backside of the hotel, looking down on the Brunswick Garden, was in the quietest part of the hotel and perfect for the purpose that brought him there. Having only been back in Rome for one week following the assignment in Paris, he barely had time to catch up on paperwork in his office and get some much-needed rest.

The call from Gene, telling him to pick the time and location for an after action meeting with the doctor was not a surprise. After each executive action mission he carried out in the past, it was standard Agency policy for him to undergo a Mental State Examination with a psychiatrist in order to determine his fitness for duty and state of mind for continuing to engage in such ops. The assignment in Paris would be no different, and he had no qualms in meeting with one of the Agency physicians. In the past, he thought that those sent out to examine him represented some of the more fascinating characters on the Agency payroll.

Dr. Richard Allen, a senior resident psychiatrist from Johns Hopkins Hospital in Baltimore, Maryland, was on regular call for his services with Agency's Office of Medical Services. However, since he did not spend any time working at the Agency headquarters in Langley, and was only used for special cases, he was perfect for meeting abroad with a NOC like Mitch in order to give him the examination. He had never met Mitch in the past, but had at his disposal the complete medical file on him. Making the trip to Switzerland to meet and conduct the exam was a special treat for the doctor and he looked forward to a week away from his duties at Johns Hopkins.

After arriving in the morning on the Swiss Air overnight flight from New York, and checking into his own hotel nearby, the doctor went over to the Le Richemond to meet with Mitch in his suite. After they introduced themselves to one another, and Mitch offered him only bottled water and juices, the doctor made his first comment of a medical nature.

"Good to see you recall that you're not supposed to have caffeinated drinks during an MSE."

"Oh yes, I remember it well. As you must know from my record, I've been through these exams several times in the past. Except for coffee in the mornings, I'm not much on caffeinated drinks anyway."

"Our meeting today will be no different from the previous ones. I've gone through your complete medical history and, for our purposes now, I am going to skip over much of the preliminary information like biographical details, etc."

"I appreciate that."

"I also will not be discussing with you today any of the specifics about the operation you recently completed that mandated this examination. I have not been read in on whatever it was that you specifically engaged in, nor should I be, for that matter. My concern is with your current state of mind, what you experienced, its effects on you, and your suitability to continue onward in your work for the Agency."

"I understand. By the way, each time I've had one of these exams, it has always been with a different doctor. Is there any reason for that?"

"I can think of no particular reason. It's probably just the rotational draw among the physicians. As you know, the Agency, for your own obvious personal security reasons, would not send out an OMS-based physician assigned to your Langley headquarters. Instead, they would select from what I understand is a comprehensive list of physicians from various parts of the country. This time I lucked out, and I must say I could not be more pleased to come to Geneva this time of the year."

"That's good. Yes, Geneva and the surrounding area is a great place to spend some time in, regardless the season. It's a beautiful city throughout the year."

"As a caveat to the questions I am going to put to you, should I happen to touch on any area that you feel impacts at all on the operation you were involved in, just stop me, and I will work around it."

"That's fair enough, Doctor."

"I started the exam as soon as walked into the room. That will also enable me to skip over a few of the areas I would normally take up during our meeting. Only if I feel a particular area has a direct bearing on you, will I subsequently ask a question."

"OK. I think I understand, but how about giving me an example?"

"Sure. In the few minutes since we started talking, I have already been able to begin observing your physical behavior. This includes some of your mannerisms, the way of presentation, appearance, verbal and non-verbal behavior, and even your level of attention to me when I am speaking. These things all serve to indicate something about your current state of mind. As we continue, I will be able to learn a lot more about you along these lines."

"I follow you. There's nothing like not having to start off with my name, date and place of birth."

"You've got it right. Let me say that in meeting with you today I am seeking to develop a 'picture,' so to speak, of you that will enable me to determine the sort of person you are. I want to learn about your personality characteristics, along with what I can tell are your strengths and weaknesses. This kind of information from you provides insights into the relationships you have with other human beings, especially those that are closer to you. In the end, I should be able to assess your current life situation as well as your development through a complete range of social maturation."

"Wow. All of that in one exam today?"

"Sounds like a lot, doesn't it?"

"It certainly does."

"To start off, Mitch, how do you feel about coming here to meet with me and take this exam today?"

"I currently live in Rome, where I feel thoroughly at home given my Italian background, and don't mind at all coming the short distance here to Geneva to meet with you. In my job, if you do not have in your blood a love of traveling, you are in the wrong occupation. Insofar as you are concerned, I have yet to be disappointed in meeting with any of your colleagues sent out by OMS. Every one of you has been intriguing conversationalists whom I have enjoyed talking with. Some talk more than others did and some listen more than others. Nevertheless, overall I have not really minded these exams at all."

"How do you explain that kind of attitude?"

"When I am in a place such as this, and not engaged in any kind of covert operation for the Agency, I am prone to feeling safe, relaxed and comfortable. It allows for me to be at peace with myself."

"Could it mean that you view such an exam as a challenge, especially since it is taking place in a location familiar to you and you prepared for it as well?"

"The enjoyment of a challenge is really a constant one for me. I am thoroughly up to confronting the challenges of daily life at any time. Life is all about change and that in it is part of the challenge. My work as an intelligence officer, in particular, requires that I be able to face head on these daily challenges in order to move forward successfully. Since I have come to enjoy what is asked of me in the assignments I am given, the last thing on my mind is to cave in and think about not giving a task my best shot, so to speak. I don't want to think about ending the enjoyment that I have in my work."

"People whom you know of who become ill, whether it is physically or emotionally, sooner or later develop problems. Have you known, or do you know, people that fall into this category?"

"I have probably met some like that over the years. Fortunately, though, I never got to know them well, or for very long."

"Does that mean you would have no interest in helping them in a time of need?"

"It means I did not get to know them well enough, as in a bonded friendship, for example, to be inclined to want to help."

"Could you characterize yourself as being such a person with a problem?"

"Not in the least. I consider myself able to cope with any issues that have come my way and where required, overcome and move forward."

"Of those people who you have developed personal friendships with, either in your work or otherwise, in social relationships, for example, has any of them developed problems that have come to your attention?"

"None that I have ever known."

"Who are those that you have a bonded friendship with, as you have termed it? You do not have to name them, just describe them?"

"Two groups of people would be applicable here. First, in my company, at the home office in San Francisco, the owner, who was my mentor in college, along with the CEO, who is my best personal friend since college days, I count as two close friends. Second, in terms of Agency personnel, Jack, who is my original and current supervisor, I count as a good friend. After that, it would be Gene and the remaining five members of our support team. They are the ones that keep me alive in the field overseas. I have come to appreciate them the most, since I depend upon their professionalism and skills in order for us to function so well together when called upon. I have bonded with them and consider them not only trusted colleagues but friends as well."

"If you came to know that any of them had physical or emotional problems, how would you react?"

"I would make myself available to provide whatever kind of assistance was needed. When you come to enjoy and depend upon these kinds of people, you cannot do enough when called upon. I would expect no less from any of them."

"That is an admirable response."

"That's just me."

"I see from your records that you abruptly lost your father when you were 12 years old. What effect did it have upon you then, and how has it come to affect you as an adult?"

"This is one question that is always asked during the MSE's, as well as the originally screening exam when I joined the Agency. I don't believe my responses, each time, has ever varied, nor should as far as I am concerned. The loss hit my mother and I severely. I was preparing for what I hoped would be a sports career in high school and college, and my father was my biggest fan. He was an astute businessperson, and he provided well for us. My mother picked up the reins after he passed, and saw to it that I received an excellent education and matured into a responsible adult. I gradually learned to live without him and have always tried to succeed in ways I thought would make him proud."

"Tell me about your dreams, including those that you can recall, following the death of your father."

"Looking back on that period, I can only remember good dreams of him cheering me on during track meets I participated in, and he and Mom always at my side, whenever I received an award or commendation."

"Were these repetitive dreams when they were at your side for positive achievements?"

"Yes, they were always good dreams of us being together as a family."

"Do you still have those kinds of dreams?"

"No, they gradually subsided after I got in my 20's."

"Did you ever have dreams back then that were emotionally upsetting, or caused you anguish?"

"None that I can ever recall."

"What do you dream about now?"

"I dream that I am the fastest runner among a large group of guys, and always able to be out in the lead, in front of the pack."

"Do any of them ever catch up and go ahead of you?"

"Not so far."

"What do you experience in the way of mood swings? For example, do you know depression, fear, anxiety or anger?"

"All of them once in a while, especially when driving my car in Rome's traffic."

"That's understandable. Try and be more specific in your answer."

"I believe we all experience some of these moods in varying degrees of intensity. I am no exception. However, I consider myself a positive person who has learned to cope with what I consider to be the minor difficulties that can crop up from time to time. In those specific instances where I experience anger, for example, I try and recognize it as nothing more than a small aspect to some particular event I am experiencing and move forward and away from it as expeditiously as possible."

"How about having feelings of resentment, suspiciousness and, sometimes, a desire to die?"

"In terms of resentment and suspiciousness, I can recall from my childhood and adolescent years experiencing them both on occasion. Especially if I lost out in a game or event, and I felt that I was not given an equal opportunity to prove myself the better choice or winner. As for having a desire to die, of course not. I know that the day will come, but that will be after experiencing a full life, including probably having some body parts that are not functioning correctly. That is when it is time to hang it up."

"Let's spend a few minutes on the topic of the line between homicide and suicide. Some scholars of note believe it is a very thin line. How would you respond?"

"I never gave any thought to putting the two together and making a comparison."

"Alright then, do you ever think about suicide?"

"Yes, I have on a few occasions. However, it would only come into play if I were cornered and had no choice. Under those kinds of circumstances, I would want to take out as many others as I am up against in the process of sacrificing my own life."

"What about in the case of just giving up on life and deciding to end your own?"

"No. I have too much to live for and so much more in life to enjoy in the coming years. Suicide, just for the sake of no longer being interested in living, would not be an option for me at all."

"You are showing me a strong, well-developed trait toward what I would call rugged individualism. How would you respond to this assertion?"

"I believe in self, my own self, and it entails maintaining the conscience of an individual. I don't care for what I would call the group conscience, wherein we meet and co-exist as a group. I don't consider myself a part of a group. I am not interested in consensus, finding common ground in a group setting, or, and it is a word I don't care much for, compromise. When a group of people meet, consider and reach common ground through a consensus, or compromise, they have surrendered their individual right to a conscience. I want no part of that."

"In your personal files, I noted your strong interest in individual sports, particularly your participation in long distance running events and marathons. Could that kind of background have been instrumental in you developing this sense of individualism?"

"I believe so, but I would have to add to that the influence of my father before he passed away. I remember his encouraging words to me about the value of individual sporting events, not only for the development of the body but for the mind as well. He also told me that the achievement of my goals and successes in life was predicated on being able to do it on my own. The achievements I would garner would come to the attention of those who would help me to get ahead, but whatever I was to do would be done on my own. I never forgot those words."

"He obviously provided you with very wise counsel."

"How about the influence of religion on the kind of individual you have grown up to be, including to the current stage in your life?"

"My father, a Roman Catholic, provided the initial impetus for me. After he died, my mother, a practicing Muslim took over. I should note here though, neither of them in any way force-fed me their religions. What I did come to accept in the existence of a supreme being, my God, I learned from my mother. Since she is to this day a gentle woman, I believe like her that it is best to hold my views on religion within me. I do not seek to spread my faith in any way. My religion is a very personal thing. It is between me and God, and no one else."

"How would you justify such a view or belief with what you can be called upon to do by the Agency?"

"If I am called upon to take an action against a government or individual that I have come to believe represents something wrong in the world, something that is inimical to mankind, I am prepared to eliminate it in order to ensure that peace in the world will be the result. I know that sounds lofty, but it is what I am able to live within my own conscience."

"Do you believe, therefore, that you have God's approval for whatever you may be called upon to do?"

"It is not God's approval that I either seek or need. I alone am the one that has to render my accounting in life to God. I will be examined for all that I do as an individual in the eyes of God. This is what my individualism means to me. I stand alone in my actions and accept what I do on my own as being what I believe is the right path to take."

"All I say to you at this point, as I end this discussion with you today, is that you possess what I would consider is full awareness of well-developed thought processes. You indeed stand as an individual and as you have demonstrated to me, you are at peace with yourself and with what you do for the Agency."

"Doctor Allen, I thank you very much. Is this your first visit to Geneva?"

"Yes, it is."

"May I interest you in having dinner this evening in a special French restaurant that overlooks a most beautiful lake?"

Chapter 25

Once the two rental periods ended on the apartments that Laura and Monica had leased, they departed from Paris without incidence and returned to the U.S. The week after their return, Jack called all the team together, except for Mitch, for a after action meeting at a summer resort just outside the town of Lake Placid, in upstate New York. The Adirondacks in early summer is a gorgeous location for relaxation and enjoyment of the scenery. However, unless reservations for lodging are made well in advance, finding any rooms, let alone five of them for eight people on short notice should have proven impossible. However, Jack persuaded a dear old friend, who happened to be one of the owners of the Lake Placid Lodge, and the five rooms became available.

Over a three-day period there, Jack, Gene, Hassan, Rena, Laura, Monica and Beau spent the first day relaxing and enjoying their surroundings together, followed by two days of debriefing on the Ahmadinejad op, from the start to finish. Jack, the senior Agency staffer that oversaw the op from headquarters, had Gene moderate the meeting, since he had been the team leader on the ground in Paris, and coordinated all the various aspects of the op as it played out, including the staggered and orderly departure of every member of the team.

Jack, before turning over the discussion to Gene, opened by saying: "I realize we are here without the benefit of Mitch being with us. It is unfortunate but we all know his status as a NOC and the different conditions from our own that he operates under. I talked with him three days ago. He is back in Rome following a detailed exam with one of the OMS doctors in Geneva. He asked that I express his very best personal regards and sincere thanks to every one of you for making the op in Paris a success. He also said to tell you how grateful he is for each of you performing your individual parts that melded together so well at the end.

If it had not turned out as flawless as it did, we certainly would not be meeting here like this today."

What followed for the next one and a half days entailed Gene walking the team through all the myriad details involved in staging the op. They dissected and justified all of their actions during the many days spent leading up to the hit, followed by their separate well-planned orderly departure scenarios. When it was time for winding up the discussions, Jack took over to guide the final comments. He said that the last two areas for consideration would be discussing how the op could be improved upon if they had to do it all over again, and the counter-intelligence and security posture they experienced in Paris during the entire time the op was underway there.

He led by saying: "From a headquarters perspective, and the degree to which we maintained contact with each of you there, we could find little, if anything, to find fault with in terms of the way all of you inter-related to each other and went about performing your separate tasks. We are immensely proud of you, but let me qualify the 'we' in my comments. Due to the tight hold on who would come to know about this op, for obvious reasons, I can only say that the 'we' means the DCI and me. Unless DCI Wicksford broke the cardinal rule himself, this was an extremely secure and tightly held op."

"Jack, I can only say that I, likewise, was highly pleased the way all on the team did their jobs and, now that it has been concluded, can take a rest and find solace in remembering their significant contribution to ridding the world of Ahmadinejad. None of us has any illusions about his demise meaning that major changes of benefit to the U.S. are going to happen overnight in Iran. We do not believe that will be the case. However, we are hopeful that the op would lead the ruling mullahs, from Ayatollah Ali Khamenei on down, to realize the futility in standing up another president like Ahmadinejad. We hope it leads them to moderate their overall policies in dealing not only with the west but also internally towards their own people."

"Gene, that was well said, and it echoes the feelings of all of us," Jack replied.

"Alright people," Gene said, "since we are nearing the end of this meeting, now is the time for you to get in your last comments along the lines suggested by Jack. Namely, could we have done it better, and lastly, what did we think about the French reaction to our action?"

Rena, the oldest member of the team and, along with her husband, Hassan, the most experienced in counter-terrorist as well as executive action type ops in the past, spoke up first.

"Gene, Jack, we knew this part of the after action discussion would be coming up. As a result, it was decided that I speak for the rest of the team is saying that as far as we are concerned, not only was the op well thought out and executed, it turned out to be surprisingly easy given where it took place. It's not that it was flawless or a textbook quality op made successful. It will go down to stand on its own as how to conceive, on relatively short notice, an intricate plan and execute it in a difficult environment. Therefore, instead of addressing what could have made it better, what is more worthy to talk about is the absence of what we expected—the well-known French ability to come down hard on any violation of French laws on their soil."

"Rena," Jack replied, "that is the real puzzle to this whole affair. Before leaving headquarters to come here, I had a conversation along these lines with the DCI. He said, by the way, to extend to all of you his sincere appreciation for all that you accomplished in the success of the op. He knows that he asked for a lot from you, and certainly knows that is what he got in return. Insofar the French, he said that he can only believe that they reacted the way they did, or in this case they held back on their reaction, due to their poor state of relations with Iran, particularly in their dealings with the administration of Ahmadinejad."

"I think that is exactly right," Gene replied. "Knowing of the capabilities of the French intelligence and security services, let alone their police force, their reaction on the ground just left us stymied. Once the hit occurred, we expected the French to quickly move all of their forces on the scene there out across the Champs De Mars green space from the foot of the tower to the southeast and the Ecole Militaire. We were also expecting that the apartment buildings that line the area on both sides of the tower would promptly be inspected. However, nothing apparently happened, as best we could determine, in any of the buildings at all."

"From where Rena and I were sitting in the street café outside of Monica and Laura's apartment building, on Avenue Charles Floquet," said Hassan, "we could hear the sirens just after the hit. However, to our amazement, no one came anywhere near our location."

"The DCI," Jack replied, "told me that the move by the Iranians to take the body of Ahmadinejad quickly away in the SUV to the airport and back to Tehran, did not surprise him. He said their abhorrence for western scrutiny, along with their penchant to providing for Ahmadinejad's security, dead or alive, left them no choice."

"Regardless where in the world Ahmadinejad was scheduled to appear, either in public or private, his security team must have concluded that removing him away from the area quickly was an integral part of their overall security plan. In this case, it did not matter that they were in France, or even that the French authorities could have been of assistance to them," Gene added.

"The DCI's last comment to me," Jack said, "was that in a cable from COS Paris, it stated that a French plainclothes security officer managed to get in close to see the body on the ground after the hit. Peering through the group of the Iranian security detail around Ahmadinejad, he watched as one of them moved in and turned over the body. When the Frenchman saw that the back of the head and neck were gone, he knew nothing could be done to save him."

"With that," Jack said, "one final area I would like to go over pertains to the team's use of the encrypted cell phones. None of you reported any signs at all of hostile surveillance coverage during the entire op. Headquarters is confident that the French services, or any intelligence service in the world, for that matter, can't crack our encryption used when making secure calls. However, it is their use of GPS to determine the area you are calling from that is a serious security concern to us. Since none of you reported on picking up any surveillance moving in on you, or even appearing to arrive nearby and set up against you, tells us something about the way you all kept on the move. It also tells us that you limited your talk time on the phones. You are to be commended for that as well."

"Jack, thank you for that," replied Gene. "All of us have a very healthy regard for French technical capabilities. As a result, we made sure we kept our airtime short, along with quickly leaving areas from where we were talking. It must have worked since once we cleared immigration at Charles De Gaulle, and the aircraft was airborne, we could breathe easily in knowing we had gotten away safely."

"The best part is," Jack added, "with the investigation by the French now fully underway, and speculation appearing in the press pointing fingers in numerous directions, who knows where it will lead. We can forget what the Iranians are saying in their press. The U.S. and Israel top their list as the perpetrators. However, their articles show nothing in the way of evidence to back up their assertions."

CHAPTER 26

Even though Gene had become Mitch's point of contact in place of Jack, Mitch was surprised to hear from him and learn that he would be coming to Italy and wanted to play a round of golf with him.

It had been five weeks since Mitch had returned from his mental state exam in Geneva, and he was productively back at work signing up new clients and making job placements for existing ones. He thoroughly enjoyed the work routine and realized how fortunate he was to have a high quality office manager, Mr. G (short for Guido), handling all of M&T's business affairs during his frequent absences.

Guido Vespucci was said to be related to one of the Italian seafaring explorers of the same name several centuries back. Unfortunately, his claimed susceptibility for seasickness prevented him from ever going down to the sea in a ship.

However, what he lacked in seamanship he made up for in business acumen. He held an MBA from the SDA Bocconi School of Management at Bocconi University in Milan. Following his schooling there, he spent 12 years managing a small gold jewelry syndicate's operations in Florence. While there, he befriended Mitch's uncle, which resulted in the introduction to Mitch who had just relocated to Rome from the U.S., and was in need of an office manager. Originally from Rome, Mr. G. signed on with M&T and quickly came to realize he had found not only an enjoyable new job, but also in Mitch a new boss who was also turning out to be a good friend as well.

Whenever he could find the time, which was not very often, Mitch played a round of golf at course where he could play his best, Circolo del Golf di Roma Aquasanta, a 20-minute drive from his apartment. The first golf course to open in Italy, in 1903, the course lies near the ruins of a number of ancient aqueducts. While it was not a particularly long or difficult course, Mitch found he enjoyed the layout and the picturesque scenery dotted with aqueducts. He also found several new Italian friends to play with, whose company he enjoyed as well.

Now he could look forward to entertaining Gene on the course and learning the latest news from home, including a possible upcoming assignment. He knew something must be up, or Gene certainly would not be traveling to Italy to play golf. Gene, likewise, had a fascination for the game but, like Mitch, also did not find the time to play regularly.

It's no wonder Romans leave their beloved Eternal City during the month of August every year. From July through September is usually unadulterated sweltering heat. The July day when Mitch and Gene chose to play their round of golf it was going to be hot and humid, with temperatures in the 90s. This prompted them to get an early start in the morning before the stifling heat of midday could settle in.

"I cannot believe the setting for this course," Gene said. "It's beautiful."

"I know. Each time I'm here, I notice something different. This time of the year, with the hot weather, the course is fortunately not crowded."

"There is nothing like the privacy of playing alone together, on a quiet course, to allow for discussing the real reason I chose to visit you, old buddy."

"It's about time. I'm ready for your data dump."

"I presume you know by now that Jack brought the whole team together a week ago, at Lake Placid, for the after action debriefing. We missed you not being there but all went smoothly and many accolades went around, to you, in particular, for the way the Paris op turned out. After a first day of relaxing along the shore of the lake, we settled down for two more days of detailed discussions."

"Would you rather have been with me and experienced what I did along the shore of a lake, in my case meeting with a shrink at Lake Geneva?"

"No thank you. I am interested, however, in the shrink's assessment of you. Are you still considered to be normal?"

"Normal my ass. I am about as abnormal as they come, and you, of all people, know it. So much so, that I'm considered fit to do it all over again. The doctor told me that based on my overall record of accomplishments, I can consider myself to be an automaton, whatever that implies."

"It means, Mitch, that you function so well in what you do, you are a self-operating machine."

"I can handle it that."

"Anyway, we finished with the debriefing at the lake, and the team departed, Jack asked that I remain behind to discuss the next item on his agenda."

"With a few bad guys still out there perpetrating terror around the world, I'm sure the target selection has been carefully thought out and determined."

"Indeed it has, including one that is going to be extremely difficult to accomplish."

"You just significantly narrowed down the list."

"How would you feel about taking out the leader of North Korea, Kim Jong-Il, in the capital of China, Beijing?"

"You know me, I won't say it can't be done, but it does have the potential to be my final assignment."

"Now you're being overly dramatic."

"I'm still listening attentively."

"First off, the two of us are to travel to Beijing separately, obviously, and conduct the pre-hit survey. Headquarters has accumulated a limited amount of interesting information on Kim's previous trips to Beijing, which are always by armored train from Pyongyang. He arrives at the same station every time, the one that all trains from China's northeast area use."

"As I recall, Beijing has at least five train stations that handle passengers and freight from all parts of China."

"Yes, Mitch, that's on the mark. In Kim's case though, it's always the Beijing Railway Station, located in the center of the city."

"Isn't it unusual for him to visit China? I mean, isn't it once every several years or so?"

"According to our analysts at headquarters, his visits are usually predicated by North Korea's need for economic aid, due to major food shortages, for example, or needing an extra bit of political support in the U.N. for standing up against sanctions to be imposed on Korea."

"If I recall correctly, Gene, his last visit was around 2010. Furthermore, around that time there was talk about his poor state of health, to the degree that one of his son's was selected as his successor. Does headquarters have any indication another trip to Beijing is in the offing?"

"As I understand it from headquarters, they usually are able to learn, about one month in advance, his travel plans. I realize that is not much time to prepare, but it is thought that now is the time for the pre-hit survey in order to determine the feasibility of even trying to make the hit while he is Beijing. Meanwhile, they have no specific information or timetable that a trip is being planned at this time."

"I can certainly schedule a plausible trip there for purposes of laying the groundwork for a new program personnel screening program for M&T. I could renew contact with some professors at several of China's best universities for the placement of newly graduating engineers and physicists with U.S. and European firms interested in hiring them. It would be much like what is currently done with the high quality engineers from India, for example, that are brought to the U.S. for work in Silicon Valley, Phoenix, Boston, etc."

"I like it. That should be a good cover for status there. For me, I would use my photojournalist cover to do some shots of the latest architectural accomplishments, particularly in Beijing and Shanghai. Some of the new buildings being completed are quite spectacular and would provide good cover for photo shoots that will allow me to roam around a bit."

"What else did you learn from your meeting with Jack?"

"The most interesting for the pre-hit survey is from headquarters satellite imagery analysts. In going back over the overhead coverage of Kim's last several visits, they have come up with some good stuff. When that is combined with what the photojournalists obtained on the ground there during his visits, like at the train station, for example, it will give us a number of leads to follow up on during the survey."

"I've used the overhead analysts' stuff in the past. It is always quite accurate and revealing. When matched up with what we should be able to do on the ground in Beijing, it should help us a lot."

"Jack even gave me a couple of suggested hotels for us to stay at there, both allowing for us to be in and around the train station. For you, they suggested the Beijing Marriott Hotel City Wall. For me, they named the Beijing Harmony Hotel. They are located near the station. The analysts believe a couple of the buildings next to the hotels offer potential for good line of sight, particularly when Kim's train is starting to move out of it, and he usually likes to stand in one of its windows waving to the onlookers on the station platform. It apparently is one of the few times that he is that exposed to the public."

"That's one of the best reasons for us being on the ground there. Can Jack get us some samples of the photos to look at showing Kim at one of these sendoffs, as well as the hotels they are suggesting?"

"He is going to pull together what he can, and we should be able to view it before leaving for China. He also is going to include some reporting on the Marriott Hotel, including the physical drawings and schematics from when the hotel was built. The analysts believe these materials will be crucial to having you make some observations while staying there."

"This is the kind of survey stuff I really enjoy. You mentioned you and me going to China. Who else will make up the team?"

"Mitch, this bit of news is interesting. However, Jack said it will only come to pass if you approve of it."

"Always considerate, that Jack. What do you have?"

"I'll start with a short explanation about our SAD organization at headquarters. When they go abroad to engage in sensitive ops, it sometimes involves a joint team effort with DOD's SMU organization. If you don't already know about them, it stands for Special Mission Unit. They conduct paramilitary ops, for example, to counter the guerrillas in Columbia, go up against the Taliban in Afghanistan and Pakistan, etc. Some of their teams can be as small as six or seven operatives, primarily focused on operating in the countryside versus in cities. They also make extensive use of military snipers."

"Gene, are you suggesting we are going to have a joint goat rope op take place in Beijing, of all places?"

"No Mitch, not at all. One of their SMU operatives, a female, was described by Jack as a superb NOC officer who has specialized not only with SF teams in jungles, but also makes extensive use of commercial cover on the ground in major cities around the world. Her work as a NOC includes frequently using alias identities in her ops as well. In addition, she also is a gifted linguist not only in English and Arabic, but in Spanish, her native language, as well."

"Sounds interesting. Please go on."

"If you agree, Jack suggests you consider using her ostensibly as an assistant to you and your cover firm. You will also assign her to do her share of the pre-hit survey. Her usefulness to us in Beijing, along with an ability to work at your level of expectations, will determine whether she returns to Beijing for the actual hit on Kim. What do you say?"

"I'm willing to give it a try. I can see using her in a role as my assistant. However, I have to insist on meeting with her for a thorough interview before I consider taking her anywhere."

"That's a fair request and what I expected."

"Let's pick a date to leave for the survey, cut it in half, and make that the date I meet with her. In addition, I would like her to have a brand-new alias and set of documents, including an age-dated U.S. passport. The Chinese authorities note things like fresh versus old documents, and we would not like her to start off drawing scrutiny."

"Where do you want to meet her?"

"If she is going to be under cover as my assistant, I would like her to come here. She has to know something about what M&T is all about, see the office in Rome, meet my office manager and get to know at least a little something about Italy, especially if it will be for the first time."

"That's a reasonable request. Jack would like us to be in Beijing in about three weeks, four at the most."

"Fine. Call me in a week or so to say when she is due to arrive, and let me know her new identity. I'll then be able to get her local lodging. If everything turns out well, possibly we can leave for Beijing from here. Will that work for you?"

"Sure, that will be good. However, we should plan to link up for a short meeting, say in Seattle, on the way out there. I will want to show you the package of overhead materials from headquarters, and that is only viewable in the U.S. You know the Agency's prohibitions and sensitivities on how that kind of stuff has to be handled.

Headquarters can have the imagery sent to the station in Seattle and brought out for us to see there."

Chapter 27

In a completely uncharacteristic move, Mitch held a sign above his head that in bold letters, eight inches high, spelled out the letters of his first name. He was standing inside the main concourse at Rome's Leonardo da Vinci-Fiumicino Airport, awaiting the arrival of Gabriela. When she cleared immigration and customs controls, and exited out into the part of the terminal where the throngs of people were awaiting for those on arriving flights, she had been instructed to look for the sign with his name on it. As a backup, if that did not work, she had his secure cell phone number.

Thirty minutes earlier, as he was walking in the airport parking garage, Mitch received a call on his cell phone that was much unexpected. It was Jack calling; that in itself was certainly a surprise. He did not expect to be in contact with him any time soon. However, it was the news Jack conveyed to him that jarred through every bone in his body. Mitch frequently thought about what he would do should the opportunity present itself to exact a much sought after revenge.

"Mitch, it's great to hear your voice. How are you?"

"I'm at Fiumicino and about to meet up with the military NOC sent for me to look over. I am fine though, and glad to hear your voice too."

"I'll keep this short. Islamabad Station has a reliable source they meet with on an infrequent basis that is privy to some of the comings and goings of Dr. Ahmad, your old terrorist leader mastermind from the Sellafield truck bomb attack and the Dulles Airport anthrax attack."

Mitch stopped short in his tracks in the parking garage, took a deep breath and replied, "Can I get anywhere near the bastard in order to ensure his early arrival with the vestal virgins in the Muslim paradise heaven?"

"That's why I'm calling to give you the first choice, and determine if you are interested in going after him should we be able to put an operation into motion. I believe you just gave me your positive response."

"You've got that one right, Jack."

"The reporting source, a Pakistani from Ahmad's village, has become a support assistant of sorts to him, and is used to run errands, buy stuff for him, convey messages, etc. The doctor is living in seclusion, but regularly changes locations in and around the outskirts of Islamabad."

"I can understand that. I'm sure he also still remembers that the big vacuum cleaner up in the sky called NSA is listening in, and he should not make much use of cell phones."

"The source reported that Ahmad is gearing up for something big, and it will be in the U.S. again. Unfortunately, the source, although confident he will be able to learn more details with time, could not provide anything further."

"Jack, when the source is next given more tasking from us, please be sure to include him getting a current and detailed physical description. Furthermore, I would like for you to resurrect for me the picture of Ahmad from his ID card at the hospital in Paisley, Scotland."

"Consider it done. I know you have a lot on your plate right now, but should we get something going, and you are able to play in this one, I'll be back in touch."

"Thanks Jack. Keep me posted." Mitch could not believe his good fortune to have the opportunity to go after a nemesis he vowed he would hunt down whenever and wherever possible.

As Mitch ended the call and resumed walking towards the main terminal, he could feel the nervousness pulse through his body. Just the possibility of going after the evil doctor again caused a swirl of thoughts to rush through his mind. Dr. Abdul-Karim bin Ahmad, the mastermind terrorist who planned and directed the two devastatingly successful attacks at Sellafield Nuclear Processing facility in England and at Dulles Airport, was still on the loose. He successfully made it back to Pakistan following the anthrax attack at Dulles that left thousands dying over a period of weeks as they traveled from the airport to their homes and jobs all over the world. Progressively becoming weaker and wracked with pain in their chests, they experienced severe respiratory collapse and failure due to their breathing in the deadly anthrax spores that had been released in the airport's heating and air conditioning system in the main terminal building.

Since that deadly airport attack, Mitch traveled through many more airports in various locales, and each time he could not but help think about the air he was breathing while inside the terminals. This meeting now, to link up with Gabriela inside Fiumicino's main terminal, would not be an exception.

Looking straight ahead at the people coming through the constantly opening two sets of double doors, he tried to focus on females who appeared to be traveling alone.

With the sign still held above his head, he was not having any luck making eye contact with any of them. Hell, he thought, many of the people near him were holding signs, but his was the only one with his name on it. Just as he was starting to lose interest in the doors, he heard a strong voice to his side say, "Mitch, I'm Gabriela Torres."

Feeling stupid to still be holding the sign above his head, he pulled it down to his side. "Gabriela, I'm Mitch Vasari. Welcome to Italy."

"I hope this will not sound trite," she said, "but I know your face from somewhere. It'll come back to me soon."

"I like the way you travel, one suitcase and a backpack. Let's get out of here, find my car and head for the city. I hope you will enjoy your visit. Italy is a fascinating place."

"It's my first time here so I will be looking for you to be my guide."

"I have a room reserved for you in a nice hotel between my office and the coliseum. If you want, you can rest up there, and then we can regroup and talk."

"I sleep well on planes, so I feel good right now. I'd like to check in, stow my clothes and follow your lead."

The drive from the airport into downtown Rome took most of an hour, with Gabriela experiencing the chaotic driving habits of Italians the closer into Rome they went. During the drive they made small talk about what it's like living in Italy and they exchanged some of the details of their upbringings. They also discussed how they each came to be intelligence officers.

After getting Gabriela checked in at the hotel, Mitch left her to unpack and freshen up. He returned to his office to meet with Mr. G, the office manager, and catch up on his mail and messages from clients. His cover work was a full-time job when he was not away on operational assignments. Mr. G could keep the office functioning smoothly but was not able, obviously, to handle the various aspects of doing executive recruitments and making subsequent job placements.

After returning to Gabriela's hotel, and learning that she enjoyed long walks, they strolled over to Trevi Fountain. Having recently received a sprucing up and cleaning of the marble, the fountain was in all of its spectacular glory. Sitting on the marble along the water's edge was relaxing and pleasant, even as it started to become crowded with locals as well as the ever-present tourists. Finding Gabriela very easy to converse with, including being able to switch into Arabic with her, Mitch decided it was time for more serious talk about her getting involved operationally in the assignment to come in Beijing. They continued with their walk, this time over to the secluded outdoor terrace of the Intercontinental De La Ville Rome, overlooking the top of the Spanish Steps.

"What can you tell me about your work in SMU, Gabriela? I am not familiar with what they do, types of ops, etc."

"Since you are from the Agency's SAD, I would have thought you were already familiar with us over in DOD."

"I only moved with my team to SAD from our Counterterrorism Center four months ago. Before that, I specialized in counterterrorist ops for the past seven years. Up until now, that is what I have found I do best, including engaging in executive action ops, or what is it you guys call it, targeted killings?"

"Ah, yes. That is what we call it, but a hit is still a hit, isn't it? No different. By the way, from what I understand, per the limited briefing I was given on you, your shooting skills are truly exceptional, and you are not known to miss."

"Why thank you. I appreciate hearing that. Tell me, have you been satisfied with your work in SMU?'

"Yes, most definitely so. I'm relatively new to SMU, having earlier spent five years in SF, primarily in Latin America and the Middle East. All the ops I've engaged in have been good for me. I have learned a lot and gained considerable experience."

"By the way, I've enjoyed speaking Arabic with you today. Your pronunciation is very clear and easily understood. You should be proud of your professional accomplishments."

"That's kind of you to say so. Thank you. My work has been rewarding for me, and I would say suited to my capabilities. At least from my first SMU ops assignment, it appeals to me a lot. However, I should add a caveat that it is more appealing when I can avoid being jumped from behind and wacked over the head and robbed, as happened to me in South America."

"Can you tell me where you were when it happened?"

"I was in Brazil and working separately from the rest of my team. It was unfortunate but I am now completely recovered and eager to move forward. When asked if I was interested in working on a joint op with your Agency for my next assignment, I jumped at the chance."

"How do you like working alone?"

"Well, like you, from what I understand about your ops background, I also trained as a case officer and have come to enjoy functioning in NOC operations. I thoroughly enjoy the challenge of being on my own in the field. My years though, on a SF team, were very satisfying for me as well. It may sound like a contradiction, but while I easily function as a member of a team, but I am equally at ease on my own. Does that make sense to you?"

"It certainly does. I know it well myself. In my case though, it may be a little different. I always know my team is around me, particularly when guarding my six, yet I seldom see them as they go about supporting me. For us, secure comms, like I'm sure you have come to depend on, keeps us all in contact as need be."

"Since you have not teamed up with an SMU before, and likewise, the same for me in not working with the Agency, you are going to have to bring me along in terms of what is expected of me, how I will function, etc."

"Well, for starters, the op that we will engage in is being treated with an extremely high level of compartmentation. I can only think of three, possibly four Agency personnel, starting with our DCI, that are read in on it. In fact, saying 'read in' is not actually correct. Nothing is being written down in the first place. Information is being conveyed only verbally, with no written record of any kind."

"I realized that was the case due to the way I was called in by my CO. After I reported for duty following my last op in LA, the CO, Major Green, informed me that the sensitivity and classified nature of the op we had just completed required that our own SMU team be broken up and disbanded. He said this was due to a matter of policy within JSOG, and had nothing negative to do with the team itself. As a result, all of my fellow team members moved on to other SMU units.

"Green then went on to inform me that I had an appointment with the CO of JSOG, who would provide a briefing on a possible new assignment for me. Even Green turned out to be unaware of my being offered a chance to take part in a joint op with the Agency. Since I was originally selected for SMU work by SecDef Panetta himself, and he personally briefed me on that assignment, it would appear that, like in your case, only a few people in DOD are aware of what we will be taking on for this upcoming op."

"Were you briefed on who the target is going to be?"

"Yes, its North Korea's President, Kim Jong-Il."

"In order to get the op off the ground, we will be going to Beijing first, in order to conduct a pre-hit survey since it will be the location for the hit. We will be a three-person team composed of you, Gene, who is my support team leader, and me."

"What kinds of commercial cover will we be operating under?"

"Gene will be a photojournalist, a cover he has used effectively all over the world. He actually is a superb photographer who, along with comparable observation skills, possesses street smarts that you would not believe."

"I'm looking forward to meeting and working with him."

"I will be in my true name, and working under commercial cover for McKinsey and Trotter, a San Francisco-based executive recruiting firm that specializes in high technology job placement. It serves as my actual NOC cover company."

"That's a great field, especially being so applicable to China right now."

"For your cover, Gabriela, do you think you could handle being my executive recruiting assistant, who is accompanying me to China? Our purpose in going there is to scout out Chinese educational institutions that offer potential for supplying graduates in the fields of engineering and the physical sciences."

"That sounds like something I can handle and get excited about."

"The end goal of such an effort for M&T is offering up these graduates to applicable high tech firms in the U.S. and abroad. This same kind of approach has worked well in India over the years, and it has resulted in thousands of engineers and technicians from the best schools there signing contracts to come and work in the U.S., in Silicon Valley, for example."

"I can recall reading articles about the value that these Indian workers have added to high tech firms in the U.S."

"Gene will be in Beijing separate from us, with no connection at all to M&T or us, for that matter. He will stay in a different hotel, but still close to where Agency analysts believe the hit on Kim is most possible when his train is pulling out of the Beijing Railway Station."

"I assume the three of us will be in limited contact via our secure cell phones, correct?"

"Yes, as necessary. We just have to practice good phone security in making sure our calls to each other are short, and we quickly move away from where the calls take place. I am sure you have found this the same in your own SMU ops. Hostile governments and intelligence services are quite capable of using GPS to track down cellular points of origin on calls they are able to intercept, even if they cannot decrypt them."

"Oh yes, it's the same for us too."

"If our pre-hit survey is successful, and it appears that we have a making of a viable op, it will all be based on getting back into Beijing and in position once word is learned that Kim has scheduled another trip from Pyongyang. We could be on standby for some time, based on his history of making the trip only every couple of years.

Lately, though, with North Korea facing severe shortages of food and fuel supplies, Kim travels more frequently to appeal to China for new aid. Seeking China's help in dealing with the West on stalled nuclear disarmament talks is also a factor in his stepped-up travels."

"What about the appointment, not very long ago, of one of his sons as heir apparent? I would think that also could provide a good reason for going to China, to introduce him and gain their support in his future plans as well."

"Yes, that is being suggested by our analysts as in the offing as well. It points to a trip to Beijing sooner rather than later. All the more reason for us to be prepared, should we have the makings of an op that can succeed."

"What is the timeline for getting the survey underway?"

"As I understand you being detailed to the Agency for this op, and assuming the survey works out, we should plan on leaving here in two days time and meet up with Gene in Seattle. We need to meet with him inside the U.S., for purposes of looking at sensitive satellite overhead coverage of Beijing. Our analysts have made some observations they believe could be crucial in our planning for the survey. That will take less than a half a day there, and we can then proceed to Beijing. In the meantime, if you still wish to be part of this endeavor, I would count on you as part of the team. What do you say?"

"Please, count me in on this one. You will find that I am very comfortable on the streets, including as it relates to surveys, plus serving as your assistant for your company. I will be a value-added commodity there at all times."

"I had the feeling that was going to be your answer. Over the next couple of days here, we will spend time at my office. I will introduce you to the office manager, Mr. G, as well as tutor you a bit on the executive recruiting profession in order to bring you up to speed on your new cover. I also will have business cards made up for you in your alias identity and have you fully prepared and ready to leave for China.

CHAPTER 28

He lifted his wet, sweat-soaked head up and off the damp pillow, and rolled over, trying but failing to find a dry spot so he could doze off back to sleep. Unfortunately, further rest would elude Dr. Ahmad for the remaining hour he had hoped to have before getting out of bed. Ahead of him, following the afternoon Dhuhr prayers, he would be having an important meeting with his longtime friend, Jamil Amin, the primary assistant to al-Qaeda's former number two, Dr. Ayman al-Zawahiri, who took over leadership of the terrorist group following the death of Osama bin Laden.

It was risky for Jamil, a known terrorist and senior operative in al-Qaeda, to leave North Waziristan and travel to meet with Ahmad in Islamabad. However, the importance of what he would convey to Dr. Ahmad made the journey an exception. Ahmad, currently in the weapons selection stage for his next major attack against the U.S., planned on simultaneous catastrophic bio-terrorism incidents in the form of utilizing some of the most deadly toxic substances known. These attacks would be timed to take place in cities across the U.S.

The question that Ahmad needed to resolve before proceeding further, however, was what would be the choice of one or two of the bio weapons that was stockpiled in large enough quantities to make the attacks across the U.S. as effective as possible. He would have his answer with the arrival of his old friend, Jamil.

"May peace be with you," Ahmad said with a profuse shaking of Jamil's hands.

"And to you be in peace together with God's Mercy," Jamil replied.

"We have not seen another in too long a time. Tell me, what is your situation?"

"After we finish here today I will not be returning to our village. Instead, I will go to Karachi where the command structure is now totally relocated on the orders of our new leader, Dr. al-Zawahiri."

"That is good news. I have heard rumors suggesting such an eventual move, but I had no idea it was already complete. It will certainly provide for better security and living conditions for all of you."

"The attacks from the infidels coming across from Afghanistan, combined with the increasing drone attacks, were making life in the villages miserable. We were frequently required to change locations, as well as be constantly on alert to who among our brothers had turned against us and was providing information on our whereabouts."

"My own move here last year from Miran Shah took place under similar circumstances. I no longer felt safe there since many of the brothers around us could not be trusted. Furthermore, too many strangers were regularly coming around and that only put my own security into question. Here in Islamabad, however, it feels like I am almost hiding in the open. While I don't go out of this house very much, having so many of our own people in all the surrounding houses here does provide for a much better feeling of security."

"I do bring you good news of our research and stockpiling efforts since the move to Karachi, but first I want to hear about your upcoming plans for dealing with the Great Satan."

"Over the past 10 to 12 months I have held detailed conversations with our own people here in the immediate area. As a result, I have been able to determine who has relatives living in the U.S., what cities they live in and what kinds of work they are doing. By having some of them come here to meet with me, or meet with the brothers I have sent to them, we have developed what has turned out to be a number of teams of trusted brothers there who are currently living in the cities I have chosen as targets. While a few of them are working in some of the industries from where we will launch the attacks, others have succeeded getting new jobs in these industries at my direction. Therefore, we have in place the right people in the right places, all awaiting further instructions."

"In other words, you now have trusted brothers pre-positioned and poised for launching the jihad."

"That is exactly correct. Furthermore, during this same period of time, I have conducted extensive research on the subject of bio-terrorism, particularly in terms of what is being done in the U.S. to combat it and the current state of readiness there. The result is that I have been able to determine where the weaknesses and vulnerabilities are and the best ways to exploit them. Only in a democratic society like that found in the Great Satan, is such a weak state of affairs found to exist. This indifference and freedom of choice are what I will be able to feast upon in order to make our jihad succeed."

"What are you looking at in terms of a timetable?"

"Adjustments will have to be made later in the U.S., but that should not affect the timing at all. The key to setting a time now will depend upon the news you have for me on the stockpiles."

"When we spoke of this last year, the research effort underway toward building up the stockpiles was still taking place in the border villages of Waziristan. Of the three substances that you asked us to focus our attention on, Clostridium botulinum toxin, Anthrax spores and Ebola virus, their development and stockpiling continue as we speak. The difference now, however, is that our efforts are taking place in three state-of-the-art laboratories, all with clean rooms, and located in three separate and secure safe houses, all near each other in Karachi. The dedicated groups of people currently involved in culture growing and processing includes five highly skilled microbiologists and seven technicians."

"This is wonderful news. It is obvious that, like I have found living here, being in and around masses of people is, in itself, a form of security, as long as you can control and maintain restricted access to yourself. I commend your ability to continue working with three of the most deadly diseases known to mankind inside a sprawling city like Karachi."

"It has turned out well indeed. The question we need to address now though, are the amounts that you believe will be required. I don't have for you today the specific quantities currently stored by the researchers in Karachi. Once I arrive there tomorrow and am briefed by them, I will be able to get that information to you. I know now that the culturing of the Ebola virus is proceeding at a much slower pace when compared with the stockpiling going on with the other two."

"I know exactly what the researchers are experiencing. The Zaire species of the Ebola virus that they are developing was originally obtained by going to that country and obtaining blood samples from villagers with the infection. It is the most lethal of the species, with a greater than 90 percent death rate for those exposed to it. Unfortunately, it is also going to be difficult for the researchers to alter the virus for the best and effective weaponizing, namely, for airborne applications. It requires the researchers to wear protective clothing, double-door access zones, use of special biological safety cabinets, etc. It can be a nightmare to handle, let alone successfully propagate."

"When I first visited the labs in Karachi, after they initially became functional, I saw very little of the original equipment that was brought out of Iraq following the Gulf War. Everything now is brand new and the whole staff is Pakistani. The Iraqi researchers you knew from when the labs were on the border with Afghanistan are all gone."

"Needless to say, I look forward to learning from you the total amounts being maintained there. Based upon the current state of planning here, the use of the botulinum toxin and anthrax spores have become my primary focus for weaponizing. While we previously proved, for the attack at Dulles Airport, that transporting the anthrax spores into the U.S. turned out to be the least of our difficulties during the operation, it should be no different this time. In fact, I expect that for the travel phase going to and moving about inside the U.S., the use of smaller containers will be possible. This week I am meeting with our concealment device specialist and am considering the use of altered ballpoint pens for hiding the custom designed vials inside."

"Do you want me to convey to the researchers that you prefer they concentrate on the botulinum toxin and anthrax spores, and do nothing further for you with the Ebola virus?"

"Yes, definitely for now. Once I know the amounts you have for each of the two, along with their projections for the next couple of months, I will then decide to go with one, or possibly both, for use against the selected targets in the U.S. As we both know, my brother, the researchers' growth of the cultures and processing takes considerable time. Therefore, the amount accumulated will determine the timetable. I have full confidence in the researchers and praise to Allah for their effort underway. We will be successful in our jihad."

"Praise be to Allah as well for our success. Do you plan on transporting the vials of your choice to the U.S. yourself, like you did for the Dulles attack?"

"I'm unsure right now. If I do, it will mean altering my facial appearance once again and, given that the infidels have good pictures of me from my work at the hospital in Scotland, I am not inclined to take the chance.

Besides, the way I am organizing this much greater jihad, it will probably mean that I do not directly need to go there."

"I know from comments by Dr. al-Zawahiri that he believes you are a most valued commodity that is to be given whatever you ask for in planning the jihad."

"With all the costly things he has done for me here in Islamabad, I can live securely and conduct my research and planning for the attack. For now, and until it is time to take the attack to the Great Satan, I cannot ask for more. I do know for sure that, once again, we will be successful. Remember my brother, we are here to serve Allah, the merciful, and we will prevail in driving the infidels off the face of the earth. We are his instruments available for him, however he chooses to use us. That is our only value to Allah in what he commands us to do."

"May Allah bless you, my brother."

"And may Allah bless you too."

Following the success of the attack at Dulles Airport, and the devastating death toll in the aftermath of the previous year, Ahmad had made his escape from the U.S. and returned to Pakistan determined to plan for a great series of attacks with even more catastrophic consequences.

During his subsequent extensive research on the state of affairs on bio terrorism in the U.S., he found that serious vulnerabilities existed throughout the country, particularly in the food industry. The weaknesses that he found offered considerable potential for producing havoc throughout the general populace. In particular, beverages such as milk, fruit and vegetable juices, particularly juices that are not from concentrate (since they require pasteurization) and are ready to drink, attracted his attention at the onset. The processes through which beverages are collected or harvested, extracted, filled or packaged, stored in large volume and then rapidly distributed, makes them a uniquely inviting target for the bio terrorist.

Pasteurization, however, plays a key role in reducing the extent of poisoning. If a product such as milk, for example, is pasteurized, the effectiveness of botulinum toxin is significantly reduced. The most acutely toxic substance known to mankind can have its effectiveness reduced from 98 per cent to 68 per cent. Between the 9/11 attacks in 2001, and the anthrax spores released in the attack at Dulles Airport in 2011, the U.S. Government instituted changes across the country designed to make more secure the nation's water and milk supplies as enforced by municipal, county and state governments, plus private companies. In actuality though, Ahmad found that the changes contained a loop hole he would be able to exploit. The safety guidelines issued by the Food and Drug Administration as well as the Department of Home Security called for voluntary rather than mandatory compliance.

In the case of water supplies, better security controls were instituted around the country but, again, not necessarily on a mandatory basis. A problem though, for botulinum toxin in fresh water, is that it becomes naturally inactivated within three to six days. Therefore, unless the toxin can be introduced into the piping system at the point where the water is leaving a reservoir for direct flow into city pipes, this kind of attack is a non-starter.

For the milk supply chain however, better susceptibilities were found by Ahmad to exist. For example, no mandatory requirements are in effect to keep milk tanks and trucks locked when not in use. In addition, there is no procedure calling for at least two people to be present whenever milk is to be transferred from one stage of the supply chain to the next. Furthermore, no mandatory toxin tests are in force to be administered by tank truck drivers to detect any of the seven serologically distinct botulinum toxin types.

The more Ahmad thought about the choices that lay ahead for him, and what he particularly liked about the food industry's specific vulnerabilities in the U.S., his inclination turned towards the use of botulinum toxin, versus the anthrax spores that the authorities were more up-to-date in guarding against since his successful Dulles jihad. Fortunately, with no timetable to worry about this time, he could easily await the next progress report from Jamil.

Chapter 29

No sooner had the aircraft leveled off upon reaching cruising attitude and the seat belt sign lights went out, when Gabriela leaned over and quietly said: "Do you remember when we first met, Mitch, and I said you looked familiar to me?"

"Yes, I do. You said it would soon come back to you what the circumstances were, and apparently, I believe it just did. Obviously, you felt the line worked well the first time, so now you want to use it again, right?"

"See, already you are able to read my mind. However, it was not a line I was using with you. I really did recall seeing a picture of you. I believe it was taken in Atlanta sometime last year, and you were getting out of a car in a hotel parking lot. I'm not usually mistaken on these things."

"Now that is of real interest to me. Please go on."

"I was at JSOG, in Fort Bragg, and attending a SF briefing on hostile surveillance and the handling of physical encounters with a target person of interest. The main point made during the brief was how not to engage a suspect person who turned out to be too well prepared for the encounter."

"OK. It sounds like one of your teams had me under surveillance, due to my coming to the attention of the local authorities in Atlanta. Perhaps it was something like my physical appearance or apparent actions on the street. Is that about right?"

"That's a possibility. However, I would say it probably was due to your patterns of travel and movements in cities that came to the attention of our intelligence officers. Subsequently, your name and basic bio information was entered into one of our computer data bases and, upon you surfacing in Atlanta, our SF representative from JSOG detailed to the Atlanta Police Department volunteered to have our team personally check you out to determine what you were doing there."

"Now isn't that nice. There I am, conducting legitimate executive recruitment interviews, minding my own business and, because of my pattern of behavior I am profiled as someone possibly up to no good. We like to think these kinds of things are not supposed to happen in the U.S. What a joke. Even so, I have learned to try and understand and cope with it."

"Look at me, Mitch. Don't you think I have been subjected to undue attention?"

"Of course you have. However, it is not for the same reason as in my case. You are a very beautiful woman who would easily attract attention."

"Why thank you, Mitch. You don't look so bad either."

"I am going to take that as a nice compliment too. What else did you learn at the briefing?"

"The briefer said it was a three-person team, with one member selected to enter your hotel room to see what could be learned about who you were, and the purpose for being there. The other two members were providing surveillance from outside the hotel's main entrance."

"Obviously, those two guys either failed to see me return and warn their guy inside, or he went into my room all stripped down of any identification or even a cell phone, and was prepared to handle me on his own."

The briefer never said anything about that part of the op. However, when he referred to the physical condition of the SF member whom you found in your room, and he was wheeled out of the hotel on a stretcher and placed inside an ambulance, all kinds of laughing busted out in the briefing room. Including from me, I might add."

"Well, I knew that something different was behind the attack on me that night in the room. It did not seem like a burglary gone wrong."

"You should know that the guy did mend well, but for awhile he was the butt of jokes among a number of his colleagues, especially all the while he was walking around on crutches from a broken leg. You did a really thorough job on him, with the leg and busted ribs; It dampened his overly cocky attitude. He settled down though, became somewhat quieter, and I believe he moved on and is now serving on one of our SMU teams."

"He appeared to be in good physical shape, but he did have a mouthful of bad words for me when he wasn't squealing like a baby pig taken away from its mother."

"I won't let that comment get back to my SMU colleagues. He would never live it down."

"I hit him hard and quick, just as I knew I had to, in order to survive the encounter. I had no idea what I was walking into, but knew swiftness was the key for me. Should you see him again in the future, wish him well. Just tell him to practice more on how to operate successfully in the dark. It certainly is my kind of environment, and he could learn to make it his as well."

"Mitch, can I buy you a drink?"

"Why Gabriela, you certainly may. I thoroughly enjoy Bloody Marys while flying."

During what remained of the 14-hour flight, from Rome to Seattle, the two of them discussed at length how Mitch conducted recruiting interviews, watched an in-flight movie and read from some books they brought with them. Gabriela's readings were from Mitch's M&T training manuals, and dealt with what the work of a personnel recruiter is all about.

Gene met them upon arrival at Seattle's Sea-Tac Airport, and they drove into town for a meeting at an Agency safe house with the Seattle Chief of Base. The purpose was to view overhead satellite imagery of the central portions of Beijing encompassing the Beijing Railway Station and hotels in the immediate area. Gene and Mitch could quickly tell from reading the accompanying headquarters analysts' comments that a number of areas in the imagery offered excellent leads for them to follow up on during the pre-hit survey. They were also, based on the materials viewed, able to divide up their tasking areas since, once on the ground there, Gene would be staying in a hotel separate from Mitch and Gabriela, and would be maintaining limited contact only via their encrypted cell phones.

Gene had the benefit of already meeting Gabriela for a two-hour introduction before she flew to Rome to meet Mitch. Now, after driving the two of them back to Sea-Tac Airport, Gabriela went inside the main terminal building ahead of Mitch in order to use the restroom. Gene would not be on their flight and, instead would depart for Beijing the following day. While unloading Mitch's luggage, they had a few minutes alone to exchange impressions about her.

"Mitch, since we played golf in Rome, and I returned stateside, I was able to read a fairly extensive summary from her file. It even included comments by SecDef Panetta, from when he appointed her to one of JSOG's SMU teams for her last assignment."

"I'm interested in hearing what you learned from it. So far, I've come away very high on her. She is bright, quick on her feet and easy to bring up to speed on what my NOC cover job is all about."

"From her record, she performs exceptionally well both as a singleton in the field and as a team player. She is looked upon as imaginative, and a critical thinker who projects a strong no-nonsense attitude toward her work. Panetta commented that he believes she represents the best DOD has to offer for special operations, including executive action ops. During an SF op in Columbia, while providing automatic weapons support to a Columbian Army SF team, they were ambushed and one of her team members was seriously wounded. The medical attention she provided saved the guy's life and afterwards, following their successful extraction, her CO wrote up an assessment for her file that said he had a hard time keeping her from wanting to get back into the same area in order to exact revenge on the guerrillas that had ambushed them. He added that the cool and relentless intensity she brings to her work makes him think she belongs in the category of the original vengeful femme fatale."

"What about the attack on her in Brazil and any lingering physical or mental side effects?"

"Nothing at all from what I have been able to learn. Her file is distinctly blank on whatever happened there and what the op involved. That also applies when I tried to probe some of my own SF friends. The word is apparently out in JSOG that SMU ops are totally off limits for discussing at any time."

"The same for our restricted access ops as well. That is exactly the way it should be."

"The next-to-last entry in her file is from a physician at Fort Bragg, following her return from Brazil. He evaluated her as fully recovered and fit to return to duty. The final entry just notes that she is reassigned to SMU and detailed to an Inter-Agency joint operation with us."

"For what it's worth, Gene, keep in the back of your mind what we heard on the broadcast news after I finished up on Ahmadinejad in Paris."

"Yes, such a coincidence, what happened to Chavez in Venezuela."

"As I recall, while catching up on all of the news several days later, during the train trip from Paris to Lyon, the Venezuelan authorities were looking for a team that, according to video camera coverage from a hotel in Caracas, included at least one male and one female member. Apparently though, the video coverage did not provide sufficient facial views to be of much use."

"Yeah, I saw that too. I believe it also included mention of finding the rifle, a Dragunov, as well as some Russian language materials, whatever that meant.

"That's interesting, to say the least. If it was an American team making the hit, use of that particular sniper rifle makes for an unusual twist to the story."

"I agree. Needless to say, I look forward to seeing how Gabriela performs for us in Beijing. I'm hoping that both of us are going to be pleasantly surprised."

CHAPTER 30

The City Wall Relics Park is located on the southern edge of the Beijing Railway Station, in the center of the city. Arriving the day after Mitch and Gabriela, Gene checked into the Hademen Hotel, just along the southwest edge of the park. His first task for the pre-hit survey would be to reconnoiter the park complex, from his hotel to the opposite southeast side along the edge of the train station, which runs west to east directly parallel to the park. From this eastern end of the park, he expected to have unobstructed views of the railroad tracks that enter and exit the station, including direct line of sight possibilities across the tracks toward the Beijing Marriott Hotel City Wall, where Mitch and Gabriela had already checked in the night before.

Posing as a photojournalist who specialized in architectural and commercial photography, Gene carried a Hasselblad modified FlexBody camera and a professional tripod. Leaving his hotel the following morning, he started out on the park reconnoiter. Fortunately, he could talk his way past friendly enough guards into several areas of the park walls and adjacent guard towers that had restricted entrance signs but overlooked the east side of the train station tracks. There, while capturing photos of the ancient wall and towers, he also could view the main Marriott Hotel building nearby and across from the 15 sets of railway tracks leading into the station. He noted the hotel's two outlying maintenance and housekeeping support buildings located between the hotel and the railway tracks.

The grounds of the park consist of walls and towers that were first built almost 600 years ago. They are situated in surroundings of classic simplicity, with more than 70,000 square meters of lawns, flowers, arbors, paths, bridges, pavilions, murals and sculptures. As a fully developed scenic spot of an ancient architectural relic, it represents an important symbol of Beijing. After spending full three hours there, including being able to capture some shots with a high noon sun on an unusually clear day for Beijing, Gene exited the park and made his way the short distance to the main entrance of the train station.

Mitch and Gabriela, after arriving at the Marriott at two in the morning following their direct flight from Seattle, slept in and did not get to work on the survey until early afternoon. Dividing up their tasks for the hotel itself, they both took separate walks around the perimeter and immediate area, followed by Mitch going over near the train station to get a feel for the distances involved between the hotel buildings and the tracks along the east side of the station. All the tracks entering the station come from this side, and dead end inside. Therefore, all departing trains must exit from the same east side, including trains arriving from Pyongyang, North Korea's capital.

While Mitch was becoming familiar with the environs outside, Gabriela returned inside and approached the hotel's events and banquet staff to inquire about holding business meetings and receptions for potential new clients for M&T during their next stay at the hotel in the near future. Dressed in business attire and appearing very much the professional businessperson, she carried with her a clipboard upon which were attached several M&T letterhead forms that she could use for taking notes and recording details from the meetings. After spending over an hour in discussions with members of the staff, she asked for a walk-around tour of the hotel's facilities. When they'd viewed the overhead imagery, the headquarters analysts' comments stated they believed that underground passageways connected the hotel and the two small buildings on the west side, nearer to the train station.

While being shown the hotel's conference and reception room, Gabriela asked to see from where in the hotel the logistical and housekeeping support facilities are based. With that, she was given a brief tour, below the ground level, on two of the hotel's lower floors that contain housekeeping support and maintenance areas, including some of the kitchen and food service areas. Not having a legitimate reason to ask to see the hotel's outer buildings next door, she was, however, able to notice two doors along the west wall of the hotel that she believed went in the direction of these two buildings of interest.

During the process of moving around on the lower floors with the two assistant managers from the events and banquet staff, Gabriela made it a point to be sure to make direct eye contact with as many hotel employees going about their work there as she could, including while walking through the hotel's laundry department. She anticipated being able to return to this area alone during the late hours. Therefore, it would help to be seen in the company of the manager and, therefore, accepted as working on the hotel staff.

Meanwhile, Gene had gone inside the train station. While there he spent a good hour and a half casing the entire physical layout, including the facilities and amenities available to passengers and visitors and the tracking system for train arrivals and departures, including the track assignments for trains, depending upon where they were arriving from. Like most modern stations around the world, passengers and visitors are free to roam around, including being able to venture out on platforms alongside the tracks.

With Gene still carrying his camera bag and tripod from the park photo shoot, he fit right in, looking like a passenger soon to depart for somewhere. Upon locating the track used for trains that make the trip to Pyongyang, he walked out on the platform eastward, past the overhead of the station roof. Noting from the large electronic schedule board that at 5:30 pm, the K27 Beijing to Pyongyang train was due to depart, he walked alongside it as it was preparing to leave the station within the hour. Obviously, the train was not the heavily armored version that Kim traveled in, but its size and location on the dedicated track were all the information Gene needed.

He learned two very valuable pieces of information while walking out on the platform alongside the K27 train. Namely, the platform itself was located on the north side of the tracks. This meant that when Kim's train slowly pulled out of the station, the side of the train that he traditionally waved from through an open window would be facing in the direction of the grounds and buildings of the Marriott Hotel. The equally important second piece of information learned was that while standing on the platform, just about where the overhead rooftop ended, Gene had a clear line of sight to the two smaller buildings next to the hotel.

Looking in the direction of the hotel from where he was standing on the platform, he was unable to determine whether the windows in the two buildings opened outwards from the inside. That piece of information would have to be learned by Gabriela, during one of her forays around the inside of the two buildings. Should it turn out that she could develop access in order to case inside the buildings, and determine the type of windows present, Gene would be prepared to return to the railway station's platform and obtain a line of sight reading with a rangefinder to calculate the distance from the windows to the platform.

After his own walk in the area surrounding the hotel, Mitch returned to his room inside and placed calls to the five institutions of higher learning that he previously communicated with prior to leaving Rome. They were the Beijing Normal University, Tshinghua University, Beihang University, Beijing Institute of Technology, and the University of Science and Technology in Beijing. Based upon his research and two trips to Beijing in the past, where he established good relations with a number of professors at the schools, he believed that their graduates were the best trained and qualified engineers and scientists available. The only other area in China with similar well-trained job candidates from their schools was from Shanghai, and going there was not a part of this particular trip. By the time he finished calls to the job placement offices, as well as some of the professors at the five schools, he had scheduled eight appointments over the next three days.

By the time evening approached, and with all reconnoiters and the casings finished, Gene, Mitch and Gabriela were all satisfied with the results. Gene subsequently left his hotel alone and being in the city for the first time in his life, went to enjoy a duck dinner at the Beijing Quanjude Roast Duck Restaurant. By prior arrangement with Mitch, the two of them would talk on their cell phones in order to compare notes from their activities of the day, while they were walking around the neighborhoods prior to dining. Mitch's plan for dinner called for taking Gabriela, who, likewise, was a first t ggime visitor to Beijing, to Sanlitun Village South, near the outskirts of the city, where they could explore the village shops there plus experience a hot pot dinner at Hai Di Lao, a restaurant favorite of Mitch's. The stroll in the village would also be a good time for a quick phone chat with Gene.

Once that call was over, and Mitch and Gabriela continued on their walk around the village, he related to her the gist of the conversation with Gene. She particularly noted what Gene told Mitch about the line of sight description from the station platform to the hotel's two outer buildings.

"Those two building," she said, "have the most potential for getting you into a position from which you will be able to make your shot."

"That's what Gene thought as well," Mitch replied. "He thought anywhere from the fourth to seventh floors looked the best to shoot from. However, Gene was not able to tell which way the windows opened."

"When I walked around the buildings exploring the grounds and the building exteriors, I wasn't able to tell either," Gabriela told Mitch. "However, I could locate where the passageways would be underground in relation to where I'd been standing near the two doors on the lower floors inside the hotel. Both doors, about 12 feet apart from one another and with key locks, lead from the hotel to the buildings."

"What are your thoughts on accessing them?" Mitch asked.

"I packed my favorite lock picking kit. I should not have any problems at all opening these two locks."

"I like what I'm hearing. Are you thinking about making a late night visit downstairs and getting through the passageways to the buildings?"

"Yes, I will at least try for one of them to see what the building is like inside and find out how I can get upstairs to check out the windows and views toward the train station platform."

"What about your cover for action?"

"With clipboard in hand, a look of authority and dressed in business attire, I hope to be accepted by anyone I encounter as one of the numerous American employees of the hotel. Should I be challenged, I will have to revert to my working for M&T and checking out the hotel's facilities, as weak a story as it will be."

"It's still worth the risk. Are you game for trying it tonight?"

"I sure am. Wish me luck?"

"I don't believe you need any. You've got plenty of skill and panache on your side already."

CHAPTER 31

When Islamabad Station case officer Rahim Zahedi received the coded signal on his cell phone he knew it was his recently recruited agent penetration of al-Qaeda, Ibrahim Lodi. As previously agreed upon between them, the signal would serve to trigger a meeting at a specific time and location. Sitting in his office inside the embassy, Rahim would now be able to cable headquarters to inform them and advise of the plan to meet with Ibrahim within 24 hours in a discreet out-of-the-way cafe on the outskirts of Islamabad. Hopefully, Ibrahim would have new information about Dr. Ahmad's physical location in the city, along with plans and intentions for the next terrorist attack.

As a case officer representing the Agency's CTC counter terrorism center, Rahim was in his third year at the station. In that time, he set about compiling an envious record of successes against a number of terrorist groups operating in Pakistan and across the border in Afghanistan. He not only was recruiting agents who were penetrations of these groups, but was also obtaining from them disseminable intelligence information of highly significantly value to the entire intelligence community.

Rahim was in the U.S. to Pakistani parents who immigrated to Florida in the 1960s. They instilled in the three children they subsequently had there the traditions, culture and language of their native country. While attending college at Florida State, Rahim majored in chemistry and, at one point, gave serious thought to becoming a medical doctor. However, growing interest in events taking place in the Middle East captivated him to the degree that he applied to work for the Agency.

Normally, because of his parents' origins in Pakistan, the Agency would not allow him to serve there. However, since neither parent had relatives still alive inside the country, the rule did not apply in Rahim's case. As a result, Islamabad Station was pleased with his assignment and fortunate to have the benefit of a highly successful case officer among their ranks. At 30 years old, and a bachelor, he had no interest in local Pakistani woman due to the practice of arranged marriages and all that entails, including the traditional period of courtship. An intention to marry a non-U.S. person would also present complications for his Agency career, unless the woman was successful in passing a detailed security screening and vetting process, as well as a polygraph examination.

Leaving his apartment the following day to hold the meeting with Ibrahim, Rahim avoided going to the station in the embassy. Instead, he set out on a complicated and lengthy three-hour surveillance detection run designed to determine if he was under surveillance. Needing to get in the black, or free of any surveillance, he pre-arranged to have five other station officers counter-surveil him along certain portions of his SDR. This would allow them to assist in identifying threats and if necessary, prevent anyone from continuing their effort against him.

Nearing the agreed upon meeting time, 12:15 p.m., and satisfied he was in the black, Rahim made his way to the Pompei Station Café. Situated in the rear of the Shapes health club compound, the rustic café afforded good privacy due to the numerous small meeting room areas inside, with well spaced tables. As an added precaution for the meeting, two members of the counter surveillance team of station officers were already in position inside, prior to his arrival, in order to provide additional coverage of him in the event anyone who knew of the meeting was there ahead of him. They also would be able to assist in the event Ibrahim found himself in any kind of hostile situation.

All station officers serving in Pakistan are personally armed with their choice of handguns. Rahim is no exception and carried in a hip holster a Browning Hi-Power 9 mm semi-automatic. Casually dressed in tan Dockers, a light blue sports shirt and a beige hunting vest, he was shown to a table in one of the small rooms of the cafe. Having ordered a glass of tonic water over ice, he took his first sip as Ibrahim entered the room and was shown to a chair at the table across from him. It was precisely 12:15 as they warmly greeted each other in their native Urdu and began their conversation.

"Did you have any problems getting here today?"

"No sir. None at all."

"What about your family and new baby? How are they doing?"

"They are just fine. Abdel is growing fast, and my wife only has to feed him once now during the night."

"That is good news. I have two small gifts here, one for your wife, and one for Abdel."

"You are much too kind, my friend. Thank you."

"Tell me the latest news. I was very glad when you signaled for this meeting."

"Since we last met I was contacted twice by Dr. Ahmad. Both were cell phone calls. The first one was to give me an address and name of a person to meet there. The second call, three hours later, was to tell me when to go to the address and see that person."

"As I'm sure you know, that is his way of injecting some security precautions into his calls to you."

"Sure. Ever since meeting him for the first time two months ago, I knew he was an extremely cautious person. Given his wanted status outside the country for his jihad attacks, it is perfectly understandable. Nevertheless, within our family and tribal groups throughout the border area, he is truly a hero for his successes."

"I can understand that. However, just think of all the Pakistanis like you and myself, who fervently believe he is an absolute traitor to our Islamic faith. He has turned his back on what our beliefs are all about."

"I have written down for you the name of the person and the address he sent me to. It is a sparsely furnished office, and it belongs to Dr. Kamram Rabbani. Two blocks away though, is a laboratory and medical supply house that Dr. Rabbani owns and operates. When I went to meet with him, he told me a little about himself and his relationship to Dr. Ahmad."

"This is very good information. I thank you very much."

"Dr. Rabbani is a pleasant man and is about the same age as Dr. Ahmad. He said they went to medical school together in Lahore, at King Edward Medical University. He dresses well and appears to run a very successful medical supply business."

"Did he say anything about his own meetings with Dr. Ahmad?"

"Only that their meetings are not very frequent. However, he expects they will pick up soon since Dr. Ahmad has been calling him more. He anticipates that he will be asked, once again, to assist in the planning for the next jihad."

"It sounds like Dr. Rabbani opened up somewhat in talking this way with you, a stranger meeting him for the first time."

"Yes, I agree completely. He even related to assisting Dr. Ahmad in preparing for the anthrax bomb attack that took place in the U.S. at Dulles Airport."

"What did he say about his involvement?"

"He said he was responsible for getting a custom-made flattened-out glass bottle fabricated to hold the anthrax spores. Just before Dr. Ahmad departed for the U.S., he met with Dr. Rabbani, who gave him the anthrax sealed inside the bottle. He added that he even watched as Dr. Ahmad placed the bottle inside the bottom of a leather carrying valise that served as a concealment device."

"Do you know if Dr. Rabbani provided the spores as well?"

"No, he didn't say. However, I know that answer myself. The spores came from a batch originally cultured by Dr. Sa'eed Jassim al-Naseri, while he was working under Saddam Hussein in Baghdad."

"I know his name well. Ibrahim, how do you know all of this?"

"I know it because I was introduced to Dr. al-Naseri about three months ago in Karachi. He is the senior microbiologist responsible for the labs that al-Qaeda has set up there since moving from the border area as a consequence of the drone attacks and U.S. military forces getting closer in their forays across the border from Afghanistan."

"Ibrahim, this is excellent information. We will be exploring what is going on in Karachi shortly. In the meantime, I want us to focus more on trying to identify where Dr. Ahmad is located here in Islamabad. In addition, you need to keep me informed, as much as possible ahead of time, when you know Dr. Ahmad will be at a particular place and time."

"This is my top priority for you. I would not expect though, that I will know when he is going to see Dr. Rabbani before I know where he actually lives."

"That is because he is probably not yet fully trusting of you. It will come in more time. You watch and see."

"For now, it is just running errands, buying things, knowing where Dr. Rabbani has the office, etc."

"What kinds of errands, for example?"

"He had me buy him a shirt, for example. He described the style, color and size, and then directed me to a particular store to buy it. He apparently seldom goes out of the house where he is living, due to concerns for his security.

"What about his need for foodstuffs?"

"No, no food at all. Apparently, he has a cook or housekeeper who takes care of those things for him."

Knowing that Ibrahim had provided valuable information, Rahim thanked him, and they finished their lunch together. Next, they pre-arranged plans for another meeting, which would again be triggered by a cell phone call, and take place at an agreed upon out-of-the-way location.

After parting, Rahim left the restaurant and started a detailed SDR before making his way back to the embassy. He knew that CTC at headquarters would be pleased with the information Ibrahim provided and this would move the operation to apprehend Dr. Ahmad one step closer. He also knew it would probably result in the death of the doctor, and he could well be called upon to assist in some way. He looked forward to taking part in whatever was asked of him.

CHAPTER 32

Following Mitch's three days of meetings with professors and job placement officials from the five universities, all of his goals were set for a near future placement seminar to be held at the Marriott. Once he was back in to Rome to await word from headquarters that the dates for Kim's next trip to Beijing were known, he would be able to re-contact the schools, as well as the hotel, and set in motion the dates for the job placement seminar. Since past trips to China by Kim never exceeded three or four days in duration away from Pyongyang, Mitch did not anticipate any difficulty in arranging the schedule for him and Gabriela to be in Beijing at the same time.

Late in the middle of the night following Mitch's first day of meetings at the universities, Gabriela was able to successfully access one of the locked doors in the hotel's basement, leading to one of the two buildings next door. Immediately after opening the door she checked for any kind of wiring or the presence of a sensor that could trigger a silent alarm in the hotel's security center. Nothing was found. Without encountering a single employee, or anyone else for that matter, she made her way down the 120-foot dimly lit passageway that connected to the building. At the end she encountered an unlocked door and went inside. From what she could initially see, the ground floor turned out to be a hotel supply and excess furniture storage facility. None of the doors she found in the darkened interior were locked, so she had unfettered access, wherever she wished to go. Using a small flashlight with a red filter that provided just the right amount of light for her purposes, she proceeded upwards in the building. Although it had an elevator, she chose to use the stairway to the upper floors in order to avoid any unnecessary noise.

Upon reaching the sixth floor, she headed in the direction of the side of the building overlooking the railway station. Entering a large room that was filled with mattresses, new pillows in wrappers, assorted pieces of hotel room furniture and a multitude of packed large cardboard boxes, she made her way over to the windows. She was relieved to see that each of them had latches that opened both to inward and outward positions. Opening the latch on the bottom half of one of the windows, inwards toward her, it effortlessly opened. She then opened the upper half outwards as well. Both halves functioned noiselessly and provided plenty of space in between from which Mitch would be able to make the hit.

Deciding she had accomplished all that was called for, she made her way back downstairs and into the passageway. Upon returning to her room, she looked at her watch. It showed 3:35 am. Not a bad 45 minutes at all, spent fulfilling the most important task assigned to her for the survey.

Later that morning, while having breakfast with Mitch in the hotel's City Wall Bistro, she filled him in on her activities a few hours earlier.

"From the time I approached the door leading into the passageway, it was an adrenalin rush. Fortunately, I am used to it and maintained firm control of myself throughout the time I was down there, as well as up inside the building."

"The best part is that you did not encounter anyone. One of my concerns, as I mentioned to you ahead of time, was to be on the lookout for local Chinese employees who might be allowed to sleep overnight in those two buildings, when not on duty in the hotel."

"What about the second building? Do you want me to do reconnoiter that one as well?"

"No. You're all done. You did an extremely good job and I don't want you to take the chance of encountering someone there by trying to access that one. Since the one you entered is only about another 30 yards further away from the station platform anyway, distance is not going to be an issue for me on this one."

"Do you have anything remaining that you want me to do?"

"Today is yours to do what you wish. Go have some fun. Beijing is such a historic city that is just loaded with good things to see. I have several remaining meetings with university officials, plus a couple of loose ends to take up with the hotel's facilities' staff. That will be it for me."

"What about Gene?"

"Later this morning, I will give him a call and let him know which of the two buildings you were inside, the floor you were on and the approximate windows location you selected. He will return to the railway station platform for some additional picture taking and while there, use his rangefinder to determine the distance to the building windows."

"Do you expect we will have much advance word on when Kim will next be coming here?"

"That is the most difficult issue facing us on this one. As Gene and I have been told by our Agency analysts, intelligence information has provided approximately three to four weeks advance notice for the past six trips Kim has made to Beijing in the last nine years."

"Let's hope that kind of reporting continues."

"With a major succession issue over leadership in North Korea causing a lot of concerns with the selection of his son to succeed him, much like when Kim took over from his father, it's a tense time there right now. It is believed that before Kim himself decides on when he will either step down, either voluntarily or forced by health reasons, he will visit Beijing again to get the blessing of the Chinese leadership. Our analysts are counting on it happening sooner due to Kim preferring to personally introduce his son to the Chinese. These are the kinds of predictable patterns that have held true in the past. Therefore, we are counting on them to occur one more time."

"He sure looks like hell when shown in the news."

"Judging by his well-known support for terrorists, let alone making weapons deals and providing support to Venezuela, Iran and Syria, it surprises me that we were not called upon before this to remove him from the scene."

"I know. That is the same view from my end, in JSOG."

"Tell me, Gabriela, how do you feel about working with Gene and me on this op so far?"

"That's a good question and a timely one as well. Your NOC cover, and the way you handle it, is highly impressive to me. Our system in DOD for making use of commercial cover is similar. However, it is not as well developed as yours are."

"How so?"

"We usually do not get that involved in actually doing any real work for the commercial companies that provide us with cover. Instead, while they do provide solid backstopping for us, they leave us alone and don't expect we will do any actual business for them."

"I can understand and relate to that very well. Many of our NOCs do indeed have business backgrounds and, as a result, are more integrated into the companies that provide cover."

"For DOD, on the other hand, our military backgrounds don't relate all that well to commercial business, in many cases."

"You have taken well to my M&T cover, particularly in working with me on this trip."

"That's the most fascinating part of being involved in this op. We will, while engaged in the op itself, at the same time actually accomplish work for M&T in the placement of Chinese job candidates with American and European."

"I bet you don't miss the slogging around in the boonies either, right?"

"I actually do miss it. However, this is certainly a nice interlude."

"From what I have been able to see of you dealing with the people here, plus the way you went about achieving the operational goals of accessing the building next door this morning, you are an accomplished ops officer. I am pleased to have you on the team."

"Why thank you very much, Mitch. I appreciate your comments. I take that to mean you want me to return here in Beijing with you and Gene, when you assist Kim in meeting his maker, correct?"

"I wouldn't have it otherwise. In the meantime, in this envelope is a little present I have for you to enjoy, either today or tomorrow before we leave for Rome. I hope it will be a pleasant experience for you."

Gabriela opened up the envelope and, with a wide grin of surprise, said: "Mitch, thank you very much—three-hour session in the hotel's royal spa for a body treatment befitting the Empress Dowager. You can bet for sure this will thoroughly be enjoyed. Best of all, it sure beats the hell out of the jungles in South America too."

CHAPTER 33

Mitch had one more brief phone conversation with Gene as he and Gabriela were waiting for their checked luggage after they arrived at Fiumicino Airport.

"After you guys departed," Gene said, "and I was in my final day, I revisited the railway station and went back out on the extended platform with my camera gear."

"Knowing you, I bet you've got enough shots for a picture book on the station itself."

"You better believe it. Combined with my first visit, it actually will make a good coffee table book of the entire station and city wall park. The time spent there also allowed me to determine an approximate distance from the train cars leaving the station to the windows in the hotel building. I stood out on the platform and took a quick sighting up to the building windows. From where the train cars emerge from underneath the overhead rooftop and become clearly visible to your position in one of the windows, it appears the distance will be no more than 620 yards."

"That should be just fine. It's actually closer than I expected. Thank you for going back there. I checked on the projected weather conditions for the next couple of months, and it looks like the intense springtime wind storms and yellow dust that passes over the city from the Gobi Desert to the west will be totally gone as well. I have been there in the past when the winds are at their height. The suspended dust clouds cast a yellow pall that hangs over the city, and actually obscures the sun during the daylight hours."

"That's good news. By the way, when I get back stateside do you want me to make arrangements for a shipment of your toys to Beijing Station?"

"Yes, by all means. Let's go with the same as used in Paris, and be sure and include both .338 Lapua Magnum hollow points as well as armor-piercing rounds."

"Will do. Is Gabriela still there with you?"

"Yes, she is. She just stepped over to the carousel to grab her bag."

"Don't hesitate to let her know how pleased I was with her contribution to the survey. For someone new working for the first time with the two of us, she stepped right in, held her own, and certainly did her part."

"I will tell her what you said. She shows excellent street skills and already talks up a good line about my own personnel recruiting business. Unless you feel otherwise, I will be cabling headquarters to let them know we want her permanently on the team."

"No question about it. Now tell me, what is the status of you possibly going to Islamabad for a visit with the nefarious doctor?"

"I expect to go on standby status within the next 24 hours, and am prepared to go there at any time."

"What about Gabriela? Do you want her to play in this one too?"

"Yes, without question. Traveling with her at my side is a good foil since it can allow for me to get in as close as necessary. I will be asking headquarters for approval for her to accompany me and take part as need be."

"That's a good decision, Mitch. From what I've seen of the cable traffic from Islamabad, the case officer running the agent penetration will probably not have much advance notice of an opportunity for confronting the doctor."

"That's my read too. It will mean a quick trip there, with little notice at all and, hopefully, an even quicker exit and return here to Rome. I'll keep you posted if I hear anything further at my end."

"Please do, old buddy."

Over the course of the following two weeks, Mitch moved Gabriela through what he termed the "advanced stages" of her post-graduate training as a professional executive recruiter. Working out of the office in Rome, she got on quite well with Mr. G, even conducting mock interviews with him serving as a engineer under consideration for employment. Mitch also took her on two trips, one to Geneva to interview officials from an electronics firm looking for new talent, and the other to Hamburg to interview several prospective job candidates.

His primary goal was to bring Gabriela up to speed in order to perform credibly when they returned to Beijing and ostensibly interviewed Chinese candidates during the conduct of the op against Kim. Mitch could not have been more pleased with the way she was rapidly growing to conduct herself as a seasoned professional recruiter.

When not working full time in each other's company on M&T business during the week, on weekends Mitch proudly showed Gabriela around Rome and the outlying areas. He tried to maintain as much of a professional relationship as possible, but it was starting to become distracting for him when he caught himself staring at her, whether it be when she was experiencing difficulty in talking with someone in Italian or walking behind her beautiful, well-built body. While nothing of a romantic nature had entered into their relationship to date, something more than just friendship was definitely in the making.

During one of those evenings when they were dining at a restaurant in the heart of the old Jewish Quarter of Rome, Gabriela began revealing, after several glasses of good Chianti, details of her childhood while growing up in Puerto Rico. Mitch could discern a soft, yet understanding realization on her part of love for her parents and relatives there. In what were becoming more frequent conversations on family backgrounds and interests, they played a game with each other by lapsing into Arabic when searching for phrases that described relationships between people. He respected her language skills It was becoming easy for him to see a lot of respect on his part for her language skills and enjoyed the ease with which they could relate to each other. To him, it was as if he was looking after a little Arab sister, though he certainly did not want her to know he was thinking of her in those terms.

Midway through the third week, Mitch received a cable from headquarters saying that per his previous referenced request, two handguns had been pouched to Islamabad Station for use by him and Gabriela following their yet unknown arrival. Both with suppressor packages, a Walther P22 was being held for Mitch and a Sig Sauer 9mm P226 for Gabriela. The cable also said approval was granted, including from the JSOG command, for Gabriela to participate along with Mitch in the possible op against Dr. Ahmad. With that, the ball was in Islamabad Station's court, and all that Mitch and Gabriela had to do was wait for when the best opportune time became available and the station said to come immediately.

*   *   *

Ibrahim could feel the excitement in his body as he approached one of the terraced garden walkways in the nearly deserted Rawal Lake View Park overlooking Islamabad and Rawalpindi. Located in an isolated section of the Margalla Hills National Park, he had previously met with Rahim along the same path about a year earlier. Sitting on one of the many benches in the area, or conversing as they walked together, it was a good meeting location that provided the privacy and security they needed.

"Thank you my brother, for coming out to meet with me again on short notice," Ibrahim said. "While I don't yet have the most important information on Dr. Ahmad that you asked for, I did learn from my cousin in Karachi a few things that I think are almost as good."

"All of our meetings are important since you never let me down each time we are together," Rahim replied. "What is the news you bring this time?"

"I visited with my cousin at his tiny home there, and he updated me on the state of the three labs set up for growing what he called the worst kinds of weapons of mass destruction imaginable."

"Do you mean what you already reported from your previous trip to Karachi?"

"Yes, it is still the anthrax spores, the Ebola virus and the botulinum toxin. The only difference now is that the complete leadership structure of al Qaeda, including Dr. al-Zawahiri, have relocated to Karachi as well. Along with his two of his senior aides and security personnel, he lives in a well-furnished air-conditioned villa inside well-constructed and guarded walled compound."

"Did you learn this information from your cousin there?"

"Yes, it came from him.

"What about their specific locations in Karachi?"

"The few remaining senior members of al-Qaeda are living in separate quarters from each other and separate from the three labs as well. I do not know their specific locations. Please understand that I have to be very careful when talking with my cousin. I trust him completely, but cannot ask for too many details. He was an orphan and grew up with my family. We are more like brothers than cousins."

"I completely understand and encourage you to exercise caution as well. At our next meeting, I will work with you on ways to ask questions that can obscure what you are really interested in finding out. It will help you out when talking with anyone, for that matter."

"That will be good. Thank you. From the way my cousin describes how he goes about serving al-Qaeda, it is much the same as my relationship here in Islamabad with Dr. Ahmad."

"Do you mean that you and your cousin are being held at arm's length, and not fully accepted or trusted yet?"

"Yes, that is basically right. Actually, we may never be fully accepted. This is due to al-Qaeda's practice of 'layers' or 'rings', where those of us serving are only allowed to learn details up to a certain level of importance."

"I understand. With the U.S., that is what we call being compartmented or restricted to only having access to a certain level."

"I know of the high level of interest you have in learning not only the location of Dr. Ahmad, but al-Qaeda as well. Please be assured that my goals are to learn this information for you as soon as possible. I want to see the al-Qaeda way of waging jihad, in violation of our sacred tenets of Islam, to be totally destroyed."

"Ibrahim, we both know so well that the true meanings of our faith are inviolate. Our faithful brothers the world over are embarrassed by their disregard of these teachings."

"Rahim, my brother, you are so right. I watched the way al-Qaeda treated my father, exploiting him only for their own ends. He was a skilled worker with metals, a truly gifted engraver. Even so, when he took sick and could no longer do their bidding, they discarded him. That is what convinced me to turn against all that they stand for and practice."

"You are on the right path and we will prevail in the end."

"I decided that at some point, after bearing witness to what they did, I had to take a stand. I am not betraying my family nor am I betraying my faith. Instead, I am getting even for the wrong they have done to my family and, as I now believe, our faithful followers of the faith everywhere."

"Please keep me advised when you learn new information."

"Whether the news comes from my cousin, or from what I learn here, you will know it soon, too."

"May Peace be with you, my brother."

"And may Peace be with you as well."

CHAPTER 34

When NSA communications intercept analysts had earlier begun reporting that the chain of events taking place in North Korea were clearly indicating that a succession struggle to replace the ailing Kim Jong-Il was underway, it coincided with similar reporting from the South Korean intelligence services. Unlike NSA intercepts though, South Korean information was based on primarily on humint reporting from their agent sources on the ground inside the hermit kingdom to the north. What was fascinating for both the U.S. and South Korean analysts was their recollection that this was the same kind of chain of events reporting experienced when Kim's father, Kim Il-Sung, the founder of North Korea, was ailing and subsequently succeeded by Kim.

This latest information being received now, though, was showing that various family members of Kim, along with senior military officers and members of the Worker's Party, were in the process of laying the groundwork for planning to leave the country should it become necessary. Funds were being secreted out of the country for safekeeping in banks in Europe as well as the Caribbean. This money trail could be seen, as well as the exit routes being planned, regardless whether it would be on short notice or for unknown future departure dates. With over six decades of rule by the same family, dating back to the late 1940s, the type of harsh rule personified by Kim Il-Sung was the kind still recognized and accepted by the populace. The populace felt an authoritative leader was necessary for their country, but he had to be stable and uniformly consistent, rather than the current brutal and mercurial rule personified by Kim Jong-Il.

The big unknown factor, however, would be the North Korean military's reaction should Kim proceed to hand over power to one of his sons, or any family member for that matter, all of whom were lacking in any kind of leadership, let alone military, experience. With the general population barely surviving at a near starvation level, it was the Worker's Party and the military that received the benefits of additional food rationing, which served to keep them well-fed and in line. Whether that would now continue to be the case with prospects of a young untested son of Kim's taking over, and the delicate balancing act of maintaining support from the two mainstays of power found in the military and the party, would remain to be seen.

Some of the North's younger generals in the military were known to enjoy solid relationships with their equal rising star colleagues in China's military, including several that served on the Central Military Commission. Recent intercept traffic between the generals indicated a stepping-up of establishing escape plans out of the North, as well as offshore banking accounts be opened in Europe with help from inside China. Without the benefit of having more definitive information on events unfolding in Pyongyang, the analysts were left with only broad speculation on where these signals would lead.

The one regularly appearing sign, however, continued to be Kim's trips to Beijing and, once again, it looked like another trip, this time possibly to introduce the heir to the leadership in Beijing, was about to take place.

Fortunately, Mitch was regularly receiving status reports by cable now from headquarters on the interpretation of events taking place in North Korea, as speculative as it usually turned out to be. He also maintained infrequent secure cell phone contact with Gene, making sure all loose ends were coming together for the op in Beijing once word was received that Kim would soon be on the move. Mitch even did a little speculating on his own on what the possibilities were that, should Kim take the young heir along with on the trip, a hit on both might be in the offing.

Having Gabriela in the Rome office every day, as nice as it was in Mitch's mind, was turning out to be an addition to the workload that had to be balanced off with an increase in M&T's executive search business conducted out of the office there. As a result, both were starting to travel separately around different parts of Europe and the Middle East, establishing new client relationships as well as interviewing job candidates to fulfill positions at the clients' manufacturing facilities. Mr. G, who had come to accept Gabriela's, found her a nicely furnished apartment within two blocks of the office. In the eyes of both the Agency and DOD, the M&T office in Rome had come to represent the first one-of-a-kind joint NOC endeavor between the two agencies.

One evening following their work at the office, while finishing a pleasant dinner at a nearby family-run trattoria, Mitch and Gabriela talked about the decision-making process involved in bringing the U.S. President to the realization that diplomacy has failed, such that he decides that ordering a hit on a sitting head of state is a choice, rightly or wrongly, available to him.

They held a similar conversation before starting out on the trip to Beijing for the pre-hit survey. However, this time Mitch had Gabriela read a cable containing an intelligence community disseminated intelligence report had received earlier in the day, which served to reaffirm in their minds the necessity of the decision the president had made that resulted in bringing the two of them together to work operationally.

"You know, I read it like the opening of a spy novel, where loud bells are set off ringing their ominous sounds of dread," she said.

"Yeah, I thought the same thing. I recall reading earlier, at least six months ago, a cable citing Iranian technicians being sent to North Korea for training in nuclear missile technology."

"I remember seeing something to that effect, as well. This new information though, in today's report, describes a dirty bomb project underway in North Korea, with a goal of selling it to al-Qaeda. It casts an entirely different light on propagating weapons of mass destruction."

"To me this means the president has all the justifications he needs to avoid continuing down the path of the U.S. always being on the defensive. We both know wars are not won this way. By taking the initiative, we can eliminate the problem. It may not be once and for all, but it will certainly serve notice."

"I don't recall reading that North Korea has a bio-weapons program as well."

"Well, as I understand it, they do, and it involves advanced aerosol technology. Did you ever hear of 'Cab-o-Sil' before reading about it in today's report?"

"No, I haven't. What is it? The report you showed me today didn't provide that much detail about it."

It is a synthetic form of silicon dioxide. Because it is an inert substance in an extremely fine particle state, it is used in foods such as ketchup, shampoos and cosmetics, where it serves as a thickening agent."

"What are its bio-weapons applications?"

"Well, the technology involved in producing it involves placing it inside aerosol cans. When it is combined with something like cultured anthrax spores under pressure inside the cans, it becomes a formidable bio-weapon. Another application would be to combine Cab-0-Sil with plague under pressure in the cans."

"As an employable weapons system then, I would think it could be used as a spray from aircraft, or even circulated inside auditoriums and arenas in the air conditioning and heating systems."

"You got it right, and those are two good examples. With the North Koreans being able to move advanced aerosol technology from their research labs to their manufacturing facilities, it changes the whole picture in how to best deal with the regime there."

"I don't even like to think about it. Just imagine all the places we go where we find ourselves in a closed environment and breathing in what could be deadly air."

"It's very scary, to say the least. Nevertheless you know, combating these kinds of things is what we signed on to do with our choice of occupation. I know this may sound overly trite, but whenever I'm faced with taking someone's life away, I am reminded of an oath I took a long time ago. I agreed to follow the orders given me by the President of the United States. Each time I find myself in a situation where I think about that oath, it enables me to move forward strongly and carry out those orders without any hesitation."

"I know it well. I feel very much the same way. I sum it up for myself by believing that no president, or no government, for that matter, exists to go out and solve their problems by assassination. However, when faced with circumstances requiring methods short of committing large numbers of troops in combat, for example, I am able to turn to the selective removal of tyrants and terrorists in hopes it will lead to more moderate policies at the heart of states that have gone astray from the accepted norms of civilized nations. That is where I like to believe we find ourselves today, in having to turn to the measures we have been ordered to undertake."

"Why Garbriela, you said that quite well."

"We started this conversation out with you talking about the Iranian technicians sent to North Korea for training. Are we seeing a pattern here as it applies to us?"

"I don't know. What do you mean?"

"Another tyrant and supporter of terrorist causes recently was taken out of action, along lines similar to what we are planning for Kim."

"OK. I presume you are referring to what happened recently in Paris, correct?"

"Sure, but since it's only two examples, I don't suppose we should call it a pattern yet, right?"

"Not unless you want to add what happened in Venezuela, right?'

"Mitch, you are right."

CHAPTER 35

When Ibrahim called Rahim for a non-scheduled meeting at one of their pre-arranged sites, it triggered what would be the next chapter in the life of Dr. Ahmad. In the meeting. Ibrahim told Rahim that the doctor asked him to be prepared to assist him in several errands the following week. Rahim immediately cabled Mitch, as well as headquarters, requesting that Mitch and Gabriela fly to Islamabad for the op against the doctor.

The following morning, the two of them departed from Rome for the 12-hour Qatar Airways flight, via Doha, the capital of the state of Qatar, located on the Persian Gulf. Upon their early morning arrival at Benazir Bhutto International Airport, on the outskirts of Islamabad, they entered the immigration arrivals hall, where an officer inquired about the purpose of their visit to Pakistan. Mitch responded that they would be doing a short survey of universities in the city as well as the neighboring city of Rawalpindi, inquiring about the availability of qualified engineers and technicians to work in Europe for various high technology firms. Admitted without any further questioning, they collected their luggage, cleared customs and took a taxi for the 45-minute ride to the Serena Hotel nearby the Margalla Hills section of the city.

As cities go, Islamabad is unusual in that it was built from scratch starting in 1961, becoming the capital of Pakistan in 1963. The resultant modernity is especially apparent when compared to its much older twin city next door, Rawalpindi, a scant nine miles away. The city is laid out along classical straight grid lines and right angles. As the seat of government and administration, Islamabad is a relatively quiet city of greenery divided into sections of government buildings, residences, shops and parks that are connected by broad new roads and modern commercial office buildings.

Before taking a few hours of rest in the hotel, Mitch held a secure cell phone call with Rahim, arranging for an early evening car pickup in a parking lot behind a large restaurant 15 minutes by taxi from the hotel. Never having laid eyes on Rahim before, Mitch gave him a physical description of himself and Gabriela over the phone. Subsequently, Rahim flashed the lights of his white, non-diplomatic-plated SUV at them as they walked toward him in the back of the car lot.

Once all three of them were inside the vehicle, and the introductions were made, Rahim started the drive to Daman-e-Koh, a scenic lookout point above the E-6 section of the city with great views of the expansive capital below. After parking the SUV in a vista viewing area, he gave them the handguns, along with extra clips of ammunition that had been pouched to the station by headquarters. Rahim then went on to suggest what he believed could be their game plan for the next several days.

"Dr. Ahmad has been in touch with Ibrahim and has sent him back to meet with Dr. Rabbani. As a result, Ibrahim has identified the locations of both Rabbani's laboratory and supply company, as well as the separate office he maintains nearby."

"Did your agent learn anything about Ahmad's location?"

"No. He remains very guarded with Ibrahim at all times. I don't believe it is because of any serious mistrust, but rather the wall of personal security he surrounds himself with in all of his dealings with other people."

"What did you learn about Rabbani's locations?"

"I like both. They are about four blocks apart, in what I would call a semi-industrial area of small buildings and shops. During daylight hours not a lot of people are out on the streets either."

"How about any vehicles in the area?"

"Just enough cars and small trucks on the streets to provide good cover for us to get relatively close to both locations."

"Sounds like we've got some good surveillance work ahead of us?"

"Yes, we do. Ibrahim expects to receive soon a call from Ahmad, whenever he wants to meet with him at either of Rabbani's two locations. He will then immediately alert me, providing the time they are to meet and possibly what Ahmad will be riding in."

"We can then get set up there and await Ahmad's arrival. Rahim, it looks to me like we could use at least two more people to assist us in the setup. What do you have available to you in the station?" Mitch asked.

"Besides myself, my branch in the station has two other Pakistani-Americans. They are briefed up, prepared and ready to assist us whenever I call upon them. With Rabbani's facilities physically located two blocks apart, along the same street, I can have each of my guys provide blocking cover support at opposite ends of the street from both locations. That will allow for the three of us, with me driving, to get the two of you up as close as possible to Ahmad when he arrives."

"I like it. You've got a good plan, Rahim. Both Gabriela and I would like to have a drive-by through the area though, as soon as possible, in order to get a better feel for what things look like there."

"Certainly, that was going to be my next suggestion. I would like to do that first thing tomorrow morning, since we have no idea just how fast this thing will start moving once the doctor calls Ibrahim."

"What about our escape routes out of the area once we have concluded our business with the doctor?"

"I've already scouted out at least three routes away from the area, depending upon the time of day, traffic conditions, any potential opposition we encounter, etc. I'm comfortable using the roads throughout that area and know my way around quite well. I will be showing you these routes as well in the morning."

"How about contingency planning for a last-resort situation?" Gabriela asked.

"If all goes according to plan, and we make it cleanly away from the immediate area, I will drive the two of you on a short SDR to satisfy ourselves we're in the black. I will then return you to the hotel. If we need some assistance, my two station colleagues in their cars will be able to assist. They will be near us at all times during the escape phase. However, in a worst-case scenario, if we are spotted and fail to complete the mission or get away cleanly after completion, I have the approvals to bring the two of you inside the embassy compound and into our station sanctuary."

"I have one more question, Rahim," Mitch asked. "What about your agent, Ibrahim, in the event he is right there with the doctor, and witnesses this whole thing coming down?"

"A fair question. If I were to let him go armed, I believe he would want to assist you in taking out the doctor. He has no respect for him and wishes that all of those who practice the doctor's perverse form of Islam be eliminated."

"We can live with that," Mitch replied.

"Hang on a minute," Gabriela said. "I would like to know what Ibrahim will be doing, should he witness what we are about to do."

"He will know to immediately leave the area. If, however, he is stopped and questioned, he will be the classic stone dummy. He will claim that in the confusion, he dropped to the ground and is not able to give any physical descriptions of us, or the direction we head in afterwards," Rahim replied.

"Good," she said.

Early the following morning, at 6:30, Rahim picked Mitch and Gabriela up in front of a small food store several blocks down the street from their hotel. Twenty minutes later, they arrived in the vicinity of the Golra Railway Station, in the west side of Islamabad, near where Dr. Rabbani's facilities were located. With few people out on the streets at that time of the morning, what followed was a systematic drive through most all of the streets in the area. After 15 minutes of crossing and criss-crossing the streets, Rahim drove them by the fronts and backs of both the facilities buildings.

Before departing from the area and returning closer into the city where Mitch and Gabriela could catch a taxi back to their hotel, they agreed on the two locations that could best serve as blocking positions for the two other station officers. From there, they would be able to park their cars on side streets but be in a position to observe the front entrances of the two buildings. Just as Rahim was going to point out the semi-concealed alley way where their SUV could be positioned, Gabriela spotted it and stole his thunder. They all agreed it would be the perfect spot for being able to observe Dr. Ahmad's vehicle as it approached either of the buildings.

Later that evening, Mitch and Gabriela returned to their rooms after enjoying a flavorful dinner of mutton tikka, chickpeas, potatoes and Kulcha naan bread, in a nearby local restaurant that Rahim had recommended. Mitch had no sooner undressed and got ready to take a shower, when his cell phone rang. It was Rahim—Ibrahim contacted him to say that he would be meeting Dr. Ahmad the next morning, at 9 am, at the front entrance of Dr. Rabbani's laboratory building. He said that Ahmad would be arriving in a black Mercedes driven by his security guard.

It was agreed that Rahim would pick up Mitch and Gabriela at 7:30 am and proceed to the alley way about 100 yards away from the laboratory's front entrance. Rahim said he would have his two colleagues in place at both ends of the street. Mitch called Gabriela's room to give her the news and arrange to meet downstairs for an early breakfast, before they met up with Rahim in front of the same food store as used the day before.

Mitch woke up early to a calm, clear, windless day of 64 degrees. With an expected full day of abundant sunshine, the late afternoon temperature was forecasted to be 94 degrees. Preoccupied with thoughts of his approach to Dr. Ahmad's Mercedes, and the physical moves he would subsequently be making, he was not very talkative with Gabriela. He didn't notice it, but Gabriela was not very talkative either. Like Mitch, her thoughts were also caught up in her approach to the drivers' side of the Mercedes, and her moves to render the security guard unable to respond to the plight of the doctor he was supposed to be protecting.

During the drive to the laboratory, Rahim, knew well what was going through the minds of Mitch and Gabriela. So he respected and practiced the same silence as they neared the location where they would finally confront the notorious terrorist responsible for the horrendous attacks in the U.K. and the U.S. Both attacks cost over ten thousand lives, and even though two years had passed, the death toll was still rising due to the lingering complications from cesium radiation and anthrax poisoning.

By the time Rahim's SUV was situated in the alleyway, with Mitch and Gabriela patiently waiting inside, suppressed handguns loaded and at the ready, the time was 8:50 am. From their location, they could not see the two vehicles occupied by the other two station officers at each end of the street. However, Rahim called them on his phone and confirmed they were in place. Glancing each way down the street, Rahim and Mitch, in the front seat, could count at least a dozen other broadly spaced vehicles for a distance totaling approximately 350 yards along the length of the street. All of them appeared to be unoccupied.

At two minutes past nine, with the sky just as clear and windless as when Mitch got up that morning, the black Mercedes came down the street. With the tinted glass in Rahim's SUV, the driver of the car or Dr. Ahmad himself would have had difficulty seeing anyone sitting inside. Once the Mercedes was past the alleyway and within about 75 yards of the entrance to the laboratory, where Ibrahim could be seen standing with his back up against the side of the building a few feet from the entrance door, Rahim slipped the gear shift lever from park to drive and slowly pulled out and turned in the direction of the Mercedes.

Rahim timed the slow rate of his speed perfectly. Once the driver of the Mercedes parked parallel to the front of the building and had opened up his door in order to walk around to the other side to open the back seat passenger door for the doctor, Rahim pulled up behind the back of the car to within six or seven feet of the rear bumper. The driver, after shutting his door, turned his back to the rear in order to walk around the front of his car. This gave Mitch and Gabriela the needed time to quietly slip open their doors of the SUV and walk up the rear opposite sides of the Mercedes.

By the time Mitch had pulled open the rear passenger door opposite from where Dr. Ahmad was sitting, Gabriela was walking past the doctor's side and ready to confront the driver as he turned around the front bumper on the passenger side. With guns drawn and in their firing positions, what looked like two perfectly choreographed moves in synchrony with each other unfolded quickly and deadly.

Although they had not talked about it ahead of time, each executed their own style of the classic doctrine of double tap shooting, but in virtual tandem with one another. With a firm grip on her Sig Sauer, Gabriela placed two shots that landed almost simultaneously, squarely in the same spot in the middle of the driver's chest. Absorbing the impacting trauma from both rounds forced his body backwards, and he slumped to the ground on his side alongside the right front wheel and bumper of the Mercedes. Not knowing if the driver was wearing body armor, Gabriela quickly stepped forward and precisely placed a third round from her weapon into his temple.

At the same time, Mitch flinging open the car door surprised Dr. Ahmad so much, he just twisted his body to his left with a frozen-like gaze straight at Mitch. He did not even notice Gabriela by his side of the car. With only soft puffs of sound, the two rounds from the Walther P22 hit the doctor squarely in the same spot in the center of his chest, as both rounds merged into one due to Mitch's single aiming point there. It was a perfect example for the making of a double tap.

Dr Ahmad had a look of startled awe. Mitch then leaned forward as if to climb inside the car. Instead, and with a deliberate and measured degree of concentration in order to resume shooting accurately, he placed the third shot in between the doctor's unbelievably wide-open eyes.

After the firing had stopped, all remained eerily still. No other person on the street could be seen, except for Ibrahim, as Gabriela watched him hastily walking away from the side of the laboratory building. She turned and, with her weapon still in a ready to fire position, scanned the surrounding area as she purposely strode over to the SUV. Holstering her weapon on her waist belt, she climbed into the front seat next to Rahim.

Before leaning back to bring his head and upper body out of the back of the car, Mitch took one final look at the evil doctor who was no more of this world. Both of his eyes remained open, while his mouth and lower jaw protruded openly in an ugly downward sag, as if seeking to suck in a last breathe of air. Just before straightening up and turning toward the SUV, Mitch heard a long, low groan being exhaled from the still body. Turning in the direction of the SUV, he continued to hold his weapon at the ready while glancing around to check if anyone could be seen observing what had taken place. He climbed into the back seat as Rahim, in a measured pace, began to drive out of the area towards the Saidpur Village in the foothills of the Margallas overlooking the city.

*   *   *

Having been caught totally by surprise when Mitch yanked open the door and looked straight at him, Dr. Abdul-Karim bin Ahmad never felt the two bullets as they impacted in his chest. Instead, all he could sense was a damp darkness closing in upon him, and he felt his anal sphincter muscles immediately give way as he began to soil all over himself in the back seat of the Mercedes. With all light fading from his eyes, he sensed an utter calm and sensation of beginning to float in the air, upwards and outside of his body. His last recollection was one of the heat rising up through his neck and into his head. He could feel his tongue expanding and growing fat inside his mouth. At that last moment of his life he felt terrified as a flood of pain spread throughout his body. If any of his victims from the two attacks against the innocent people killed at Sellafield and Dulles Airport could see him now, sprawled in the back of the car, they could conjure up that he died a quick death. However, to Dr. Ahmad, he instead died in sheer agony knowing what terror was all about.

*   *   *

The two station officer colleagues of Rahim observed the actions of both Gabriela and Mitch in and around the Mercedes from their observation posts at opposite ends of the street. They watched as Rahim drove the SUV out of the area, and remained in their parked positions for no more than 30 seconds after Rahim had passed by one of them. Then they drove away, in the same direction, with one of them catching up yet maintaining a discreet distance behind the SUV. Knowing the route that Rahim would be taking to drop Mitch and Gabriela off at a morning bazaar market that would be starting to fill up with shoppers, both of the station officers remained in their counter-surveillance positions until the SUV came back down out of the foothills and stopped at one of the entrances to the bazaar.

Before exiting the vehicle, Mitch and Gabriela gave their weapons to Rahim and said their goodbyes. He told them that once they got back to the hotel later in the day, the same two officers would again be taking up counter-surveillance positions in support of them until late in the evening. One would be inside the main lobby area of the hotel, and the other would be parked in his vehicle at the entrance of the road leading into the hotel grounds. He also said that they should plan to remain in the bazaar for at least a couple of hours and then call him in order to determine the conditions at the hotel.

Later that afternoon, after returning to a relatively quiet hotel, Mitch and Gabriela agreed to take their dinner separately in their rooms, and pack their clothes for checking out early in the morning for the flight back to Rome. They knew that the adrenalin rush of the morning's events would surely take a toll on them and, as a result, they would probably not be good company for each other that evening. As they packed they each watched the local television channels to see what news might be reported on the happenings that morning in front of Dr. Rabbani's laboratory on the west side of the city. Nothing was being reported at all on the newscasts.

It wasn't until their flight landed in Doha, when they changed planes for Rome, that television stations and newspapers were reporting the death of the notorious mastermind doctor wanted for the terrorist attacks of over two years ago in the U.K. and U.S. Vivid details were provided on the grisly scene found when his body was discovered in the back seat of a car in a run-down, semi-industrial part of Islamabad. He was cited as being hailed by many of his countrymen as a Muslim hero when he had returned to Pakistan from the U.S. attack. However, another article described the day's event as the inglorious end of the doctor considered by many others of his countrymen as receiving a just reward for being a betrayer of the faith.

Chapter 36

Mitch awoke the next morning in his bed, back in Rome, with an uneasiness sweeping through him. During the night, he had a wonderful dream about being together with Gabriela but, just before waking up, he experienced loud noises pounding in his brain, and a sense of dread began to overtake him. He had a feeling of being tossed around on a storm-swept sea, and it startled him into immediate consciousness. The part he couldn't explain was the feeling of something having gone very wrong during their op against the doctor in Islamabad.

After making coffee, he booted up his laptop and turned on the TV to check on the latest news stories. He then sat down and tried to think through the state of his relationship with Gabriela. Both had taken the lives of others in the past. When they had talked about what they both had done, they'd agreed that neither had any feelings of remorse for lives lost. Instead, they soldiered on, believing that they were right to follow the orders given them by their superiors.

This time, however, as best Mitch could rationalize it, the difference was that what took place in Islamabad was in view of each other when they took someone else's life. Should it even matter, he asked himself? Why was he getting stuck now with these kinds of thoughts? He wondered what her thoughts were on them being together during the hit on the doctor and his driver. Could she possibly be having a problem over what took place as well? He felt the need for a frank and open discussion with her.

When he arrived at the M&T office an hour later, Gabriela was already there and talking with Mr. G on what transpired during their absence. Mitch joined the conversation and, within half an hour felt up to speed on the state of work in the office as well as several items he would have to address in the near term. Based on Gabriela's comments and input during the discussions with Mr. G, he became even further convinced that she had a natural flair for the executive search field of work and had turned out to be a definite value-added commodity, not just to M&T, but to the Agency as well.

Looking for an excuse to be alone with her in order to discuss these earlier nagging thoughts about Islamabad and their own relationship, he suggested they step outside and go down the street to a new coffee house that recently opened for business.

Although located on a busy street for pedestrians due to the many retail shops lining both sides of the street they found the shop not at all crowded. Getting their cups of American coffee and finding a corner table in the back to their liking, Gabriela was totally unaware of the troubling thoughts on Mitch's mind.

"Since leaving the hotel in Islamabad, and during the flight back here, it seems like we have barely talked to each other," Mitch said. "Is there something on your mind? Have I done anything to upset or offend you?"

"Mitch, nothing is bothering me at all. I am sorry you even have these thoughts," Gabriela replied.

"I realize we only met two months ago, but since leaving Islamabad, I sense a pensiveness or deliberate quietness about you. I hope it is not due to anything I did. If that is the case, I am truly sorry."

"Mitch, you are really showing a soft and thoughtful side of you I have not seen before. Thank you for the concern. While I certainly have no problem or issue at all with what we did during the op, any quietness you notice is my way of reflecting back on what took place there."

"I am relieved to hear that. Up until now the things that we have discussed about the work we engage in has convinced me that we are a lot alike in many ways. Nevertheless, I guess that, in this case, we do react differently in the aftermath of a targeted killing. I'm sure it's just me being over-attentive, particularly when it involves you."

"Now it's my time to observe something in you, dear Mitch."

"What's that?"

"I believe I am detecting some serious affection from you. Is that true?"

"I could say that I thought you would never ask, but it would be trite. Of course it's true, and I'm glad you've observed it. I also hope you know, Gabriela, that if you let me continue to talk to you this way, it will be shooting all to hell our established professional relationship."

"I'm mature enough to handle it and, by way of further observation, I believe that what you are saying is true."

"Over these last two months we have basically been in each other's company every single day. That means we did a lot of things together in a short period of time. As a result, I've come to not only respect the professional skills you bring to our work, but also to admire the sincere and wonderful personality you have as well. I'm grasping for the right word now, and I believe it is affection. That is what I am coming to see with us."

"Mitch, how sweet you are. It's my turn now. Working closely with you here in Rome, as well as in Beijing and Islamabad, I am convinced that we were made to work with each other. We have the symbiotic synergy—how's that for a term—to make a formidable team of two. Based on what I was told about you before we met, and now that I have experienced working directly with you, I am a very lucky person.

"While I am also interested in the direction our relationship is heading, my concern is for our being able to continue to work together without letting feelings of affection cloud our thinking or our actions."

"Mitch, I have an idea how we can make it work."

"I sure want to hear it."

"If the professional desire to succeed is what drives our working relationship together, let's make sure that it comes first. That way, the affection we have for each other becomes the subsequent icing on the cake."

"I like that. To me, that would mean regardless how sweet that icing might be, the basis of our working relationship lies underneath, and that is what will prevail."

"Exactly. Given our line of work, and being employed by two distinctly different agencies, we don't know what kinds of future assignments lie ahead for us, where they will take us, or, even if we will be together again. Therefore, I believe we should just let events play out as they may."

"I'm glad we got all of that out of the way. I feel like tonight could be one of celebration for us. What do you say, Gabriela?"

"I agree. How about we go back to the office, finish up the day, and then find out what you have in mind to celebrate?"

The rest of the day went inexorably slow for the two of them. On the positive side, though, Mitch was able to remain occupied with Mr. G, plus shuffle paperwork and move ahead with plans for appointments with both potential clients as well as prospective candidates. Gabriela, once she completed her assigned calls to three new client firms, was left with idle time to think about how she would prepare herself to enjoy the evening to come. Deciding to leave the office early, she told Mitch she made an appointment at a nearby salon to have her hair styled and herself made up for the special evening that lay ahead.

With Mitch determined to make it as thoroughly pleasurable an evening for them both, he chose two of his favorite spots—one for a sumptuous dinner, the other for an after-dinner drink—that he had come to enjoy a number of times in the past. The dinner selection, La Rosetta, in nearby Piazza Navona, is known for its excellent seafood. Accepting the waiter's suggestion, they each started out with an appetizer of a dozen French oysters on the half shell. For their entree, they shared a four pound Maine lobster, with drawn butter. For dessert, they chose a locally made cheese with wildflower honey.

Exchanging furtive glances at each other as they dined, they made light chatter about their earlier days and the various kinds of foods they enjoyed eating as the result of all their travels. They also joked about the oysters they ate and whether they would produce the legendary aphrodisiac effects on them. Gabriela decided that, if so, they should probably not spend too much time at the spot Mitch chose afterwards for a nightcap. That was all the signal Mitch needed to tell him the icing was forming on the cake.

Leaving La Rosetta, they walked arm in arm the short six blocks into the neighborhood known as Trastevere, and a bar called Freni e Prizioni, overlooking the Tiber River. As they waited for their drinks to arrive and agreed that the Tiber, with its shimmering, sparkling lights aglow on the surface of the rippling water was definitely a romantic setting, they both realized that the inevitable could not be held off any longer.

"I wonder how long it will take for a taxi to get us back to my place."

"Mitch, I thought you would never ask. I've been wondering when you would try and bed me down."

"Can you hold off until we finish our drinks, or should we just chug-a-lug them down?"

"I'm not so sure I can wait much longer. I think the oysters are kicking in."

"Looking at you across the table a few minutes ago, as you were ordering, is when my oysters started to kick in."

"Now I know, Mitch. We definitely think alike."

With that, their drinks, two Bellini cocktails, arrived. Due to the stunning beauty of the shimmering waters of the river, they actually took their time in drinking them. As they glanced at one another with increasing desire, Mitch asked for the bill, paid in cash, and they departed by taxi for his apartment.

As he showed her in, Gabriela glanced around for a couple of moments in silence, and said, "Mitch, what a wonderfully decorated apartment. It certainly shows you in the choice of décor. Definitely, on the masculine side, subdued in color and very tastefully done."

"Thank you. Look around and make yourself comfortable, while I fix us something. Would you like coffee, a glass of wine, or maybe a digestive? Just name it."

"A glass of white wine would be fine, Mitch. May I use the bathroom?"

"Sure. It's inside the bedroom over there, the first door on the right."

He went into the apartment's small kitchen, got the wine out of the refrigerator, and returned to the living room with two glasses of well chilled white wine which he placed on the coffee table in front of the beige leather sofa. After turning on some soft music, he glanced towards the slightly open bedroom door. The bedside lamp was being dimmed. Walking slowly over to the door and stepping inside, he could see that Gabriela was lying in the bed covered by only a sheet.

Propped up on one elbow and looking straight at him, she said, "I have a surprise for you."

"I can see that you certainly do."

He retrieved the two glasses of wine from the living room and set them down on the side table next to the lamp. Sitting down on the edge of the bed, he began to unbutton his dress shirt as Gabriela attentively watched.

"This morning," he said, "while we were having coffee, I knew right then and there that it was time you came here tonight."

"I knew it too."

Stepping out of his slacks and underpants, he slid beneath the sheets beside her. He could smell a mild sweet musk from her sultry perfume as she lay on her back with her head on the pillow, her hair glistening in the soft glow from the lamp.

My God, he thought to himself. She is truly beautiful. And her hair, it is not blond, it is actually golden.

He slowly began kissing her firm breasts, one after the other. She raised her head up slightly, and bit him gently on the side of his neck. So soon they yielded to each other in a willing, powerful, and assertive manner. They quickly and totally opened up to one another. Eagerly experiencing their pleasure with abandon, what seemed like an eternity turned out to be but minutes, until they both climaxed together, and he moved to lie down alongside her. Without a word being spoken, they both fell into a deep sleep with their arms wrapped around each other.

CHAPTER 37

The icy cold wind that swept the dark waters of the Sea of Japan had no effect on Captain Toru Otani, or his ship, for that matter. They silently cruised underneath, at a depth of 200 feet, on a northwesterly course 150 miles off the coast of North Korea. Considered by Japan's Ministry of Defense to be the most skillful and proficient submariner in their navy, he was proud to be in command of Japan's latest advanced Soryu-class fast-attack submarine, the SS-504 Akagi. She was launched in October 2010, and named after one of the World War II aircraft carriers that attacked Pearl Harbor. The Akagi is the largest and quietest of Japan's diesel-electric boats, and incorporates the Swedish supplied Kockums Stirling air independent propulsion system serving to enhance the vessel's stealth and special operations capabilities.

While Captain Otani was finishing a sashimi and sushi dinner in the wardroom with his fellow officers, the ship's Chief Petty Officer from the Communications Center entered and handed him a decrypted cable from the Kure Naval District Headquarters, located in Hiroshima Prefecture. The cable ordered the captain to take the Akagi to a new position off of North Korea's South Hamgyong Province, southeast of the major submarine base at Chaho. More than half of North Korea's 90 mini subs use this base as their home port. The port is home to a number of older Russian-built Romeo and Whiskey-class submarines as well, and also serves as the training facility for North Korea's East Sea Fleet.

The cable stated that the U.S. Navy's Advanced Deployable System (ADS), an undersea surveillance system that is used for detecting diesel electric as well as nuclear submarines, had picked up signals from four mini-subs, as well as the confirmed signal from North Korea's newest and only Kilo class diesel electric submarine that was recently acquired from Russia. All five vessels were reported running close together on parallel courses coming out of the Chaho base and were proceeding southeastward out into the Sea of Japan. The course the captain was ordered to take would interdict this small flotilla of subs.

The ADS is a portable fiber optic based system and serves as a powerful listening device that is deployed along the sea bottom off of the entire South Korean coastline, as well as significant portions of the North Korean coastline on the east coast side of the country. The system is operated under the joint command of the South Korean Navy and the U.S. Navy. Its predecessor is the popular Cold War SOSUS system that was used so effectively, for decades, in detecting and tracking Soviet submarines coming out of bases in both the North Atlantic and North Pacific Oceans.

North Korean submarines regularly infiltrate South Korean waters to land ashore special forces commando units from the Reconnaissance General Bureau, the highly secretive intelligence organization created in early 2009 that is charged with conducting all espionage and special operations against the south. With the south sorely in need of a modern countermeasure system, the answer proved to be ADS. By providing early warning notification of the north's operational forays, the south can intercept the north's ships and landing parties and, in many cases, either sink, capture or force their retreat back to the north.

These military incursions on the part of the north were inherited by Kim when he succeeded his father and began his own dictatorial reign in 1994. In keeping with his father's policies, these aggressive military actions also served to placate and keep under control the high command, which has come in recent years to growing increasingly restless with the failed economic policies of Kim's harsh rule. Military leaders prefer achieving reunification with the south via force but, at the same time, recognize that their own populace, their source of manpower to conduct war, must be better fed through more enlightened free-market economic policies.

In October 2010, when North Korea held the debut of the heir-apparent and self-chosen successor to Kim, his younger son, Kim Jong-Un, the stage was set for further consternation and concern within the high command. Besides naming his own successor, Kim concurrently named him a four-star general in the military, and also appointed him to be vice-chairman of the Workers' Party Central Military Commission. This served to place him on the party's Central Committee as well. It is this Central Committee of the Workers Party, particularly its powerful political bureau, which shares power in the country with the military. However, in order to placate the high command after anointing the "young general Kim" as his successor, Kim adroitly selected two rising military officers to the ranks of general at the suggestion of the Central Military commission.

*　　*　　*

To add further strain to the often volatile relations on the Korean peninsula between the north and the south is the yearly joint military exercises staged by South Korea and the U.S. For the first time, in 2010, just after ADS became operational, the exercises were expanded to include a limited number of contingents from the naval, air and ground forces of Japan, Taiwan, Singapore, Australia and New Zealand. By the time the same enlarged joint exercises were staged the following year, Captain Otani and the Akagi participated as part of the Japanese Navy's contingent. It was a first for him in working closely in exercises with both submarines and surface ships from other participating nations.

One particular ship's commander, from the South Korean navy, impressed Captain Otani with his skillful and disciplined handling of his ship under difficult circumstances. In one part of an exercise designed especially for South Korean and U.S. vessels to combat North Korean naval incursions, the Akagi was required to run a course directly underneath the South Korean commander's vessel, under silent running conditions and in close proximity. Unable to detect the presence of the Akagi, but being required to follow a limited version of a zigzag course, the commander piloted his ship smoothly and accurately through the exercise to its error-free conclusion.

At the end, when the Akagi was running nearby on the surface and all the participating ships had raised flags to express appreciation of their country taking part in the exercises, Captain Otani held a brief radio-telephone conversation with the South Korean commander. He commended him on his highly professional seamanship, and they both expressed hope they would, once again, have the opportunity to be in the same waters together. It was an amiable conversation that Captain Otani enjoyed and would remember.

With a length of just over 280 feet, and a weight of 4,200 tons, the Akagi can make a surface speed of 20 knots, and over 35 when submerged.

Carrying a complement of 10 officers and 60 enlisted men, the ship has a cruising range of 6,200 nautical miles. The most impressive features of this state-of-the-art diesel electric boat is its armament—with six torpedo tubes, the Akagi is able to fire a combination of 36 Boeing Harpoon Block II UGM-85 anti-ship and anti-land missiles, as well as 16 Type 89 II torpedoes.

The ship can remain submerged at depths in excess of 1,000 feet and go undetected for months at a time. Producing its own oxygen and drinking water from the sea, the only limitation to the crew's endurance is the amount of food that can be carried. Typically, that means cruises not lasting more than ninety days. However, in the decades leading up to the 1980s, most cruises for Japanese submarines were much shorter in duration since the boats spent more time in waters closer to Japan, in the nearby stretches of the Pacific Ocean, the Sea of Japan and the South China Sea. With changing government foreign policies due to Japan's expanding role in world affairs, along with the accompanying need for the latest in underwater technological advances, subsequent newly launched submarines in the Soryu class completely altered Japan's blue water naval capabilities.

When the cable from Kure directed Captain Otani to take the Akagi further westward into the Sea of Japan, it included giving him instructions for linking up with a South Korean Navy missile armed patrol vessel PKG-716, the Sub Hoowon. Upon reading this portion of the cable, his face broke out in a wide grin as he immediately recognized the name of the vessel as the same one he had worked with during the joint exercises some months earlier. He wondered if the ship would still be under the command of the captain he talked with at the conclusion of the exercises.

Not knowing what the North Korean intent was in sending four mini-subs and a full sized Kilo-class boat eastwards into the Sea of Japan towards Japan, Captain Otani could only guess at this point about what might soon take place. He would follow his instructions from Kure and his own instincts as called upon. He did know though, that the Kilo boat was certainly no match for the Akagi. With the stealthiest of ultra-quiet running advances on board, the Akagi could close in virtually undetected either alongside or directly underneath any of the North Korean vessels they were on an intercept course with. Combined with her more than 28,000 acoustic panels covering the surface of the ship to mask its sonar signature, the Akagi can lurk around undersea, unheard and unseen.

A more disturbing question on the captain's mind, however, was the absence of a North Korean mother ship, usually disguised as a cargo vessel, that would serve to provide refueling for the mini subs, in order for them to remain in the area, much less return home. No such ship had been reported anywhere in the vicinity. Needless to say, the captain knew that as he brought the Akagi ever closer toward the five vessels, as well as closing with the South Korean patrol ship, he would be receiving additional information from his headquarters at Kure.

As the evening wore on and midnight approached, neither the Kilo boat nor the mini subs had any inkling that the newest fast-attack submarine from the Japanese Navy had picked them up on long distance radar and was tracking them. The sooner they dove beneath the waves together, it would only become slightly more difficult to track them via the Akagi's sonar at that distance. Upon being advised by the tracking officer of their course and speed, Captain Otani ordered the Akagi to rig for and commence silent running.

As one of the Akagi's Petty Officers 2nd Class exited the communications center to make his way to the navigation table in the center of the control room, he approached the captain with a new message in hand. The first two sentences of the cable from Kure described the purpose of the North Korean vessels as that of a training mission that would probably not take them much further out into the Sea of Japan. The captain, with that, breathed slightly easier until he read the next two sentences. Citing South Korean communications intercepts picked up from the North Korean port at Chaho Base, the cable said that each of the four mini subs carried on board four Iranian Navy submariners. They were on board the vessels for purposes of becoming familiar with the operating characteristics of the vessels, as well as gaining experience with the latest versions of electronics equipment carried on the vessels.

Apparently, the cable added, these mini subs were new, upgraded types of the Yono class of boats previously provided to Iran. After arriving in the country from North Korea, they were slightly modified and introduced to the world as the Iranian-made Ghadir class submarine for use in the Persian Gulf, the Gulf of Oman and through the Strait of Hormuz into the Arabian Sea. Finally, the cable advised, the South Korean patrol vessel, the Suh Hoowon, would shortly be contacting the Akagi in order to coordinate their approaches toward the North Korean vessels and any actions on their part, as necessary.

In order to establish encrypted radio contact with the approaching Suh Hoowon, the Akagi would need to come up from her current running depth to one averaging 80 to 90 feet. Once there, a radio antenna would be raised that would break the surface of the sea and allow for instant communication. Instead, however, Captain Otani ordered the Akagi to a periscope depth at 60 feet which, besides radio contact, would also provide visual coverage as the two ships neared each other. He knew that at his current speed of 30 knots, and the last known position of the Suh Hoowon, it would not be long before radar contact would be established, and he would be receiving a radio message from the captain of the Suh Hoowon.

Retiring to his cabin for a brief rest, Captain Otani ordered up from his orderly the latest information, both classified and unclassified, on the status of relations between North Korea and Iran. Within a few minutes, the orderly returned with several classified readings kept on file, as well as two recent articles downloaded from the Internet. He subsequently read through the materials and, before dozing off for a short nap, he learned several interesting things that provided a good perspective in revealing the extent of cooperation between the two countries, and where their aggressive naval policies, in particular, were taking them on collision courses with their own local neighboring states, as well as with the U.S.

Being knowledgeable and well read in on North Korea's aggressive naval tactics in and around the waters of the Korean peninsula, what was new to him in these readings was learning of the similar practices by the Iranian navy in the waters of the Persian Gulf, the Gulf of Oman and out into the Arabian Sea. Similarly, he also learned that the Iranians make extensive use of different kinds of mines, including contact and sea-rising types. They were used with devastating effects on local shipping, another practice obviously improved upon from the tactics of the North Koreans. What impressed Captain Otani the most though, was the high degree of military cooperation, including technology transfer, sales and training, between the two countries involving ships, aircraft, missiles and nuclear weapons technology.

The next to last article he read dealt with the assassination of Iranian President Mahmoud Ahmadinejad during his recent trip to Paris, and how part of his visit there was giving a major speech on the purported peaceful intentions of Iran's nuclear program. The final article was a classified South Korean intelligence report dealing with an agreement signed between North Korea and Iran on nuclear missile technology and training from North Korea in exchange for Iranian oil.

As he could feel himself starting to slip off into a light sleep, the last thoughts on his mind were the complications that weapons of mass destruction lead to, especially when it involves their development by rogue nations of the likes of North Korea and Iran. In particular, he resented the intrusion of nations like these into the open waters of Sea Japan itself, and the potential effects this could have on his career as a Japanese navel officer.

CHAPTER 38

No sooner had twenty minutes passed, when the Captain was awakened by his orderly, advising him of the radio telephone call coming through from the captain of the Suh Hoowon.

"Otani-san, is that you?" asked ROK Navy Captain Lee Jae-ho.

"Lee-san, it's good to hear your voice once again. It has been a while since the exercises. I hope you are well."

"All is fine, Otani-san. I am pleased to be working with you. This assignment could turn out to be an interesting time ahead for us, to say the least."

"What is the latest situation as you currently know it, Lee-san?"

"From the recent cable received from my headquarters, it looks like the four North Korean mini subs are on a training mission, accompanied by the Kilo boat. They all are currently running close together on the surface. However, I believe that could shortly change. While I am relieved about it purportedly being for training purposes, I am bothered by the extent to which they are heading further eastwards into the Sea of Japan. They should, as based upon what I know are their usual configurations and lengths of time engaged in exercises, be making a turn soon to commence their training exercises in a westerly direction back towards their coastline and base."

"I share your concern, Lee-san, even though I also am glad to learn about their mission being an exercise. Is there anything further, Lee-san?"

"Yes, there is more information. Since you have been running submerged, you probably have not picked up their mother ship, a surface vessel disguised as a cargo ship, heading eastwards toward them. I currently show the ship on radar on a course directing coming up the stern of their subs, at a distance of 50 miles away."

"Ah, yes, Lee-san. We are picking it up on our extended sonar. The ship is a real noise maker, and has some serious engine problems that are going to soon be in need of repair."

"For us though, close in our local waters of the ROK, that kind of ship still represents a threat."

"I certainly understand, Lee-san. From what my headquarters and U.S. forces have reported, their Kilo boat is a different story. While Kilos are older boats, this one is a newer upgraded version and, unlike the surface vessel, is actually running quite well right now. I believe it is being used for the first time by the North Koreans on a training mission, since it was acquired from Russia."

"Yes, that is my understanding too."

"Otani-san, I know you are very aware of what took place in late March last year, just after our own joint training exercises were completed. The North's sinking of our Po Hang-class corvette, the Cheonon, was done by at least one mini sub thought to be of the same type as the four we are sailing towards."

"Yes, Lee-san, I was saddened by the loss of so many of your brave seamen. I would like to think though, that with Iranian Navy personnel reported to be on these mini subs, it may well be as we have been told, namely, it is a training mission or familiarization exercise, instead of any form of hostile intent against your ship or anything else in these waters."

"I want to think the same thing, especially since the Kilo sub is certainly aware of my presence as I steam in their direction. By the way, Otani-san, you may want to call up your shipboard information on the class of the mini subs accompanying the Kilo. All of them appear to be in the Yeon-o class, also sometimes listed as the Yono-class."

"Yes, I am familiar with them. It is believed to be the predecessor of the Ghadir—class now in use by the Iranian Navy. At 29 meters in length and carrying a crew of 18, they are diesel-electrics, not particularly very fast and have a limited battery capacity when running submerged. However, they are relatively stealthy due to their quiet running capabilities, and each of them is armed with two torpedoes. I would not be surprised at all that what we are facing in these four mini subs is the latest upgraded version of this class, and Iran has it under consideration for further adoption into their own fleet."

"I completely agree since it would explain the Iranian presence onboard them here in these waters."

"Lee-san, my orders originally instructed me to take up a position of initial monitoring of the vessels similar to what we both practiced in last year's exercises, meaning, namely, from a discreet distance. As you know, that will require me to remain submerged and on ultra quiet running in order to go undetected by them. I will only use the radio telephone to talk to you, as necessary. They will be hearing many kinds of other radio traffic from ships all over the Sea of Japan, encrypted and in the open, and we should fit right in with it, depending on what they are able to perceive as your specific traffic, and who it is you might be talking to."

"That's fine, Otani-san. I will play a shadowing role, per my own instructions. Anyhow, I am sure we have already been picked up on their radar and they have been able to specifically identify my ship within the last 20 minutes or so. They have my engine signatures in their data files on ships of my class, and by now no doubt realize I am a well-armed ROK vessel."

"Assuming, Lee-san, they are waiting for the mother ship to close in before commencing their training, I would expect that will be when we see them beginning to make significant moves. It may be to either make a 180-degree turn to face back toward their coastline and commence engaging in their exercises, or take a different tack and decided to play cat and mouse with your vessel. I suppose a third option, should they do a 180, would be to remain on the surface and make haste for their home base."

"Otani-san, we do have ROK Air Force maritime surveillance aircraft on standby, as need be. The two aircraft that were available to be airborne in this area had developed some minor mechanical troubles that prevented them from taking up positions above us for at least another hour or so. However, I've been informed that fighter aircraft are currently sitting on takeoff pads and could be here in a matter of minutes. The concern though, is not to give our hand away by showing too much of a presence. In the meantime, I'm instructed to just stay on a surveillance track and monitor their positions to determine what they are planning to do."

"My orders call for surveillance and monitoring as well, unless they make hostile moves. Since the sinking of your corvette last year, the whole game plan for dealing with the north has changed. Their conduct of engaging in numerous so-called training exercises that take them miles offshore now, have sparked concern obviously in both our countries, let alone in the U.S. In Japan, for example, we don't take kindly to them launching long-range missiles on what they say are testing runs over our northern islands."

"Otani-san, we will shortly be abeam of each other on a course that will take us directly on a northerly heading onto their starboard side. May I suggest we consider what our initial moves be, depending upon their response to your presence nearby?"

"Yes, Lee-san. At present, I have you on my port side, and you are three miles ahead. When my ship is abeam of you, we should only be separated by about three-quarters of a mile. With you being visible to them, you decide your opening move should they take an aggressive posture and make any hostile moves against you."

"Obviously, with you to my starboard side, I will either move to port, or it will be straight toward them, providing, we are not in too close at that point. What is your thinking, Otani-san?"

"My primary concern, naturally, is with the Kilo sub. Should she turn toward you, and I receive any indication she is preparing to dive and open torpedo doors, my own high-speed torpedoes should suffice. Kilo boat electronics for going into firing sequences usually are quite detectable and provide ample time to respond if I am already on a solution course and ready to fire. To do that, I am prepared to open a couple of torpedo doors ahead of time to continue to forestall them from having any inkling of my presence. With the noises being received on their sonar from the mini subs and your heading in their direction, they will not detect the doors' opening."

"That's excellent, Otani-san. I will take responsibility for the four mini subs. Should any of them turn towards my ship and provide any indication of hostile intent, my own armaments will be quite adequate. Submerged, they will not be making enough knots to prevent me from tracking them. If they stay on the surface, which I do not think they will do, my anti-ship homing missiles should easily be able to handle them."

"In that case, Lee-san, should they go hostile, I will swing inward past the Kilo and go for a flanking movement on the starboard side."

"Otani-san, I believe we have a plan."

"I agree."

Just as the two captains described it, the Suh Hoowon and the Akagi took up their positions in tandem, and slowed their speed in front and to the starboard sides of the approaching North Korean Kilo sub and four mini subs. While the Kilo boat was totally unaware of the Akagi's presence, the Suh Hoowon was a different case. A half hour earlier, when the Kilo first picked up the Suh Hoowon on radar, the Kilo's captain radioed in the situation to his home port at the Chaho submarine base. Providing course and speed of the Suh Hoowon, the captain asked for instructions on how he should proceed and the kind of offensive or defensive posture he should project, particularly insofar having the four mini subs there on a training and familiarization mission.

The first response from Chaho base advised that the mother ship was increasing its speed to their location, and should shortly be showing up on the Kilo's radar. Further, when the mother ship was in position close enough to the mini subs, the Kilo was to dive and take up a new position that would allow for going on the offensive against the Suh Hoowon, should it become necessary. In the meantime, the Kilo captain was ordered to proceed as planned and commence the exercises once the mother ship was closing in to the sterns of the subs, regardless the presence of the Suh Hoowon. Lastly, the captain of the Kilo was instructed to be sure his monitoring position, following his ship's dive, would allow for the Kilo to be in a firing solution position against the Suh Hoowon, again, should it become necessary. Satisfied with the instructions, the Kilo boat captain went about ordering his ship to be ready for diving as well as quiet running conditions, as the mother ship approached.

The Kilo boat captain was completely unaware of the changing situation back home in the country's capital of Pyongyang. With the grandiose announcement and subsequent pageantry and celebration of the naming of Kim Jong-Il's son, Kim Jong-Un, as his successor during October of the previous year, Pyongyang became the scene of the start of a period of progressive jockeying on the part of military officers and Workers Party members alike. In the quest for positions with more power, this included the formation of new alliances as well as the repledging of heartfelt loyalties, until the death, of their dear leader, Kim Jong-Il. It only had been five months earlier last year, in April, that Kim promoted 100 senior military officers in order to further coalesce and strengthen his hold on the key positions of power in the country. At least 50 senior party loyalists were promoted as well.

The additional military loyalists, who were now further committed to serving the wishes of Kim Jong-Il, included those from the National Security Agency, the Air Force Command, the Navy Command and the

Artillery Command. The one loyalist who did not need another promotion, regardless whether he wanted it or not, was the closest confident of Kim's, General O Kuk-Yol. Known as the consummate strategist who holds the highest of trust by Kim, General O is also given credit for his success in convincing Kim, a number of years ago, of the importance of military policies that place particular emphasis on the use of special forces and extensive intelligence resources. With General O thoroughly immersed in the masterminding of infiltration, strike, reconnaissance and special ops missions into South Korea regularly, his crowning achievement came with the February 2010 formation of the super-sensitive Reconnaissance General Bureau, from which mini sub operations are an integral part.

The clinker in the coal bin though, would come to show itself in the form of the Reconnaissance General Bureau's Commander, Lt. General Kim Yong-Choi, thought to be a long-time protégé of General O. In the short time span of six months, following the naming of Kim Jong-Un as the successor to his father, the RGB Chief took young Kim as his protégé and brought him along to understand and be prepared to give orders in conducting the kind of deadly operations against the south for which the RGB was known to engage in under the leadership of his father. With the RGB Commander having his own aspirations for leadership that placed him at odds with the aspirations of Kim Jong-Il's powerful brother-in-law Chang Sung-taek, the stage was set for a dangerous period of instability that could lead to the collapse of North Korea with the passing of the ailing Kim.

Another unknown for the captain of the Kilo, as he was about to get the training and familiarization mission underway: Young Kim Jong-Un, the chosen successor to his father, was at RGB Headquarters on that fateful afternoon when the captain's radio message was received indicating that his ship and the four mini subs in his flotilla were coming to be shadowed by the lurking presence of the ROK patrol vessel, the Suh Hoowon. With his father's ailing poor health taking its toll on his frail body, would the young Kim decide to use this as the opportune time to exercise his own authority for the first time? Could the scene starting to play itself out in the Sea of Japan enable him to take up the reins of leadership and make his first decision that could lead to a military confrontation with South Korea? Or, would he let his mentor, the RGB Commander, inform the ailing Kim of the situation and let him decide on the course of action to take? It all came down to a chance for the young Kim to project boldness and decisiveness in the face of the ROK enemy to the south. The decision to come would be the classic one for the young general Kim. Play it safe and hold off until such time as experience would come to prevail over his growing ego and self-assertiveness? Or, move on his own to show he is a worthy successor to his father?

CHAPTER 39

The arrival of the cable from headquarters did not catch Mitch by any kind of surprise. He was anticipating its arrival almost daily during the two week period following his first night with Gabriela in his apartment. Now they could put their plans into action for returning to Beijing and the mission to end the life of the Supreme Leader of North Korea, Kim Jong-Il.

Headquarters, or rather Jack, Mitch's supervisor in SAD who no doubt wrote the cable, asked for a meeting with Mitch prior to the trip to Beijing. He suggested it be in California, since it would be plausible for Mitch to stop off at the M&T home office in San Francisco just prior to continuing onward to China. Jack was still honoring Mitch's proviso about the two of them not being seen in public together for reasons of Mitch's personal security. However, he knew that the mention in the cable of wanting to discuss the possible use of the "Boogie Box" as a means of exfiltration from Beijing, if need be, would serve to get Mitch's attention and subsequent agreement for the two of them to meet.

When Mitch went into the office that morning, after reading the cable at his apartment, he immediately filled Gabriela in on its contents, except for the part about the Boogie Box. Since its existence and use was highly classified by the Agency, any information about it would have to come from someone like Jack at headquarters, or even someone senior to him. Special tools and techniques involved in certain types of exfiltration ops is a restricted subject within the Agency, where it is considered a compartmented program that requires a separate briefing for each person selected to be read in on the program's existence.

Upon learning the contents of the cable, Gabriela was glad to know that solid intelligence reporting indicated that Kim was preparing for the expected trip to Beijing, including a date for his arrival there, in four weeks' time. The reporting cited two primary reasons for the trip—a personal request from Kim to China's premier for a massive increase in food aid as a consequence of North Korea's disastrous crop shortages over the past year, and also to introduce the younger Kim to the Chinese leadership as his chosen successor.

"Would you be interested in spending a few days with your parents and family in Puerto Rico, before heading on to Asia?" Mitch asked.

"Why Mitch, that would be wonderful. Yes, I would."

"We could link up in San Francisco afterwards, and then fly direct to Beijing."

"What about Gene? Would we link up with him ahead of time for a meeting before leaving the U.S.?"

"No, I don't think it will be necessary, since I believe that between Gene, us and headquarters, we have all the remaining details covered, and he should be able to proceed on his own to China."

Mitch didn't say anything to her about his cable response back to Jack, asking that since Gabriela was an integral part of Mitch's cover for the ops mission to Beijing, including posing under commercial cover with Mitch in the M&T company, she could not be left exposed alone there should he have to beat a hasty exfil out of the country immediately after the hit. Before saying anything to her about it, he would wait for Jack's reply, indicating she would be given the security briefing on the Boogie Box system during their stopover in San Francisco.

The next several days in the office together, along with Mr. G, involved purchasing their air tickets and making hotel reservations back at the Beijing Marriott, including arrangements for the use of hotel meeting rooms for conducting interviews and briefing sessions for a number of their university professor guests. Mitch sent emails to his university contacts at the five schools, advising them of the dates for hosting the event at the hotel. He also included mentioning that his M&T colleague, Gabriela, would be accompanying him and involved in conducting the interviews as well. Gabriela took the opportunity to call her parents to let them know she would be paying them a visit in a few days time, and how much she looked forward to seeing them. They were overjoyed, to say the least, to know she would be coming home, even if for just a short visit.

In the evenings leading up to their departure from Rome early the following week, Gabriela and Mitch enjoyed quiet, intimate dinners together, revisiting several trattorias and osterias, the small family-run restaurants they previously discovered and had come to enjoy so much. After returning to Mitch's apartment in the evenings after dinner, Gabriela would go to bed first, around midnight. Mitch, on the other hand, would usually remain up and spend an additional hour reading. During that time, after she fell asleep, he could not but help come into the bedroom to check on her, and watch the rise and fall of her chest as she gently breathed, laying either on her back or on her side. With an occasional turn of a hand, or movement of an arm, he was fascinated to watch as she repositioned herself and settled in for a sound night's sleep. Fearful of waking her if he tried to softly stroke her hair on the pillow, he hesitated and would retreat back out into the living and resume his reading.

He knew what was happening to himself as he further came to respect and admire what he had found to be a complex woman who, when called upon, could be wonderfully warm, loving and highly passionate, on the one hand, yet deadly, violent and cunning on the other. Savoring the feel of her skin on his, when they were pressed together at the height of their lovemaking, the silent question that lurked in the back of his mind was whether this was the kind of woman he could choose to spend the rest of his life with.

*   *   *

Their departure from Rome's Fiumicino Airport had an air of foreboding about it since a thick fog permeated the entire area, resulting in a darkness that prevented the noonday sun from shining through. Fortunately, though, after taxiing out to one of the main runways following a half-hour delay, the fog showed signs of lifting, and they were on their way.

"I don't like the feeling of leaving in this kind of weather for a major operation on the other side of the world," she said.

"Why Gabriela," he replied. "With your background and experiences all over the place, and all the flying it entails, I'm surprised you would show many concerns over a thick fog."

It's probably the darkness more than anything else."

"By the time we get to New York, and you go onward to San Juan, I'm sure you'll be in much better spirits. Just think about your family and what a good time you're going to have during your visit with them."

"You're right, you know. I'll certainly be up for seeing them. I guess what really is bothering me though, is the prospect of what's to come for us once the op in Beijing is over."

"How so? What do you mean?"

"As far as we know, this will be our last time working together. I was assigned to the CIA to work with you, originally, on this one op. I realize we took a detour and made a stop along the way in Pakistan, in order to pay a serious house call on your doctor friend there. However, now we are back on track and as far as I know, this is it. I will revert back to JSOG at Fort Bragg, and you will resume what you do best, a singleton NOC with a solid track record of successes."

"Thank you for the compliment, but why does it have to turn out the way you have described it?"

"It's my military way of thinking prevailing over my own instinctual desire to carve out a new kind of future that involves us continuing to work together and to always be together."

"Gabriela, let me share something with you. As far as I am concerned, I would like to think my instincts right now are the same as yours. However, I will not let them interfere with what is at hand for us in this op. We both realize what a successful hit on Kim will mean, not just for our country, but the world as well. I want us to be successful in accomplishing it, including getting out of China and safely back in one piece so that we are prepared to go forward with whatever future assignments might be made available."

"What does that say for us and our working relationship?

"It means, Gabriela, let's give this op our very best, and make it work. After that, how about we go and relax in some memorable part of the world for a vacation where we can talk this whole thing out? How does that sound to you?"

"You're right, of course, and it makes the most sense, including our going off together afterwards. I just thought that while at home with my family, I might finally be able to tell them I believe I have found 'Mr. Right.' Now, however, I think I'll hold off until after the op in China is over."

"I know better than to say that you're thinking like a man, since I know that the elbow I will feel abruptly in my ribs will cause me to throw this glass of champagne I am holding all over the place. In reality, you're thinking for both of us, and that is what counts."

"The hell with whatever instincts are involved. Let's just not spill either of these glasses of good champagne."

"I do want you to know that I look forward to meeting your family, and hope it will be soon."

"I believe you will like them a lot, since I know they are going to enjoy meeting you. Have you ever been to Puerto Rico?

"Actually, yes I have. I was there twice several years ago to conduct interviews and sign up some new client firms. Both trips were successful and I thoroughly enjoyed myself as well."

"What did you like the best about being there?"

"That's easy. The rum, especially when it's in Mojitos."

"Thanks sport. I asked for that."

Chapter 40

The Inn Above Tide, situated on the water in the heart of Marin County's bayside town of Sausalito, just minutes from San Francisco's Golden Gate Bridge, provided the seclusion and perfect setting for meeting with Gene and holding the briefing for Gabriela on the Boogie Box program. Mitch arrived in San Francisco four days earlier and was able to reconnect with his M&T home office colleagues, and catch up on the latest developments in the company's recent business activities. Gabriela, after leaving Mitch at JFK Airport in New York, flew onward to Puerto Rico to spend four days in San Juan with her parents, as well as visiting longtime friends and catching up on news from the home front. By the time she departed for San Francisco to link up with Mitch, she was relaxed and satisfied in seeing that both of her parents continued to enjoy good health and the company of their brothers and sisters living nearby. Being the only child, and going off at the age of 18 to college, followed by starting a career in the army, resulted in lingering feelings of guilt for Gabriela, especially when it was time to leave them behind and get on with her own life.

Prior to Mitch and Gabriela arriving at the inn, where Jack rented a comfortable suite at the far end of the property, literally a few feet above the waters of the bay, Mitch told her about a briefer who would be there from headquarters to read her in on a compartmented program. Jack greeted the two of them warmly, especially Mitch, who he had not seen in close to a year, and introduced them to the briefer. After serving coffee, Jack suggested that he and Mitch step out on the veranda while the briefer stayed inside with Gabriela and provide her with the details of the restricted access program.

For the next 35 minutes, Gabriela sat motionless and transfixed on a sofa facing the briefer as he explained what the extraordinary Boogie Box program is all about. He told her it really is a box, barely large enough to hold a person, and is used to secretly and securely transport a person safely out of a country without the knowledge of that country's host government authorities of any kind, or anyone else, for that matter, who is not privy to the contents of the crate. The box is constructed to look like a well-made wooden packing crate used to transport commercial goods of all types.

In reality, the box is an ingenious concealment device that functions as a sealed, self-contained, short-term survival capsule capable of supporting life until such time as an aircraft can reach international airspace. Once the person to be transported is inside, and the windowless crate is closed, the crate is moved with as much haste as local traffic conditions will permit to the nearest airport for transport out of the country.

Typically, a wide-body or jumbo long-range passenger aircraft is employed under the command of a senior pilot who is aware of the Boogie Box program to the extent of knowing that a special person is inside the box below in the aircraft's cargo hold. Once airborne and in international airspace, the pilot leaves the flight deck with the copilot in command, and climbs down into the cargo hold via the access hatch below the flight deck, to open the crate and release the person inside.

Gabriela, continuing to show no emotion, yet fascinated by what she was hearing, waited until the briefing was over and asked if she had any questions.

"Yes. I do have a few. To start, has anyone inside ever been discovered and arrested by local authorities before the aircraft could depart?"

"Not once since the box was invented and subsequently used. By the way, are you in any way claustrophobic?"

"No, I'm not. However, this kind of experience will really put me to the test."

"Do you see having any kind of problem with it?"

"Not as long as you don't tell me that I am actually the first person to use it."

"Rest assured, it has been used numerous times in the past. I know of no instance where it has not been successful."

"I don't suppose I can bring along my luggage."

Having a hard time holding back a laugh, he replied: "It can only be what you are wearing on your back."

With the briefing finished, she signed the required secrecy agreement for being read in on the program, and thanked him for the time spent and the information he provided. After saying goodbye to her, Jack and Mitch, the briefer asked Jack to step outside the suite with him, for a moment or two. What he did not reveal to Gabriela while telling her about the Boogie Box was that he was an Agency staff psychologist. Besides providing the briefing, he also was there to evaluate her suitability and state of mind, in order to judge her ability to remain in the box for an extended period.

"Well, Doctor," Jack said, "what do we have on our hands here?"

"Besides having a sense of humor I can relate to, she is calm, collected and handles herself quite well. Her body language revealed nothing noteworthy at all. She was not defensive, but rather took it all in stride."

"Did she have many questions to ask?"

"Not really. She claimed not to be claustrophobic but we both know any normal person would be concerned about being able to spend any amount of time inside the box, especially knowing they are also in the belly of an aircraft flying thousands of feet up in the air."

"Doctor, let me tell you something. She is not your garden-variety person. We consider her to be very special."

"I believe I can see that in her. She definitely shows a military bearing in the way she carries herself, and appears strong-willed and well-disciplined. On that basis, I am confident she is capable of successfully experiencing the Boogie Box.

"Doctor, thank you very much for coming all the way out here to conduct the brief. Now let's hope we don't have to end up using the box."

"The pleasure was mine. With this beautiful setting on San Francisco Bay, how could I resist a chance to get away from headquarters and experience this part of the country?"

Going back inside to finish up the meeting with Mitch and Gabriela, Jack filled them in on how the use of the box, or in this case, two boxes—one for each of them—could come into play, should the situation require their deployment.

"Two of the boxes are being shipped to the embassy in Beijing. They will be configured and ready for use if it appears the authorities are in any way aware of your presence and moving to capture either of you."

"What will be the extent of the station's security setup around the hotel?" Mitch asked.

"It will consist of an armed surveillance team covering all the entrance points around the hotel. We will also have two manned vehicles on standby inside the hotel's parking lot area for your extraction, if necessary."

"What about local communications?" Gabriela asked.

"Our commo people inside the embassy will be monitoring the complete spectrum of bands and channels that the police and intelligence services are known to use. This will include their VIP channels as well. At the first hint of their suspecting that Mitch's firing came from the hotel or building alongside it, we will advise both of you to move to the nearest extraction point, where the vehicles will be located, in order to get you clear of the area and over to the embassy."

"I would expect," Mitch said, "to be making my way out of the building and across the underground passageway back into the hotel by the time anyone can figure out the location from which I was firing."

"The key," Jack replied, "is going to be your ability to get back into the hotel unnoticed and to your upstairs location in the business center where you and Gabriela are conducting the interviews. How will you handle the rifle afterwards?"

"The tennis racket carrying case I use to carry it into the building and upstairs to the firing location will be used to carry it out as well. Once back downstairs and through the passageway into the hotel building, I expect to meet up with Gene before using the stairwell up to the business center. I will pass it off to him, and he will take care of getting it to one of the station's security officers for return to the embassy."

"Gene will be a busy guy, between moving from the train station to the hotel basement, picking up the rifle and getting away from the hotel as far as possible to hand it off."

"I agree, Jack. However, we all know Gene. He can hustle with the rest of us. I know you've got the details for your end of the op planned out just as well as ours. For us, Gabriela will be continuing with the interviews in the hotel while I'm doing my thing up in the window of the building next door. She and I have talked it through a number of times, and both feel very good about being able to pull this thing off without a hitch."

"To assist me in the interviews," Gabriela added, "I've made arrangements to have a couple of business center staff work with me in and around the meeting area. Mitch, you will be meeting them ahead of time, when we first start interviewing a couple of days ahead of shooting day. They will function to attend to the candidates waiting to be interviewed. For example, they will serve refreshments, as well as bring people into the interview rooms. It will appear that, during your absence, you are also inside one of the interview rooms. In your case though, it will be me who will be the person bringing candidates to you. I will make it appear as if I am doing this when not engaged in my own interviewing."

"Jack, as you can see, we're ready to get this show off the ground. What are your final comments for us before Gabriela and I leave for the airport?

"I have only one comment to make before you leave. It's about the use of the Bogie Boxes. Their use is an extraordinary occurrence for the Agency. They are seldom employed, and then only under the most secure of conditions. They will be on standby inside the station and used should it become absolutely necessary after extracting the two of you from the hotel compound."

"We'll be prepared for it too, Jack, if necessary. Moreover, if everything falls into place as planned, Gabriela and I will be wrapping up the interviews inside the hotel, followed by watching local TV coverage of what took place earlier at the nearby train station. Following that, we look forward to sticking with our schedule and departing from Beijing the following day."

"I have no reason, Mitch, to expect otherwise."

"Is there anything else, Jack?"

"The director has instructed me to follow you guys, in two days time, to Beijing. I will remain there, inside the station, and act on his behalf should it become necessary. He asked that I pass on to both of you his best regards and expectations for your success."

"In other words, it would appear to me that the situation with North Korea and China is such that your presence there may be necessary should our successful hit against Kim escalate tensions with the Chinese and you need to carry a message on his behalf."

"Leave it to you, Mitch, to make a perceptive observation. From what the director told me, our Agency's growing relationship with China's national intelligence service, the Ministry of State Security, has begun to blossom. Part of that relationship entails exchanging information on Kim, his regime's ambitions, their nuclear program, and now, what the naming of his younger son to succeed him means for China. Some years ago the director personally took the lead in establishing this delicate liaison relationship with the MSS. I would have thought though, that our COS in the station could certainly do the same job if called upon. However, the director said his preference is having me on the ground in Beijing instead."

"Obviously, Jack, this will not have any impact on what Gabriela and I will be setting out to accomplish. Moreover, it's good knowing that other things are going on that certainly could come into play should we have anything but a clean successful hit and subsequent safe departure from the country."

"With that, you two, you've planned for success, now go and achieve it."

CHAPTER 41

The sky was just beginning to lighten as the early dawn beckoned all of the ships to come closer to each other. Captain Otani stood at his command post in the Control Room of the Akagi. The sub was gliding effortlessly at a depth of 200 feet, and on a parallel course with the North Korean Kilo sub that submerged just minutes earlier. Running at a periscope depth of 65 feet, the Kilo was about to maintain visual contact with the four mini subs running on the surface one mile away.

Ordering the diving officer to take the Akagi up to 78 feet, and remain on course, Captain Otani would be able to establish communications with both his own headquarters in Kure, as well as with Captaine Lee aboard the Suh Hoowon, which was continuing to run in tandem from a position a few miles astern. As the sun continued to rise further into a clear sky in the east, visibility on the sea surface was becoming very good.

With the North Korean mother ship now in a position astern of the mini subs, the initial exercise for them commenced. They proceeded to separate into two groups of two each and take up adversarial positions. While two of them remained on the surface, the other two boats dove to their periscope depths and, in tandem, proceeded to move away for a distance of three miles. At that point, the exercise called for the two submerged boats to plot simulated torpedo runs on the two surfaced boats.

For the next several hours, by which time the sun reached its apex, the Suh Hoowon and the Akagi observed from a respectful distance the four mini subs as they took turns making torpedo runs on each other. They also practiced regrouping in a wolf pack of four vessels and making a practice run against the mother vessel. None of their exercises involved any movement towards their submerged Kilo, which stayed in a shadowing position in between the four vessels and where the Suh Hoowon continued to steam in an oblong ring along the outer fringe of the exercise area. For the time being, both the Suh Hoowon and the Akagi, for their part, maintained radio silence since no hostile moves had been made by any of the North Korean vessels. The Akagi, being fully aware of the Suh Hoowon's location, maintained a submerged intersecting position of protection in the event the situation towards the ROK vessel on the surface changed.

Change was indeed about to come when the young general Kim, who was continuing to monitor the radio traffic with the Kilo and the mother ship from RGB headquarters, decided to exercise his authority as a recently appointed four-star general in his father's army. He instructed his mentor, the RGB Commander, to order the mini subs to play a cat and mouse game with the Suh Hoowon by making a series of feinting moves towards the ship's position on the fringe of the exercise area where the ROK continued steaming an oblong circle. The commander suggested to young Kim though, that only two of the mini subs become involved in such a provocative move, while the remaining two move closer towards the mother ship's position. Young Kim agreed and the commands were radioed to the mother ship, the Kilo sub, and the four mini subs.

When a radar operator on the Suh Hoowon first spotted the mini subs changing course that resulted in two of them turning to head towards his ship, he immediately informed the bridge. This potentially hostile move prompted Captain Lee to break radio silence and inform Captain Otani aboard the Akagi.

"Otani-san, we have two of the mini subs heading toward us on a bearing of 280 degrees, and a distance of 12,000 yards."

"Lee-san, I can confirm that. We have them on radar as well. Our position is to their starboard side at 8,500 yards. How do you intend to handle the situation?"

"As you can see, Otani-san, we are already well within their torpedo range. Therefore, I will not be waiting much longer if they continue their present course towards us. Have you been able to detect that they are arming their torpedoes and preparing to fire?"

"Not at this point, Lee-san. Stand by for a moment."

"We have our anti-ship missiles ready to fire, Otani-san. They should easily eliminate the two subs, but it will then require us to use our higher speed to outmaneuver their torpedoes if they are fired first."

"Lee-san, they are increasing their speed towards you and remain running on the surface. They have just now armed their torpedoes. We will provide cover for you against the Kilo, and the remaining two mini subs if they change their posture and make any aggressive moves toward you in any way."

At this point, Captain Lee ordered the firing of two ROK Sea Star Anti-ship Missiles, and the chaos that comes with an opening battle at sea began to unfold.

No sooner had the missiles been loosed from the Suh Hoowon, than Captain Lee ordered a hard turn to port and emergency full speed ahead. This move served to begin taking his ship away from the anticipated unknown number of torpedoes that could well be coming his way from the two mini subs.

At the same time, Captain Otani ordered battle stations and taking the Akagi up to 150 feet in order to float the buoy that would enable the electronics warfare officer to commence signal jamming of all shipboard wireless data communications that might be emanating from North Korean ships in the area. Although it would block his own efforts to maintain radio telephone contact with Captain Lee, it also meant that the North Korean vessels would be prevented from transmitting any messages back to their home bases or even among themselves. Initially, none of these vessels would be aware of the jamming, until they tried to receive incoming messages and found them to be unreadable due to the random noises, tones and pulses blocking out all receptions.

Even the mother ship, bristling with antennas and capable of instant communications with bases in North Korea, would be helpless in face of the broad spectrum massive power output being sent out by the Akagi's generating equipment, specifically designed to play havoc with enemy communications, whether it be obvious, as in this case, or subtle during which no sounds at all are heard on a ship's receiving equipment.

In quick succession, the captain of the Kilo sub, whose radar picked up the firing of the Sea Stars, immediately ordered a deep dive from the shallow periscope depth where he had been cruising between the mother ship and the mini-subs. Believing that his ship might be the next target, that unfortunate move on his part prevented the Kilo from being in a position to respond timely against the Suh Hoowon. By diving deep, precious minutes were lost in being able to recover and return up to a shallower depth and come to a favorable firing position for retaliation.

Within just a couple of seconds after the launch, the turbofan engines from the Sea Stars powered the missiles quickly up to a speed of Mach 1 and onto their targets. The resultant total obliteration of the two mini-subs took place in a thunderous cacophony that was accompanied by two huge upward spirals of white water where the two subs had been a moment before.

Captain Otani called for the Akagi's sonar officer to report on the status of any torpedoes that may have been fired by the two mini subs that were no longer in existence. His reply was, "nothing in the water, sir."

Turning to his diving officer, the captain said: "Give me a firing solution on the Kilo. I also want bearings on the remaining two mini-subs as well as the mother vessel. Maintain silent running and alert all the crew for possible quick evasive action," he added.

With that, the two helmsmen, who were seated five feet away from the captain, each instinctively knew to reach down and pull tighter their seat belts that held them in front of their control wheel stations. If the Akagi was going to go up against the Kilo, they knew the kind of roller coaster ride the crew could experience.

"Open bow torpedo doors one, two, three and four. Flood the tubes and arm the torpedoes."

"Aye, Captain," the diving officer replied. "I have a firing solution on the Kilo, sir. She took a steep dive and is leveling out at 400 feet. She also is running at a 20 degree angle on our starboard side, and is beginning to commence a turn and make a run toward the Suh Hoowon."

"Fire tubes one and two," the captain ordered.

With that, only two slight lurching movements forward could be felt inside the Akagi, as the Mitsubishi Heavy Industries-made Type 89 II homing torpedoes leaped in a massive eruption of air bubbles out of their tubes.

"Tubes one and two fired," was the reply.

Set to reach their maximum speed of just over 80 miles per hour, this latest generation of Japanese wire-guided torpedoes covered the 9,000 yards distance in less than two minutes. Rapidly transitioning through their three phases of moving into the vicinity of the target, maneuvering for acquiring the target and, subsequently, the final pursuit or homing in on the target, the Kilo was easy prey for such sophisticated technology brought to bear against it.

The Kilo sub's sonar operator barely had time to holler out that the two torpedoes were coming in their direction, than the captain ordered a full astern and hard port maneuver in a last-ditch attempt to try and take his ship out of harm's way. He also ordered that decoys be launched to try and attract the incoming torpedoes away from his ship. Within seconds, he then ordered full stop and rudder amid ship in a futile attempt that would serve as the last order he would ever give. The initial effect of the full stop order resulted in an immediate drag on the ship's propeller, causing a massive amount of bubbles to form, encircling the entire rear section of the ship. The captain was hoping that this cavitations maneuver would further serve to distract the incoming torpedoes as the Kilo's forward momentum allowed it to glide away from the patch of bubbles.

The maneuver came too late, and both torpedoes impacted near simultaneously in the center of the Kilo's control room compartment amidships. A muffled roar from the explosion was immediately heard back on the Akagi, accompanied by a slow jiggling vibration felt as North Korea's latest addition to their submarine fleet ceased to exist. The two sonar operators on duty aboard the Akagi could hear the tumultuous crackling breakup of the Kilo as it commenced its plummet in a multitude of pieces to the bottom of the Sea of Japan.

Maintaining his course and speed, Captain Otani ordered the jamming of all communications signals to continue as he raised one of the Akagi's attack periscopes and scanned the choppy waters to check on the status of the mother ship and remaining two mini subs. While the two boats appeared to be motionless in the water, the mother ship was underway and slowly headed in the direction where the Kilo went down. After receiving the bearing and distance of the Suh Hoowon's heading, four miles away on a southerly course, Captain Otani focused his attention on the remaining threat posed by the two mini subs and their compliment of deadly torpedoes capable of being launched at any time. When the diving officer informed him that sonar was detecting a course change for the two remaining mini subs that would take them directly behind the mother ship on a northerly course, the captain hesitated from issuing the order to fire two more torpedoes from tubes three and four. With the three North Korean vessels appearing to be making preparations to go into a search mode nearing the Kilo's last known position, the captain decided to continue southward in the direction of the Suh Hoowon, since he no longer considered the mini subs or the mother ship a threat.

Ordering a halt to the jamming of communications signals, the float buoy's low frequency antenna was used to send an immediate Emergency Action Message to the Akagi's headquarters at Kure. The news of a Japanese submarine and a ROK patrol boat involved in the sinking of a North Korean Kilo submarine and two mini subs in the Sea of Japan, resulted in the U.S. Air Force Global Strike Command issuing a special alert. Included in the call up were more than 40 B-2 and B-52 strategic bombers from Anderson Air Force Base on the island of Guam, along with more than 100 fighter aircraft from the 5th Air Force stationed in Japan. In the event of hostilities on the Korean Peninsula, these would be the primary aircraft to be used against North Korea. Captain Otani was ordered by Kure's headquarters to provide escort duty for the Suh Hoowon, as she steamed southwest on a course for the patrol boat's home base in South Korea. Re-establishing secure radio telephone with Captain Lee, he and Captain Otani thanked each other for the assist and, once again, pledged their willingness to come to each other's aid whenever called upon.

"Lee-san, remember some time back when you told me about your liking for western movies?" asked Captain Otani.

"Yes, Otani-san. I remember it well. You told me that you also enjoyed them a lot."

"Well, in fine western movie fashion, we just bushwhacked some of the bad guys."

"Including the mini subs and the Kilo, Otani-san, they all are no more. You did a great service for both our countries. Thank you."

"Likewise, Captain Lee, you did the same. I thank you too."

What started out as a routine surveillance exercise of North Korean naval vessels venturing further out into the Sea of Japan than previously known, turned into a major incident costing the lives of 92 Iranian and North Korean sailors. With not a single loss of life on the South Korean and Japanese sides, it was unknown if this event would trigger a larger conflict to come, once the mother ship was able to re-open jammed communications with its home base in Chaho and RGB intelligence bureau headquarters in Pyongyang. No doubt, upon young Kim hearing the news, he would have much to think about regarding his foray into exercising his new powers in the arena of military gamesmanship.

CHAPTER 42

After receiving word from Agency headquarters that communication intercepts revealed that the dates were set for Kim Jong-Il and his son, the young Kim, to visit Beijing, Mitch, Gabriela and Gene immediately booked their flight and hotel reservations for their return there. Fortunately, late spring is not yet a busy time for the tourist hordes to descend upon the major cities of China. As a result, no problems were encountered in making their reservations.

Gabriela also telephoned the business center at the Marriott City Wall Hotel to finalize with the staff there the dates for the job candidate interviews in the business center. Mitch completed his emails to the various university professors he met with during his earlier visit, so they would coordinate with the student job candidates on their availability during the dates selected for meeting at the hotel.

Insofar Jack, since he would be going separately to Beijing as the DCI's representative in the event that meeting with MSS intelligence service officials became necessary, he made his own separate flight arrangements. He sent a cable to the station in Beijing and requested he be provided with lodging inside the embassy compound during his stay. He also confirmed that Mitch's sniper rifle and ammo had gone out in the pouch, along with encrypted short-range commo devices for the team's use during the op.

During their final evening in San Francisco, Mitch and Gabriela enjoyed dinner at an upscale French restaurant on Nob Hill. They both knew that, like themselves, a father and son were also in the process of making their own plans for a trip to Beijing. Only their trip would be by train, from Pyongyang to Beijing, and would last for 26 hours. The following day, by the time Mitch and Gabriela had completed their uneventful non-stop flight from San Francisco to Beijing, and were resting up in their separate Marriott rooms, Kim Jong-Il and young Kim were departing from Pyongyang for Beijing and their four-day visit with the Chinese leadership, including a couple of days for Kim to show his son some of the tourist sites there.

The trip was designed to introduce young Kim to the very leaders he would come to rely upon once he took over the reins of power with the passing of his father. While China's influence over the bellicose, isolated and insolvent state was limited, the aid and protection that it provided served as a form of reassurance to the concerns of what a collapsed North Korea would mean for the entire region of North Asia. Foremost in the mind of China's military leadership was the need for stability on its border with North Korea. Unfortunately for these same leaders, they had come to realize that under the erratic rule of Kim Jong-Il, and his success in building a nuclear weapons' stockpile, stability on the border had become elusive.

Furthermore, due to an unfortunate turn of events, Kim Jong-Il was arriving in Beijing in the foulest of moods. Only a few days earlier he learned of his son's precipitous actions that resulted in the loss of North Korean and Iranian sailors, as well as the sinking of North Korea's single Kilo submarine and two mini-subs. Inasmuch as Kim sought to establish his son's military bona fides, he was infuriated to learn the young Kim took it upon himself to go that fateful morning to RGB headquarters and order the provocative course of action resulting in the subsequent disaster. Knowing that China's intelligence agencies would have picked up intercepts of North Korean naval message traffic before and after the disaster in the Sea of Japan, the last thing he wanted to be compelled to do was start off the visit in Beijing with having to make an explanation in front of the Chinese leadership.

*   *   *

After meeting with the hotel business center staff, inspecting the meeting room facilities and choosing from a selection of light refreshments to serve the visiting candidates over the course of the next several days, Mitch and Gabriela settled in at the hotel's third floor lounge to discuss their game plan.

"Mitch, do you expect anything will appear publicly in the local press or on TV announcing the arrival of Kim and his son?"

"No, not really. From what I recall from the Agency briefing on his last couple of trips here, the only real indicator is the change in train track schedules for trains arriving from China's northeast provinces. The primary track into the Beijing Railway Station for trains from Pyongyang will be blocked off and reserved for his heavily armored train, plus the identical twin dummy train that travels with it. With the announcement of the canceling of that track for other trains, the local press will pick up on it and ferret out a limited amount of information, which subsequently will make its way onto TV as well, in announcing the anticipated arrival of Kim and his entourage."

"The amount of secrecy and security arrangements surrounding this guy is nothing less than astounding."

"I like to think of it as deep-seated paranoia about being assassinated. It is thoroughly ingrained not only in Kim himself, but throughout the thinking of his protective security staff as well. At least we know that, based upon his previous trips, he is predictable, fortunately, for both the time he arrives in Beijing and the time he departs. Moreover, upon departing, he likes to stand at the open window of his train car and wave to the station onlookers as it slowly pulls out of the station. For me, that is all the predictability I need to do my job. Everything else in his schedule, plans and movements, are all quite unpredictable."

"It's fascinating to think about these little quirks that people have about themselves. Some of them can make excellent sense from a personal security perspective, while others can be a person's undoing. I've seen this in other targets that I have worked against, and it always seems to remain true.

"I have no reason, Gabriela, to think it will be any different this time."

"By starting our interview sessions with the students on the day of his arrival, with both of us spacing out the number of interviews as the four days pass by, you should be able to have a solid alibi to cover the period of time you are actually next door in the hotel's storage building."

"I just hope you succeed in covering for me by making it appear I am behind a closed door in one of the interview rooms. By the way, we both need to remember the protocol about limiting the use of our secure calls between us, as well as with Gene. The local services intercept capabilities are first rate, even if they are not able to decipher what is being said. I would expect that several mobile vans or stationary observation posts near us and the train station will be on duty when Kim arrives and departs, and capable of triangulating by GPS our positions."

"How did you leave it with Gene then, insofar advising you on Kim's movements?"

"He will be on the outer periphery of the large open area in front of the railway station's main entrance, when comes time for Kim to arrive there by car and be escorted into the station and to his train. Gene will call and all I will get is a couple of beeps giving me the heads up. That will allow me to get into my setup mode up in the window."

"With me, at that point continuing on in the meeting rooms with the candidates, I am confident of being able to make it appear you are there as well."

"Once I receive Gene's beep, he will proceed on foot over here to the hotel in order to take up a position to observe the train station platform from the top floor bar. Once I finish the job, I will then beep him, and he will take the elevator down to the basement level in order to do the brush pass of the rifle in the bag."

"During our earlier trip here for the pre-hit survey, he mentioned that he can walk the distance between the station and the hotel in approximately six minutes."

"After the pass, I return to the meeting rooms and join you in continuing the interviews. Hopefully, by that point, only a few candidates, at most, will be remaining there. As for Gene, he will take a taxi out of the immediate area, eastward and away from the hotel, and meet up with the security officer and give him the rifle to take back to the station in the embassy."

"Mitch, what about the Boogie Box? I still cannot get over the briefing you arranged for me in Sausalito. I had no idea such a thing existed, much less used so successfully. Was I overly surprised? No, not really. However, for me to be inside one, wow."

"As I understood it when your briefing was over, two of the boxes will be on standby inside the Agency station here. It's a possibility that one or both could come into play once the hit on Kim is made."

"Knowing it may only require that I be inside one for a few hours will make it doable. I'll by O.K. How do you feel about the way everything else is shaping up now?"

"I feel very good right about now. I'm up to the task. When I finish, I know I'll be on a real high. My only problem, deep down, is being able to learn to turn that high feeling off and walk away. What are your thoughts?"

"I feel good as well. We've proved to be a real team and forged a bond between us as a result. It will enable us to succeed in this one as well."

The clock continued counting down and, in two days time, while the candidates were beginning their interviews with Mitch and Gabriela in the hotel meeting rooms, the train arrived at the nearby Beijing Railway Station carrying Kim Jong-Il and the young Kim.

CHAPTER 43

Armed with his trusty Hasselblad digital camera and shoulder carrying bag, Gene returned to the area around the Beijing Railway Station. This time, however, he focused his attention on the sprawling, park-like, 10-acre main front entrance on the north side, instead of the south side along the ancient city wall that he reconnoitered during his previous visit to the city. Doing a repeat of timing his walk from the station directly eastwards along Maojiawan Hutong Road to the Marriott City Wall Hotel, where Mitch and Gabriela were in the second day of interviews, again, only six minutes were needed to cover the short distance.

Going from the hotel back to the station, this time he walked around it to the south side, along the old city wall park area he covered so extensively during the pre-hit survey. Walking to the east side of the station, he could look out over the track marshaling yard. From there he could see the two all-black armored trains from Pyongyang, parked on one of the station's long spur tracks leading eastward away from the station.

By pre-arrangement with Jack, now ensconced inside the Agency's station inside the embassy, Gene expected that, in two day's time, during the afternoon, he would receive the coded beeping signal on his cell phone indicating that Kim Jong-Il, young Kim and their entourage had completed their visit and were returning to the train station for their departure back to Pyongyang. That would mean Gene should make sure to be in a position in front of the main entrance to the station to confirm that Kim and party had arrived and were entering through the guarded VIP entrance for escort to the train platform and their waiting train.

Mitch was also expecting to receive the same coded beep message as Gene, except that, in his case, he would already be holed up in one of the upper floor windows. It would serve to let him know Kim arrived at the station and would soon be boarding his train. By making his way along the hotel's basement passageway to the building before sunrise on the day of Kim's departure, it meant Mitch probably would be spending close to ten hours in position there. In order not to be seen by any of the hotel's staff in traversing through the passageway, he had no choice in the matter. Gabriela, in the meantime, would continue with the day's interviews, including making it appear that Mitch was in one of the rooms doing his own interviews as well.

Before they parted company and retired for the evening after three days of interviews, Gabriela gave Mitch a key to the locked passageway door for his use early the next morning. During their previous stay at the hotel, she was able to make an imprint of the lock when she picked it to enter the passageway for her first foray into the building next door. She tested the copy out late one evening after their return to the hotel. It was perfect.

Neither of them slept very well knowing what lay ahead the following day. Tossing and turning most all the night, Mitch was only able to get about two hours of sleep before his alarm went off at five a.m. He got up, showered, shaved and dressed. He put on a business suit, white shirt and tie that he would wear all day long, including when he returned to the hotel to resume a last remaining interview or two.

He felt good about the way the interviews for him and Gabriela had turned out over the past three days. He was also able to spend a fair amount of time with a number of the candidates' professors who came to the hotel to talk further about the personnel recruitment and job placement process, as well as talk about some of their student candidates. He was left with the distinct impression that the overall cover for the operation was holding up very well. He also was more than satisfied with Gabriela's solid performance in the conduct of her interviews going into the final fourth day. She showed a high level of business acumen, and was turning in a credible professional performance in her own right.

For Mitch, all he could do was to wait it out in a section of the seventh floor that he created for himself by moving around a number of large cardboard storage boxes around the window from which he would be shooting. He built a small area in front of the window that could conceal him entirely. He could not be seen by anyone when exiting the elevator, or coming up the stairwell. While quietly moving around the boxes to fashion his hideout, he was reminded of building a fort when he was a kid and using it when playing games with his friends.

He purposely traveled light since, once the hit was made, he would have to restore the area to what it looked like before he arrived. Wearing surgical gloves throughout his time inside the building, in order to avoid leaving fingerprints, he carried the sniper rifle concealed in an oversize tennis bag. It was designed to hold several rackets, a few cans of balls and some sports clothing. However, it turned out to be perfect for the rifle, suppressor, supporting tripod and ammo. Mitch even had enough room left for two bottles of drinking water and a couple multigrain energy bars to sustain him through the day in front of the window.

Just a few minutes after three in the afternoon, while he was looking out the window overlooking the rail yard and observing one of the armored trains moving into position to back into the station and the platform where Kim and his entourage would be boarding, Mitch received the signal on his phone indicating Kim's motorcade would shortly be arriving at the station. Mitch moved to get himself into position behind the window, and the cardboard boxes stacked there to serve as the shooting platform. On top was the rifle with its tripod extended. The window remained closed. What followed was the second beeping signal on the phone, this time from Gene. This told Mitch that Kim was about to enter the train station and make his way to the platform.

Having earlier done the set up for the L115A3 rifle, it now sat on top of the sturdy and packed boxes at the ready. What remained was to open the window upwards for a distance of no more than four to five inches. This would provide a clear view from which to shoot. The sound suppressor on the end of the barrel would not even protrude out the window and, with no lights on inside the basically semi-darkened room, Mitch and the rifle would be unobservable from the outside world around the building.

Not knowing if the window of the train that Kim would be standing in front of and waving from would be open or closed, the magazine in the bolt-action rifle was loaded with .338 Lapua Magnum armor-piercing rounds. No protective bullet-resistant window glass material was known to be available anywhere in the world that could stop the penetrating power of a magnum round from this superior sniping rifle. With the short distance involved from up in the building's window firing position down to the train's window as it began to slowly pull out of the station, Mitch's level of confidence in succeeding in his mission was high. Of more concern though, was not in taking the shot, but rather in being able to exit the building unobserved, go through the brush pass with Gene and return upstairs in the hotel to the business center.

For one last time, Mitch stood next to the window and leaned forward to the edge of the window sill to check on the position of the sun outside, as well as the wind conditions. Facing directly westward, towards where the sun would soon be setting, he experienced a degree of glare and brightness that could be a factor in his shooting accuracy. In terms of the wind being a factor, Mitch looked across the rail yard to several flags hanging limply from poles next to the ancient city wall to the south of the station. He also spotted two flags on poles two buildings over from his, about 150 yards away. Again, these two were hanging limp as well, with barely a ripple of a breeze noticeable.

He was soon to make the most significant hit of his career, the third one in a short time span of only four months. However, it did not seem to register, or have much impact on him now. What mattered more was evading attribution for the shot and a clean getaway out of the country once the hit was made. It would now just be a matter of minutes and it would be over.

For young Kim, a hectic four days were coming to a close with the arrival of him and his father in the armored limousine back at the railway station. Following two days of high-level meetings with China's senior Communist Party officials, as well as the key military leaders, the last two were spent being shown a number of the more prominent sights of significance in and around Beijing. What intrigued young Kim the most was the size, scope and engineering that went into the construction of the Great Wall. After that, the Ming Tombs and the Temple of Heaven were of particular interest to him, given his own growing feelings of greatness being bestowed upon him since being named as his father's chosen successor. As much as he marveled at these sites of such historical importance in China, he knew very well that back in North Korea, long known by westerners as the "hermit kingdom," few similar sites of greatness could be found.

Walking just to the rear and side of his father as they were being escorted through the VIP section of the station, young Kim was looking forward to resting up during the trip back to Pyongyang. After being constantly at his father's side for the full four days, and still being reminded and harangued by the senior Kim about the fateful decision made to provoke the ROK ship in the Sea of Japan, he wanted to be left alone and out of sight of him.

One last duty to perform, that of standing in the windows of the train and waving their goodbyes to the controlled crowd of Chinese onlookers and staff workers from the North Korean embassy, and it would finally be over.

Out on the street in front of the station, Gene, upon seeing both the Kims alight from the limousine and walk into the station, made his way for the last time toward the Marriott City Wall Hotel and the waiting brush pass with Mitch in the basement. He too was looking forward to completing their mission, getting out of the country and returning home for some much needed rest.

CHAPTER 44

Mitch glanced at his watch; it showed precisely 3 p.m. Looking up and out of the window, he could see the all-black armored train began its slow movement out of the station. He moved to open the window around four inches, noting that the titanium suppressor at the end of the barrel of the rifle, was just within two inches of where the closed window glass had been. Stepping back and assuming his seated shooting position, he was able to lean comfortably forward, with his elbows resting on the boxes, and grip the rifle.

Before peering through the Zeiss Hensoldt scope, he could see that the turret knob on its side was adjusted to the full 56 millimeters variable maximum. He easily lined up the cross hairs with no parallax error, on each of the successive car windows as they started to come into view. At this relatively short distance of 620 yards, he anticipated being able to see blemishes on Kim Jong-Il's face, once his car came out from under the extended station roof. Fortunately for Mitch, the angle and glare from the sun was not going to be a problem.

By the time the third car with windows came outside from underneath the roofing, with no one seen standing or moving in any of the cars corridors, Mitch knew that was about to change. With that, he immediately saw movement as the windows of the fourth car came into view. Men wearing dark suits were standing in each of the eight windows as the car glided slowly by. As the fifth car's windows started to come into view, no one was standing until the middle of the car. There, slowly coming into view was Kim Jong-Il and the young Kim, standing side by side and waving out of the closed windows at the last standing group of people there to see them off. They were both wearing the classic style Mao Tse-tung blue tunics, buttoned up to the neck.

Continuing to control his long breaths as he sighted on the upper portion of the kill box that framed the torso of Kim Jong-Il in his crosshairs, Mitch thought that at this range, he would hit his target directly in the center of the infrasternal notch. In other words, the .338 Caliber, 162 grain match grade armor-piercing projectile, would impact in the center of the upper chest at the sternum. With the train still straining to gather increased momentum as it slid out of the station, Mitch firmly aligned his scope sight, barely leading the target at all, as Kim continued his waving.

Taking up the slack on the trigger, he slowly applied center pressure with his trigger finger; he knew he must avoid disturbing his sight alignment until the weapon fired. By not knowing exactly when the weapon would fire, he would avoid any kind of flinching or jerking motion of any kind. He knew that this would provide him with the trigger surprise he sought as the rifle fired, and a steady shot would be assured.

In one last controlled breath, as he held the sights on the top center of the kill box, he continued squeezing the trigger with slightly increased pressure. The bullet fired and all that was heard was a spitting, phfft-like sound, as the round made its way past the titanium suppressor at the end of the barrel. It found its target through the resistant glass of the window of the fifth car. Kim Jong-Il was immediately lifted off his feet and thrown backwards against the compartment door wall behind him before he could wave that one last time to the people on the platform. The impact point was four inches below Kim's laryngeal prominence, or Adam's apple, exactly where Mitch was aiming for.

Since the copper jacket around the steel core of the bullet began to expand once it impacted and went through the resistant glass, the entry hole it subsequently made in the center of Kim's upper torso was two inches in diameter. As it coursed through his chest and exited through his spine, the steel core gave away to the innermost core of lead. As a result, the exit wound was massive. Kim was dead instantly as he was thrown back and began slipping down the wall of the compartment, to the corridor floor of the car.

Still wanting to maintain a sight picture after the firing of the round, Mitch continued with the rearward movement of his trigger finger after it had been fired. He could barely make out a small diameter hole through the window glass where Kim had been standing. The elder Kim was gone and Mitch caught a glimpse of young Kim falling over off to the side of where his father had stood, entirely disappearing from view.

In the dim and fading light that was left inside the room, Mitch took one last glance at the still moving train as it continued to gather speed coming out of the station. He could see a number of dark suited people, all quickly converging from both ends of the corridor to the center of the car from where Kim had been standing. With only 20 or so people waving at Kim at the end of the platform, all they would have seen was Kim collapsing backwards as the bullet entered the glass window, and he was gone from view. Moreover, with Kim's security personnel massing around the crumpled body on the corridor floor, the train continued picking up momentum as it made its way onward out of the station heading eastward in the direction of Pyongyang.

Lifting up the rifle and folding the tripod underneath the barrel, Mitch collapsed the rear stock of the rifle as well. He then packed it back inside the tennis bag, along with the two empty water bottles. Replacing all the packed cardboard boxes to where he found them in the room, he took one final detailed look around the area where he had spent the morning and a good portion of the afternoon. The last thing he needed was to leave behind any evidence of his presence up inside the storage room on that fateful day.

He encountered no one as he made his way down the stairs of the building and into the passageway leading back inside the hotel to the closed door at the end. He opened it slowly, glancing down the 80-foot lower basement hallway, with stairs and elevators located at the far end. Once again, he saw no one. Moving steadily down the hallway carrying the bag with the rifle concealed inside, he was about to reach the stairway when one of the elevators next to it opened. Out stepped Gene with a large grin on his face.

"How did it go?"

"Perfect. Exactly as planned."

"Congratulations Mitch. You still know your stuff."

"I wonder though, how much we will learn about it on the news."

"How's that?"

"As far as I could tell, the train did not stop. With his body on board they are still heading towards Pyongyang."

"Well, I'll be damned. That's an interesting development."

"Give me the bag, Mitch, and I will pass it on to a station officer within the hour."

"Thank you, Gene." Handing him the bag, followed by the pair of surgical gloves he'd worn throughout the day, Mitch added, "How about taking care of these as well?"

"My pleasure."

"What's your timetable for departing?"

"If I am able, I will try and re-book for a flight home tomorrow evening. What about you and Gabriela?"

"We should be winding up the interviews either late this afternoon or tomorrow morning, at the latest. We will try for a flight back home for the day after tomorrow."

"Do you have any reason, at this early stage, to expect complications, or anyone coming to the hotel to talk with you?"

"No, none at all. I'm confident that I left the shooting nest upstairs exactly as I found it, with no trace of my ever being there. The whole event just could not have gone any smoother."

"Just the way we like it. Take care and see you back home."

"You too, guy. Thank you."

Gene boarded the elevator and went up to one of the upper floors just above the hotel's main lobby. Switching elevators, he returned down, this time to the lobby level and, with the tennis bag in hand, strode out the front doors of the hotel and caught a taxi. After a 15-minute ride, he arrived at the Meisong Golf Driving Range, located east of the hotel. Entering the range's coffee shop next to the front entrance, he sat down, ordered an iced coffee and waited for a station officer to arrive and relieve him of the bag.

Mitch also took one of the elevators from the lower level, up to the business center level located one floor above the main lobby. Before going into the center, he took off his suit jacket and, entering a men's toilet next to it, proceeded to act as though he was cleaning the jacket off, as if he had spilled something on it. Leaving the toilet and going into the center, he made his way to the interview rooms. When one of the center's attendants saw him, he approached her and said he had to clean some coffee stains off of his jacket. Asking that a fresh pot of coffee be brought to the interview room assigned to him, he went inside it and acted as if he had been there all along. He knew that, depending upon how Gabriela was able to cover for him during the day, he might well have a plausible story to use, should it become necessary.

When the room door opened and the attendant stepped inside with the pot of coffee, she was followed by Gabriela. As the coffee pot was being set on a sideboard next to the interview table and chairs, Gabriela turned to Mitch and asked: "Mr. Vasari, are you ready for your final interview of the day?"

"Why yes, I certainly am," he replied. "It's been a long day for both of us."

Once the attendant left the room, she went on to describe how she had covered for him during portions of the day, including telling some of the business center staff that he had gone on some errands near the hotel, plus was holding another interview meeting at a different location since one of the graduate students was unable to come to the hotel. "No one on the staff here specifically asked for you," she said, "and I had no trouble making it appear as though you were in the room doing your own interviews. By the way, with that Cheshire grin on your face, I take it to mean all went well for you today."

"It could not have gone better. Everything took place exactly as planned, including the loss to the world of one of the last remaining despots."

"Does that mean we are going to celebrate together tonight?"

"Yes, it certainly does. In addition, I hope it will last as far into the night as possible too."

"I will do my best to make sure that happens."

CHAPTER 45

No sooner had the United Airlines wide body aircraft carrying Mitch and Gabriela lifted off from Beijing Capital International Airport, when the secure landline telephone rang inside the Agency station chief's specially constructed telephone booth inside his office at the embassy. The entire eight-story main embassy building, which stands inside a ten-acre compound, is known as a sensitive compartmented information facility, or SCIF. The Agency's station inside it occupies 20 percent of the building. The COS' telephone booth, also fashioned as a SCIF, serves as a double layer of security when used for discussing sensitive information.

The call was from the office of the chief of China's premier intelligence service, the Ministry of State Security. Geng Huichang was appointed as Minister of the MSS in 2007 and, throughout his tenure, maintained a direct liaison relationship with whoever was assigned to Beijing as the Agency's Chief of Station. As a protégé of an earlier MSS Minister, Jia Chunwang, Geng also exhibited a fondness for dealing with the CIA, and enjoyed his occasional meetings with the COS. This call to request a meeting would be no exception, except that Geng asked to meet with Jack Benson instead, the special visitor from headquarters. The COS, taking the request in stride, since he did not want to ask how Geng even knew about Jack, said he would see to it that Jack was at the requested place. The meeting location was thought by the COS to be unusual, especially given the demise of Kim Jong-Il two days earlier on Chinese soil. The COS did not know what to expect.

Geng asked that Jack, if at all possible, met with him within the hour, at a guesthouse located inside Zhongnanhai, the restricted Communist Party and State Council central headquarters area, on the west side of the Forbidden City. Replying in the affirmative, the COS was further told that Jack was to only be accompanied by an escort driver. Geng apologized to the COS for this kind of request, but said it would be for the best this way.

The COS, by coincidence, had Jack at his side in the office when the call from Geng first came through. Jack readily agreed to Geng's request with an affirmative nod of his head. Before Jack left the embassy, the COS sent an immediate precedence cable to headquarters in order to get Geng's unusual request to meet with Jack on the official record. He also used his secure office telephone to call the Chief of China Operations in the East Asia Division at headquarters, since he was the COS's predecessor and had met with Geng on numerous occasions. As he was about to leave the embassy for the meeting, Jack stopped by the ambassador's office to advise him of going to meet with Geng, along with the location inside Zhongnanhai for the meeting.

Beijing has a multitude of picturesque sights throughout the city, many shrouded in a long history of mystery and intrigue. Few compare with the area in and around the Forbidden City, particularly on the west side around Beihai Park, which comprises the center of Zhongnanhai. Completely surrounded by vermilion walls, the area has long been known as China's Kremlin. Jack, as a student of China's history and cultural traditions, wondered what he was getting himself into as his driver made way, in light traffic, to the guarded entrance on the northernmost section of the complex.

At the restricted gate area, one of the two uniformed and armed People's Liberation Army soldiers there instructed the driver, in excellent English, to drive through and park in any of the several open spaces just inside the gate and remain at the car. The driver did as he was instructed. Jack opened the door and stepped out of the car and found himself looking at a fit man in a dark suit who had pulled a golf cart up alongside the car. He introduced himself as Zhou and asked Jack to accompany him to the meeting with Geng.

Driving on a well-maintained concrete path, they went to the central lake area that comprises one of the three small bodies of water in the complex. They stopped alongside a lush garden of flowering plants, dense foliage and recently trimmed camphor trees. In the center of this quiet and secluded area, along the edge of the water, stood a small ornate guesthouse that was constructed in the classical Chinese design. Jack was asked to enter through the carved wooden door and step inside where Geng was waiting.

Greeting Jack effusively, Geng shook his hand and, with a warm grin on his face, invited him to step out the back of the guesthouse onto an open deck area overlooking the body of water which was virtually choked with blooming pink and white water lilies. Known as the "Central Sea," it was, along with the other two lakes, called the northern and southern seas, constructed in the early 1400s as irrigation projects in support of the building of the imperial palace next door that is now known as the Forbidden City.

"I want to thank you, Mr. Benson, for accepting my invitation to meet on such short notice," said Geng.

"The pleasure is mine. Please call me Jack. I would speak to you in Mandarin, but I am long out of practice, and would be an embarrassment to myself."

"Don't worry, Jack. Let's stay with the English. I hope though, I won't be the one that is embarrassed."

"You underestimate your language capability. You are doing very well."

"Thank you. You are very kind. I asked to see you today before the events that took place two days ago grow old, and their true meaning gets distorted as the news media the world over tries to explain what happened."

"I'm certainly fascinated to learn what you are about to say."

"Your coyness belies one of your significant attributes as an intelligence officer. Are you sure you don't have some Chinese as ancestors in your past?"

"I wish I did since it would make me a much wiser man."

"I asked your COS to send you here alone today because we know that you were sent out with a special mission in mind—a mission that should not require you to do anything except enjoy your visit and return home. The only exception would be if some part of the mission went awry, and it became necessary for you to contact me first, to request a meeting, instead of the other way around."

"What can I say? I am in your country as a guest, and in a position where I much prefer to listen."

"By the way, I hope the COS is not insulted by my not inviting him as well today. We have a good relationship, and I enjoy his company, whenever we are together. If he is upset, please reassure him of no disrespect on my part. The state of my relationship with him is on a different level, and quite separate from the subject of this meeting."

"I will let him know what you have said."

"If it had been possible for me to meet today with your DCI, Ben Wicksford, then he would be with me now in your place. He and I enjoyed an especially good relationship for a number of years, starting when he was posted here as the COS. We started out by playing cat and mouse with each other, trying to size each other up and determine where any exploitable vulnerability, as you call them in your recruitment process, might be found. Neither of us could find any, at least I was not able to find any in him."

"Ben was not able to find any because he realized you are a true man of Han."

"Now that, Jack, is your Chinese side coming out. It was spoken like a true Confucian at his best.

"Many years ago, a Chinese acquaintance told me that the Chinese looked upon themselves as the Jews of the Orient. When I disagreed with him, I could tell he was upset, and I had hurt his feelings. That was until I followed up my statement by saying that, instead, I preferred to think of the Chinese as the jewels of the Orient.

That solidified my relationship with the fellow, and I thought I had found a true friend. However, he was not open to recruitment either."

"This tells me why Ben can trust you with the mission he sent you here for. With his well-developed appreciation for China, I would bet the two of you are on the best of terms."

"I certainly believe so."

"I am going to continue to tell you about why you are here with me today. Two days ago, on our Chinese soil, a team from your Agency was successful in ridding the world of a troublemaker whom we in China, as well as many of you in the U.S., no longer had any reason to see continue to live. The death of Kim Jong-Il turns out to be a good omen for both our countries. By the way, if you don't already know it, after the shooting, Kim's security detail aboard the train made the decision to continue out of the station, and take the body directly back to Pyongyang without stopping."

"What about the people who were watching from the station platform? I have not seen anything in your local media the past two days of what might have been seen?"

"I could do nothing about the Korean embassy people who were on the platform and might have witnessed him going down inside the train car. But I ordered a clampdown on any Chinese there who might have witnessed it."

"I would expect some of the details will begin to leak out relatively soon. It sounds though, that you certainly have things under control."

"As much as our government, and particularly my own ministry, does not tolerate such unilateral action by another government in conducting an assassination inside our borders, your Agency's selection of doing the job here was obviously the best choice. We both know that keeping track of Kim's whereabouts is not an easy task and, since we are literally the only other country he travels to, your decision was the correct one."

"You have me in a very awkward position right now. Because I so value our intelligence liaison relationship with the MSS, and in particular, the personal relationship that you and I have established with our DCI, I certainly hope no damage has been done that will affect our dealings in the future."

"Fortunately, your Agency decided to choose a target whose time had come. Since we obviously would not undertake doing the job ourselves, and he travels literally no where else, we allowed you to do it here instead. As far as I am concerned, better your people doing it than mine. I should also mention that your team's planning and execution appears to have just about been flawless. I see no reason for your actions to affect the relationship in any way."

"What can I say to that?"

"I would say to start by commending the team for pulling it off so successfully."

"It would appear that your MSS managed to oversee what was taking place all along. Is that what you mean about the operation almost being flawless?"

"I don't like taking credit where it is not due, but your two principal members of the team, who are by now out of Chinese airspace and safely on their way back to America, are on that aircraft because we allowed it to happen. Nevertheless, except for a very few unprofessional slipups on their part, they still would probably have been able to pull it off, even if we were unaware of what was going to take place."

"I am intrigued by you saying that Kim's time had come."

"Yes, inasmuch as we have tolerated him for years, in order to have stability on our border with his country, his demands on us have become too much. With him ruling over a ruined economy, but overemphasizing instead building a nuclear weapon capability, it convinced us his demise was in order."

"We in the U.S. have the same deep concern about a nuclear weapon-armed North Korea, especially when it includes long-range missiles. Kim was becoming unpredictable, and we have also begun receiving evidence of certain ranking military figures and senior members of the Workers Party secreting funds out of the country and laying the groundwork for future exit routes."

"Our sources have also picked up on these same developments and now that he went ahead and selected his young son to succeed him, our interest in taking action appears to have crossed paths with your own."

"What is your view on the young Kim being able to rule the country?"

"Not very good at all. His older sister and her husband show signs of wanting to take over, but we believe the aging military will not stand for it. The Korean people need an authoritative leader, and we judge the people as willing to be ruled by a strong hand. However, the answer is not to be found in anyone else from the Kim family. The question is whether one of the senior military figures will make a move to take over from the young Kim, since your operation to remove his father succeeded and could indeed serve to precipitate such an action."

"Do you have any particular military officer in mind that would be acceptable to China?"

"Yes, actually we do. For now though, I think it best to hold off discussing it further. I will consider returning to the subject in the future. I realize that giving you that kind of information now would make for one hell of a report back in Washington."

"I look forward to it."

"Let me finish our meeting by saying the strong economy of China, along with the great wealth we are accumulating, including our valuable investments in the U.S., is not going to be wasted or jeopardized by the fall of other governments and their leaders who pursue such dangerous foreign and domestic policies."

"I could not agree with you more."

"You must understand that we do not like what you did in the hit on Kim on our Chinese soil. However, since it was in our interest as well, we will allow it to pass. I have been instructed by the highest level of my government to convey to your government that both of our countries are poised to keep the world at peace through cooperation. Because of the strengths of both our economies, we will be able to share a destiny of leading the world together."

"Your message will be favorably received and much appreciated in Washington. By the way, would you mind if I asked about the slipup that the team made here during the operation?"

"Ah yes, I knew that you would come back around to my earlier comment, and not let it pass. When your team made a visit to Beijing several months back, we did some routine background checks on, I believe, three people. One of them, an actual professional photographer, turned out to be of interest due to his background of being in places around the world at times of high interest to your Agency, as well as mine. The other two, who I will refer to by the names they used here, Mitch and Gabriela, turned up of mixed interest. Although we did not find any useful information about her, the covers she used and past activities in her background gave us nothing to indicate she is an intelligence operative. She, nevertheless, is known to turn up where paramilitary and counter terrorist operations are occurring.

"For Mitch however, our delving into his background did indeed make us suspicious. Even though he has gone by a number of identities over the years, he has a penchant for showing up in parts of the world where other successful hits have taken place. Most recently, and this is what focused most of our interest in him, he turned up in Paris during the successful hit on Ahmadinejad, another one of the world's despots we could all do without."

"The MSS certainly does their homework."

"What we even learned about you is interesting."

"Is there no end to this?"

"We have you going all the way back to Laos, and other parts of Southeast Asia, where you operated for many years in both true name and a host of aliases. However, I do not believe you were engaged there in operations against us in any way. Therefore, you were left alone."

"Nothing like keeping good records."

"Insofar your op here, your team's tradecraft was basically excellent. Their communications among themselves, being encrypted, was disciplined and limited to sending signals. Even trying to track them by GPS failed, since they limited their time to just a few seconds, and we were unable to triangulate in any way. They also made sure to stay on the move, not giving us enough time to close in on him if our plan had been to apprehend them. Instead though, our decision was to let the operation play itself out in order to confirm our suspicions as to the identity of their target. It is when we turn to the unprofessional slips of the tongue on the part of Mitch and Gabriela, that we could pull things together identifying Mitch as your shooter. On the evening after the hit on Kim, their escapades during the night in Mitch's hotel room, combined with his veiled references about his success mentioned to her upon arriving back from his shooters nest in the building next door, identified them as the two key members of your team."

"Since you believed something in the way of an op was in the making though, dating back to their earlier trip here, were you in any way concerned that something could be in the offing, possibly against one of your own officials?"

"After the earlier trip, we believed it was going to be Kim due to the emphasis the team placed in the observations in and around the Beijing Train Station. No high level Chinese officials, civilian or military, make use of it. Kim, however, has used it six times in the past four years. By the way, are you aware of the minor war we have been engaged in with North Korea for a number of years?"

"If you mean the war with your military in the border area that resulted in North Koreans invading one of your PLA bases and killing some of your soldiers there? Yes, we did learn about it shortly after it occurred."

"A number of our senior generals were enraged and although it happened a few years ago, to this day they stand by the recommendation that we stage a coup in North Korea and remove Kim, as well as the entire military hierarchy."

"I can certainly see that both our governments have walked a parallel line on how Kim was ultimately to be dealt with."

"By the way, do you expect to be in touch again with your team that was here?"

"I certainly can if you have a message for me to give them."

"Please congratulate them for me on their success. For Gene, let him know that if he puts together a pictorial book on the pictures he took around the old city wall, I would like to have a signed copy. As for Mitch and Gabriela, tell them that while we found them an engaging and attractive couple together, including our listening in on their pillow talk in the hotel room, neither of them will be welcome should they ever try to return to China."

The End